The Cursed City

Laurence O'Bryan

This novel is a work of fiction. Any resemblance to actual persons, living or long dead, is entirely deliberate.

Acknowledgements & Dedication

I'd like to thank my editors, Alex McGilvery & Sheryl Lee, and early readers, Tanja Slijepčević, Roy Hunt, Guillaume Fichot & Susana Zabarskaya. All remaining errors are mine alone.
This novel is dedicated to my son, Justin who has had a lot to put up with.

Historical Background & Recap
from The Road to the Bridge, the second novel in this series

This final novel in the series takes place in 326 A.D. Since his victory at the Battle of the Milvian Bridge, Constantine has issued an edict of toleration for Christians and consolidated his power over the empire. He disbanded the Praetorian Guard, started a building program in Rome and other cities and defeated his final rival Licinius, Emperor of the eastern provinces. He decided soon after to move the capital of his empire to the newly named Constantinople. In 326 A.D. Constantine, and many in his court, went to Rome for the celebration of his twenty years as emperor. Below are the historical figures we encounter in this fictional retelling of a crucial period in world history.

Main Characters

Emperor Constantine, later to become Constantine the Great, fifty-five years old in 326 A.D.

Helena, Constantine's mother, had separated from Constantine's father (now dead) the Emperor Chlorus, many years before this.

Crispus, the son of Constantine by a previous consort, from before he became involved with Juliana, is thirty-one years old in 326. He was not in Rome when Constantine took the city at the Battle of the Milvian Bridge, as he was too young to campaign and was not living with his father. Five years after that battle he was appointed Caesar by Constantine in 317 and then, still at a young age, Commander of Gaul. In a series of subsequent battles he confirmed his status as a brilliant general and appointed successor to Constantine.

Fausta, Constantine's wife in 326, daughter of the Emperor Maximianus, now dead, and sister of another emperor, Maxentius, also dead.

Juliana, a fictional character I created to help tell the story of Constantine's life. Her son with Constantine died in Rome during the Battle of the Milvian Bridge.

Axel, the son Juliana had with a Saxon warrior. Juliana persuades him to fight for Rome.

Lucius, another fictional character, a Christian, I created to help tell the story of Constantine's life.

Place Names Used At The Time (326 A.D.)

Bithynia – A Roman province in what is now western Turkey.

Eboracum – The Roman city, now York, in the north of Britannia.

Gaul – A Roman province, now largely France.

Germania – Germany, most of which was outside the empire at this time.

Italia – Italy, the home province of the Roman Empire.

New Rome – what later became Constantinople and is now Istanbul.

Nicomedia – The Roman city, capital of the Eastern Roman Empire at the time, now the city of Izmit in Turkey, on the Sea of Marmara.

Pola, now Pula, a Roman city at the tip of the Istrian peninsula in what is now Croatia.

Treveris – The Roman city, now Trier, in western Germany, on the River Moselle, inside the Roman Empire, capital of the western Roman Empire at that time. Also known as Augusta Treverorum in official records of the period.

"When evil men advance against me to devour my flesh, when my enemies and my foes attack me, they will stumble and fall,"
Psalm 27:2.

Prologue

Rome, 326 A.D.

The blade plunged fast and deep into the slave's body. A gagging stench erupted as stomach fluid and hot blood flowed. The wounded man grabbed at the dagger, hoping to stop its progress.

"Noooooo," he screamed, jerking back.

Crispus pushed the blade upward, aiming it for the slave's heart. The slave's fist connected, sending Crispus' head back.

Crispus kept pushing the blade. His hand was deep in the man's stomach, his arm wet. Still the slave struggled to get away, grappling with Crispus, pulling him down and to the side.

The knife almost slid out.

Crispus moved the blade around, as he'd done many times in battle to end a man's life.

The slave bleated like a lamb being slaughtered. Then with a final jerk, the noise stopped.

A jingling from the courtyard below the palace on the Palatine Hill signaled the arrival of a troop of cavalry to escort Crispus to the Procession of the Knights.

"Goodbye, my friend Seutonius," whispered Crispus, as the slave fell out of his hands, ending up lying beneath him.

The slave's eyes were wide. Crispus closed them with fingers dripping blood. He staggered to his feet, his body shaking with the effort of killing. He stepped back, pressing his lips together. He had to control himself.

It was time for the Vicennalia, the celebration of twenty years in power for his father, the emperor.

I

The Imperial Palace, Palatine Hill, Rome, 326 A.D.

The Circus Maximus glowed as torches sent sparkles into the air all along its upper walls. It was mid-summer. A hot breeze had been blowing all day. The sky was darkening now, and the roars of the spectators echoed as the last chariot race reached its climax.

"Sit near your father," said Fausta to Crispus, holding his bare arm tight. "He will want his victorious general by his right hand."

Crispus pulled his arm away and headed up the giant dining hall to the table at the top, decorated with gold cloth, trimmed with purple silk. He sat to the right of his father.

Slaves were bustling about carrying trays of sweetmeats and olives, boiled eggs of various sizes, stuffed dates and doormice, wine glasses, golden pitchers, gold plates and candle holders, and giant fans made of peacock feathers.

Trumpets blared. A buzz of excitement filled the far end of the hall, where a marble bridge connected the Imperial Palace to the emperor's covered box at the center of the circus.

More people entered the room. The row of red cloaked imperial guards checking for weapons was almost overwhelmed, but it held its ground at a row of yellow marble pillars which marked the edge of the dining area.

"He'll be here soon," said Fausta, smiling over at Crispus. She was sitting on the far side of the giant gold covered, purple cushioned chair where Constantine would sit.

Crispus stared out the window to his left. Mars had risen above the circus. It was a sign. He turned to Fausta. Her eyebrows were raised.

"I will ask him what you suggested. Do not say anything to him, stepmother." He gripped his wine glass.

Fausta put a hand on the table, leaned toward him. Her white gown was trimmed with purple silk. A thin diadem decorated with pearls and diamonds sat on her hair, which had been pulled tight into a bun.

The gown was split down the middle but held together with gold pins so only a little of her pale skin was visible.

"This is your moment, Crispus. The great Emperor Diocletian set aside his rule at the celebrations on his reaching twenty years in power. Your father will be open to this. I know he looks forward to traveling to Jerusalem. For the sake of the empire, please press your case hard."

The hubbub of noise, shouts and shuffling almost drowned her voice out. A crowd of spotless-toga wearing high officials and senators, and senior officers in shiny leather breastplates decorated with medallions, poured into the hall to take their places at a series of tables that stretched down the center of the giant room.

Then a hush descended.

Everyone in the room stood, turned to the entrance and bowed. Fausta and Crispus too. A peal of trumpets blared. Surrounded by six of his personal bodyguard, each wearing a gold breastplate, Constantine strode into the hall, tall, dignified, at the height of his power, walking fast with his purple cloak billowing behind him, showing the hard expression he'd adopted to deter those who wanted to take advantage.

The guards didn't break from around him until he was right beside his golden seat at the top of the room. He waved at Fausta and Crispus to sit as he did.

"We missed you at the last race, Crispus. What happened to you?"

"I had a meeting with an informant," said Crispus, softly.

Constantine shook his head, as if displeased. "Another informant, eh. I hope you're not wasting your time. Did this one tell you anything interesting?" He almost shouted the word *interesting*.

"Nothing we do not already know." Crispus motioned for one of the hovering slaves nearby to bring wine for their goblets.

"You are a diligent son," said Constantine. "But for the rest of this evening you will stay here, by my side. No more running around after shadows, understood?"

"He has the best intentions," said Fausta, loudly.

Constantine turned to her. "And how is my loyal wife this glorious evening? I am told you've been busy with every aspect of this feast. There are more egg sizes on the trays around this room than I thought existed."

"That is the way they do things in Rome, dear husband. And I'm well when you are happy. That is all I need." Fausta looked down the room, then back at Constantine. "Where is your Saxon bodyguard tonight?"

Constantine smiled. "Juliana won't be joining us. There are a lot of security preparations needed for tomorrow's parade."

"No doubt she'll report everything to you in person later," said Fausta. Then she smiled in a fake way that would only fool idiots.

Constantine lifted a gold knife from the table in front of him and banged it onto the table by the end of its handle.

"I'll get my reports any time of the day or night I wish, dear wife." He pointed the knife at Fausta. "Say nothing more about Juliana."

Fausta stared back at him, as if daring him to stab her in front of all their guests.

Constantine pointed his knife at a slave nearby holding a large golden tray, clearly meant for his table. The slave, a slim Nubian, held the tray down for him. Constantine speared a large egg and turned back to Fausta.

"You can be my taster tonight, dear wife. Swallow this."

Fausta still did not change her expression. She reached forward, took the knife and ate the egg in two bites.

"It is perfect," she said.

Constantine waved the slave nearer and took other eggs from the tray, placing them on his plate.

"Will you be staying for the entertainment?" asked Crispus, taking some eggs from the tray for himself.

"I've no wish to see a clutch of Roman senator's daughters dancing. They'll all be looking at you in any case. You are the hero these days and I'm glad of it. I'll listen to the lyre players. Then I'll go."

"There will be speeches, Father. Please stay for them." Crispus smiled at his father.

Constantine shook his head. "You can report what they said about me tomorrow when you come to me after the parade."

"You are still not coming to that, either?"

"It has taken the elders of this city a long time to get it into their thick Roman heads that I don't venerate their old gods any more, nor do I care for long flattering poems when everyone knows most of them would stab me in the eye in a moment, if they had a good chance."

"And if the mob starts baying for their emperor?"

"You must satisfy them. Better to have the next emperor with them than the last."

Fausta coughed.

Constantine looked up. "Lucius Armenius, I was wondering if you'd show up."

Beside Lucius stood a broad young man with long blond hair, wearing a Saxon style breastplate with swirling patterns painted on it in dark browns and blacks.

"Axel, you are welcome too."

Axel and Lucius bowed deeply.

"Up, up, you know I don't like all that," said Constantine.

"How is your mother, Axel?" asked Fausta.

Axel stared at her as if she had two heads. Finally, he replied, "Good."

"You are as talkative as ever, dear Axel," said Fausta. "That's what you get, I suppose, for having a Saxon father. Now, why don't you both find a table and rest your legs."

Constantine raised his hand and pointed at the far side of their table. "You must sit at our table," he said.

Lucius bent down toward Constantine. Axel went and sat at the end of the table.

"Has my emperor had time to consider the situation of the Christian rowers in Crispus' galleys?"

Constantine stared up at Lucius. "I cannot see to every petition personally, my old friend. Have you taken it up with Crispus?" He pointed at his son.

Lucius kept staring at Constantine.

Constantine groaned. "You cannot have the world fixed instantly for you, Lucius."

"I know," said Lucius. "But this is important. And we have waited a long time already."

Constantine pointed at Crispus.

The room buzzed with noise. Lucius looked around. Slaves were rushing, delivering trays of food and jugs of wine. The older men were grabbing at the younger female slaves.

Constantine pointed down the room. "Do you see what they're like? Rome's patrician class are as bad as ever. Do you think they'll change overnight? People have to be worked on, Lucius. And they are worse here than in any other city in the empire."

"They are used to having whatever they want," said Fausta.

A scream rang out. A slave girl ran for a side door, her tunic half off.

The man who did it stood and bowed toward Constantine.

Constantine called the head of his personal guard to him. The man came forward quickly, his scabbard knocking noisily against the sectioned leather lower apron of his uniform.

"Have that pig thrown out," he said, pointing at where the man was retaking his seat.

Lucius was still on the other side of Constantine, standing between his and Fausta's chairs.

"That man is the son of one of the most powerful senators," said Fausta.

A shout rang out as the man was picked up from where he'd been sitting and half-carried, half-dragged from the room.

"Good, a lot of people will hear about what happened to him," said Constantine. He banged on the arm of his chair. "You are right, Fausta. These chairs are much more comfortable than lying down on couches."

A messenger in a plain white tunic came rushing toward them. Another of Constantine's personal guard raised a hand and stood between the messenger and Constantine.

"My emperor, I have a message for you from the Saxon woman."

"Let him through," said Constantine.

The messenger went to his knees and bowed, his head touching the floor.

"One of your personal house slaves has been found dead, my emperor."

Constantine breathed in fast through his nose. "Which one?" he said.

"Julius Seutonius."

Constantine growled. His growl grew louder and louder until everyone at the next table stopped talking.

He reached a hand toward Lucius and grabbed his arm, pulling him down. "Find out what happened, Lucius. Julius Seutonius was supposed to be doing something for me." He pulled Lucius closer. "Report only to me. This is a personal matter. And bring Axel with you."

II

The Imperial Palace, Palatine Hill, Rome, 326 A.D.

Juliana walked fast through the maze of tunnels under the Imperial Palace. Ahead of her strode one of the highest-ranking imperial slaves, a wiry man with a bald head who'd served Diocletian personally when he came to Rome more than twenty years before and made sure to tell everyone about it.

"I discovered him while the feast was starting." The old slave glanced back at Juliana. "We heard you were looking after the emperor's personal protection. You were one of us once. I heard that too."

"A long time ago." Juliana tucked part of her long tunic up under her shiny leather belt to make it shorter, so she could walk faster.

"Once a slave, always a slave, isn't that what they say?" said the old man.

"I am proof that isn't true."

The old man slowed as they came to a set of rough stairs leading up. "And I trust you more for it," he said.
He led the way up the stairs. Near the top, the tread changed from wood to marble. They went through a door and were immediately in a long corridor. The hunting scenes painted on the wall in shades of yellow and blue effectively disguised the door when it closed behind them, so that it appeared to vanish.

Down the corridor three imperial guards were standing around a body on the floor.

"I must have this corridor cleared as soon as possible, Juliana, but I knew you would want to see your master's slave exactly as we found him."

"Stand aside," the old man shouted, as he came near the legionaries.

They stepped back to let Juliana and the old slave through. Blood had spread out in a slick red pool under the slave and oozed down the corridor. The old slave was careful not to step in it.

Juliana looked at her gold threaded sandals, shrugged, stepped into the blood and leaned down over the body. The dead slave's face was turned up. His eyes were closed. Blood smeared his face. Juliana held her nose. The smell from man's open stomach was strong. What had he been eating?

A large wound was visible in the man's belly. Grayish-purple intestines bulged out. Whoever had done this was used to killing people.

She looked at the man's hands to see if he was holding anything or had blood and skin under his fingernails. He did, someone's skin was piled under the fingernails of his right hand. All she could tell from it was that whoever he'd scratched hadn't been a Nubian.

"How often do people use this corridor?"

"Rarely. It connects the main hall to what used to be Emperor Licinius' private quarters. After Licinius was defeated by your master, no one used his rooms. We were waiting for your master to take up residence in Rome." He bowed, smiled at Juliana.

"Do not worry, we will all be gone soon enough, and you will have the place to yourselves again," said Juliana.

She looked at the legionaries. "Did any of you see a sword or a dagger here?" she asked, her voice loud.

The older legionary answered without looking down. "There was no weapon visible when we arrived. We touched nothing."

"Then help me move the body, so we can see if there is anything under it."

The legionaries lifted the body and moved it to lie face up on the far side of the corridor. There was no weapon underneath it.

Juliana went through the side pockets of the tunic. She found two gold coins, aureus minted under Diocletian in one pocket, and a curved wooden key in the other, the type usually used for rooms in a better insula, one of the tall apartment buildings in the city.

"He smells bad," said the old slave. "We need him gone." He tapped Juliana's arm. "You will provide the statement of what happened to the head of the imperial household, yes?" He rubbed his hands together. "I will be the witness, if needed, to how the body was found."

Accounting for slaves was a task that all Roman patrician families took very seriously.

"Yes, you can take him away. But keep his body somewhere cool until tomorrow night in case the emperor wants to see him. After that, burn the body." She looked into the old man's eyes. "Do not throw him into the Tiber. He was a respected imperial slave."

The old man bowed his agreement.

Juliana stepped back, awkwardly wiping her sandals on the dead slave's tunic as she did, then walked away fast with the two gold coins and the key in her hand. The old slave stared after her. As soon as she had gone, he spoke loudly to the legionaries, ordering them to carry the dead body away.

Seutonius had been tasked by Constantine with investigating threats against his person while they were in Rome. Had Constantine also given the slave access to an apartment and money to bribe people? Slaves rarely carried gold coins, though they sometimes did carry keys, if they were trusted.

She listened to the distant sound of lyre music. The feast was getting going. She turned a corner. Coming toward her, at a brisk pace, strode Lucius and Axel, her son. Lucius had gray temples now and his face was creased. He looked concerned.

"What news, Juliana?" Lucius sounded grateful to have found her.

She told them everything she'd found out, omitting that she'd discovered a key and gold coins. These things were best discussed first with Constantine.

"Why would anyone kill Seutonius?" asked Lucius.

"He was investigating threats against Constantine," said Juliana.

Lucius looked up and down the corridor. "Perhaps we should go back to the feast. Whoever murdered Seutonius might be about to do something stupid."

"Yes, go back. Tell Constantine what happened and that I'll report to him later."

"Where will you go?"

"I want to see Seutonius' room."

"You know more than you are telling. I can see that in your eyes, Juliana," said Lucius.

III

The Imperial Palace, Palatine Hill, Rome, 326 A.D.

"The bishop of Alexandria requests to approach," said the slave. "He is at the last table." He offered Constantine something from the tray of honeyed sweets he was carrying.

Constantine ignored the sweets.

The slave pointed down the great hall. A thin man with a white beard, dressed in a long off-white tunic, was standing by the last table. When he saw Constantine looking at him, he bowed.

Constantine waited until the bishop looked back up at him, then waved the old man forward.

"I see that Bishop Alexander has come to make trouble," said Crispus. "Do you want me to get rid of him, Father?"

"No need," said Constantine. "I heard he's not well. He won't be able to cause any more trouble soon."

The bishop went down on one knee as he came near Constantine's table.

"Arise, brother Alexander," said Constantine loudly. "What brings you all the way to Rome?"

"I am here to see you, my emperor, to pay my respects on your twenty-year anniversary."

Constantine smiled at the old man, motioned him closer. "How can I help you?"

The old man pressed his hand to his chest and coughed. It sounded as if something was rattling in his throat.

"I was advised not to come, my lord. But there are grave matters I must report to you."

"What matters?"

"Lewd acts in the temple of the great mother in Alexandria continue, my lord. The priestesses sell themselves more brazenly than ever. They claim this is allowed here in Rome and that I have no authority to stop them."

"Is that all you wish to report?" asked Constantine.

The bishop bowed again. "Christian slaves have been beaten for coming to our services, my lord, but we are dealing with this matter ourselves. The problem we need help with is these wicked priestesses."

"Be assured, Bishop, we will take care of this matter. Provide the location of their temple in Alexandria to our governor in the city and he will have their temple confiscated. Come back in two days and a letter will be waiting for you to take to the governor."

The bishop smiled. "May we have the land of this temple for a church, after cleansing it, of course?"

Constantine looked at the man. This was most likely the real reason for the bishop's visit. "Yes, if you welcome all to it, including any priestesses who change their ways."

The bishop looked about to say something, but a shout rang out. Everyone looked for its source. Halfway down the room a man stood, clutching at his throat. A woman screamed, rose up, clutching at the man who was now coughing blood.

Constantine pointed at Crispus. "Get that man out of here and get all the trays of food sent back to the kitchens and not thrown out."

He pounded a fist on the table, then stood, raising both his hands. His table was set on a small plinth, but he was still taller and broader than most men in the room when he stood.

"We have all feasted enough, good friends. Not one more bite will you place in your mouths. It is time for us to finish the feast. I wish you all well."

He pointed at Fausta. "Let us leave."

He walked around the table and went down the room to where the man who had been shouting was lying on the floor. No one was beside him. It looked as if he'd been taken over by a daemon, people were keeping such a distance from him.

Blood was dribbling from the man's mouth as Constantine came near him. A voice behind him said, "My emperor, do not go near him."

Constantine didn't take any notice of the warning. He held the man's hand and bent down low over him.

"We will look after your family," he whispered. The man tried to smile. Blood bubbled from his mouth.

"What did you eat?"

The man gurgled.

A woman's voice behind them interrupted. "He ate everything he was offered, my emperor."

"I am glad to hear that," said Constantine, turning.

The woman had a pale blue dress on. It wasn't half see-through, like the dresses many of the other women wore. It was also cut high around her neck.

The woman was shaking, her hand reaching out toward Constantine and the man who had been poisoned.

"Is this your husband?" asked Constantine. He motioned her to him, passed his hand to her.

"No, he is my landlord." She gripped his hand. "If anything happens to him, I do not know what will happen to all us tenants." She stopped, as if she'd thought better of saying more.

Constantine waved at one of his bodyguards standing nearby. "Take this man to the infirmary. Say he is to be admitted on my orders. Tell them to do all they can for him, and at my expense."

Three legionaries bent down, picked the man up and carried him from the hall. The woman went after him. Most of the people nearby were up now and moving toward the door at the end of the hall.

Constantine's guards were standing in a circle around him. They followed him as he headed back to where Crispus and Fausta waited.

Fausta ran to him as he got near. "What did he eat?"

Constantine shrugged. "Everything." His expression was stiff. He placed a hand on his chest, then made it quickly into a fist.

He walked to the side door that led to the older part of the palace, where Constantine and his family had taken over the large rooms previously used by the Emperor Maxentius, Fausta's brother, when he had celebrations in the city to attend to.

The rooms were set around a courtyard with a small fountain at its center, water flowing from the mouths of three nymphs.

"We will use food from our own supplies from now on," said Constantine angrily, as they arrived in the courtyard.

"We still don't know what killed the man, Father," said Crispus.

"I was warned about coming back to Rome," said Constantine, sitting down heavily on one of the wide marble benches covered in thin cushions, near the fountain. He took off the thin diadem and handed it, stiff-armed, to a slave waiting nearby.

Crispus stood near his father. "Your Saxon shield maiden does not know the future. You can't believe everything she tells you."

"I don't," said Constantine.

"So, when will you announce me as your successor?" Crispus sounded angry now. "Tonight was the moment to do it. When will you do it?"

Constantine looked up at him. "I never said I would announce it tonight. You are getting ahead of yourself, Crispus."

Crispus let out a gasp. "But we discussed it, twice. You said this was the right moment, after celebrating twenty years in power, the moment Diocletian announced his making way for new emperors after his twenty years in power. You agreed it. What has happened?"

Constantine shook his head. "We agreed it, but not the date when it'll happen. There are still some things I need resolving. The plan remains the same, my son, but the moment to announce it is not now. And not here in Rome."

Crispus sighed.

"Sit down, you are making me jumpy," said Fausta.

Crispus sat on one of the other benches.

"The transfer of power must be done properly, or the people will not follow you, Crispus. My advisors say we should make the announcement back in the east, at the new capital, at New Rome."

"What advisors?"

Constantine just stared ahead.

"New Rome is not ready for big ceremonies yet," said Crispus.

"No, but it will be soon," said Constantine. "And your half-brothers are there."

A thud echoed from the entrance corridor. The sound of running feet followed. Everyone looked to the door leading back to the main part of the palace. Constantine stood up, his hand at his ornamental dagger, as if expecting he might need it.

A moment later Paulina appeared from the corridor. Her hair was pulled up high on her head and she wore a heavy white tunic down to her ankles, but there was no disguising that she'd put on weight since Constantine had last seen her.

Paulina bowed low when she saw Constantine.

"I'm sorry to disturb you, my lord," she said, "but there is urgent news and you said to come to you if I found anything out."

Constantine waved at her with both hands to rise up and come forward.

"If anyone has permission to come to me without warning, it is you, Paulina. Now, what is your news?"

She came close to him, lowered her voice. "There will be a ceremony tonight, my lord." She looked around. Fausta and Crispus were sitting on the bench at an angle to the one Constantine was sitting on. Two slaves were hovering nearby.

Constantine waved in the air toward the slaves. "Be gone," he called out. "We will call if we need anything."

The two slaves disappeared.

"You can talk now," said Constantine.

Paulina stared at Crispus as she talked. She spoke in a low voice.

"The ceremony is a secret one. It will bind all those who attend to a cause." She paused. "May I sit?"

Constantine pointed at the bench.

Paulina sat, leaned up toward him. "They want to meet you."

"Where?"

"Under this palace."

Constantine looked at Crispus. "You want to meet these people?"

Crispus shook his head. "If we chase every shadowy group in this city, we will be worn out by the time we leave."

Constantine turned back to Paulina. "Can you take me to where they're meeting?" He rubbed his hands together.

Fausta stood beside him and held out her hand to Constantine. "My emperor, do not get involved with these groups. Crispus must go. Order him to."

"No, I will do this myself, Fausta. I don't want to rely on second-hand reports. Paulina can be trusted."

Paulina looked from face to face. "These people will do anything to take us back to the old ways. I've spent the last ten years in Rome trying to get the building work that the emperor ordered completed. But at every turn something is put in our way. Slaves disappear, contractors die, fires break out. This is a chance for the emperor to meet the people we need to support what we are doing. The emperor should meet them."

"Do you trust these people?" asked Fausta.

"I do not know them," said Paulina.

IV

The Imperial Palace, Palatine Hill, Rome, 326 A.D.

Juliana turned to Axel, opened her arms. "It is good to see you, my son. Your centurion has given you time off, or did you break out of the old praetorian camp?"

"I'm a centurion now, Mother, and no, I didn't break out of the Praetorian barracks. There's hardly anything to break out from anyway. We've been tasked with dismantling all the remaining buildings and walls still standing."

"It's about time they finished that job." Juliana put a hand on Axel's bare arm and squeezed it. "I'm glad you're helping erase every memory of those bastards."

"Juliana, sorry to interrupt, but have you any thoughts about who might have killed Seutonius? Constantine will ask," said Lucius.

"Someone wanted his mouth shut," said Juliana. "I expect whoever killed him was someone he knew. Most likely someone we know."

Juliana strode ahead with Axel at her side. Lucius trailed behind.

"After we see Seutonius' rooms we must head back quickly to tell Constantine what we've found," said Lucius.

"Agreed," said Juliana. She held a hand out and gripped Axel's upper arm.

"I am glad you are here," she whispered.

At the stairs down to the slaves' quarters, Juliana went down first. The stairwell changed after one turn. The marble wall covering did not extend into the lower part and when they reached the bottom a wide, brick-lined corridor stretched away in both directions.

It needed to be wide, as it was busy. Slaves in pale purple, brown or off-white tunics were hurrying about.

Some of them wore wooden medallions, a few had smaller silver medallions hanging around their necks.

Juliana was looking for a slave with a gold medallion and a white tunic. The slaves ignored them as they walked past, carrying trays or amphora or bundles of cloth or sacks of different sizes.

The corridor opened into a large, low roofed hall. Corridors branched off, and at the center of the hall stood tables, where slaves with silver medallions sat, shouting orders to the other slaves hurrying around them.

Juliana went straight to a table where a slave in a white tunic sat. His face was red. He stood and bowed as the three of them came near.

"Masters, there is no need for you to be down here. If you send a message, we will do whatever needs doing and report back quickly." He bowed low.

"I know how the palace works," said Juliana. "We are here to look at the sleeping place of Seutonius, one of the senior imperial slaves who came with the emperor a few days ago."

The slave was wire thin and had a face lined with creases, as if he had been out in the sun too long.

He didn't ask any questions. He just motioned another slave over and spoke quickly to him, pointing to the far side of the hall.

"This man will take you there," he said, and bowed again.

The sleeping quarters were in another hall, not far away, and down another staircase. On each wall of this hall niches had been cut into the rock of the hill. These niches contained just enough space for a man or woman to lie down, and a tiny shelf at the back, where a tunic could be placed or a small figure of one of the gods.

The niche they were taken to was bigger than the ones on the other walls. It was deeper and wider and had a black leather curtain pulled across its front.

Juliana pulled the curtain aside quickly and gasped. Two young male slaves lay behind the curtain, sleeping naked in a loving clinch.

The slave who had brought them there started shouting. He used his hands to slap at the naked slaves, who jumped out of the niche, pulled their tunics on and ran off, with indignant screams following them.

The slave bowed low. "I can have both of those slaves gelded in the morning if you wish."

"No," said Juliana. "What I am concerned about is if anything has been taken from Seutonius' bed chamber."

"Those two weren't carrying any more than a tunic," said Lucius. "Let's get this over with." He looked upward, as if concerned that the low brown, unpainted roof above their heads was about to collapse at any moment.

"They will both be searched and their sleeping places too," said the slave who'd brought them. "Shall I get that done now?"

"Yes," said Lucius. "Find us in the emperor's rooms."

The slave hurried away. Slaves were coming and going to niches around them and pulling curtains across to get some privacy. It appeared that slaves were sleeping in each niche all the time, sharing them with others when they were not using them.

Juliana ran her hands around the shelf at the back of the niche, looking for a hole where anything could be hidden. She also shook out the stained blanket and the thin mattress, crunching the hay interior to see if there was anything sewn inside it. Then she turned to the pillow. It was small, but it had a purple cover and looked to be the only thing that Seutonius might have owned.

When Juliana picked it up and squeezed it, she felt something in it.

V

The Imperial Palace, Palatine Hill, Rome, 326 A.D.

"Who will be at this meeting?" asked Constantine.

"Senators, officials, people like that. People I need on our side to get things done."

They'd walked quickly to the large basilica building, which had been built by the Emperor Septimus Severus over a hundred years before. Now they were three levels down beneath the main hall. Each level had a lower ceiling, until finally the roof of the corridor they were walking down was so low Constantine had to bend his head.

Paulina walked in front, leading the way, carrying a small flickering torch she'd taken from the wall in the first underground level. It was the only torch they had seen.

"I was here before, a year ago. That was a meeting to agree a truce between followers of the old gods and us Christians. The room is near."

The corridor branched. Paulina took the left turn. This was the narrowest passage yet. Ahead, Constantine could see a glimmer of light coming from a doorway.

Paulina put her torch down as they approached and left it on the floor, turning it so the flame doused. She put her finger to her lips as the last of the flame died.

A murmur of voices came from up ahead. They moved slowly forward, Constantine in the lead this time. He wondered if Fausta had been right. Might he be in danger down here? Should he have called a unit of his personal guard to come with him? He stopped and held his hand up for Paulina to stop as well. One thing was sure, they would not have been able to approach this meeting so quietly if there had been a dozen men with him. Whoever was here could have scattered fast in this warren of underground tunnels.

He listened. Yes, he could make out a voice.

"Take our offering, lord of the darkness. Take our offering queen of the light. We come to you with these gifts that you might hear us."

A jingling sounded. Small bells ringing.

Constantine moved toward the open doorway, his hand near his dagger. He smiled grimly as he breathed in the damp smell of the earth. His personal safety was always something others were more concerned about than him.

Paulina came up beside him. He could see part of the room they'd reached now. Men and women dressed in everyday tunics and a few older men in togas were crowded into a candlelit space a few steps below the open doorway. They had their backs to them. The room was long and as Constantine and Paulina put their heads forward to see more everyone in the room began to hum.

It sounded as if a human beehive had come to life.

A scratching noise came from behind them. Constantine turned. Behind them were two older women. They were smiling.

"Come inside, join us. You have nothing to fear," said the oldest of the two women. "Our door is always open."

"We are expecting you," said the other women. "We were watching to see if you would come alone or bring your men. You are welcome to join us."

Constantine turned and stepped down into the hall. A few people turned and a gasp ran up the room as the whole crowd turned.

A collective intake of breath followed, as if something predicted had happened.

Rows of benches ran up the room. There was an empty corridor in the center between the benches, leading toward a plinth, on which stood a large black urn with small flames leaping from it. The roof of the hall was blackened almost entirely and the walls too. The room looked older than any other part of the building he'd been in.

A woman and a man stood one on either side of the urn. They were both dressed in long yellow robes.

Constantine walked up the center corridor between the benches. He knew some of the people in the room. They were senators and officials and members of the best families in Rome, mostly from the older generation, but with a few younger people too.

The woman at the top of the room had a snake wound around her body. Its large black head was to the side, and it too watched as Constantine approached. The man had a large raven on his shoulder. He walked slowly. He knew the difficulties taming snakes and ravens from birth and that they would protect their owners if they felt danger.

Both the man and woman held their arms wide as Constantine came near. He held his own arms up in greeting. If these were the people holding Paulina back, he needed to find out if they could be turned to his will or if another way would be needed.

The man and woman bowed their heads a little as he approached. When he was almost at the urn they stood in front of it, as if protecting it. The man spoke.

"We hoped for many years that you would join us. This flame," he waved at the urn behind him, "was lit five hundred years ago and has not gone out since. It is renewed every year from a different source and every five years we hold these ceremonies to renew our vows to the old gods. Will you join us in the renewal?"

Constantine looked around. The faces of the crowd, there must have been a hundred people at least, looked expectant and happy.

"I will," he said, loudly.

The raven cawed.

A bell tinkled. A hush descended.

Constantine sniffed. He could smell frankincense and something, possibly lavender, in the air. The man and woman looked beyond him, over his shoulder. He glanced around. A young woman, perhaps eighteen years old, was being escorted by a man wearing a bull's head, with giant horns.

The young woman was wearing a thin gown. She had her hands out in front of her. Lying across one palm was an ornamental knife, with a curved blade. In the other was a golden bowl. At the back of the room Paulina raised a hand and gave him the thumbs up.

The young woman stood still in front of him, expressionless.

"Choose," said the man. "Either you will drink blood with us by cutting the flesh of the sacrifice, or you will drink from the bowl. Which is to be?"

"Choose, choose, choose." A low chant went up, starting at the back of the hall and spreading forward. Every time he went to a meeting they wanted him to join them.

There was a threat in the chant. He breathed in deep. He knew how to turn these people.

"Do not be afraid. I will drink from the cup first, so you see there is nothing to fear," said the woman behind him, by the urn.

"And I will make a cut on the sacrifice's breast so you see the blood can flow from her and that you will not be in danger from that."

"There is no need for that. If you," he pointed at the woman, "drink from the bowl I will follow you."

She took the golden bowl, sipped from it, and passed it to Constantine. He looked down the room at Paulina. She had her thumb up. He took in the faces staring at him. Had he been seeking this danger? Paulina was smiling her encouragement. She knew what he'd been through, how he'd come to blame himself for what had happened to his father. She knew the choices he now faced, about when he would hand over power and how it would be shared. They were the same choices his father faced.

He took the bowl, turned, and faced the room.

"I drink this for you, to show that I respect you and that you can trust me to do what is right." He drank a little from the bowl, passed it back to the young woman.

The older man put a hand on Constantine's arm and squeezed it. He raised his other hand for silence.

"The emperor is one of us now. We have dedicated this night of the horned moon to the old gods of light and darkness once again with an emperor, as we should." He squeezed Constantine's shoulder, leaned toward him and said in a low voice, "It is good that you show us the same support in public as you do for the new Christian god, which your friend Paulina speaks for here in Rome. Equal treatment in your empire is all we ask."

"I expect you to support Paulina in her work," said Constantine.

"The gods are watching you and your will must be done, Emperor," said the man.

"See to it," said Constantine. He blinked. His eyes were betraying him. It seemed as if the red earth wall at the side of the room was turning to liquid.

"I must go," he said. He walked as confidently as he could to the back of the room where Paulina was waiting.

"What in Hades name was in that bowl?" he whispered to her.

"Do not be concerned, Emperor. The effect will pass by morning. Let us go."

Constantine took one last look up the hall before he left. The young woman who had given him the drink was standing naked with her back to him. In front of her the older man and woman had their arms up and were reciting something. The room answered. Constantine headed for the door. He didn't want to watch. He had seen many different ceremonies to the sun and the moon and all the horned gods in his time and had no need to see more.

VI

The Imperial Palace, Palatine Hill, Rome, 326 A.D.

Juliana pulled the small folded letter out of the slit she'd cut in the cushion with the Saxon dagger she kept in a leather sheath on her belt.

She opened the parchment. It was an agreement to rent a room near Nero's Circus on the other side of the Tiber on the Via Castello, near Hadrian's tomb. The rent was one gold aureus per week. She showed it to Lucius.

"Wow, that must be some apartment. You could rent a villa with an orchard by the sea for a month for that."

Juliana pulled the wooden key out of her pocket. "This could be the key for the apartment," she said. "I found it in his pocket. We should go and have a look."

"Now?" said Lucius.

"Well, if I know how fast slaves pass news around, if there is anything interesting in the apartment it will be gone by morning."

"Should we go to the stables and get some horses?"

Juliana shook her head. "We can walk there in the time it will take for them to get three horses ready. I know a shortcut, let's go."

The short cut took them along the side wall of the Circus Maximus. It towered to their left with the wind whistling through its giant, now dark, upper arches. Homeless people huddled in the deep shadow of the circus wall. The scene was peaceful, but Lucius and Axel kept their hands on the pommels of their swords, just in case. Juliana had a small axe on her belt.

The good part of going this way to get to the Tiber was that the city watch patrolled here constantly.

"I need a dirty cloak," said Lucius, as they strode on. "This breastplate will attract too much attention."

"Buy one from them," said Juliana. A group of men were gathered around a fire up ahead. Lucius went straight up to them, pointed at the cleanest looking man and asked, "How much for your cloak?"

The man laughed. "It's the only one I have." The others laughed too, nudging each other. They might have done more, but the sight of Lucius and Axel with their hands by their belts would be enough to stop any but the most confident thieves.

Lucius took two silver denarii out of his money pouch and held it forward in his palm.

"You'll be able to buy the best cloak in Rome in the morning with that," he said.

The man slipped off his dark, greasy looking cloak and took the coins.

As they crossed the river by the Aelian Bridge Lucius had his new cloak wrapped tightly around him. They looked a lot less like escapees from an imperial party. There were more men from the city watch at each end of the river, but after skirting Hadrian's Tomb the buildings became run down. When they turned into the Via Castello they were met by a completely different sight.

The street was lit with torches outside many of the buildings. Singing echoed. And flute playing. The first tavern they passed was overflowing with revelers, many drunk and falling about. The tavern girls' dresses were pulled off either one shoulder or both, exposing one or more of their breasts.

Further on the taverns were tightly packed and the street was almost full from side to side with people of all types.

"I didn't know this place existed," said Axel.

"I want you to forget it exists after tonight," said Juliana.

A group of legionaries, possibly centurions, though they wore no medallions of rank, were pissing at the side of the street, aiming their urine into a wooden pail that a urine collector was holding.

"I bet he makes a lot of money on this street," said Lucius.

"She," said Juliana. "She's a woman."

Lucius was looking up at the names of the apartment buildings on small wooden plaques on the first floor level of each building.

The walls of many buildings were painted in vivid scenes of debauchery, satyrs running after nymphs, their giant organs leading them, men on top of swans, multiple naked figures in a circle of debauchery.

"No wonder the rent here is expensive," said Juliana. "The question is, what does an imperial slave need an apartment here for?"

"For entertaining new friends," said Axel. "I know a few legionaries who'd love access to rooms in this street." He was staring at two young street girls who were blowing kisses in his direction and waving at him.

"It's this building," said Juliana, grabbing Axel's arm and pushing him toward the high doorway to what appeared to be one of the best buildings in the street.

The tavern on the ground floor of the building had two tough looking doormen. The door they were guarding had a beaten silver covering to it with a satyr embossed on it.

"I'll find out who lives here," said Lucius. He went up to the doormen and pointed at the building above them. One of the doormen leaned back and laughed. The other placed a finger on Lucius' chest and shouted something in his face. Lucius backed up and came back to where Juliana and Axel were standing.

"He says we have to go into the tavern to ask who lives upstairs. Their master would make that doorman eat his own eyeballs for breakfast if he told me anything."

"Let's go in then," said Axel, eagerly.

Juliana looked at the closed door, which gave access to the upper floors. No one had gone in or come out since they'd been outside.

"Looks like we'll have to," she said.

Lucius headed into the tavern. Juliana and Axel followed. The doormen nodded as they entered. Inside it was dark, with only the candles at each table and a raised area at the end of the room illuminating the crowd of people at the tables or standing by the walls. Everyone was watching a pair of actors, two young men, performing a scene on the stage.

One of them had a purple cloak on and was carrying a shield with a Christian cross on it. The other was wearing a bull headdress. The two were circling each other. A slave girl in a short red tunic approached Lucius and motioned him toward a table at the edge of the seating area. Two young men were already at the table, but there were four empty stools they could sit on.

They sat. Lucius waved the slave girl to him.

"We are looking for the service you provide in apartment thirty-four," he said.

The girl stared at him as if Lucius had grown a second head. She looked across the room to a thin man who was watching them. She held three fingers up, turned and went away. Lucius stared after her. Juliana was watching the thin man approaching. A cudgel with a silver handle dangled from his wide leather belt.

When he reached their table he smiled at Juliana, then leaned down and whispered in Lucius' ear.

"Speak to all of us," said Juliana, loudly.

The man threw up his hands, looked at Juliana and spoke. "I did not know you were all interested in what we provide on level three."

"What is the fee?" said Lucius. "We have had our fill of simple pleasures." He put a hand on Juliana's bare arm and squeezed it.

The man raised one finger. "Each," he said.

"A silver denarius each. That's a lot of money for a brief interlude."

The man shook his head. "Not one denarius," he said. "One gold aureus, each." He started at Lucius, then at Axel and then at Juliana.

Lucius slapped his thigh. "This is more like it," he said. "So please, tell me exactly what we'll get for this."

The man looked around the room.

"Do you see the serving slaves? You can pick any of them. Perhaps that girl you just spoke with. Or do you like young men, or children? The youngest here is only ten, and then you do whatever takes your fancy to them." He leaned forward, looked around, smiled. "The tools for this can be yours or we can provide them."

"And what about afterward?" asked Juliana.

"We take care of the bodies, if that is needed," said the man.

Juliana looked at Lucius. He seemed to have gone pale.

"And how much time will we have for this?"

"You can play with them until dawn."

Lucius banged the table. "We will come back."

He stood and walked toward the door. The man bounded after him, as did Juliana and Axel.

As they left the man's voice barked in their ears. "If you think you can complain about what we do here to the consuls or to the senate, know that we have entertained all the senators and consuls of Rome here for the past hundred years."

The door slammed behind them.

"So that's what senators of Rome view as entertainment," said Lucius. "No wonder they are too busy to think about changing anything in this city."

"The rich can pay for anything," said Juliana.

"There may be another way in around the back," said Lucius, heading up the street. He turned to see if Juliana and Axel were following. The man with the silver cudgel was outside now, talking to the doormen and pointing at them.

At the end of the block he turned left to go around the building. The lane they were in soon turned to near darkness. When they reached the end of the building there was another street, running parallel to the street they'd been on. Only the light from a torch at the next crossroads showed them what was ahead.

"Stop," said Juliana. "Our eyes will adjust. There are plenty of stars out."

They stood and waited in the darkness, listening to the echoes of singing and shouting. A door banged halfway along the street. A man with a giant stomach stepped outside and whistled. From another lane, further away, a cart rumbled. Two men were pushing it. They stopped at the doorway, where the man with the stomach banged twice on it as they arrived. The door opened and two men carried what could have been a body into the street and placed it on the back of the cart.

The cart moved off, coming in their direction. As it came near Lucius stepped into the middle of the street and put a hand up.

"Is there anywhere to sleep things off around here?" he asked, as the cart came closer.

"At the end of this street you'll find a good place with a soft mattress and not too many fleas," replied one of the men in a Greek accent.

"Your friend will need somewhere to sleep things off," said Lucius, pointing at the prone figure in the cart.

"He's in Hades now. He won't be worrying about fleas."

"What happened to him?" said Juliana.

"We don't ask," said the man. "We just take people to the quacks who take out the brains and the livers for use in potions."

"What about the man's family?" said Juliana. She was trying hard to suppress her disgust.

"He should have thought about them before he drank himself to death in the Via Castello."

The men and the cart passed them by.

"Never come to this area on your own," hissed Juliana, standing close to Axel.

"I wouldn't, anyway," he said.

"Swear it," she said, angrily.

VII

The Imperial Palace, Palatine Hill, Rome, 326 A.D.

Paulina tugged at the sleeve of Constantine's purple tunic. "Before we go back to the others we need to talk."

"Yes," said Constantine. They stopped at a marble bench in the long corridor outside the rooms for the imperial family. Constantine sat, then patted the space beside him for Paulina to sit.

She sat at the other end of the bench.

"Equality between the old gods and the new, what do you think about that, Paulina?" He gave her his stony glare.

Paulina didn't reply immediately. She stared at the pink marble floor.

"Will this promise of equality for the old gods impact my work at Nero's Circus?" she said, still staring at the floor. "We are still without a proper plan for what we put up after the circus is razed."

"See to it then, Paulina. The road is clear. All are free to worship however they want. That's what I promised down there, and they know they will have freedom for their ceremonies if they don't stand against you," said Constantine.

"Yes, but they will use your promise to demand an equal share of any new buildings." She made a fist with one hand, held it with the other. "I have dealt with these people for too many years. They twist everything, demand to have ceremonies in our new churches, whenever they want. They will want shared control of the other new churches too. Some say we are just replacing one temple with another." She sounded exasperated.

"I saw some faces I knew among them," said Constantine. "I expect you knew a lot of them too, did you?" He rubbed his hand along the smooth edge of the marble bench.

"Most of them."

"Give all the names to Juliana in the morning." He didn't look at her.

She let out a whistling sound. "What will you do?"

"Some will be arrested, to encourage the others."

"What charges?" She didn't sound surprised.

"We will find something."

"Is this the right way?"

"Yes, I keep my oath, to defend their right to profess any faith they want. They can claim a cat is their god, or a mouse, for all I care, but I never swore to protect them from arrest."

"And what will you do to them, the ones you round up?"

Constantine stood up, walked on ahead.

"Give Juliana the names. That's all I need from you." When he reached the double doors to the imperial rooms, they were open. Guards were standing to attention on both sides. He headed inside to the atrium to see if Crispus and Fausta were still there. They were. He could hear them arguing as he approached.

"You never listen," shouted Fausta, as Constantine came into the atrium. She was standing with her back to him. Beyond her sat Crispus, on the opposite bench in the seating area.

"The emperor is back," said Crispus loudly, cutting her off.

Fausta swung around and rushed toward Constantine. "Thank the gods," she said. "You have returned safely. I was about to send men looking for you." She hugged him, smiled up at him. "Never do that again, promise me. This city is a den of wickedness."

"I can't promise, and well you know that," said Constantine, hugging her lightly. "But you are right. It was no place for an emperor to go, though the news is good. I have found out much that is helpful."

"What do you mean?" asked Crispus.

Before Constantine could answer a knock resounded from the door into their rooms. An imperial guard appeared moments later.

"Lucius, Axel and Juliana are here to see you, my emperor."

"Send them in," said Constantine. "This is turning into an interesting night."

Lucius, Axel and Juliana came in, and related everything that had happened, with Juliana doing most of the talking.

"Take twenty imperial guards with you tomorrow night and go through every floor in that building. I want that tavern closed and the owners on their knees outside begging to keep their heads."

"You want them to lose their heads?" asked Juliana.

"You know the answer to that," said Constantine. "Anyone who dares to kill slaves without reason must be punished. An eye for an eye. A tooth for a tooth.

"And this is not just about killing slaves. These people are polluting the city. Every time I come back here I find something worse. This has to be stopped." He made a fist. "I don't care how many have to die, we need to make an example of these people."

VIII

The Via Castello, Rome, 326 A.D. The Following Evening

Juliana walked behind the troop of imperial guards as they went up the Via Castello. It was at the first hour of darkness, but there was still a hazy light from the west and red clouds on the horizon.

The revelers in the street were not as drunk as they would be later on, but there were still idiots willing to heckle the imperial guards.

"Come and join us for a drink," shouted one man. Another ran into the street to remonstrate with the centurion leading the troop. The centurion kept walking, until the man put a hand on his arm greaves.

The centurion, without breaking stride, pulled his sword and slashed at the man's arm. The man screamed and ran. The street went quiet. No one else came near them. When the troop reached the building they were interested in, it appeared closed. No one was outside and when they pounded the door, no one answered.

The centurion motioned one of his men forward. The man, a giant bursting from his uniform, had a short battering ram on his back with an iron head and handles so many men could grab it. Two men took a hold on each side and the battering began.

Lucius and Juliana waited, watching everything from the street. Axel had been instructed to return to his unit.

It took only four blows for the door to burst open. The metal covering didn't help. The men with the battering ram dropped the ram and went inside, their short swords out. The rest of the troop followed, except for four men who were posted at the door.

Juliana and Lucius went in after them. There were no customers or staff inside. The centurion pointed at a small door at the back. It was closed. It looked more solid than the front door.

"Bring your ram next door," said Lucius.

They went outside and battered at the next door, which gave access to the upper floors without going through the tavern. That door broke open in two blows. The imperial guards were getting into their stride. The blows resounded down the street. The noise from the people watching was like the buzzing from a very loud beehive.

Two men were posted on this door and the others went up the narrow stairs inside with Juliana and Lucius in the middle of the entourage. Juliana heard a cry from above and saw a body on the stairs as they continued up. The dead man had a leather apron smeared with stains. His eyes were wide open in death.

It was the only resistance they encountered before room thirty-four. The fourth and last door on the third floor. The centurion opened this door himself with a sharp blow from the pommel of his sword.

"They make these apartments too easy to break into," he said, bowing a little to Juliana, then stepping inside. "They expect the door down below and the doorman, who you saw, will be enough to protect them." He looked around the large, dark room.

"Anything in particular you're looking for? This area has a bad reputation. Our men are all banned from it."

"Why?" asked Juliana.

The centurion touched his hand to his lips, looked up. "I don't want to be talking out of place or annoying the gods with malice talk. All I will say is that is what I know. A few years ago some of our men, who we knew were on their way here, never came back to barracks. We asked around. Never got any answers. No officers cared."

"We might find answers here," said Lucius. He was standing at a large oak chest on the far side of the room. He opened the lid and winced as he looked inside.

He closed the lid.

"What's in it?" asked Juliana, coming up beside him.

"Torture tools," said Lucius. "I think we have enough evidence of the evil work going on here." He waved the centurion forward. "Have this box carried back to the emperor's quarters," he said.

"I want to see what's in it," said Juliana. The centurion's eyes were wide. He nodded, agreeing with Juliana.

Lucius put his hands up. "If you both insist," he said. He turned back to the box and lifted the lid.

Juliana looked inside. A selection of knives and saws lined the inside of the box. But what Juliana couldn't take her eyes off was four skulls, two large, and two small, in the bottom of the box. Each had a small candle inside and each was stained with black smoke, as if they had been part of many ceremonies.

"Whoever owned this apartment was busy," said the centurion. "Do you know who lived here?" His voice was a growl.

"We know who had a key to this room, and he is dead already," said Juliana.

Lucius looked around, put a finger to his lips. "Let's not talk any more until we are back at the palace, Juliana."

The crowd on the street had grown when they came out. Two guardsmen carried the box, one at either end.

Shouts went up when people saw it. The crowd was getting bigger.

"What now?" asked the centurion.

"Tell your men around the back to start a fire and chain up any who try to get out. The same this side."

They waited. Then waited some more.

People started passing them in the street, bored with watching and nothing happening. The music from a tavern across the road had started up again. Lyres and flutes echoed. Most of the imperial guards were standing in a line outside the building now, as if guarding it. Juliana and Lucius were in the middle of the street.

Then, with a shout, a group of men charged out of the door. The two giant doormen were in the front. Each had a short legionary's sword in his hand. They didn't try to engage any of the imperial guards. They headed straight for Juliana and Lucius.

Juliana had her dagger out quickly. Lucius had his sword in front of him. As the doormen came near, Juliana took a deep breath to steady herself. Then she threw the dagger at the face of the leading man. She still practiced throwing her knife almost every day. It was second nature to her now to pick a target and hit it, though hitting a moving one charging you was always a bigger challenge.

The doorman, who had a large face with scars down one side, ducked as he came forward. Juliana had anticipated that. She'd thrown low. The dagger impaled the man in the forehead, a little off center. It didn't go in far, but it did go in. Though it didn't stop him. He kept coming, the knife sticking out of him like a horn on some mythical beast.

"Back," screamed Lucius.

Both of them stepped back. Juliana's mind raced. The twang of arrows sounded. Other men had appeared in the doorway. They had bows. One imperial guard was down. The others had their shields up.

This was not going to be easy. But she'd been in many fights.

Lucius stepped in front of Juliana and raised his sword to protect them both. The injured doorman was almost upon them, and behind him was the other doorman. Both were shouting some garbled ancient curse in a strange language.

IX

The Imperial Palace, Palatine Hill, Rome, 326 A.D.

"Stop walking up and down," said Fausta. "You are driving me mad." She put her wine goblet down with a bang on the low table.

"I have to know what's going on," said Constantine. "I should have sent more men with them."

"Stop. They will be back soon. Better to send a troop than a cohort, Constantine. You know what the senate here is like about deploying troops in the city."

Constantine was pacing faster now. "I swear," he said, "this is the last straw." He punched the air.

"Every senator will have to come for the inauguration of New Rome. I will refuse permission for them to leave. I don't want to have to come back here ever again and deal with all the corruption and decadence in this place." He growled. "This city is not fit to be the capital of the empire. It's a shame on us all."

He stopped, took the gold cup waiting for him, drank from it and threw it across the private dining room at the life size statue of Augustus near the window that looked out over the city. The noise of Rome in the evening, of horses, men, and the early evening carts all mixed to make a low rumble like a beast rising from the deep.

None of the imperial slaves, who stood with eyes down at either end of the room, went to pick up the cup. They knew better. They only did what was asked of them with the emperor, lest they enrage him more.

"Another cup," he shouted.

A slave ran toward him carrying a gold cup. She was perhaps twenty years old and strikingly beautiful, but the emperor didn't even look at her.

"The apartment was being rented by one of your slaves," said Fausta. "I don't think that is entirely the fault of Rome. He came to this city looking for debauchery."

"My point exactly," said Constantine. "Everyone knows this city is the center of every evil practice. It brings out the worst in people when they come here." He pointed at Fausta. "We are all supposed to be living a life that can be an example to the people. We are supposed to be living up to the rules this Christ god passed to us, which his priests keep babbling on about. Am I mistaken?"

"No, you are right." She looked around. "Did you send Crispus with Juliana?"

"No, Crispus is on another mission for me, equally as important." He knocked back his wine, held his cup out to be refilled.

"You know I hate this city, Fausta. It has too many secrets. Too many cabals. It's all about smug defiance here. I have a good mind to burn this city down." He drank again from his wine.

"You can't do that," said Fausta. "The first Roman emperor to follow Christ cannot burn down the city where his empire began."

"Well, I want to do something they will all remember for a long time."

"Moving the senate and all the senatorial families to our new capital. That will do it. And take the best statues and all the gold from the temples and they will definitely remember you."

"You know we need a better name for our new capital than New Rome," said Constantine.

Fausta raised her voice as she replied, "I told you, the city of Constantine. That's what everyone will call it."

"No. If I agree to that, the name will be changed again when the next emperor wins a few battles and decides he deserves a capital named after him, too."

"If you name your son as your successor perhaps the name will last longer." Fausta drank from her cup.

"I suppose, that's another good reason to anoint Crispus. You are good at finding them, Fausta."

"It is the right thing to do." She smiled at him.

"I know. Let's talk about Paulina. I'd like your advice about her."

"What do you mean?"

"Do you think the Christians have taken to her being their leader here in Rome?" He sat near her on a marble bench. He stroked the marble. It was cool. The heat of the evening hadn't penetrated it.

"Yes, of course they have." Fausta smiled at him in a way he knew meant she was hiding her real thoughts about the subject.

"It is important that they do," said Constantine. "I've put her in charge of the money we're going to contribute to all the new churches here." He laughed. "It will be good, don't you think." He slapped his thigh. "It will stop them spending all their money on young boys."

"You heard about that?"

"Why do you think I put Paulina in charge of their money?"

Fausta took a gulp from her wine, looked away.

"It's not because she warms my bed, woman." Constantine stood, went to the window for some breeze and looked down on the stables courtyard below.

A row of flickering torches attached to the wall of the palace gave a golden glow to the cobbled courtyard. The sound of horses neighing and their feet on cobbles rose up to him. He leaned out.

"Who came?" he shouted.

"Crispus," came the reply.

He went to the door to their apartments and ordered the guards to open it. The stairs down to the stables were directly ahead. Soon the sound of voices reached him. Crispus appeared with one of the imperial guards.

He turned on his heel and went back into the imperial rooms.

Crispus followed.

Constantine shouted at the slaves in the atrium to leave. When they were all gone, he turned to Crispus.

"Have the arrests happened?" His tone was impatient.

"We found two of them from the list, that's all. The rest must have been warned."

"Who would have warned them?"

Crispus shook his head, slowly. "I don't know."

"Someone who wants people in their debt." Constantine paced up and down. "Two senators. That's a joke." He pointed at Crispus.

"Who else knew your orders, Father?" Crispus sat down near Fausta. She was staring at him.

"Paulina? Is that who you mean?"

"I don't want to say."

"What do you know?" Constantine shouted at his son. He was on the same path his father had taken with him, pushing his son away, but he couldn't stop himself.

It seemed for a long moment as if Crispus might defy his father.

Then he replied, softly, "She took gold from the treasury to give to the temple girls who used to work for her, and to the eunuchs who used to fill that temple she was a priestess in."

"I gave her permission to pay off the temple debts." Constantine glared at Crispus.

"I know, but she's stealing from the treasury and giving gold to anyone who claims to have renounced the old gods. Did you know that?" Crispus' expression had become a sneer. "And she sent your mother to Jerusalem."

Fausta leaned up. "It's almost three hundred years since Christ was crucified. Every scrap of Jewishness has been scrubbed out of that city. I don't know what she thinks your mother will find."

"Helena wanted to go," said Constantine.

Fausta shrugged. "A woman cannot lead the Christian church, Constantine. I told you this before. You just refuse to listen."

X

The Governor's Palace, Zion Gate, Jerusalem, 326 A.D.

"Today is the day you will tell me," said Bishop Macarius. "You can't hold out any longer."

Helena motioned the giant Nubian with the ostrich feather fan to come closer to her.

"Beat faster," she said, looking up at the blank faced giant.

As the breeze from the giant fan increased, she sighed. "I have no idea why so many people love this city," she said. "It's an oven in the summer and in the winter there's just officers' wives all squabbling with each other. The tenth legion has more hangers-on than any legion I have ever encountered."

"Don't change the subject, Helena. Why did you insist I come with you on this crazy mission? We'll never find anything in this godless dump." He waved at the city beyond the small grilled windows of the room Helena had been given by the governor. They were stuck in it because it was part of the stone walled Roman camp on the south western corner of the city. Jews had been barred from the city after their revolt almost two hundred years before. Most of the people living in the flat roofed houses were either Roman citizens or a mix of Persians, Greeks and Egyptians who had come to call the city home.

Helena was glad not to be spending too much time in the main part of the city. The smells of eastern spices filled many of the streets.

"Are you sure you want to know?"

"Yes, please. I left my brother priests, and my flock, behind in Rome and for what? We are here nearly a year and we have found absolutely nothing. Not an inscription, not a record, not a tomb. Nothing." He shook his head. "If we go back to Rome empty handed your son will not be pleased. If we can't find any evidence of Jesus, he will look like a fool for sending you here." He pointed at himself. "I don't need proof of an actual Jesus to believe in him. I don't care if we can't find his family. It's the message he brought that is important."

Helena hummed.

"Well, why did you insist I come here?"

"Will you go rushing back to Rome if I tell you?" It sounded as if she was mocking him.

"Should I?" He sounded angry now.

"I don't see any reason why, but you may feel differently after you hear what I have to say."

"Go on then, tell me." He had his hands out, pleading.

"It wasn't me who insisted you come to Jerusalem."

"That's it? It was someone else who arranged for all this?" He waved around himself, dismissively, at the scuffed wooden chairs, the chipped black marble table and the half size statues of Augustus and Vespasian, painted to look real with purple cloaks and odd gold faces, trying to look like gods.

He stood up. "Who did this? You have to tell me."

"Sister Paulina."

"What! You're not serious. That bitch." He swung around. "She just wanted me out of the way. I should have guessed." He sat down on one of the high-backed wicker chairs. "Maybe I should go back to Rome and spoil her fun."

"Maybe, but our main problem still remains, Bishop Macarius."

Bishop Macarius threw his hands up in the air. "Have you listened to any of the people who have come to visit you in the last week?"

"Yes, I've listened to a hundred soothsayers and more necromancers since I came here. I've had enough of them all. Send them away. They just want gold. Not one of them told me anything useful. And every time someone sounds like they might know something it ends up that they want to take me to their cousin's house or their uncle's villa and that they want us to buy it and dig underneath it."

"Did you know it is the feast of Tisha B'av today, Helena?"

"No, what is that? It sounds like one of those Persian festivals."

"It's a Jewish festival, actually. Today is the only day in the year that Jews are allowed back into Jerusalem. I think we should listen to the Jews who've come to see you today. This was mostly their city three hundred years ago. They are far more likely to know where to find traces of Jesus than all those Armenians, Egyptians, Persians and Romans put together."

Helena stood. "That's asking for trouble. The Jews are desperate. They'll say anything to be allowed stay here. You see them if you want to, but don't let them take you in. I've a meeting with the legate of the tenth legion. We need him to commit more men to leveling the temple of Venus."

"You'll be lucky to get anything more from him. I expect the temple priestesses' bribes are slowing things up."

"Bribes and all the rest."

"They are all hoping we'll go away so everything can go back to the way it was." He went down on one knee in front of her.

"Helena, I beg you, come with me to meet the Jews. You are right that they are desperate, but everyone in Jerusalem will be persuaded if we get information from them. They judged Jesus and they buried him. Please, join me. You can meet the legate after."

She stood. "I can see why they made you a bishop."

The bishop bowed and left the room. Helena went to her bed chamber on the opposite side of the tower and with the help of her body slave she prepared herself. It was important that anyone who met her would know immediately that she was the mother of the emperor.

She'd heard that some who met her, or her son, were so consumed by the meeting that their dreams were filled with the imperial family. Others made up stories, lies about what had happened at a meeting, which they spread about for years.

It was important to give anyone who met her something to remember, and to embellish.

She wore a thin gold and jeweled diadem through her hair and a purple stole over her shoulder. Her gown was a cream Egyptian linen sheath reaching down to her ankles.

She held her head high as she walked into the main room of the basilica the tenth legion had built to replace the previous building burnt down during the Jewish wars. The room was double height and had a row of thin marble pillars down each side, but it was still a stable compared to the basilicas in Rome. Perhaps a hundred people could fill it, standing or sitting on the wooden benches that lined the too-hot room that afternoon.

The legionaries who managed what remained of the palace and the new buildings had left the main doors of the building open to catch the midsummer breeze, which some days came from the far-off sea, but there was not much of it that afternoon. Guards stood, clinking by the doors. They searched all who entered the building to ensure that no weapons would be carried into the room by a zealot or anyone else with a grievance.

Helena arrived through the door at the back. A double row of legionaries, carrying javelins held tight, surrounded the area at the back of the hall while she spoke with the three officials charged with ensuring any audience went off well.

The three men bowed as she approached.

"Up, up," she said. "I need you to do something for me."

"Yes, my lady," said the oldest man, a white-haired Greek with a flat nose.

"We see only the Jews today."

One of the men smiled, shook his head.

"My lady," he said. "There are very few…"

"Be quiet," said the older man, cutting in.

"Yes, my lady," he went on, then bowed.

Helena waited with her back to the audience room while orders were shouted. A great shuffling and muttering went on and on until she thought it would never stop.

Then, finally, the hall quieted, and she was ushered to the golden governor's chair at the top of the room. The only people in the room now were Roman officials in togas, Bishop Macarius, Roman legionaries and five bedraggled looking men and one woman wearing a black gown, similar to those she'd seen the women of the desert wearing.

"One at a time, please, Bishop," she said as the bishop approached to stand beside her throne.

"One will come forward," said the bishop loudly.

The first man had a limp and white hair. He begged, quietly, for the right to be buried on the Mount of Olives when he died.

"Granted," said Helena.

A scribe at a desk by the wall waved the man to him to take note of the decision.

The next man asked for the prohibition on Jews entering the city on all other days to be lifted.

"Not granted," she said, with a wave of her hand.

The man went to his knees. "I beg you, my lady," he said.

"Take him away," said Helena.

Two guards strode forward, picked the man up under his arms and took him out of the room. He screamed as he was thrown from the building.

Next came the woman. "My lady, you are searching for records of the one they call Jesus?" she said, after prostrating herself.

"Everyone in Jerusalem knows that by now," said the bishop. "Can you help us?"

"I know where the devil is, my lord. Does that help? And I wish to be buried on the Mount of Olives."

Helena shook her head, waved the woman away. The final two supplicants repeated the begging of the others, to be allowed to be buried on the Mount of Olives. Helena granted their wishes. As they were about to leave there was a commotion at the main entrance to the hall. A shout went up and a guard rushed over to where Helena and the bishop were talking.

"The woman says you agreed to her request too," said a guard as he approached Helena. Then he bowed.

"I didn't agree to anything for her," said Helena. "Tell her to go."

"I'll do it," said the bishop. He turned to Helena. "I'll follow you back to the rooms. Have some apple tea. They just got a new supply."

Helena was back in her rooms and in a simple tunic with all her jewels boxed up when Macarius arrived back.

"What else did that woman have to say?" asked Helena as the bishop sat down on the couch in her dining room.

"The usual tale of woe," said the bishop.

"Explain," said Helena.

"Her name is Bina. She claims to have seen Jesus in a dream." He sat on the Egyptian wicker chair opposite Helena. "She is a troublemaker."

"Why?"

"Her family call her a traitor, so she says."

"Why is that?"

"For talking about Jesus, calling him the messiah. She says she's lost everything because of her dreams." He sighed. "I expect she's looking for a reward."

Helena stretched her arms. "What was all that about knowing where the devil is?"

"That's part of her dream. She says she sees the emperor in her dream. And that he comes back to her almost every night."

"Is she still below?" Helena pointed to the hall where she had held the audience.

"I had her arrested," said the bishop.

"For what?"

"Cursing you and making up stories to trick you."

"Have her brought to me," said Helena.

"She is a good liar, that's all."

"You're probably right, but she might provide some entertainment."

She looked at her hands. What she really needed, if she couldn't find any evidence of Jesus, was a few good stories to take back to her son.

XI

The Imperial Palace, Palatine Hill, Rome, 326 A.D.

Paulina bowed as she entered the yard. Constantine was talking to the head of the imperial stables, a man he'd met fourteen years before, when he'd first occupied rooms in the palace after taking over the city.

"Come and talk with me, Paulina," said Constantine. "I always enjoy the stables before the rest of the house is up." He put a hand on the stable master's arm. "I'll be taking your advice about when to exercise the mares in New Rome, my friend. Thank you." The man bowed and left them. Constantine walked into the stable building. It took up one wall of the courtyard and had two wide doors for horses to go in and come out.

The only other people in the stables were two stable boys sweeping. The sounds of horses whickering and distant shouts and the early morning rumbles of carts from the city were all that could be heard. The smell of the horses, a mixture of sweat and drying manure, was strong.

"There is a private room up here," said Constantine, walking away from Paulina, heading toward the end of the building, where chariots were lined up against the wall. He walked around them and headed for a small doorway in the stone wall. It was barely big enough for him to get through. She was right behind him.

"I'll go first. The last time I was here it was full of cobwebs. You don't want them all over you."

"Where does it go?" she asked, coming up beside him. She had a light green summer cloak on. It was loosely tied and he could see the swell of her breasts

"That's why they'll never make you bishop of Rome," said Constantine, pointing at her cleavage.

"They were never going to anyway. Covering up like an Arab woman would not make any difference."

"Maybe, but you don't make it easy for the men who run this city. They like women who do what they're told." He was going up the stone stairs fast. They were just wide enough for two people to pass. He pushed away cobwebs as he went up.

"I don't think anyone has been up here for years," he said, as he reached the top. The attic space they were in was as long as the stable. The floor was white with dust.

"You take me to all the best places," said Paulina. She slipped the cloak from around her shoulders and went over to a long wooden box against the outer wall, put her cloak down and sat on it.

"What was this room supposed to be for?"

"For the emperor's secret meetings."

"What? Surely there are better places than this."

"Not if you like stable boys."

"So, there hasn't been a lot of use for it recently." She smiled, brushed at a pile of dust with her foot. "You stay well away from Rome."

"I've a good excuse, unifying the empire and defeating all my rivals."

"Not all," said Paulina.

Constantine sat beside her. "Who is my rival now, dear Paulina? No one would dare raise an army against me."

"It's not an army that will defeat you. There are other ways to lose power." She turned to him, put her hand on his bare knee. His purple summer tunic had a gold edge to it. She ran her hand along the golden edge.

"You look perfect, Paulina." He closed his eyes, breathed in her perfume. "I expect all the wives of all the servants of Christ hate you."

"Does Fausta?"

"I have no idea." He shook his head slowly. "Tell me, do you have any other news besides my imminent doom? I can have a hundred soothsayers predict that every single day."

She pulled her hand away. "Have you considered my request for more funds for our church at Nero's circus?"

Constantine sniffed. "I've been told by the master of my treasury that I should wait until Macarius returns to allocate further funds." He looked around. "What is that smell?"

A trickle of smoke appeared from the doorway they'd passed through.

"Fire," said Paulina softly. She looked around. "Is there any other way out of here?"

Constantine touched the dagger at his side. "We can cut through the roof if we have to." The roof would not be easy to reach. They looked around. They could stand on the box they'd been sitting on.

A stamping and then wild neighing came from below.

"I have some wonderful horses down there. Let's see what we can do to rescue them."

The stairs were full of smoke as they went down. When they reached the bottom, they were confronted by a wall of flame in the stables. The chariots were blazing. In the distance they could see panicking horses racing for the doors to the yard and the stable boys running about, opening the doors to allow the horses to escape. Flames were billowing in their direction.

Constantine turned to Paulina. "That dress of yours will be your death shroud if it catches fire."

She backed up the stairs. "Can we get out through the roof?" She started coughing. Her hands were against the wall, shaking.

Constantine looked at the flames again. He could run through it, but even if he carried Paulina through it naked her hair might catch fire. He waited to see if the fire would abate. And then a crash echoed. A beam from the roof had fallen where he was just about to race through the inferno. The whole upper floor might fall in if they didn't act fast.

"Back up." He coughed. His eyes were stinging. His chest felt heavy.

This couldn't be the way he would go, could it? How in Hades name had this happened at the exact moment he was in the attic area?

XII

The Governor's Palace, Zion Gate, Jerusalem, 326 A.D.

"Tell me your story," said Helena. They were in her rooms in the tower overlooking the city. The bishop sat back in his wicker chair. The two guards who had brought the woman stood near the door.

"I am so grateful to you. So grateful that you see me." The woman went to her knees, then prostrated herself on the cool stone floor.

"Up," said Helena. "Tell your story."

The woman stood with her hands crossed over her chest, as if protecting herself from a blow.

"We were a rich family, once. We had olive groves. I and my husband were happy." She started whimpering. "But my sister was jealous. She turned my husband against me. She told him I was possessed by demons, that I would never have children because of it." Bina's head bent more. "She said it was because I loved the stories of Jesus that a preacher had spoken about in our village when I was young." She sighed.

"My husband left me for her. He told me to go. So I found refuge with a group of Christians at the edge of the desert. They kept me alive. They pray every day for Jesus' return, they say the end times are here, upon us. They say we will all be taken to heaven soon."

Bina stopped talking. She was staring at the floor, as if remembering something.

"Why did you come to see me?" Helena said in a bored voice.

"Because of my dreams."

"What dreams?"

Bina took a step forward, put her hands out.

"I see Christ on the cross. Then I see where they lay him out. It is Jerusalem before the rebellion. My grandmother told me stories about the city bustling with Jews, not the way it is now."

"You know what we are looking for then?" said the bishop. "We look for proof that Jesus was here. A dream is not proof."

"My grandmother's family supplied the trees for the crosses the Romans used back then." Bina looked around. "I think this is why I'm cursed. What my family did has been visited on me."

"We are not punished by God for things that our fathers did," said Helena.

The woman shook her head, raised her hands. "But I feel the weight of it all on me. I cannot stop thinking about it." She sniffed, holding back her tears.

Helena stared at her, an idea dawning. Constantine would be interested in where the cross of Jesus had come from. Others might be too. "Where did your family put the old crosses after they were used? Did your grandmother tell you that?"

Bina shook her head. "No, no, I do not know that, but I can show you where their workshop was."

"Good," said the bishop. "Let's go there."

"First," said Helena. "I want to hear more about your dreams. Tell me everything you see. And tell me about the devil."

The woman licked her lips. "I see your son, the emperor. I see a daemon behind him." She glanced at the water jug on a small table near Helena.

Helena took one of the glasses and passed it to the woman. She drank eagerly from it.

"Thank you. You are as good as they said you were."

"Tell me more about this daemon." Helena leaned forward.

"The daemon is cloaked in fire, my lady and behind him there are others. His consorts, male and female, old and young, all naked except for the flames and smoke that surround them."

"These are the dreams of a disturbed woman," said the bishop. "There is no need to believe any of this."

Bina turned to the bishop, pointed at him and said, "I saw your face," she said. "Among the daemons."

XIII

The Imperial Palace, Palatine Hill, Rome, 326 A.D.

Constantine poked his dagger through the thin gap between two roof tiles. He sliced the blade up, then down. Then he put the blade along the other side of the tile and did the same thing. Shouting rang out from the yard. The attic space had smoke all through it. He waved it away. It got thicker.

He was standing on the box they'd been sitting on and reaching up to the corner of the sloping roof where it met the wall. Paulina was below, coughing.

"I feel dizzy, my lord," she called up to him.

Constantine banged the tiles with the jeweled end of the dagger. They moved, bounced back into place. He banged the tile again. The biggest gem fell from the end of the dagger. The tile moved. A gap opened. He hit the tile again, harder. It broke. Part of it fell back into the room, just missing him. A rush of smoke streamed out of the hole. He turned his head away and kept bashing at the tiles around the one he had moved.

Soon there was a gap big enough for Paulina to get through. He looked around. The flames had been encouraged by him opening the hole in the roof. Part of the floor was on fire. Flames were leaping out of the doorway to the lower floor.

"You go up first," he said to Paulina. "It's big enough."

"I am not leaving you," she said.

"You have to go first," he said. "I can lift you up. You can make the hole bigger as you go through."

She hugged him, coughed. He made a cup from his hands and pushed her up through the hole. She peered back down at him, pushed some tiles away, then put her hand down to help him.

He reached for the edge of the tiles instead, to pull himself up. A tile came down on top of him, bouncing off his shoulder. He reached for more tiles, pulled them down too. The hole was a lot bigger now. The wooden beams holding up the roof were visible.

"Get back," he shouted at Paulina. "The roof might cave in." He reached with both hands for an exposed wooden beam and kicked with his feet against the wall. For a moment he thought he wouldn't make it. His eyes were smarting and his mouth bone dry from the smoke moving past him.

He kicked again and managed to get an elbow over the roof edge. Heat from the flames touched his bare legs. He pulled himself up, fast. A lot of shouting echoed from the yard. Fire spreading was one of the biggest fears people had in Rome. A relay of water jugs would not be enough to douse this. They would have to flood the floor of the stables below and hope the flames didn't spread to the palace.

He pulled himself onto the roof and lay on the tiles, spreading his weight, relief pouring through him with each breath of clean air. A scream came from a palace window above. He looked up. One of the slaves was at a window pointing down at him.

"That way," he shouted to Paulina, pointing at the end of the roof. They reached it and looked down. It was a long way to the ground. A stable boy below spotted them and pointed up. A Nubian slave nearby ran off and came back moments later with a rope. He threw it up to them. It took three throws before Paulina, reaching out dangerously to her side, grabbed it. They tied it to a wooden beam.

Paulina went down first. Then Constantine. A group of slaves held their hands out for them to break their fall, if they slipped. They ended up with bruises and scratches from scraping the wall, but nothing else.

He brushed himself down, angrily, then gave orders for the trough at the end of the stable yard to be opened and the water usually used for cleaning the yard to be directed onto the floor of the stables. The last of the horses were being led out of the stable yard by the gate at the far end. Smoke still billowed from the stable doors and an acrid smell filled the air, making the horses whinny and rear up as they left.

"The stables are gone," he shouted, when the water was flowing across the stable yard toward the burning building. He turned to the master of the stables, who was overseeing a line of slaves passing water buckets being thrown into the burning building without much effect.

"Get the fire hooks, fast. We'll throw them up to the top wall and bring the building down. We may need a hundred men to do it. Get the imperial guards and any other legionaries you can find. Go."

He stared at the frantic activity. How had the fire started? Had someone seen him heading up into the roof space? He pressed his fists to his sides. They'd had a lucky escape. The sooner they left this city the better.

Constantine and Paulina stayed in the yard until a troop of the imperial guards arrived with fire ropes and hooks. Experienced throwers had the grapples over the top edge of the stable wall quickly. One group had a section of the front wall of the stables down in no time. Then another section was pulled. Soon after, the whole front wall came down. A great whoosh sounded as the wall collapsed. Dust and debris rained into the yard.

People coughed and stepped back to the far wall.

Constantine ordered the imperial guards to work on the wall at the end of the stables, where the gate was, as the fire was still burning there. A great crowd had gathered outside and when the end wall came down there a loud cheering broke out as dust, smoke and sparks filled the air.

"Block the stables off from the palace," said Constantine, as he coughed. "Every door and window must be mortared up until the yard is working again," he said to the head slave of the Imperial Palace, who was at his side.

"Douse the stables with water for three days, non-stop. I do not want to see this fire springing up again."

"We will look after it, my emperor," said the man, bowing. Four imperial guards were standing around Constantine. People in the street, visible through the open gate, were pointing at him. He turned to look around. Paulina was by the door back into the palace. She bowed at him and was gone a moment later. Coming toward him was Fausta. She had her arms raised and was screaming.

"Why are you here? We have slaves and so many, many people to do all this work. Come away, Constantine. The crowd has seen you."

"I'm not afraid of my people," he said.

"These are Romans," she said, bowing a little in front of him. "I don't trust the mob. This could have all been done to attract them." Her voice was high pitched. She stared at the still burning wreck of the stables. "How did this happen?"

"Someone wants me dead."

XIV

The Governor's Palace, Zion Gate, Jerusalem, 326 A.D.

"This woman is evil," said the bishop. "She should be locked up."

"Take her to a cell," said Helena. "And treat her well." She straightened her back, smiled to herself. This woman's story might not be what they'd hoped for, but something could be made of it.

The guards took the protesting woman away, pinning her arms to her sides.

"You don't believe any of it, I hope," said Bishop Macarius when she was gone.

"I don't know who to believe, sometimes," said Helena. Then she smiled at the bishop and changed the subject. "How is that young deacon who sleeps in your room? Is he well?"

"As you know, I provide spiritual guidance for the boy. That is all. And he is well, thank you."

"I am sure he is, with your care. Now, I am tired, Bishop, perhaps it is time for you to go back to your deacon. Daily guidance is good for us, I hear."

The bishop stared at her. His mouth opened and closed, as if he wanted to say something, but thought better of it.

When he was gone, Helena ordered her house slave to fetch some Persian wine and some local white cheese and the dark bread from the Greek bread shop.

She drank alone in her room, sipping at the watered-down wine, remembering days from long ago with Constantine's father, until the sun was half-way down to the horizon and the heat of the day had passed.

She called a guard then and asked for Bina to be brought to her. When the woman appeared she was shaking. Her hands were bound by rough rope.

"Take the rope off," Helena shouted at the guard. "I never asked for her to be tied up."

The guard bowed. "A guard was struck by the prisoner. The rope was put on after that."

"I am sure if she hit one of you, she had a reason." Helena pointed at the wicker chair where the bishop had been sitting. "Please, Bina, sit, have some water and wine. There is plenty of bread and cheese too."

The woman stared ravenously at the food. She went first to the bronze tray the food was sitting on and stuffed her mouth, as if afraid the food would be taken from her any moment.

"Sit, eat slowly, drink some water."

The woman looked at the wicker chair but sat on the floor. She cradled a piece of white cheese in one hand and a hunk of bread in the other. She bit at them as Helena spoke.

"I want you to take me to where your family had their business in the city, supplying crosses for criminals to be crucified."

"Why?" asked the woman in a curious tone.

"I want to see what is left of this business your family once carried out."

"Every wall was broken down when Jerusalem was destroyed by the Emperor Hadrian. That is the truth, Empress."

"Does your family ever talk about what street your ancestors had their business on, what district?"

"Hadrian was here nearly two hundred years ago. The city has been rebuilt. It would not be easy to find."

"Someone must know where your family business used to be in Jerusalem."

The woman's cheeks were bulging. She bent over, coughed and spewed half eaten food over the floor.

"You want my help?" she asked, sobbing, on her knees, looking down at the food.

"Yes," replied Helena.

"We all need help too," said Bina, sniffing, half-crying. "Christians are also banned from visiting this city, if they were ever Jews. We must be allowed into Jerusalem. And," she looked up, "we need a church so that we'll be ready for the second coming, when our Lord Jesus returns." She put her hands on the top of her head, bowed, as if marking something.

"I can help you all, Bina," said Helena. "I have already given orders that all followers of Christ be allowed into the city no matter if they were once Jews or not. That should already have happened."

"It hasn't. They use Hadrian's edicts against Jews to turn us away." Bina groaned loudly.

Helena called out for a slave to come and clean up the floor.

"I will change all this," said Helena, softly. "I intend to start a great church here. A church that will stand over Jesus' tomb. I believe that tomb is under the temple to Aphrodite. We will start building work soon. The site is almost clear." Helena leaned forward, lowered her voice more. "But we need more than an empty tomb. We need to find proof of his suffering and his resurrection."

The woman shook her head. "There is no proof. How can there be? We must simply believe. That will be enough." She nodded over and over.

"Take this woman away, bathe and dress her," said Helena, turning to the imperial slave standing behind her. She looked back to Bina. "We will go out together into the city in the morning."

The slave went to Bina and put her hand on Bina's shoulder.

Bina went with the slave, but turned at the door and said, "I cannot tell you exactly where my family used to work. All I know is the street name."

"That is enough," said Helena.

"Will the bishop be with us?" Bina asked.

"No."

Bina smiled.

XV

The Imperial Palace, Palatine Hill, Rome, 326 A.D.

Constantine paced from side to side of the giant audience hall. At the far end a row of imperial guards stood to attention, their hands on the pommels of their swords. The head slave of the Imperial Palace was standing near Constantine, waiting for instructions.

"Did you find out if anyone was seen at the stables before the fire started?" Constantine's tone was sharp, his anger clear.

"Emperor, we asked everyone who was there, the stable boys, the Nubian who was only there to walk the horses around the yard, everyone. No one saw who started it." He smiled, showing yellowed teeth. "I recommend they all be tortured. A crushed finger or toe usually loosens the tongue."

"You will not torture any of them. I want them watched. I want you to report if any of them meet with anyone unusual." He growled his dissatisfaction.

"It will be done."

"Do any of you have a theory as to how the fire started?"

"Some say this is the old gods sending a message."

"What message?" Constantine shouted. "I simply assume this was started deliberately. Perhaps the gate was left open in the morning and someone was hiding in the stables, and when they saw me go up to the attic they started the fire and slipped away. That's a better explanation than a message from the gods."

"That is certainly possible, my emperor." He paused. "Did many people know about your meeting?"

"I told nobody," said Constantine stiffly.

The old slave sighed, put his head to one side. "Perhaps your friend spoke about her meeting with you. It is a big thing to have a private meeting with an emperor early in the morning."

Constantine stared at the man. "Have you talked about who I was with?"

"I never speak about an emperor's private meetings." He sounded indignant.

A knock echoed from the end of the hall. A purple tunicked slave came through the door and hurried toward Constantine.

"Juliana the Saxon wishes to see you, my emperor."

Constantine waved his hand. "Let her in." He turned to the old slave. "The empress wishes to see you. Go to her." The man hurried away.

Juliana walked fast up the empty hall, her sandaled feet echoing. A small axe dangled from her belt. Her leather uniform shone as she passed through shafts of light from the small grilled windows high up.

"You're dressed for a fight, not a feast," said Constantine, holding his arms wide to welcome her. "What happened on the raid?"

Juliana bowed, briefly, then came close to him. "We were attacked. Lucius is injured. He may lose his hand."

Constantine stepped back and raised his fist. "You didn't bring enough men. I knew I should have sent more."

"They had well-armed veterans defending the building."

Constantine's voice rose. "I want the head of whoever owns that building."

"I expected you would say that." Juliana paused, rubbed her hand across her mouth, then went on, "The owner has been arrested already, but there's a problem. He claims to have imperial protection. He's been asking for someone from your household."

"You've questioned him? Where did you find him?" Constantine's pulse was quickening.

"We spoke briefly. After we killed the owner's guards, he slunk out of the building like a rat. I took him to meet my Saxons and he shat himself when he saw a few giant axes and the men carrying them."

"Who does he claim protects him?"

Juliana paused, looked at the marble floor.

"Spit it out." Constantine was becoming angrier.

"Crispus." She said it softly, then looked at Constantine.

"Holy Jupiter! That's not possible. My son doesn't frequent those places. Why the hell would he be giving his protection to such a man?" Every word was shouted.

"That's what I thought, so I did some digging before I brought this to you."

"And?" Constantine looked around to make sure there were no slaves nearby. There were none.

Juliana lowered her voice. "Seutonius rented rooms in the building. He had a rental agreement. It had a seal on it from a well-known lawyer. I found the lawyer's rooms near the forum and I persuaded him," she rattled the axe on her belt, "to tell me who paid for the rental and for his seal." She looked straight at Constantine.

"Crispus paid?" asked Constantine. "Surely not. Why would he pay for Seutonius to have rooms in that debauched house?"

Juliana put her hands up. "All I know is that Crispus provides the protection, that he rents rooms and he was involved with Seutonius in some way." She looked up at Constantine.

He stared at her, his mind working. "Was he involved in Seutonius' death?" His expression had darkened. "I don't believe it. I want to see him now. Find him, bring him to me."

Juliana headed away.

Constantine shouted after her. "Do not tell him why he is summoned, just get him here."

He walked around the hall, looking at the wall paintings. They showed scenes of the lives of previous emperors, Augustus winning the battle of Actium, Vespasian taking Jerusalem, and his own victory at the battle of the Milvian Bridge. He looked at the picture and wondered what other battle had been portrayed in that spot before they'd painted this scene.

He pinched his nose, breathed deep to calm himself. He would keep himself in check with Crispus. He had a reason for doing this.

He would not let any of this come between them. He would not fall out with his son the way he had with his father.

Thoughts of his father's death had dogged him in the last year, as Crispus' demands to succeed him grew petulant, reminding him of his own words to his father and what had happened at the end. It had not been right. He could see that clearly now.

He could have avoided it.

He would still have become emperor.

Footsteps echoed. Juliana was returning. She came quickly up the room.

"Crispus has left Rome," she said.

Constantine let out a loud groan. "Where has he gone? I did not give him permission to leave."

"No one knows. His rooms are empty. Perhaps he's gone back to his fleet."

"His fleet was taken from him," Constantine shouted. "Send messengers to each city gate and find out which direction he took." Memories of arguments with his father filled his mind, while an emptiness filled his gut. He couldn't lose the son he was so proud of, but could he let Crispus defy him?

How had it come to this?

Juliana bit her lip. "What do we do when we find him?"

"I want Crispus arrested. He has a lot of questions to answer. Now go. See to it."

XVI

The Governor's Palace, Zion Gate, Jerusalem, 326 A.D.

"Come along," said Helena, turning back to Bina.

Bina was standing near the door into the tower. Around Helena, in the parade area in front of the tower, there were six imperial guards with shields and spears in their hands, ready to defend Helena if anyone dared to attack her.

Bina hurried to Helena's side. The gate to the Roman camp at the edge of the city was open. More guards were standing on the rampart and by the tower, which formed the northern corner of the Roman camp on the edge of the city.

It was early morning, so the heat of the day had not fully hit, but there were still traders outside the gate, waiting to sell their wares to the Romans.

News that the mother of the Emperor of Rome was visiting Jerusalem had traveled far in the time she had been here. Spice merchants from the Hind and beyond mixed with silk traders, slavers from all corners and the usual merchants from Egypt. All hoping to make a lasting relationship with the empress.

"Clear a path," shouted the centurion in charge of her guard unit.

Helena and Bina followed him. Around them the imperial guards matched their pace.

"Please, Empress, stop, look at our wares," came a shout. "Empress, please help us," another shout went up. As they passed through the stone gateway the shouts became more urgent. A press of faces pushed in toward them. Helena could smell old sweat and pungent spices.

She knew what it was like to be in need like many waiting at the gate, but it was decades since she'd found favor with Constantine's father and become the mistress of a Roman general. In that time, as her partner rose to become emperor and then discarded her, bitterness had found a place in her heart. Many supplicants she had helped over the years had forgotten that help too fast. She was wary now. Eaten bread is soon forgotten.

Bina's head went down onto her chest at the sight of the crowd.

Helena put her hand on Bina's arm. "They will not all follow us to the temple. Some are waiting to see the quartermaster. He comes out to select who he will buy from at this time each morning."

And she was right; as they made their way to the cardo, the main street running north-south through the city, the number of followers diminished. Most of the shops and taverns under the colonnades on each side had not opened yet, but the bread makers had and there were lines of people, women and slaves mostly, waiting to buy from the piles of flat bread sitting on the shop counters. The bread gave a welcoming smell to the early morning city.

Everyone gawped at the empress and her bodyguards as they went by. When they reached the forum, that too was mostly empty. A few birds with bright crowns on their heads pecked at the stone paving, looking for food. A line of slaves waited with dull red amphora for their turn at the water fountain, before heading off to their masters' quarters in the poorer parts of the city.

The entrance to the temple of Venus still stood, a narrow gate in the western wall of the forum. Waiting at the gate was the legate in charge of clearing the site. He saluted as they approached. Bina gripped Helena's arm as they came near the entrance.

"That is the street," she said, pointing to the north, where a lane headed off toward the northern wall.

"That was the edge of the city in Jesus' time. The executioner's gate was just here, and there were workshops in this area serving the Roman demand for chains and nails and crosses."

"Not an auspicious trade," said Helena.

"My family were one of the few who did this work. We were outcasts even then."

"From the lowest will come the help you need, that was predicted," said Helena.

She raised a hand in greeting to the legate, then tapped the arm of the centurion leading her group. "Not into the temple area today, up that way," she said, pointing to the lane where Bina's family had once had their business.

They turned as one and headed toward the lane, leaving the legate staring after them, his hands on his hips, his mouth open wide. The lane was only large enough for two donkey carts to pass each other, so the legionaries pressed close to Helena and Bina as they entered it. It was darker here than the forum too, but after a moment Helena's eyes got used to it.

"How far up?" she asked, tugging urgently at Bina's arm.

"Where it bends," came the reply.

Helena peered forward past the backs and shields of the legionaries. The bend was further along, past rows of tall shuttered houses and workshops on their right and the high wall to the grounds of the temple of Venus on their left.

A shout, as if from a child, echoed and above them and a shutter banged open. Something fell into the street in front of them.

"They still throw garbage into the street?" asked Helena.

"I don't know," said Bina. "I'm not allowed to live here." She looked up at the open shutter. A red-haired woman was peering down at them. She had her hand to her mouth. She stepped back out of view when she saw she'd been observed.

"We heard Gauls had been settled here recently. Retired legionaries from the third," said Bina. "They are dirty, not like us."

They'd reached the bend in the lane. Beyond it, the lane changed. It had houses on both sides. At the corner stood a large double doored workshop. The doors were closed and dusty, as if the workshop was no longer in use.

"Knock on these doors," said Helena to the centurion, pointing at the two bigger doors and another smaller one to the left, which gave access to the rooms on the two floors above.

The centurion knocked with his fist on one door and other legionaries knocked with the ends of their spears on the other doors. They pounded harder and harder, as if trying to break in.

After a few more thuds shouts came from above.

"I'm coming. We have done nothing. Our taxes are paid. We are followers of Ba'al. We are allowed to live here."

A woman was looking down from a first-floor window. She had black hair and a round face.

"Stop banging," said Helena.

The street fell quiet as they waited. The sound of a bar being moved followed, the smaller door opened, and the woman came out. Peering out from behind her was a young girl with the same wild shock of black hair.

"We need to talk," said Helena, waving the woman forward. The woman came nearer, then stopped, bowing with her hands up. Her child waited at the doorway.

"What is it I can do for the great empress?" She bowed again. Her red dress billowed out around her and a necklace with a phallic symbol in wood at the end of it fell forward in front of her.

"What type of workshop is this?" asked Helena, pointing at the two large doors.

"My family used to operate a timber business, but we have struggled since the forests of Ephraim were sold."

"Where is your husband?"

"He died," said the woman flatly. "Fighting the people who stop us going near the forest." She put a hand to her chest, bowed her head in remembrance.

"Do you still trade?" asked Helena.

"We work with sacred wood."

"What sacred wood?" said Helena.

"Wood blessed by the temple priestesses." She pointed at the temple to Venus. "They used to be just there, but they have moved."

69

"What do you do with the wood?" Helena took a step toward the locked doors.

"We make it into fertility symbols, like this." She lifted the long piece of wood dangling from her neck.

"Show me the workshop," said Helena.

Bina was standing quietly to the side. She was staring at the woman, as if she knew her from some other life.

The woman went in through the small door. Soon after the sound of bars being moved came through the doors and one of the larger doors creaked open. Beyond was a room with thick dust mites swirling in the shaft of sunlight that lit up the floor. A wooden worktable took up the middle of the room. Discarded tools lay on it and piles of wood of various shapes lay around it.

"Three of us work here," said the woman. "Me, my daughter and my sister. This work is not for men."

Bina coughed. Helena looked at her. "You want to say something?"

Bina nodded. "Where is your family from?" she asked the woman, softly.

"Ephraim."

"My family is from there too." Bina looked around. "I was told they once owned a wood trading business here, at the bend in this street." She put both hands to her chest. "I brought the empress here."

The dark-haired woman bowed at Bina. "You are welcome. My family bought this over a hundred years ago, when we were allowed come to live here by the governor at the time. My great grandfather built this building with his brothers." She pointed upward, then all around them. "There was nothing but a rubble pit here when he came. This was one of the last streets in the city to be rebuilt."

"Where was this rubble pit?" asked Helena.

The woman pointed below their feet.

In the street outside a crowd had gathered. It was getting noisy. Someone shouted, "Come to our workshop. This one is unclean, Empress."

Helena turned to the centurion who was standing nearby. "Send a man back to the camp. We need twenty more legionaries to clear the street and set up a watch system on this workshop. No one is to come or go here without my permission."

She turned to the dark-haired woman. "We will be here for a few days. Then we will be gone."

"My business will be ruined," said the woman. She looked distraught. "We will starve." She looked from Helena to Bina and back.

"No, you will never be poor again," said Helena, firmly. "I will make you an offer now for everything in the pit below us."

"Not the workshop or the building?" asked the woman suspiciously.

"No, just what is below ground. How much will you take for it all?" She could make something of this. Her prayers had been properly answered. She would get back to New Rome in time for the dedication, and they would find something here to bring back, to prove all the doubters wrong.

The woman stared, her eyes narrowing. "Ten gold solidii, the new coins your son has minted."

"You like the new coins here," said Helena. "But I will not give you ten."

The woman looked disappointed.

"I will give you twenty, if you also agree to fill in the hole below us when we are finished and never dig it up."

Bina let out a gasp.

"And you will be paid two gold solidii for bringing me here," said Helena, to Bina.

"But how do you know there is anything of value down there?" asked Bina.

"I have seen this place before," said Helena. "And I saw your face here, in a dream." She smiled properly for the first time in months.

XVII

The Imperial Palace, Palatine Hill, Rome, 326 A.D.

Constantine walked toward Paulina as she came into the atrium. The small atrium was only occasionally used by previous emperors, mostly for private meetings.

"Good to see you are well," he said. He hugged her, then pushed her away from him and looked her up and down. "Not even a scratch."

"I have a few, but not where anyone can see them."

He touched her shoulder. "Are people gossiping about us?"

"I deny it all. It's a total pack of lies. The woman you rescued from the flames was a slave who looks a little like me, but older." She smiled, shrugged.

"I never met anyone who looks like you," said Constantine. He stepped closer to her.

"We cannot go back to the past," she said. "That's what I wanted to tell you when we met."

"You are right," he said.

"You have enough women in your life."

"And I have no need to run after anyone anymore."

"You never did." She touched his bare arm. "But you must be careful now, someone wants you dead," she whispered.

"Not for the first time." He laughed. "It used to be whole armies and cities wanting me dead. Now it is just someone."

"Do not make light of it, Constantine." Paulina pushed him away. Her green gown clung to her body. She pulled at it to make it less revealing.

"You have sworn off all the sins of the flesh?" asked Constantine.

"I've been told I will suffer in the fires of Hades forever if I do not renounce all the sins of the flesh. And after that taste of the fires yesterday, I know why they will be worth avoiding."

"I can still feel the flames," said Constantine, rubbing his bare arms, then touching his face. "That was a close thing, yesterday.

"How long will these good intentions last, Paulina?"

"Until the church at Nero's Circus is built, at least."

"I'd better put aside more money for it." He pointed at the purple silk covered couches in the center of the atrium, under the opening to the blue sky above.

"Sit. Tell me everything people are saying about what happened."

Paulina sat. Constantine stood in front of her, his arms folded across his chest.

"The people are talking about Crispus. They say he's run away. They say that he must have been involved in the fire."

Constantine closed his eyes. "I will not judge him until I speak to him. No one else should until he has a chance to defend himself. He is still my son." He looked away. "It pains me that he might have had anything to do with this." His voice rose. "I could not sleep last night. Faces and memories kept coming before my eyes."

Paulina stood, put her hands on his arms, gripped him. "This is not your fault. This is not like what happened with your father."

"Do you know what Crispus' last words to me were?"

She shook her head.

"*You do not listen.* Those were his last words." He let out a pained grunt. "I remember how I was with my father, Paulina. And I remember what he was like with me. It's all come around again."

She squeezed his arms. "Crispus asked me about your father earlier this year. About how his grandfather died."

Constantine pulled away from her. "What did you tell him?"

"The truth. His grandfather was poisoned by a tribeswoman he entertained in his rooms on the night of his death."

Constantine sat on the couch.

"If he's asking what happened he may have already been told a different story. How can I know what others told him?"

"You can't."

"You know what this means?" He made a fist, shook it in the air.

"Be calm, Constantine. Yes, if he is in fear of his life, he may strike back. And he may feel he has a reason to now, even if he wasn't involved in the fire, but by going away it says something. He is not looking for confrontation."

Constantine shook his head. "You are right, but this is where that night twenty years ago has led us."

"You cannot go back, Constantine. And you are not your father. You are so much better to your son than your father was to you."

"Am I?" asked Constantine, stretching his hands forward. "I am the one delaying his appointment as emperor. I am the one who took his command away from him."

"But you have not threatened the life of the woman he loves."

"And who is that, Paulina? He left his wife in Treveris. He did not even invite her to come to Rome for the celebrations. Why is that? Who is he sleeping with? Some slave girl? I see none of them hanging around him with doe eyes." He waved his hand through the air. "I asked the slave master if any of our slaves are missing, to see if he took one with him. He didn't."

Paulina walked to the small, burbling fountain and then back to Constantine.

"Ask him all this when you see him. I honestly do not think he started the fire."

"But he must explain why he went missing at the same time. And if he had a part in Seutonius' murder."

"Perhaps that's why he's gone. Perhaps he was visiting that apartment. Perhaps he likes those entertainments."

"Those are not entertainments, Paulina. Torturing and killing people you have sex with is pure debauchery. It's a return to the excesses of Nero. If this is true, then Crispus must be stopped. How can he succeed me?"

"So you think you've discovered his secret?"

"I have not discovered anything."

"Perhaps it is time for you to leave Rome, Constantine. Whoever set that fire may do something like it again, or worse." She looked around. "There are far too many rooms in this palace, too many secret passages and too many people around here who have a grudge against you or who support Crispus."

"You are right. I need to find Crispus."

"I've been told you should look to Polensis in Istria. That's where his command ship ended up after Chrysopolis. The officers on that ship will be loyal to him. Even if he isn't there, you will need to ensure those officers are removed or tested for their loyalty to you."

"To Polensis then," said Constantine. "And you will come with me to help with Crispus."

She squeezed his arm. "No, please, I cannot. I am flattered you ask, but I'll never be able to get the church finished if I do. They will say I'm nothing but your mistress and all the good work I've done to make a place for women in the church of Christ will be wasted. You will work it out with Crispus. I am sure he was not behind the fire."

She leaned forward and kissed his cheek. "I hear congratulations are in order. You still have what it takes."

He pulled away. "What do you mean?"

"The Empress Fausta is with child. I am happy for you both." She put her hand to her mouth. "You did not know. Oh, I am sorry. I often get news early from the physicians. I hope it is good news."

She looked stunned that he didn't know.

He shrugged angrily. "I'm sure Fausta is waiting for an auspicious moment to tell me."

He cast his mind back to when they last slept together. It was months before, as they had come from New Rome separately. She would have to be quite advanced. How had he not noticed it? Why had she not told him already?

He tried to remember what Fausta had been like during her previous pregnancy. Yes, she hadn't showed for a long time.

"Well. It's another reason for me not to go with you. I will not be talked about as stealing you away when your wife is expecting. That would be the talk of the empire."

XVIII

The Governor's Palace, Zion Gate, Jerusalem, 326 A.D.

"We will go down into it today," said Helena. "I want two men you trust. That means men who won't talk about everything they see."

"None of my men talk about what they see," said the legate, normally responsible for the temple. "They know they will lose their tongues and their balls too, if they do."

"Good," said Helena. "I expect we will find things that will surprise us all."

The legate looked at her, as if he wondered if she was senile. "Let's make a start."

The tables and tools and piles of wood in the workshop had been piled up at the back. Bina was with Helena. She had found out from the owner that she'd looked down into the pit beneath the workshop after her husband died, when they were looking for things he might have hidden down there. They'd pulled up some floorboards in the middle of the room.

Those floorboards were now up again and the gap they opened up was big enough for one person to go down at a time. There was a drop of twice a man's height and a jumble of burnt wood and dust below, as if a building that had once stood here had been set on fire and collapsed in on itself.

"They searched under that rubble?"

"No, they didn't dig down," said Bina. "There may be human bones down there. No one would want to disturb ghosts, neither Jews nor followers of Ba'al or followers of Christ would do that. Such places are unclean."

"My men don't worry about that," said the legate. He turned and gave an order to the helmeted centurion standing behind them. Moments later, two legionaries, with their swords and belts off, wearing just their leather tunics and sandals, were lowered by rope into the pit.

"I will go down too," said Helena. She had a determined air.

"I do not think that wise," said the legate. He had closely cropped gray hair and now a troubled look on his face.

"Keep your opinions to yourself," said Helena. "I will do what I decide."

Soon she was going down slowly, hanging on tight to a rope. She clearly surprised them all with her agility as an older woman. The legionaries stared, open mouthed. She looked amused at their reaction. Of course, they knew nothing about her resourcefulness and the life she'd lived in a tavern before becoming the mistress of a Roman general.

A torch had already been lowered to one of the men. It had spluttered and nearly set the rope on fire as it went down, but it came to life again and one of the men held it aloft so Helena could see what was around her as she went down.

The first thing she noticed was the smell, a dry, over-ripe smell. The next thing she noticed was the rats. They scurried about, just out of the reach of the light.

She looked down as she came to the bottom. She was landing on a compacted pile of dirt. She looked up. The space down here had been used as a dump until it was closed up.

"Look around," she said to the men. "I want to know everything that's down here."

The man with the torch walked in circles around the point where they had dropped in. He held the torch low, looking at the dirt and rubble and then held it up, to look where they were going. Helena and the other man followed him. The first man grunted as he kicked with his hob nailed sandal at something in front of him.

Helena reached for her scarf and put it over her mouth. The stench of excrement was overpowering. Clearly, the pit had been used for many purposes.

"Keep moving," she said.

The man moved on. He kicked at another small pile and a skull was revealed. He grunted again. Then they arrived at the stone wall at the back of the pit. They walked along the edge of the room, then all the way around the pit, watching their feet constantly, trying to find stable places to put them, as piles of dirt, pieces of wood and stinking dust crunched beneath them.

"I've seen enough," shouted Helena. She headed back to the rope, the two men at her elbows.

She thanked each of them with a silver coin and waved for her to be pulled up. She looked up as she was lifted out.

"Did you find anything?" were Bina's first words when she reached the top.

"I did," said Helena. "Your dream was true."

XIX

The Imperial Palace, Palatine Hill, Rome, 326 A.D.

"Why didn't you tell me," shouted Constantine. "Half the city of Rome knows you are pregnant before I do." He paced up and down in Fausta's bedroom. He'd dismissed the slaves, but knew they were likely to be outside the door, listening.

"I only just found out. Who told you?" Fausta's voice was also raised.

"It doesn't matter. When will we expect the child? Soon?"

Fausta looked at him. Her mouth opened and closed. "I may lose the child. That is what the physician said."

"Why?"

"The voyage coming here was stormy. I fell. The baby may be damaged." She put her head down, sniffed, then put both her hands to her face and started crying.

Constantine went to her and pulled her to him. "You should have told me. You must stay in Rome until the baby is born. Do you still feel the baby moving?"

She nodded.

A surge of pride rose inside him. Paulina was right. He was still able to father a child. It was a special feeling, a warmth surging through him. And who was coming, another son to teach about the ways of war and ruling? Or a daughter with wisdom who would teach them all how to live again?

"I don't want to stay in Rome," said Fausta. She sniffed, looked up at him. "I want our child to be born in the new city you are making."

Constantine shook his head. "Only travel if your doctors are sure it is safe. I must go to Polensis." He hugged her.

"Polensis, in Istria?" asked Fausta. "What makes you want to go there? I heard they still have pirates on that coast."

"That's most likely where Crispus has gone."

Fausta shook her head. "No, no, didn't he tell you? He's gone back to his family in Treveris." She looked up at him. Her eyes were still wet.

"A message came from his wife to come to her urgently. You were so busy with the fire yesterday morning he didn't have time to wait and tell you. His wife is sick. She may die. He had to go. I'm sure he will send you a letter explaining it all. There is no need to go to Polensis. Stay here in Rome with me." She hugged him.

He held her to him, waited, then spoke softly.

"Well, if he is not in Polensis, I can go back to New Rome that way. I've ordered all the senators from Rome to be there for the dedication. There is a lot to do. I must oversee it all. They will all stay here if I do not go there." He stepped back and held her at arm's length. "I expect, given when we made this child, that you will be with me in a few months." He touched her stomach. "And eat. You should be showing more. Are you starving yourself?"

Fausta shook her head. "I will come as soon as I can." Her head dipped again. "Pray that I don't lose it."

"I will do more than that. I will get the best physicians in the empire to come and look after you."

She held her stomach.

"Rest," he said. "I will see you at the feast tonight. I've much to do before I leave."

He headed out into the corridor and then to the rooms of the chief treasurer. The man, a freed slave who'd risen high, was surrounded by officials in tunics when Constantine arrived. They melted away as he came into the large marble floored room.

The chief treasurer stood up behind his table and bowed low. "What can I do for you, my emperor?"

"Is the gold ready to be transported to New Rome?"

The treasurer blinked fast. "It is, but there is one thing I must tell you."

"Yes?" said Constantine.

"There will not be ten chests of gold. I am sorry to say that there are only nine now."

"What happened? When we reviewed the treasure when I arrived there were ten chests and you had set aside enough to pay for the celebrations already. Have the rats in Rome started eating gold?"

"My emperor." He looked surprised, spoke fast. "I received a letter from you to let your son Crispus have one chest. He took it away on a cart yesterday morning." The treasurer touched his lip with his finger. "I have your letter somewhere. I never do anything without your personal seal on it."

Constantine looked around. Two officials were still in the room, at small tables near the door. They seemed oblivious of anything but the scrolls they were reading. He assumed they were both listening with perked up ears.

"Here it is," said the treasurer. "I knew I hadn't put it away yet." He handed Constantine a small scroll with a purple ribbon, exactly like the ones he used to send instructions to people. He opened the scroll.

A short letter asked the treasurer to release one full treasure chest of gold at once to his son, Crispus. The signature was his and the seal, a small legion standard with his name around it, was his too. Constantine looked closely at the signature. He'd heard of people copying his signature, but mostly the forgeries were poor, as they didn't have something to copy. This signature was perfect.

If he hadn't asked for the ten chests of gold in the vaults under the Imperial Palace to be shipped to his new capital, this would never have been discovered.

"How much else have I given Crispus over the years?" He tried to sound unconcerned. He'd been appalled at how little gold remained in the imperial treasury when he'd come to inspect it after arriving back in Rome.

Ten chests of gold coins could be collected from one province in a year, and Rome still had many provinces sending taxes to the city.

Africa and Gaul and Britannia and Hispania each were broken into provinces.

Not as much gold was being sent to Rome since his diversion of much of the revenue to his armies, but there should still have been more treasure chests here.

"None, my emperor. If you are concerned about the lack of treasure, we are expecting more at the end of the summer, and your building work this year has caused an unusual outflow, but no, I have not given any other treasure chests to your son."

"Make sure the remaining chests are ready, as I requested. No other chest is to be removed until my personal guard comes to collect them." He knew he sounded angry, but he didn't care.

The treasurer bowed low as Constantine strode out of the room. Thoughts of what Crispus had done filled Constantine's mind with bitterness. Why had Crispus gone behind his back?

XX

The Governor's Palace, Zion Gate, Jerusalem, 326 A.D.

Helena walked into the parade area. The sun was low in the sky, dipping slowly through clouds streaked with orange. The heat of the day had been oppressive, so the light wind from the distant sea was a blessing.

Dust from a line of cavalry, recently returned from a patrol, hung in the air. Helena pulled her Egyptian scarf tight around her mouth. Legionaries had brought back three of the thick timber joists, which had been used to hold up the floor above the pit.

Helena had noticed, when being winched up out of the pit, that three joists holding up the floorboards above and which were set side to side, not back to front, were about the same length as a cross used for crucifixions. She'd also noticed that the three thick pieces of timber were stained with what could have been blood and had notches cut into them, where a cross piece would have been.

"Bina, do what I said now. And remember," she gripped Bina's arm. "One of these crosses is probably the one that was used at the time of Jesus. When you pick one, base your choice upon whether any of the crosses appears to cure you from anything that ails you."

The gold coins she had shown Bina, which would be her payment, were waiting back in the room. She could see the lust for them in Bina's eyes, which she'd seen many times before when people wanted something that could change their life forever.

"Make your choice freely, Bina," said Helena.

Bishop Macarius was waiting, kneeling by the three pieces of timber. His hand was on one of them.

"This one feels right," said the bishop. He stroked it, then bent down and kissed it. "I feel a warmth from it as if the warmth of Jesus' holy blood lives on in it."

He kissed it again. The legionaries at the closed gate of the compound were staring at him, as if they might have to arrest him for trouble making.

"Bina will decide which one, Bishop, so please, move back."

The bishop stood and moved away at Helena's command. Now that Helena could see them in the light it was clear that these had once been the main part of the crosses used to execute criminals. They were deeply stained, many times over.

Assuming the people who rebuilt the workshop had reused wood at the site, it was likely that these crosses had been used by the city before the Jewish revolts. And from what she'd found out from the legate, the main upright of the cross usually remained for as long as it could hold the weight of a prisoner. It was the cross beam that got replaced regularly.

The chance that these were the crosses from the time of Jesus was high.

What was needed now was a miracle to reveal which of the beams was the one that Jesus had bled into.

Bina muttered prayers as she went from one piece of timber to the next. When she reached the one the bishop had chosen, she touched it, then pulled away as if she'd been burnt.

"This is not the one. This is the cross the bad thief died on." She spat into the dust.

The bishop groaned and looked at Helena with an anguish twisting at his face.

Helena shook her head for him to be quiet as Bina moved to touch the other pieces of timber. The next one she stroked, as the bishop had done. The final one she touched only for a moment before crying out as if she'd found a lost child.

"This is the one. I feel my scars healing, look." She pulled up her long black robe, exposing her thin legs. They were scarred around the lower thigh, but whether that was recent scarring or older was hard to say. The legionaries around the ramparts nudged each other and stared.

Bina dropped her robe back down and came to Helena. "I have had a pain in my knee since my husband beat me. This has never left me since. And now, suddenly, it is gone. I am free of pain. That one is the cross of Jesus. It has miraculous powers. You must preserve it in the new church you will build here in the city where we found it."

"I will pray for you. This is indeed a miracle," said the bishop. "We can use all of this wood in the new church."

"No, Bishop," said Helena firmly, shaking her head. "A small piece of the cross will be sent to the main city in each province of the empire. Such miracles must be shared. The cross has a power to help all those who believe in the new religion of the empire."

The bishop bowed. "I am honored that I was present when the true cross was found."

"Come with me, Bina. Your reward is waiting." Helena strode away toward the entrance to the tower, where her rooms were.

When they reached the rooms, she took the bag of gold from the small chest under her bed and passed two coins to Bina.

"Return to your community. This will help them. And say only that I decided to help you. It is a gift to you all." She passed the coins to Bina.

Bina looked at them with wide eyes.

"Thank you, thank you, Empress. Everything will change for us because of this." Her step was sure as she left.

***

She headed down the stone stairs and almost ran out into the street. The road west lay just outside the compound. She passed through the high gate of the Roman camp with a few mutters coming from the guards at a woman leaving the city so late.

But Bina's community was not far away and she knew the road well. She could be with them before the moon went out of the sky.

She turned as she came near the rocky hill that marked the end of the city boundary.

She'd heard a noise. Someone was following her. She gripped her coins in her hand and started running.

XXI

Outside Rome, 326 A.D.

Constantine looked back along the line of horses heading east out of Rome on the Via Tiburtina. The port of Aternum was their objective. They had sent no messengers ahead, in case Crispus was there or someone who could warn him to move on from Polensis.

"You did not need to bring so many of your men," said Constantine, looking over his shoulder. Directly behind them rode ten Saxons, all of them young replacements for the original band that had traveled to Rome twenty years before.

Dust filled the air behind them and the smell of dust and drying horse manure from previous travelers was all around.

"They want to get out of the city. A sea voyage to Istria sounded like a good idea during a summer in Rome." Juliana stared straight ahead. They were near the front of the line, with only a small troop of forward riders in front of them, who took turns to ride ahead and warn slow carts and horsemen to pull off the road until the imperial entourage had passed.

They had left the city with no fanfare soon after dawn. Constantine did not want the great unwashed of Rome to be waiting to see him off. You could not be sure how a mob would react in Rome unless they had been paid. He sent a message to the senate to make sure they were all in New Rome for the dedication of the city to Christianity. Other messengers had warned the priests of every cult in the city to publicly pray for his well-being, or risk being banned.

"You were happy to leave too," said Constantine, as he adjusted his new, thin-leather tunic. If there was one thing that Rome was still good at, it was making light leather tunics.

"I'm always happy to be with you," said Juliana, looking at him.

"Don't let Fausta hear you say that. She'll think our affair never ended."

Juliana shook her head. "I've nothing but respect for Fausta. She is the mother of your children and soon she will give you another son."

"Juliana, the empress brought none of our children to Rome for the celebrations. Do you not think that odd?"

"She likes to keep them away from court." Juliana paused, then continued, "Perhaps she fears what happened to many imperial families when a new emperor comes to power. Her young sons might be considered competition for Crispus."

"Crispus would not dare do anything to my children with Fausta."

"Maybe, but I understand her wanting to protect them."

"She lied to me about Crispus." His tone was clipped.

"How?"

"She told me Crispus was called away by a messenger from his wife and that his wife was ill." He shifted in his saddle as his horse rode slowly on, then sniffed the air, angrily.

"And you found out there was no such message?"

"Yes, you are ahead of me."

"Have you also considered that Crispus may have lied to Fausta about it?"

"I have, but I would have expected her to express some doubt in the message, not simply defend him." Incredulity filled his voice.

"Perhaps she was worried about what you would do if you found out he was behind that attempt on your life." Juliana also shifted on her horse, leaning forward to stretch her back.

"You will fall off if you keep doing that," said Constantine.

"No, I won't." She turned her shoulders one way, then the other. "Are you sure you didn't set that fire yourself to prove your power to save Paulina and the palace all in one morning?"

Constantine scoffed. "I do not need half of Rome talking about what I get up to in the early mornings."

"You say that, but half the city is now talking about your virility, giving a child to the empress while servicing Paulina."

"That is not the reputation I am looking for in Rome." He paused, looked around. The line of their entourage was thinning out as the road headed up hill. The clip-clop of the horses had changed. He had learned to listen for such changes, though the risk here was nothing like it had been when he was fighting a war.

He looked forward. There were other things to concern himself with now.

"Do you think Crispus set the fire?"

"I don't," said Constantine. "He has no reason to. He expects to be made emperor. Why risk everything on a throw of the bones?"

"Some people can't wait for things. You know that, don't you?" She smiled at him.

Constantine considered his answer for a long time before replying. He took a swig of his watered-down wine, then put the wineskin back, hanging from the pommel of his saddle.

"You are right, but I still think Crispus is just showing his annoyance at me. He may celebrate when we arrive at Polensis. I hear they have a magnificent amphitheater. He loves a good show."

"The games there include local women fighting each other to death."

"If Crispus hasn't planned any games for our reunion I will order games myself, to celebrate the succession. That should make him happy."

XXII

The Temple of Venus, Zion Gate, Jerusalem, 326 A.D.

Helena waited inside the gate, watching workers hurrying about in the temple courtyard.

"Every reference to Venus has been removed?"

"Yes, Empress. The temple has had every image removed and the rotunda has been stripped of every statue and wall painting and every mosaic has been pulled up. It is all bare. You can do with it as you will."

"You will extend the building to cover the caves where the tombs were?"

"Yes, the architect's plans were explicit on that."

"Empress," said Bishop Macarius, coming toward her and bowing. "It is a great day. Our hopes have turned to fruit."

"Indeed, and you are prospering. This city seems to suit you more and more." She looked behind the bishop to the two good-looking young men who had accompanied him. "Your acolytes grow." She pressed her lips together to suppress a disdainful smile. Better to give him enough rope and watch as his flock turned on him if he was abusing his position.

"Yes, Empress, the appearance of the true cross has renewed the faith of many strays." He bowed. "I expect this city will quickly become a place of pilgrimage. We will need many new acolytes."

"You agree there will be no charge to enter the new church?"

"Of course, Empress. How could we charge for people to hear the words of Jesus?"

"My work here is done then," said Helena.

"You will go back to Rome first?" said the bishop.

"No, to New Rome. I have to get there before Constantine dedicates the city. He must have a piece of the cross at the ceremony. It will be a sign to all that God approves of moving the capital of the empire and dedicating the city to the God of Christ." She looked around. "Bina never reappeared?"

The bishop shrugged. "You know how fickle woman can be."

Helena shook her head, angrily. "You men are just the same. I'm sure she has her reasons for not coming back."

"There is something else I wish to speak with you about, Empress." He bowed low.

"Come and see me tonight."

Helena turned and went out of the gate to the temple grounds, her guards around her. She had to move fast, start preparations for her trip.

XXIII

Polensis, 326 A.D.

The ship Constantine had commandeered, a large trading vessel, had only places for five rowers on each side. It sat low in the water, but the late summer had seen few storms and the captain of the ship had assured them they would be across to Polensis in two nights, with the wind as it was.

So he decided not to wait, to leave the horses behind and take two Saxons and twenty of his own imperial guards, all men you would stand back from if you saw them coming. It would take a small army to stop them, and all they expected to find in Polensis was the city night watch and harbor patrols looking for thieves trying to steal from the trading vessels in the port.

"Do not raise any unusual flag as we come into Polensis, Captain," said Constantine, when they were at sea. "You can tell the tax officials who board us."

"You don't want everyone in Polensis to know that their emperor has arrived, before you put a foot ashore?" asked the captain of the ship.

"That's it," said Constantine forcefully. "We will head for the governor's palace and surprise him. The town's people will find out soon enough." He turned to Juliana.

"Just like old times." He smiled.

"Better than old times," said Juliana.

***

Two days later, as they rowed into the port of Polensis, they could all see there was no place at the dock to pull alongside.

"We'll have to wait our turn," said the captain. He pointed at the flagman waving at them from the end of the wooden dock. "We are to stand-off and wait." He shouted an order and the rowers, already at slow speed, stopped. An anchor was thrown overboard and they came to a halt in the middle of the port, the ship trembling as it stilled. A crisp smell of fish and salt filled the air. Shouts, and the crack of a whip echoed from the town.

"There are some benefits if you raise the imperial flag," said Juliana. She pointed at a skiff being rowed toward them.

"We have a visitor."

"The tax inspector," said the captain. "He will want to know what we have on board so they can tell us what bribe we need to pay them."

"You mean what tax you have to pay," said Constantine.

"That too."

The skiff pulled up alongside them. A thick, frayed rope ladder was thrown down over the side and an older man with a big gray beard appeared. He didn't recognize Constantine and addressed the captain of the ship first.

"What do you carry?" He glared around at Constantine and Juliana, as if he might decide that the ship could not dock because of them.

"If you want to keep your job, you will get down on your knees," said the captain.

The older man looked perplexed. He stared at Constantine and only then did he take in the gold armbands.

Constantine stepped forward. "I don't care about formalities, Captain. I just want this man to answer one question."

The tax official went to one knee. "I am very sorry, Emperor. I did not know it was you."

"One answer is all I need," said Constantine.

"I will answer."

"Has my son, Crispus, arrived here yet?"

The man looked up at him. "He has, my emperor. He arrived three days ago and stays with the governor. There is a lot of excitement in the city. No member of the imperial family has visited us since the time of Diocletian."

"You must wait on board while we use your skiff to get to shore."

"Of course, Emperor," said the official, bowing. "I will order my rowers to be extra careful."

"Order your rowers to come up here," said Constantine. "I will use my own rowers."

The four skiff rowers came aboard and were replaced on the skiff by four of Constantine's imperial guard. No one wore any purple and only Constantine wore medals on his chest. He asked Juliana to stay on the ship and make sure the tax official didn't go back to shore, or anyone else leave the ship. He didn't want the town talking about him before he found Crispus. He also wanted time alone with his son. It would be the best way to fix things between them.

The group rowing ashore looked like a legate with some of his men, coming to Polensis to visit or to find a mistress.

No one stopped them on their way out of the dock. The gate was open and as they were carrying no cargo there was no need to assess taxes.

The governor's palace had been pointed out to them in the center of the town. It was the only three floored building, aside from the amphitheater, and easy to find even through the hot and narrow streets of the town. They just had to head in the direction of the amphitheater.

Other people were heading there too. An evening entertainment was starting and many people whispered that the son of the emperor might even be spotted in the imperial box. Many wanted to get a seat near it, especially the younger women.

Constantine stayed at the back as they made their way to the main door of the governor's palace. It was guarded by four legionaries with helmets and shiny leather breastplates.

Constantine went to the front of his men as they came near and pointed at his medals. The lead guard went down on one knee.

"I live to serve you, my emperor. If you had warned us you were coming, we would have sent a troop to meet you."

"No need," said Constantine. "And send no one ahead. I want this to be a surprise for my son."

"Yes, my emperor. I will come with you and show you where they are."

He led the way inside the palace, through two main gates, an inner courtyard and down some wide marble stairs to a garden with garlands of roses hanging along the walls.

The sound of a group of revelers came to him as they walked to a corner of the garden. Smoke from fires drifted high and the smell of meat cooking came to him.

Laughter echoed.

Ahead was a group in togas standing around with senior officers in leather tunics, their gold medallions flashing in the early evening sunlight. He couldn't see Crispus. He walked around the group. Where was he?

"Emperor," came a shout. Everyone in the group turned and stared, then together they went down on one knee.

A small man in a toga with a wide gold edge came forward. "We are deeply honored to welcome you. Our palace is yours, my emperor. I am the governor of this lowly province."

"Thank you everyone, rise. I will not disturb your celebrations." He looked around. "Is my son here?"

The governor's face changed. He smiled warmly, shook his head. "No, he is not, we are expecting to meet him at the amphitheater. He is our honored guest. You will be too. Why don't you join us for our feast before we go there?"

Constantine looked at the back of the garden, where slaves were tending a roasting pig and other meat on racks. He could smell the food. It was enticing. His stomach grumbled.

"I wish to talk with my son. Where is he?"

The governor's mouth opened and closed. "We hoped he would stay with us, but he insisted on staying in the town. An old friend of his lives in a villa on the other side of the amphitheater."

"Is there someone who can direct me there?"

The governor looked around. He clapped his hands. "Yes, yes, my daughter, she can take you."

He waved at a tall, black-haired young woman at the edge of the crowd. She came slowly toward them, her body moving sensuously under a tight yellow dress.

"Marina, bow for our emperor."

The young woman stared at Constantine as if she'd been hit on the head, then bent low, her hand at her neck, holding her neckline tight to her skin. A faint whiff of perfume reached him.

She rose slowly. Constantine put his hand out. She kissed his imperial ring.

"My emperor, we are doubly blessed this summer," she said. "First your son, then you." She looked down.

"Do you know where he is?"

Marina nodded, then said, "Shall I take you there?"

"Yes, at once."

Marina led the way back through the garden. An older woman, a slave, her chaperone, came behind them. Marina tried to engage Constantine in small talk, but he barely replied so she kept walking, moving faster as they left the palace and headed through the narrow streets of the city.

The main streets were crowded. The smell of fried fish, fresh bread and roasting meats was powerful as they passed by street stalls and the larger taverns. The crowds were in a festive mood. Many of the women wore garlands of roses, as a local goddess was being honored that day. Younger men, as in most towns in the empire, stood outside taverns drinking their fill and commenting on the women as they passed.

Constantine's mind wandered. What would he say to Crispus? He could not be angry. He would not make things worse. Crispus would have good reasons for everything that had happened. His hopes of a clear path to becoming emperor had been dashed. Perhaps he saw his father as playing games with him, as he had seen his own father do.

He would end all this. He would give Crispus a date for him to become emperor. The end of this year would be the best moment.

That would shock him. And please him. The time for waiting was over. If he wanted a smooth transition, he would need his son to agree to the date.

He had to ensure there was no anger on either side. Setting a fire was not Crispus' style. He'd had chances to kill his father before and he hadn't. At the battle of Chrysopolis, Constantine had visited the ship from which Crispus would direct the naval engagement.

Crispus' men had surrounded Constantine. They'd been angry that their pay had not come through. Crispus could have cut him down then. He could have won the battle and claimed the throne. There was no one else who could raise an army against him.

And there were other times, many of them, when they were together alone, when he could have poisoned him or stabbed him. No, it was just unfortunate timing that he'd left the city on the morning of the fire.

They'd reached a villa with a high wall and no windows at the ground level.

Marina stopped, pointing at the thick looking wooden door.

"This is the villa."

"Do all your villas have few windows?" asked Constantine.

"Only the old ones. We had a problem with pirates a long time ago. My father can tell you all the gory details." She smiled, showing two rows of perfect teeth.

"Who lives here?"

"A retired officer from your legions. A legate who was injured at Chrysopolis, I believe." She walked toward the closed door. "Shall I knock for you?"

"No, I will." Constantine pulled the dagger from his belt and banged hard with the end of the handle against the door. Three times he knocked. Then they waited.

No one came. No one looked out of a high window. The house appeared deserted.

He looked up and down the street. No one was coming and going in this part of town. Had he been sent on a wild goose chase?

"Perhaps they have all gone to the amphitheater?" said Marina. "Shall I take you there?"

Constantine banged on the door again. "One more try," he said. "Then we will go."

His four imperial guards were talking together nearby. One of them came forward, bowed. "Shall we force our way in?"

The door of the villa creaked open. An old slave with a nut brown head peered out at them, blinking.

"What do you want?" he said, gruffly.

"I want to see my son, Crispus. Is he here?" said Constantine.

"They have gone already to the amphitheater," said the old slave. He pointed over the roofs of the houses to where the roars from the amphitheater drifted to them.

"Who will I say called for him?"

"His father," said Constantine. There was no point in hiding his presence in the city anymore.

He turned to Marina. "What is the quickest way to the amphitheater?"

"Follow me." She gripped his arm. "They have gone early. The best people do not usually go so early." She gripped tighter. "Sometimes the richest men in the city go to the houses of the courtesans and tell their families they have gone to the games."

Constantine put his head to one side. "You think my son has gone there?"

"Many men do."

"Do you know where these houses are?"

She looked at the chaperone. "No, but she does. She tells me all about what goes on there."

Constantine waved the chaperone to him. "Take us to the houses of the courtesans."

The women looked bewildered. She blinked a couple of times.

"Not for me," said Constantine. "I am looking for someone."

The old woman smiled, nodded, as if she'd heard that story before.

"Follow me," she said.

They headed for the amphitheater, but when they got within its shadow, they went up a narrow lane with two men standing guard at the entrance. They had nail studded cudgels dangling from their belts. The men stood still as they watched Constantine, his guards and the women pass.

"This is the street," said the chaperone. "Now I must take Marina away or I will be blamed for showing this to her."

Marina was staring up the street. Women were standing in a group halfway along. Their tunics were the type dancers wore, more revealing than covering.

"Yes, you can go now. Tell your father we will be back later." He put a hand out to Marina. "And neither of you mention where I came looking for my son."

Marina bowed. "Of course." She smiled up at him. "I will not reveal your secrets, or your son's."

XXIV

The Governor's Palace, Zion Gate, Jerusalem, 326 A.D.

Helena waited for the slave to leave. "You came quickly, Bishop. Did you hear they found Bina's body outside the city?"

Bishop Macarius wrung his hands. "It is terrible news, beyond grotesque. The poor woman. You must look for the bandits who did this. Jews no doubt. They must be punished severely."

"Crucified, perhaps?" offered Helena.

"No, I did not say that. I know your son has banned crucifixion."

Helena put her hands together and her thumbs to her lip. "I want to find out what happened before I leave." She looked up. "I hear you've asked for Christians who were recently Jews to be stopped from coming into Jerusalem." She sounded angry. She hadn't asked the bishop to sit. He remained standing.

The bishop shrugged. "Jews cannot just say they are followers of Christ and the next day get our privileges. They must be baptized and learn about living a Christian life before they are admitted to the congregation."

"And your fee for baptism is a welcome source of income, I am sure."

"We receive only enough to keep the church alive. We are frugal, Empress, but we do need funds to pay for new churches."

"You are right." She smiled at him. "I have decided to take the true cross to New Rome when I leave, Bishop. You can cut the top section away for use here in Jerusalem, but the rest goes with me."

He bowed in agreement, then put his hands toward her, palms up. "I have also made progress on finding proof of Jesus' suffering." He looked smug.

Helena noticed the leather bag dangling from his shoulder.

"You have something to show me? I do not have much time." She leaned forward. "What is it?"

The bishop shuffled on his feet. "May I sit?"

"Be quick."

The bishop sat on the wicker chair near Helena and opened his scuffed leather bag. He pulled a scroll from it. The scroll was small, and tightly bound with a thin, faded yellow ribbon.

He lowered his head and his hand shook as he passed it to Helena.

"This is the record of the trial of our messiah. The man is named Yeshua, his Jewish name." He held the scroll toward Helena.

She didn't reach for it. "The dates are right? The witnesses listed?"

"Everything is right. It even has a description of his betrayal by Judas. That was what made me believe it."

"Where was this found?"

"The Roman governor at the time of the Jewish revolt moved all trial records into his palace at Caesarea. Officials there, under direction of one of my acolytes, conducted a search. They found this." He waved it up and down in front of her.

"Open it," she said. There was little excitement in her voice. The timing of this arrival was either very good or very suspicious.

He undid the ribbon and pulled open the scroll. He held it open for her to read.

She peered at it. "It looks good," she said. "It must have cost you a lot."

He stared at her. "I paid for it out of church funds."

"You do know this is not the first scroll like this I have seen?"

"It is the only one to come from the governor's archive."

She leaned back. "So you say. Well, I shall take it to New Rome. I am sure that is what you want, seeing as you reveal it just before I leave."

"Take it as a gift from the church to your son," said the bishop.

Soon after the bishop left, Helena rode to the nearby villa of the Roman governor of Jerusalem with a troop of cavalry as an escort. The villa's high walls blocked out any view of the city, but she could hear sounds from the nearby market beyond the villa's walls; shouts, neighing, the banging of carts being loaded as the market closed for the day.

As soon as she was taken in to meet the governor, she got to the reason for her visit. "Were all the trial archives from the time of Jesus taken to Caesarea?"

The governor bowed. "Yes."

"What else was taken, aside from the records of trials?"

"I am not sure, records of payments to informants probably." He looked down. "I'm sorry to say we do not have copies."

"So the records in Caesarea are real? You can vouch for that?"

"Yes, and I will write a letter for you which confirms this." He smiled.

"That would be good, Governor."

"I am pleased to help. And if you travel through Caesarea you should find a place on one of the fast trading ships heading to New Rome." He puffed up as he spoke. "They have the very fastest ships and the very best olives. My wife's family is from Caesarea. They have olive groves there. Try some." He pointed at the tables heaving with food.

Helena shook her head. She had long ago become fearful of food offered, though she knew it was most likely just because she'd heard about imperial relatives being poisoned.

"What about bandits here in Jerusalem? Do you have many problems with travelers being murdered on the roads here?"

"Why do you ask?"

"A friend was murdered outside Jerusalem."

"Was she wealthy?"

"No, but she probably had some gold coins with her."

The governor shook his head, sorrowfully. "These terrible things happen from time to time. If a wealthy merchant shows his purse around he might be followed out of the city and robbed. The people who do it will only murder the man if they think he'll come back to the city and accuse them."

"That's what I thought too."

"Would you like me to investigate this?"

Helena took a step closer to him. "Yes, that is also a good idea. I will tell you all the details and if you find out anything send me a letter. I am very concerned about this. You will be doing me a great service."

XXV

Constantine kept walking. The women in the street stared at him and the legionaries with him, their swords dangling from their belts. One of the women winked at Constantine, so he went to her.

"Where is the house for rough treatment?" he asked.

She looked him up and down. "You want to give it or get it?"

"Give."

Her eyes widened. "You can treat me bad any time, your excellency."

"I want you to point out the house where I can get it any time." He reached for the purse on his belt and slipped out a new silver denarius. The other girls were crowding around now.

"I can join you for another denarius," one shouted. Another put her hand out to touch his bare arm. He let her.

"Which house, that's all I want." He held the coin toward the girl who'd winked at him.

She reached out her hand and tried to take the coin, but he closed his fingers too fast.

She pouted, pointed up the street. "The house with the bear's skull above the door. That's where you want to go." She held out her hand.

He passed the coin to her and walked on.

Catcalls followed him. "Watch out for that one. He likes it rough," was the clearest shout.

He kept walking. He was used to catcalls. Enemies would shout insults over a wall. Comrades, when asked to do things they didn't want to do, could also dig deep into their estimation of his character or motivation if he pushed them hard. It annoyed him, but he'd learnt not to let it show. It only encouraged them if you did.

The catcalls grew quieter. From some doorways, women curled their fingers at him and smiled. He kept going. He could sense the men with him looking around. He knew they would probably come back here if they were released from duty.

The house with the bear's skull, a large white one with its jaw wide open, was near the top of the street. The door into the two story building was open, but there was no one by it.

He walked straight in. The transition from bright sunlight to the dark musty interior almost blinded him, so he didn't immediately see the old crone sitting on a stool at the foot of the stairs to the upper floor. But he heard her voice. It was strong and clear. And was that smell coming from her?

"You wanna go up, you pay me."

He looked beyond her as his eyes adjusted. She was on her own. There were no guards to protect her, no cudgel lay at her side.

"I can go up without paying you."

"You'll only get fish oil thrown over you if you do. And you won't get what you want with that all over you." She laughed. "Men usually come here to enjoy themselves, not to fight us. If you want free service try somewhere else. I'm sure there are lots of girls in the town who'll give it up for a rich man like you."

"I'm not here for service," he said. "I'm here to fetch someone."

"Is that it? Well, we don't do any free services here, so if you want to know anything you'll have to pay up." She held out her palm.

"How many girls die here every year?"

She shook her head. "The gods decide who gets taken, not me."

"How many do the gods take each year."

She shrugged. "I don't keep count and it's none of your business anyway."

He turned to the man directly behind him. "Tie her up and put a gag in her mouth."

The old woman screamed. Constantine stepped back from the stairs. What looked like a bowlful of fish oil fell onto the lower stairs, followed by a shout from up above.

He turned to one of the other men. "Go around the back in case they have another way out. Take one of the others with you."

Two of his guards headed out of the building. The two other men with him gagged and tied up the old woman. She screamed whenever she could. Faces appeared at the top of the stairs. Mostly they were young girls, some still children. They all looked half starved.

He went to the gagged old woman. "This house will be sold by the end of the week and the proceeds distributed to your girls if you don't cooperate."

The old woman had a defiant look on her face. She was trying to remove her gag by bending her head, moving her chin.

He pulled the gag down.

"You cannot sell my house from under me," she said, half spitting. "If you want to fetch your friend look above, the room at the back. He has two young ones with him, but don't say anything about what they look like if you go into the room." She pointed up and to the back of the building.

"I know where that one is staying," she said. "And all his high-class friends will know about what he likes by the end of the week, if you make any more trouble."

Constantine sighed, stepped back, looked up the stairs. None of the faces peering down had blood on them, though a few had purple scars.

He went up the stairs slowly. No man looked down at him, though some of the older girls looked as if they could do you some damage if they sliced at you with a knife.

He held up a hand. "I am here to fetch someone," he said. "We'll be gone when I get him."

Smiles came then, as the girls came to the conclusion he'd not come to steal from them.

When he reached the first floor two older girls, one with two purple eyes, pointed at a door at the end of the corridor. It was closed. They giggled. He put his finger to his lips.

If Crispus was behind the door he must have heard what was going on in the building, unless he'd drunk a skin full of wine.

His two remaining guards were close behind him. One was watching down the stairs for trouble. The other stood near him, his hand on the hilt of his sword, ready to pull it out and cut anyone in two who threatened the emperor.

Constantine went near the door, listened.

He should not be here. He should not be risking everything like this. Fausta would tell him he was crazy not just sending a troop of men in to ransack the building.

But he couldn't do that. He could pay these legionaries with him to be quiet, but he'd never be able to control the mouths of fifty men. His son would gain the reputation of a sick emperor in waiting and his time in power would forever be colored by what happened here.

"Stay here," he said to the man behind him. He pushed at the door.

XXVI

Jerusalem, 326 A.D.

Shouts from beyond the wall of the Governor's garden sent all heads turning.

A scream echoed.

A guard with his helmet a little askew came marching through the garden toward the governor. He whispered in the governor's ear.

The governor turned to Helena. "Some Christian pleb wants to see you. I can have him thrown out of the town."

"Who is he?" asked Helena. She did not need more delays.

The guard was fixing his helmet. "He spoke a lot. I didn't catch all the names." He shuddered, as if throwing off water. "There was one thing he said that I remember. Something Jewish. I never heard it before."

"Spit it out, man," said the governor.

The guard's eyes were wide. "Something about Helena, the emperor's mother, and some person called Bina."

"Bring this man to me," said Helena. She turned to the governor. "Is there somewhere private I can meet him?" If this person knew about Bina, she needed privacy. She did not need everyone in the city talking about what happened to Bina, using it to throw doubt on the true cross. That could not be allowed.

"Of course, follow me," he said. He led the way through the garden to an area in the far corner surrounded by trellises with thick, lush vines running through them. Two wooden seats occupied the center of the screened off area. A pool with fish darting around lay between them.

"This is fed from the pool of Zion," he said. "It is the quietest place in the house. I'll get my guards to stay when they bring the man to you."

"Tell them to do what I say. That is all," said Helena.

A thin man in the poorest of tunics was pushed into the screened off area.

"Unhand him," said Helena, sharply. She knew how to keep a tight grip on situations, to keep all weak emotions hidden.

The man fell to the mosaic around the pool. He bowed from where he was, almost touching the mosaic with his forehead.

"Get up," said Helena. "And tell me what you want." She leaned toward him. "And remember this, I do not give gold coins away to anyone who drops a name in front of me."

The man bowed his head over and over as he spoke. "I am sorry. I am very sorry, please forgive me, Empress. Please, I swear, I am not here for anything but justice. My poor wife was found dead and she has not even had a proper burial." He sniffed, put the back of his hand to his mouth and started crying. Through the tears he kept talking.

"We do not know where to bury her. For us, she is Jewish. She always has been. But she ran off with some Christians, and claimed she was a follower of Christ."

He looked up at Helena and gulped his tears away.

"What was her name?" But she knew where this was going.

"Bina. She was seen in Jerusalem with you, my empress." He put his hands forward, imploringly. "I was shunned by my village because Bina ran away. They blame me. My sheep have been stolen and slaughtered. The village wants my house now too, as my wife is dead. I must throw myself on the street."

"This is sad news indeed, but your wife left you long before she came to me. Why do you come here?"

"Two things," he said. "First," he shuddered, then went on. "Please give me a letter for the bishop so he agrees to bury Bina on the Mount of Olives. And second," he looked up, "please, I beg you, take in Bina's daughter to your house as a slave. If you do not, I cannot feed her from a pauper's bowl. She will have to be sold to a whorehouse. I know her mother did not want her servicing men before she even became a woman herself." He bent his head forward as if defeated.

Helena's hands tightened into fists. "Where is this girl?"

"She waits for me in the street outside."

"Go, get the girl waiting outside," she said to one of the guards. "And fetch some water and food here." She waved the guard away.

"And you," she said, pointing at the man on his knees, "sit over there." She pointed at the other bench at the farthest point.

Bina's husband pulled himself to his feet and sat, his back bent.

When the little girl appeared, Helena knew at once what she must do. The girl looked less than ten summers old and was as thin as a spear. Her hair was long, black and a dirty mess. Her tunic was patched and ripped.

The girl went to her father, but she didn't hug him. She sat a little way from him and stared open mouthed at Helena. Food and water had been brought on round beaten-bronze trays, which were placed on the ground.

"Eat," said Helena, "and drink your fill."

The little girl waited until her father nodded at her and then they both drank the water and stuffed their faces with the eggs, olives, flat bread and the crumbly white cheese which had been brought.

"She is a good girl," said the father. "I ask a fair price for her, that is all."

"What is that?" She'd expected this moment.

The father finished stuffing some bread in his mouth, then burped. He held his stomach.

"The whorehouse will give me a gold aureus for her, but I may find an older man who will offer two. What do you think she is worth, Empress?"

XXVII

Polensis, 326 A.D.

The door opened easily when Constantine pushed at it. The room was small, just big enough for a bed and a dark wooden bench at the end of it. The bed was covered in a greasy wolf skin. Sitting quietly on it was a young woman of about fifteen summers. Blood trickled down the side of her face from a cut across her forehead. It looked as if she'd been in a knife fight.

Constantine walked around the bed. Lying on the floor beyond it was another girl. She had a knife protruding from her chest. Dread grew inside him. Was this what his son was like? No, it could not be.

The girl on the bed started screaming.

"Shut up," shouted Constantine. His head was pounding. The girl kept screaming.

"Shut up or I will shut you up," said Constantine. He gripped the dagger on his belt and pulled it half-way from its scabbard.

The girl stopped screaming. She started crying.

"Where is the man who did this?" asked Constantine, pointing down at the dead girl. Her eyes were open, and she was staring up at the ceiling. She was naked, too. She looked grotesque, her hands clutching at her chest and multiple purple marks around her neck, as if she had been throttled many times.

This was not the work of Crispus. He had stumbled on the murder of a whore, that was all. The tension inside him flowed out.

The crying girl pointed at the back of the room where shutters lay open and a thin window looked out over a lane.

Constantine looked down. Two of his men were in the lane, standing outside the back of the building.

"Did you see anyone come out of this window?" he shouted down.

Both men shook their heads.

He turned back to the girl who was alive.

"What was the man like who did this? Did you get his name?"

She just kept shaking her head. Her gaze flicked to the doorway where other girls were now staring in at her.

Constantine looked around the room to see if Crispus had left anything behind.

"Let's check the other rooms," he said to the legionary with him.

Both of the other rooms on that floor were empty. One looked like a sleeping place for all the girls in the building. Straw mattresses covered the floor and a little table had candles and a statue of a horned god on it.

Constantine looked for a way onto the roof, but he couldn't find one. They went back down.

"Find your friend?" asked the old woman, cackling.

They went straight out the front door.

"If I see him, I'll tell him you were looking for him. He looks like you, doesn't he?" The old woman laughed.

"To the amphitheater," said Constantine. He needed to talk to Crispus, to clear his mind of any doubts about who had killed the girl.

The street leading to the amphitheater was crowded. A line of men wearing shaggy fur-skins, with antlers on their heads, filled the middle of the street. They were slicing the air with knives, chanting and half dancing, half walking. Behind them, came a line of young women in red tunics. They had cuts on their foreheads, like the girl in the rough house and they sprinkled blood around them as they shook their heads. Drummers beat a steady rhythm behind them, on thin red hand-held drums.

Constantine and his guards headed down a side street to find a quieter entrance to the amphitheater. But the next street was the same, and this time one of the men with antlers spotted Constantine and waved the other men toward him, their knives flashing through the air like the spear dance of a Gallic tribe, the drummers behind beating to the rhythm of their dance.

XXVIII

Caesarea, 326 A.D.

"What is your daughter's name," asked Helena. She waved the girl to come closer.

The girl stayed where she was, but replied, "I am Bina, like my mother." Her face puckered as she spoke, as if she was holding back tears.

"You do not need to be afraid, Bina," said Helena. "I will be looking after you from now on."

The girl looked at her father. He smiled, held his hand out. "Two aureus is a good price for a virgin."

Helena reached for the purse at her belt. She took out a single aureus. She held it forward, then, as he reached for it, she pulled her hand back. He stumbled, then stopped near enough to her that she could smell his stale sweat.

"Have you abused this little girl, as you abused her mother?"

He shook his head, fast. "No, I swear, on my life. I never hit her mother and I would never strike a child." He sounded indignant.

"She seems frightened of you," said Helena, glancing at the girl.

"She is soft in the head. She is frightened of everything." He grinned. "For that reason, I will let you have her for one aureus with my hopes that you will help her make a better life."

Helena handed over the coin.

"You will stay here now," said the man to the young girl.

"You will not be a slave," said Helena, leaning forward with a smile. "You will help in my household and be free to leave when you are older."

"Thank you," said the man. He walked away without even looking at the young girl. She stared after him, an expression of relief on her face.

"Come here, Bina," said Helena. She opened her arms wide.

Bina stepped closer but did not hug her.

"Did your father do things to you?" said Helena.

The girl looked toward where her father had gone.

"He will not be coming back. He cannot hurt you anymore," said Helena.

The girl looked at Helena, then burst into tears, her face buried in her hands, her shoulders hunched over.

Helena went to her, put her arms around her. "Where did he hurt you?" she said, her tone soft.

The girl pointed at her crotch.

"Since your mother left?"

The girl nodded.

Evil bastard, she thought.

"You are safe now. It is over." The girl put her arms around Helena.

"Now drink some water and eat. I must make preparations for you. You are coming to New Rome with me. Would you like that?" It took all her will to hide how angry she was.

The girl nodded. A tiny smile appeared at the corner of her mouth. Helena led the girl to the trays and left her. She curled a finger at one of the guards as she walked away. It was time for retribution, one of the greatest pleasures of wielding power.

The guard followed her. When they were beyond the trellises Helena said to him, "Do you remember the father's face?"

The guard nodded.

She pointed at his sword. "I want you to put that through his heart and turn it until he squeals." She pointed the way the man had gone. She spoke drily, as if ordering more food, and inside she felt the cool pleasure of revenge.

"Do it outside the town walls. And throw his body in the Valley of Hinnom for the rats to eat. I hear they eat anything around there."

The man saluted.

"And bring back my aureus, too."

XXIX

Polensis, 326 A.D.

Constantine put both hands in the air. The men with the knives shouted, pointed at the amphitheater. They were drunk. He turned to the guards with him.

"Don't pull your swords. They want me to go with them."

The man who had flashed his knife at Constantine pulled up the antlers he was wearing, so Constantine could see his face.

"Come, come with us. The feast of the blood is starting. There will be a girl for everyone and a belly full of wine."

He reached a hand forward. It held the knife, the point facing back to him.

Constantine took the knife. The man grabbed his knife arm and pulled him into the line of antler-capped men half dancing toward the amphitheater, a steady drum-beat echoing all around them.

When they reached the amphitheater, a wide gate was open leading to the sand covered interior. As they came out from under the shadow of the amphitheater walls rows of seating rose high and steep around them. His guards had stayed with them, two on each side, but no one seemed to notice.

The excitement of the crowd infected him.

Trumpets blared as he reached the center of the pit. Men with antlers converged from four entrances and in the center a black cauldron emitted thin white smoke.

He turned around as he came near it. The trumpets blared again.

A voice cried out, "Hail, Emperor Constantine."

The cry echoed all around. "Hail, Emperor Constantine."

In the governor's box, above the entrance on his left, he could make out a group of men and women in pristine togas bowing in his direction. One of the men was waving at him to come up to them.

All around him the men with antlers were shouting, stabbing their knives into the air, lusting for blood and the hunt.

He headed for the gate under the governor's box. Guards opened a door in the passageway. He went up the stairs, followed by his own guards. The stairs opened onto the balcony overlooking the pit.

In the pit, four women in billowing white tunics were walking toward the cauldron. One from each entrance to the amphitheater.

He looked along the rows of people sitting in the governor's box. At the far end sat Crispus, with a hand up, waving at Constantine, a big smile on his face.

Constantine headed for Crispus. Everyone in the row of seats moved out of his way. A great rustling of togas followed.

When he reached Crispus, he smiled down at him. This was not the time to arrest him, with everyone watching.

"It is wonderful to see you, Father," said Crispus, rising up. He stepped forward and hugged Constantine.

"I have been looking for you," said Constantine. "A young woman in a rough house said she saw you this morning."

Crispus shook his head. "What? I've been in a tavern most of the morning with my friends." He pointed at two men sitting on the row behind. They looked like ex-legionaries you'd employ as bodyguards. They would not be the type to tell tales on their master.

He leaned toward Constantine. "Someone is going around this town pretending to be me. I have debts in taverns I have never seen the inside of."

"Why did you leave Rome so suddenly?" Constantine squeezed Crispus' shoulder.

Crispus shook his head. "I told you at the feast I was leaving early the next day. You don't remember?"

Constantine stared at him, his mind going back over the feast.

"You had drunk a lot of wine," said Crispus. He leaned closer to Constantine. "I heard there was a fire in the Imperial Palace that day. Did you see it?"

He looked about as innocent as a new-born slave.

"Yes, I saw it." A hush descended. He turned to watch what was happening in the arena. All eyes were staring up at him.

The governor was at his elbow.

"Emperor, will you throw the garland?" He had a laurel garland in his hand.

"Yes."

In the arena, below the governor's box, all the women who had come in procession to the amphitheater waited, their hands up.

Constantine went to the edge of the box and launched the wreath. Most of the women stood back to let one of their number take it. She pushed her way forward. When she had it, all the other women walked away. The men in the sheep skins were gone from the arena, and the cauldron had been taken. The woman with the wreath laid it in the center of the arena and picked up a knife that had been left there.

The watching crowd grew silent. Then, as one, the drummers, who had taken up positions in the front row of the seats, began beating slowly. Boom-boom-boom-boom, like a heartbeat.

A gasp went up and rolled around the seating.

"The entertainment is beginning," said the governor.

Constantine sat, with the governor on one side and Crispus on the other. The woman in the arena was standing, waiting, staring at the gate under the box where they sat.

Then he heard it. A low growl. Then an animal thudding.

A collective gasp echoed. He looked directly down. A giant black bear was lumbering toward the woman. It looked lean, as if in need of a good feed.

Crispus gripped Constantine's arm. "I will go down and make this a fair fight if this woman struggles with the beast." He stood and passed down to the end of the row of seats.

Constantine admired his son's courage, but he also knew that the bear was likely to have been given wine to drink and be unable to put up much of a fight.

The bear growled.

The woman raised her knife and ran toward it. The bear rose up high and let out a deep roar. The woman dodged one way, then the other and passed to the left of the bear, slicing into its side.

The bear roared at her, its mouth wide and turned and loped after her, running fast, gaining on her. She tripped and went down.

The bear reached her, reared up and opened its mouth wide in a triumphant roar, looking around.

That was the moment Crispus ran into the arena and shouted at the bear. He swung the dagger in his hand back and aimed it at the bear's head. It struck into the neck, sending the bear spinning around in pain, looking for the source of what had attacked him. The woman rolled away.

Crispus walked confidently toward the bear. It raised itself up again, as if the dagger dangling from its neck was a pin prick. Its long growl silenced the screaming audience.

Constantine looked around. Everyone was staring open mouthed at Crispus. He did not have a sword. What would he use to subdue the beast?

The drummers started again. Dum-dum-dum-dum.

The woman, who was now on her feet, shouted at the bear. It turned its head. She screamed at it. It roared back. Crispus ran toward the bear and jumped high, putting one hob-nailed sandal forward and crashing into the bear's side, below where his dagger was sticking out.

He grabbed for the dagger, but instead of pulling it out he rammed it further into the bear's neck and pushed it to the side, so the point emerged at the front. The bear toppled, swinging around wildly. One paw, topped with claws, raked into Crispus' side. The crowd gasped together as Crispus rolled away, blood mixing with sand around him.

A troop of arena handlers came running out with a wooden stretcher and lifted Crispus onto it. The woman he had rescued walked beside him as they carried him under the governor's box to wild applause.

In the arena, bear handlers were prodding at the bear. It appeared to be dead, flat on its back. A man with a black hood and an axe over his shoulder marched to the bear and with one blow and a high spurt of blood he severed its head. Then he picked up Crispus' dagger and headed after him.

The governor turned to Constantine. "This story will travel all over the empire. Crispus will make a worthy successor to you. You must be proud."

"I am," said Constantine, a rush of good feeling for his son coursing through him. "I will be announcing his succession soon, governor. Let's hope his injuries aren't serious."

"Crispus, Crispus, Crispus," came the chant, starting near the governor's box and spreading in a circle around the amphitheater. As Constantine was about to leave the box he looked back. It was a long time since a crowd had so enthusiastically called his name. The governor was following him. They went down the stairs together. At the bottom was the tall woman he had thrown the laurel to. She bowed.

After Constantine passed her, he turned. The woman was kneeling before the governor. He bent down and whispered something to her. She laughed.

Something inside Constantine shifted, like a door opening. There was more going on here than he was being told. He didn't like it. There had been trickery at the whore house, meant to distract him while whoever killed the girl escaped, and now his son had been gifted with the opportunity to appear the hero, by a woman who was friends with the governor.

XXX

Caesarea, 326 A.D.

Helena held Bina's hand tight as they stepped onto the galley. "Have you ever been on a ship before?"

"No," said the girl. No and yes were the usual responses Helena got from her. She knew it would take time for Bina to trust her and to accept that her abuser was gone forever. "It's scary sometimes, but it's a real adventure, and we will travel near the coast. I prefer it that way."

"Why are you taking me to New Rome?" asked Bina. Her brow was creased with worry.

"You are proof of the miracle that happened in Jerusalem."

The girl looked at her, a confused expression on her face now.

Helena bent down to her. "Your mother left you to become a Christian. Now you will become one too, like your mother, because of her courage. That is the miracle." She took the girl's hand and headed to the captain's room at the back of the galley. The galley officers were standing to attention on one side. She nodded at them as they passed, noting the well-scrubbed deck underneath their sandaled feet.

"Sail as soon as you can, Captain. It'll be good to be out at sea. Did your other passenger arrive?"

The captain nodded.

She pushed at the rough wooden door of the cabin. The room beyond was in almost total darkness, but as her eyes adjusted, she could see more. A narrow bed at the side was where she would sleep. A rough bench attached to the wall at the back was where they would eat. On the right a low platform with wolfskins thrown over it was where personal slaves could sleep. Sitting at the edge of the bench was a boy of about fourteen summers.

The girl flinched away when she saw the boy.

"Do not worry. This boy will sleep outside on deck."

She raised her voice. "Does the bishop know what happened to you?" she said, addressing the boy.

"No," he said. "We left Jerusalem at night, as you had instructed. He will just think I ran off."

"Did you bring with you what I asked?"

The boy reached into the pocket of his tunic. He pulled out a gold ring. "The ring."

"Give it to me," said Helena.

The boy padded toward her and passed it into Helena's outstretched hand.

He smiled at the young girl. "You don't like boys, then."

Helena's hand came up fast. She grabbed the boy by the chin.

"Never make assumptions and never speak about such things again or you will be sent to the brothers in the desert to live atop a pole." It would be best to treat him harshly now. If he spoke like this when he was older, he would get a life changing beating.

The boy squirmed. His hands came up, but he didn't dare try to release Helena's.

"I've saved this girl from the life you have been living up to this. And make sure you do not let the sailors fuck you on this ship or I will have your balls cut off with a hot knife before sending you to the brothers." She released him and pushed him away.

He stepped back, shaking, eyes wide.

"I assume the captain thinks you were to be my lover?"

The boy shrugged.

"The best way we can dispel that idea is if you make sure not to enter this cabin again until we reach New Rome."

The boy nodded. "What about my payment?" he said.

"First, try to remember everything you did with the bishop. Your testimony is what I've paid for and your new life with a bag of gold in your little hand depends on it."

XXXI

Rome, 326 A.D.

Paulina stepped off the flat sand platform. It stretched away toward the tall Egyptian obelisk that had stood at the center of Nero's circus. Around its base many Christians had been martyred.

"The Empress Fausta wishes to see you," said the slave. He nodded toward an entourage waiting nearby, on the edge of the building site. Paulina's building crew had already pulled down most of the seating that had surrounded the circus.

She walked fast and bowed as she came near Fausta.

"What can I do for you, Empress," she said, as she rose.

Behind the empress stood four giant Nubian guards with the curved swords such guards liked to use dangling from their belts. If that lot wanted your head on a platter it would be done so fast you would still be alive as your head spun through the air.

"I am pleased to see you are making good progress," said Fausta.

"We are, would you like me to show you our plans?"

Fausta shook her head. "The emperor told me all about them." She paused. "What I need is for you to stop sending messages to my husband." She raised her hand. The four Nubians stepped forward.

Fausta's voice dropped. "I cannot answer for my guards if they discover anyone going against my wishes."

"What messages to the emperor?" Paulina raised her hands, appealing to be believed.

"Perhaps this will help your memory." She snapped her fingers. A slave, who had been hanging back behind the Nubians

123

rushed forward. He carried a leather sack in front of him as if it contained a dead dog. He dropped it at Paulina's feet, then pulled it open for her.

Inside was the head of one of the young Christians who'd joined her demolition crew recently, excited by the changes going on in Rome.

"This brother is not a messenger to Constantine," said Paulina. She bit her lip to suppress her anger.

"That is not what he was claiming in a tavern last week. And when my men spoke to him, we discovered he was a runaway slave who had killed his master."

Paulina stared at her. When she spoke her tone was slow and deliberate.

"You do not need to watch everyone working with me. I will not send messages to Constantine, and I especially will not send messages about your search for someone to get rid of your baby."

Fausta snorted and spoke slowly too. "That you do not spread lies is all I ask," she said. She was angry now, her cheeks red, her lips pressed together as she finished.

"Empress, I don't lie."

Fausta shrugged.

"But if your baby dies because of the herbs you've been buying, I will make it my business to tell Constantine what I know."

The empress glared at her as if she hoped her stare might burn Paulina where she stood.

"I have not sought to end my pregnancy. I have sought out doctors so that I know all the ways people like you might try to kill my baby." She turned and stormed away.

XXXII

Byblos, 326 A.D.

Helena and Bina watched from the deck as they approached the port of Byblos. A galley was leaving at the same time and a trading vessel was also on the way out of the port. That left a space at the white stone dock near the short breakwater in the tight curve of the bay.

The captain shouted at the row master and the drummer slowed his beat so their speed decreased. The water was as still as blue-green glass that afternoon and the sun high and hot with little breeze. A column of thin smoke rose from inside a pillared temple on a low hill above the port. In the distance a row of mountains stood out against the skyline.

"What temple is that?" asked Helena of the captain.

"They worship Adonis here," said the captain. "The river that opens out here runs red with his blood at each new year and its water is a cure for many sicknesses." He pointed. "See, there are sick people there, on the dock?"

Helena looked where he was pointing. A few of the people heading out of the dock were being carried by others.

"I heard people died after coming to this temple," said Helena. "After we tie up, I want to see the priests of Adonis brought to the dock and the governor of this port brought here with every legionary he can muster."

She looked up at the mast. "I see you have done it correctly today, Captain. Make sure my purple imperial standard goes at the top so that all these people," she pointed at harbor guards running toward where they were going to dock, "can tell who is aboard."

She took Bina's hand. "And Captain, make sure you take on plenty of water, olives, bread and cheese. I will not have a hungry crew on any vessel I travel on."

The captain hung his head. "May I ask you for a few coins to pay for it all? I spent all you gave me already on supplies."

"I don't believe that for one moment, Captain, but Bina will bring you some coins before we tie up, and don't forget my instructions."

She pulled Bina after her. When they were inside their cabin she bent down to her. "Many try to take advantage of people like us," she said. "You must learn to demand high standards and to give orders with confidence, no matter how you feel inside." She put her face near Bina's and flicked her smile on and off.

Bina nodded. Then she copied Helena's fake smiling.

Helena laughed. "Pour me some water, dear Bina," she said.

It was late afternoon by the time the priests of Adonis had arrived at the port. The governor of the town, and the hundred legionaries stationed there, had already been standing to attention for some time. The sun was lowering fast, and they weren't wearing battle dress, but it was still hot on the dock where Helena sat under a hastily erected canopy with Bina, in a pure white tunic, beside her.

The priests of Adonis were all shaven headed. Each of them wore only a loin cloth and thin gold arm bands. The priests were plump looking and almost covered in blue tattoos. Behind them came a stream of the town's inhabitants in a multicolored array of tunics and head wear.

Flute players accompanied the priests' approach and singers called out in turn with high keening songs. When they reached the open area in front of the purple imperial canopy the priests bobbed about on the spot until one of their number shouted and they all went down to prostrate themselves in front of Helena, mother of the emperor.

Helena's canopy also had the two members of her personal guard who accompanied her everywhere at its back, impassive and standing with their swords out and dangling from their hands, ready to dispatch anyone who dared approach her without permission.

None of the priests looked capable of attacking anyone. They appeared bleary-eyed, as if they didn't sleep much or spent most of their time smoking the herbs the river valley was famous for from here to the gates of Hercules.

Helena waited, unmoving. An older priest with baggy eyes and a rolling belly of fat stood and put both his hands forward, palms up, in supplication.

"We welcome you to the city of Adonis, great lady, mother of a god, queen of all she surveys."

Helena put her hand up. "Stop. My son is not a god and I am not a queen. Bring people cured by your temple to me, on board my ship. Bring them at dawn, and with them two relatives for each who can attest to the previous sickness you cured. Now, take all your priests and be gone." She waved him away.

The priest put his hands on his head and whimpered.

A great muttering ran through the crowd. A man with a thin diadem on his head stepped forward. His cloak was black, as was every other garment he wore. He stopped as the priests moved away, then prostrated himself.

"Up," said Helena. "Who are you?"

The man stood, put both hands forward. "I am the leader of the Qana here. We have a treaty with Rome and are allowed all vassal privileges under that treaty. We welcome you." He glanced at the departing priests. "We are not followers of Adonis. We follow the old ways of Abraham. Please do not think we are like these priests."

"Are there followers of Christ here too?" she said.

The man turned and pointed at a small group of people standing at the edge of the crowd.

"These are the followers of Christ." He put his hands to his mouth and shouted, "Yoseph, come forward."

A thin man with a haggard expression came slowly forward. Behind him he left a woman with two young children clutching at her.

This man also started to prostrate himself, but Helena told him to stand.

"Come and see me at dawn," she said to Yoseph. "I have news for you."

She stood up, waved at the crowds, then turned, and with Bina holding her hand headed back onto the ship.

The captain held the door to the cabin open as she came toward it.

"Would you like me to find a palace near here, for you to stay at?" he said.

"We will be leaving soon after dawn, Captain. Find the governor of this port and bring him to me at once."

She went inside the cabin and looked around.

"Put your mattress on the floor, Bina. And sit quietly when our guests arrive." She pushed a wisp of hair behind Bina's ear and leaned down. "You are learning quickly, my child. I see a great future for you."

She opened the door to the cabin and whispered to her two personal guards standing outside.

Watered down wine was brought. When the governor appeared, he went down on one knee and laid his rod of office in front of her.

"Whatever you command will be done, Empress." He bowed.

"In the morning, at dawn, I want the temple of Adonis emptied of its priests."

The man's expression darkened, then he smoothed it. "My empress, I must appeal to you. The temple brings in many visitors and many people here rely on it to earn their keep."

"Yes, yes, I know all about the rites of Adonis and the many women who enjoy the services of the priests and how they spread sweetmeats and other gifts around to mark their happiness, and..." She leaned forward from the bench at the back of the cabin where she was sitting and pointed at him. "I expect you make a good living from the bribes they give you, but it is all over, from tomorrow morning."

"But, Empress, the whole town loves the temple."

"Stop it," she shouted, angrily. At that, the door banged open and two guards came in, their swords up.

"If you say one more word in contradiction of my orders your head will be set outside that temple before night falls to encourage others to obey my orders." Every word was spat out.

The governor bowed. Helena took the opportunity to wink at Bina.

"Who is the temple to be given to?" asked the governor, softly.

"The followers of Christ will be given the temple and you will protect them all. If I hear that any one of them has been harmed after this, you will be harmed to the same extent as the worst inflicted on them."

The man nodded. He was stony faced now. "Do you wish to visit at my villa outside the town?" he said.

She shook her head. "I want you to go and get ready for the morning. When the priests come here you will take over the temple and throw out all that belongs to them. Blow a horn three times to indicate it is done. Understood?"

The man nodded.

"You are dismissed," she said. The man went out. Bina laughed silently.

They ate a dark lentil stew that evening, a local delicacy, the captain said, and spent the evening on the roof of the cabin on cushions, enjoying the breeze.

The captain had released a few of the crew, those he said had earned a night away from the ship. They had gone to a tavern at the end of the dock with two blazing torches outside it. He knew where his men would be and could call them from their entertainments if he had to.

The first they knew that anything was amiss was when Helena saw the bald wet head of a priest appearing at the side of the ship.

No one was at the front of the ship at the time and the captain was resting, asleep under a half-broken palm leaf canopy beside the mast.

But Helena's guards were not asleep. They were sitting in the shadows beside her cabin, and they stood up, their swords in their hands as four priests with curved wet swords glistening in their hands rose dripping onto the ship. Helena's guards rushed at them, but they were too late to stop them coming on board.

The priests were joined quickly by another four, all obviously with some military training as they did not scream as they attacked, they simply started jabbing at Helena's guards.

The conclusion should have been without doubt, with four men against each of her guards, but they didn't reckon that Helena was also capable of defending herself.

She took the two sharp knives on the plates in front of them that they had used to cut the flat local bread and launched them at the two leading attackers. One of the knives missed, but the other went into the arm of a priest and drew blood and a shout from the man. That was the signal for a general shouting to begin and in moments the deck was alive with the captain up, crew men joining swinging cudgels, spurts of blood and screams of agony and rage.

Helena covered Bina's eyes, but the young girl pushed her hands away. One of the attackers had managed to get past Helena's guards and laughed as he came running at Helena, his sword raised.

Helena picked up a plate and threw it at the man. It hit him, but it didn't stop him. He laughed and pulled his hand back to strike.

Bina dived at his legs. Helena screamed, "No."

The man looked down and swiped his blade toward Bina instead of Helena. Bina twisted like a snake, but the blade sliced along her thigh and she screamed.

The priest, sweat and water glistening on his face, his breath coming fast, pulled his sword back to stab at Helena, who had come forward, bending down to reach for Bina.

XXXIII

Polensis, 326 A.D.

Constantine put his hand on Crispus' arm. They were in a stone walled room under the amphitheater, Crispus lying on a wooden bed.
A physician was binding up his side with a yellow linen bandage from which blood seeped.

Crispus' face twisted as the physician passed the bandage under his body.

"I hope you know what you're doing," said Constantine.

"I served for twenty years with our legions, Emperor. My job was to bind wounds and save lives." He passed the binding over and under again as Crispus groaned.

"Your son will live. The bear just cut his skin. He is lucky. Bears can pull your guts out with one blow and you don't survive that, no matter who you are."

Crispus' blood dripped through cracks in the bed onto the stone floor. Standing around the bed were the governor, the woman Crispus had saved – she had her hands together praying – and other people Constantine did not know.

"Are you finished binding the wound?"

The physician nodded. "He needs rest now."

Constantine looked around. There were too many people in the room.

"Everybody out," he said. "I want to speak to my son." He waved his arms. "Where are my guards?"

His personal guards shouted, "Here, Emperor," from where they were standing by the doorway.

"Get these people out, including the physician, and make sure no one else comes into this room."

The guards shouted and the people moved. The governor was the last to go.

"I will be at our villa, Emperor," he said.

Constantine didn't reply. He had his hand on his son's shoulder. The governor left the room.

Crispus smiled up at him.

"You were lucky this time," said Constantine, "but that must be the last time you jump into any arena."

Crispus shook his head. "I want to bring this type of games back to Rome," he said. "Did you see how they all loved it?"

Constantine took a deep breath, suppressing his irritation. "What matters is that you do not try that again. When you are the emperor people will expect you to be above such things. You are far too valuable to let an animal end your life. We will be plunged back into civil war with every governor thinking they can announce they are the new emperor. Thousands will die." He gripped Crispus' shoulder tighter.

"Tell me that you understand this and perhaps then we can agree on your succession date."

"I understand that, Father." Crispus winced. He lifted his hand.

Constantine gripped it. They would not end up as enemies. He would ask him about the missing gold when he'd recovered from his wounds. This was the moment he would tell him that he loved him, something his father had never done.

He stared at Crispus, but the words would not come.

"What brings you here?" asked Crispus. "Surely you could have sent a messenger?"

"I heard a lot crazy talk in Rome," said Constantine. He breathed in deep.

"What talk?" Crispus looked interested, and unafraid.

This alone was reassurance for Constantine. If his son had planned his death, he would not be so calm.

"It is all nothing. I wanted to see you. We didn't finish our conversation about when you will be appointed emperor."

"I leave all that to you, Father." Crispus shook his head, closed his eyes. "I knew after we talked about it, that the more I demanded it, the less likely you were to give me what I wanted."

Constantine bent his head forward. It was clear what he had to do. This near escape was a sign that he had to put Crispus into power soon, so he would stop taking such risks.

"I have made up my mind. You will be anointed my successor and I will retire at the end of this year at the Saturnalia. We will invite all the governors to New Rome and have a celebration like no other ever held. You will be emperor of a united people."

Crispus smiled. His grip on Constantine's hand loosened. He reached to Constantine's arm and gripped it, pulling him to him.

"From me and all our family, thank you. This is great news."

"Your job is to get better," said Constantine. He blinked, remembering something. "Fausta said you were called away by your family. Is your wife well?"

Crispus licked his lips.

"I love my step-mother, dearly, Father, but sometimes I just wish to get away." He closed his eyes. "I had to make up a story for her to explain my quick departure. But it was not entirely a lie. My wife was not well for a time, but she said for me not to come quickly. I decided to see some old comrades here before heading north."

A commotion outside in the corridor made them both look to the door. It was closed over almost completely.

"Emperor Constantine, my lord," came a shout. It was Lucius' voice. What was he doing here?

XXXIV

Byblos, 326 A.D.

Helena walked along the line of priests kneeling on the wooden deck.

"Your leader is not here, I see," she said. "Would any of you like to live?"

Two of the priests turned their eyes up to her. She stopped by the older looking one of the two.

"Why did you come here tonight?"

The man looked at her, then looked away, up at the nearly full moon which lit the deck like a giant lighthouse. A light breeze ruffled his hair. In another situation, it would be a perfect night for romance, with a faint musty hint in the air from the olive groves behind the town.

She poked at his shoulder with one of the daggers she'd picked up from the deck, discarded by the priests when they saw four of their number dead and the crew and Helena's guards surrounding them. The dagger had a carved black ivory phallus as a handle.

The man's hands were tied behind his back. He swayed a little as he contemplated what was expected of him.

"The high priest sent us. We are only following orders, Empress. If we do not follow all of his orders we have our throats cut in the night and our bodies thrown into the sea." He hung his head.

"Your high priest could not find any people he had cured?"

"No, there are some, I am sure, but mostly the people we cure are from far away and they go back to their homes."

"You haven't cured anyone locally?" She sounded disdainful now.

"We ask too much in payment for most of the locals. They do not come to us for their sicknesses."

"They know better," said Helena, cutting him off. She walked along the line to the other priest who looked up at her.

"Do you wish to live?"

This priest, a young man who should have been in the legions, nodded and bit his lip. He knew the most likely outcome from their capture.

She prodded another of the priests with her sandaled foot.

"What about you?"

The man looked up with pain in his eyes. "Will you believe I am a slave to these priests, bound by law to follow anything they ask?"

She nudged the last one. He looked up and said in a guttural eastern accent, "I am escaped slave. I found refuge in the temple. I do only what I am told."

She turned around. The crew and her bodyguards were staring at her.

She looked up at the moon. "We need men like you in the legions," she said, her voice calm. "If you agree to join up and to give evidence against the high priest, you can all live."

A sigh went up from the men. The captain put his hand up.

"Perhaps we can take one head to encourage the others."

"There has been enough dying for one night, Captain. One of your men is gone, yes?"

"Yes, and another's badly injured. He will have to remain here."

"Do you have enough men to get to New Rome?"

"I will recruit another at the tavern," said the captain. He pointed at where a torch lit the doorway of the tavern.

"Go find the governor," said Helena. "He must take statements from these priests."

The captain headed off. Helena and Bina went to their cabin after making sure enough guards would remain on deck to watch the prisoners. They slept badly.

Yoseph arrived at dawn.

"You will place a follower of Christ in charge of the temple," Helena told him, after he had bowed and stared, amazed, at the sight of the priests being led away by legionaries.

She called him to her and hugged him. She didn't care about his thin dirty tunic. He shook in surprise, then stood back, as if ashamed to be so close to her.

"I know the terrible things that many followers of Christ have been through," she said. "Those days are over."

His eyes opened wide. He blinked away tears. "What about all the priests in the temple?" His voice caught in his throat. "They do not like us even in the shadow of their temple."

"The most violent priests have been taken care of and their leader has been arrested. The word will spread about how they attacked my ship last night. There will be no sympathy for them."

She put a hand out to him and gripped his when he put it forward, a smile beaming now on his face.

"Act as Jesus would, think only of helping others, and this church will succeed here."

He bowed. "We live our lives that way and will continue to do so." He blinked. He seemed to be on the point of crying. "This is truly a miracle. Your miracle."

She released his hand. "This is our moment. Enjoy it. Celebrate." She waved toward the sun, coming up over the mountains behind the town, and laughed. "We are changing the empire, my friend, together."

He smiled. "And if the priests try to retake the temple?"

"Cut their heads off, with my permission."

XXXV

Polensis, 326 A.D.

"Lucius," Constantine shouted. No one came. Loud conversations were going on outside.

"Let the man in," he shouted.

The door pushed open and Lucius, in a leather guard's tunic and with one hand bandaged, came into the room.

"Emperor." He bent down on one knee.

"Lucius," said Constantine. "It is good you are here."

Crispus waved and gave him a thumbs up.

"How is your hand?" said Constantine.

"I am lucky. I have been learning to fight with my left and I find it works well." He held his injured hand up. "And this one will heal, so the physicians say."

"Better to lose your hand than your life," said Constantine.

"But you are injured as well now," said Lucius, looking at Crispus.

Constantine explained what had happened.

Crispus added, "I am now to be the hero of Polensis." He put his fist to his lips, as he winced. "And my father confirmed he will stand aside for me at Saturnalia."

Lucius' mouth opened. He bowed for Crispus. "This is big news indeed. I will have to be more friendly to you."

Crispus' eyes closed. He shook his head from side to side. "You will always have a place at my court."

His eyes remained closed.

"Did the physician give you juice of the poppy?" asked Constantine.

Crispus put his thumb up, then dropped it again.

"We will go up to the box. He should remain here all night, until the bleeding stops. I have seen injuries like this before." Constantine stepped back, then headed for the door.

The physician was outside. Constantine gave him instructions to find helpers to stay watching his son through the night, to change his binding in the morning, and to mix honey with it. He was about to go on talking when the physician put his hand up.

"I know what to do, Emperor. Your son will not be moved. There will be guards at this door all the time so he is not disturbed, and my wife and daughter will come with broth and blankets for him." He bowed. "It is my duty and our pleasure to help."

Constantine reached for the leather purse attached to his belt.

The physician shook his head. "The governor already paid."

Constantine and Lucius, with Constantine's guards behind them, headed down the corridor, busy with men coming and going, and went up the stairs to the governor's box.

As they reached a quiet point in the stairs, Constantine turned to Lucius and asked, "What brings you here?"

Lucius looked troubled, as if he wanted to talk about something.

"Not here," he said. "I have news."

"What about?"

He looked up and down the stairs. No one was coming.

"About Crispus."

Constantine shook his head.

"I will listen to no more against him. Do you understand?"

Lucius nodded, but only after a long hesitation.

"My son nearly died today. He is a good man and will make me proud as an emperor." He lowered his voice. "Be careful that you do not spread lies about him. I am convinced there is a plot to prevent him becoming emperor." He paused. "You saw him. I forgave him in the blink of an eye for not telling me where he was going."

He turned and headed up the stairs. Lucius followed.

"Sit in the place of honor," said the governor when they emerged into the box. A display of spear throwing was taking place in the arena. The target was a prisoner bound to a wooden target.

"What is the prisoner guilty of?" asked Constantine. There were already three spears sticking from his chest and his head was down.

"He was the leader of a band of outlaws who killed two traders near here. A child with them. Another escaped. The case against him was proven almost a year ago. No one came forward to appeal on his behalf. We hold such men until this annual festival so that all will see the results of going against the law of the empire." He waved at the crowd who were jeering at the impaled criminal.

A shout went up as another spear impaled the man, this time from the side and through his cheek. The pool of blood around his feet grew. Cheering rang out, echoing around the arena in a wave. The last spear thrower bowed at the governor's box. He was a small wiry man wearing only a loin cloth.

A team of other men appeared. They cut down and dragged away the criminal using hooks in his flesh.

"Your son is sleeping now?" asked the governor.

"Yes, he will stay down in that room for one night, at least."

"Everything will be done as he needs it." The governor slapped his hand on his knee. "We serve you with all we have." He glanced at Lucius. "Is this a member of your imperial family?"

"This is Lucius Armenius. He's been with me since we fought together in the east."

The governor smiled. "Yes, the famous Lucius Armenius. We have heard about you. I expect you have some good stories to tell. I hope you will tell us a few at the feast later." He turned. A woman behind them was calling his name.

He waved the woman forward.

"This is my wife. She will take you to our home. We can see you have just arrived. I am sure you will want to wash the salt from your skin."

Lucius looked at the woman, then leaned toward Constantine.

"We'll talk later." He stood and headed off with the governor's wife.

"My wife is a genius for knowing what people need." The governor looked back at the arena.

"We have a fight between two famous bears coming up, Emperor. I hope you will enjoy it." He moved closer to Constantine. "We can have more private entertainments arranged too. My wife is very good at that as well." He winked at Constantine. "Ask your son about those. She helped him find what he likes." He laughed and made a gesture with his fist, as if ramming it up someone.

Constantine stood. He could not watch a bear fight while his son was lying below.

"I'm going to see Crispus," he said. He headed out of the box and down the stairs. His guards followed.

When he reached Crispus' room, an older woman was cooling his brow with a wet cloth. She bowed and stayed low until Constantine told her to rise.

"How is he?"

"He will recover. He's in the poppy sleep now." She seemed nervous.

"Is he still bleeding?"

"No, the binding has done its work."

Crispus moaned. It sounded as if he was calling for someone. Whose name was that? Constantine leaned over his son.

The woman nodded. "Yes, he calls names. He must love his family."

Crispus moaned a name again. Constantine could not make it out.

"I will return in the morning to check on him. I'll be in the governor's villa tonight, if anything changes."

The woman nodded. Constantine headed for the door. As he opened it, he looked back.

"What name has he called, mine?"

She shook her head. "No, his mother's, the Empress Fausta."

Constantine was about to tell her that Fausta was his son's stepmother, but he didn't. Let her believe what she wanted. As he headed out, he smiled at the thought of Crispus calling Fausta's name. They would laugh about it together when Crispus had recovered.

A slave of the governor's was waiting outside with Constantine's guards. The man had a calm, sun-beaten face and eyes like black beads. He invited Constantine to follow him to the governor's villa.

"We have rooms waiting for you, Emperor," he said.

"Has anyone asked to see me?" said Constantine.

"A small group gathered with petitions when they heard you had arrived." The man looked solemn. "Will I send them away?"

"No, have you an audience hall?"

"Yes, it is not what you are used to, Emperor, but it works for us."

"We will go there first. I want to hear as many petitions as I can before the feast."

"Yes, my lord."

The audience hall was small, and the waiting area outside crowded. As Constantine walked through it with his guard a great clamor went up and scrolls were thrust in his direction.

The governor's house guards and slaves did their best to keep the people back, but it was not easy.

One shout at the back of the group caught Constantine's attention. "Two of my girls are dead. Please help me."

He looked over the heads of the crowd. The woman had a red face, as if she'd been crying a lot.

He put his hand on the shoulder of the governor's slave and pointed at the woman. "Make sure she gets to see me," he said.

The first few petitions were about land squabbles. He directed both to seek the governor's decision.

The woman with the red face was shown in next. She fell to her knees in front of him and touched her forehead to the yellow marble floor of the audience hall.

"Up," said Constantine.

"I loved my daughters," she cried out, as she rose. "They were my life. Now both of them are dead." She wailed.

Constantine waited for her to stop. He leaned back in his carved oak chair. It had gold laurels embossed into its arms and gold claws as feet.

She pounded her chest. "How am I to live when my daughters are not here to look after me?"

"Why is this my concern?" asked Constantine.

"I heard that someone staying with the governor is responsible for what happened." She started crying again.

One of the governor's guards came forward. He saluted and asked for permission to speak.

"Granted," said Constantine.

"Permission requested to remove this woman and punish her for blaming a guest of the governor for these deaths."

"What punishment do you suggest?"

"A whipping and she be expelled from the town."

Constantine looked at the woman. She was on her knees, crying. He stood, walked to her. Standing over her, he said, "Where were your daughters when they died?"

The woman looked up. "At the old witches house. The one who sells girls to men who enjoy making them suffer." She began crying again, softly this time, hunching over, as if expecting only to suffer more.

XXXVI

Rome, 326 A.D.

Paulina stiffened. She had been sleeping badly since Lucius left. Her discussions with him had led to him leaving Rome to find Constantine, but she had not asked Lucius to give him a message, so she hadn't lied to Fausta.

She looked around the room. She'd been staying in a tavern near Nero's circus since Constantine had left the city. The price was low for the room and she wanted to make sure the coin Constantine had given her would last as long as possible. Now every room in the tavern was taken by women who'd once served as priestesses in her temple, and most of them had men with them in their rooms. She felt safe, except for one thing.

The tavern was still open and the crowd in the big room below could get boisterous at times with legionaries singing bawdy songs and fighting over any minor insult.

It was something else that had woken her. And there it was again. Someone walking in the corridor.

She slipped from her bed and pulled the dagger from under her pillow.

The door to her room had a bolt of wood as a lock. As she watched in the late evening light coming in from the small window, a blade tip appeared in the gap between the door and the wall. It moved upwards to lift the bolt. She went behind the door, her breathing heavy, her heart pounding. It opened slowly.

The tip of the sword appeared in the opening.

"We know you are there. Come out, if you don't want us to lock all the doors of this tavern and burn you all out."

Paulina considered the offer for a moment, looking around the room, savoring what had been a good period of her life, leading good people.

"There is no need for that." She waited, her back to the wall as a centurion of the imperial household, a purple scarf around his neck, entered the room, his sword still up. Behind him, two other burly imperial guards followed. They filled the room.

When they saw Paulina was unarmed, they sheathed their swords.

"You will come with us. Get dressed but bring nothing with you."

"Where are we all going?" said Paulina, a smile in her voice.

"You will find out."

"Wonderful. I need a little entertainment." She raised one hand and slipped out of the thin night dress she wore. She stared back as the three guards ogled her body, then stuck her tongue out at them and went to the wooden box in a corner where she kept her clothes, neatly folded. She bent down, reached to the bottom of the box, to the last temple dress she kept for old time's sake.

One of the men grunted like a pig as he watched her back as she slipped it on. She turned and identified the man who had grunted by the slick of saliva on his open bottom lip. She smiled at him, blinked, then looked at the centurion.

"I am ready for anything," she said, with a bow. Getting men to like her had been her profession for a long time. She hated the lies but knew they could help her survive.

He led her downstairs into the main room of the tavern, which had gone quiet, presumably since the moment the imperial guards had headed up to her room. Some of the tavern guests had probably departed at that point. Legionaries who'd suddenly remembered their duties or thieves who'd remembered what they'd done.

A hiss came from the back of the room as Paulina was taken out through the front door. She turned, smiled and shouted, "I'll return."

The centurion put her in the first of two waiting heavy chariots and with the second chariot following, they headed out of the city toward the setting sun. As the sky brightened they turned into a high gate opened by slaves. A dusty path led in a gentle curve to a villa, set amid endless rows of vines. Two torches lit the main wide door. Through a window on one side Paulina could see the glimmer of candles.

The centurion stopped the chariot in a spray of dust, the horses whinnying and neighing. Grapes were heavy on the vines behind them and ahead the villa was almost covered in thick ivy.

The double doors opened and two slaves, who probably doubled as guards, bowed and motioned for her to come in. She went in, tight lipped with apprehension as to what was coming for her.

The slave led her into a room on the right. It had rows of dusty benches and a plinth at the top of the room, as if it had once been used as a temple, though there were no statues and the walls were bare. The only window was sealed shut.

"Please, wait here. The master will be with you soon," said the slave. He closed the door behind him.

Paulina went to the window. The glass was thick and green and in small squares, but she could see the chariots moving off. She walked around the room. There was no other way out. She listened at the door and eventually heard a low conversation.

She was a prisoner.

XXXVII

Polensis, 326 A.D.

"Take this," said Constantine handing the crying woman four gold aureus he took from the purse on his belt. "I do this only because of your distress, not because I take responsibility for what happened to your daughters."

The woman looked at the large gold coins in her hand. She could buy a house with them.

"Do not blame the governor or any of his guests for what happened to your daughters. They did not have to join that house."

The woman nodded, wiped at her tears and stumbled for the door.

The governor's slave stepped forward. "You are very generous, my emperor."

Constantine looked at him. "Go after her and warn her not to tell anyone what I gave her and speak of it no more yourself." He pointed his finger at the slave. "And fetch Lucius Armenius, who has recently arrived."

The man bowed and hurried away.

"Send in the next person," shouted Constantine.

A stream of litigants, many of whom Constantine could not help, followed one after the other. One man wanted a place for his son in the Praetorians and asked would they be recruiting again. Constantine told him he'd disbanded the Praetorians and would not allow them to reform. A woman wanted to know if her daughter should be allowed join a local temple. Constantine told her to join a Christian church.

The sun was lowering when Lucius arrived. He came in annoyed.

"I have to wait with your supplicants to see you now," he said, as he came up the room.

Constantine sighed loudly, shook his head. "I did not tell them to keep you waiting." He pointed at the governor's slaves and the guards in the room.

"All of you, leave now, and tell whoever else is waiting that the audience is finished."

He put his hand up and waved Lucius to him. "Come, I saw a garden at the back. Let's get some air."

They headed out of the audience hall by the back door. Constantine asked a passing slave girl to show them to the gardens. She did so and went away to get them wine.

The garden was empty.

"So, what is it you want to tell me?" Constantine sat on a rough wooden bench. It looked as if it had been in use for centuries.

"Do not blame me for what I am about to tell you. That is what I ask you before I begin." Lucius spoke softly, after looking round to check that no one had followed them.

"More intrigue. When will this ever end?" said Constantine. He pointed at Lucius' hand. "A centurion in one of my legions was injured liked this. He claimed prayer to the Christ god cured him."

Lucius moved his hand. "I must practice holding things again, so my physician says."

Silence descended. They looked at each other, as if neither of them wanted to talk about what needed to be talked about.

"Tell me what you came here to tell me," said Constantine.

"I cannot," said Lucius.

"Why?" said Constantine, getting annoyed.

"You have sworn me to say nothing against Crispus."

Constantine threw his hands in the air. "So, tell me, but do not expect me to believe any part of it."

"I will tell you something else, and you do not have to believe that either." Lucius raised his hands. "And I did not come here to spread rumor. I came here because I am concerned for you."

"Keep going." Constantine walked slowly from side to side as Lucius spoke.

"I know why Seutonius was murdered. He knew about Crispus and Fausta and threatened that he'd reveal it. He was expecting his freedom and a bag of coins."

"How do you know this?" Constantine was clearly annoyed and having a hard time suppressing it.

"A widow selling her estate outside Rome was expecting to sell it to him. He told her he was coming into money." Lucius paused, took a breath. "There are not many people Seutonius knew who could provide him with such wealth."

"That doesn't prove anything."

"There is someone else involved."

"Who, spit it out, man."

"If I say it you must promise to listen. Do you?"

"Yes."

Lucius' voice dropped. "A slave of the empress, of Fausta your wife, told a follower of Christ that her mistress followed you to the stables that morning and on seeing you go into the loft she used a candle to start a fire."

Constantine stopped walking and pointed at Lucius. "I don't believe it. Someone is trying to stir things up. First, they blame Crispus for Seutonius, then they blame the empress for the fire. I have heard this type of thing before."

"And there is more," said Lucius, interrupting. "This is only the beginning."

"Come on then, tell me the rest." Constantine pinched the bridge of his nose.

"Fausta has been seeing someone."

"Who?"

"Crispus." Lucius whispered the word.

"That is a lie," Constantine shouted. "She is pregnant with my child. This is absurd. This is gutter talk from the lowest tavern in the Subaru, where the women are painted like statues and the men are drunk from morning to night." He was becoming angrier with each word.

"They do not talk about this in the Subaru."

"But it is still just talk. Praise the gods, that you would come all this way to spread vile talk like this." Constantine stood in front of Lucius. "I should throw you out!"

"I have proof," said Lucius. He reached into a pocket of his tunic with his left hand and pulled out a thin gold band.

"Your son gave this to Fausta, to pledge himself to her." He handed it to Constantine. "Look on the inside. His name is there."

Constantine looked. Crispus' name was indeed there.

"Anyone can have this," he said. He threw the ring to the ground.

"I'm not finished." Lucius went and picked up the ring. His voice grew softer as he continued, "The empress is pregnant, but the date of the baby's birth gives a lie to you being the father."

"What? That is too much. This will be proved as a lie when the baby is born soon enough." For the first time in the conversation Constantine hesitated. Fausta had looked very small when he last saw her. Was it possible he was not the father? No, surely not.

"You cannot tell me that Crispus is the father!" He stepped back, a tremor of shock running through him as a queasy feeling grew unexpectedly. He wanted to go back to before he'd heard these words coming out of Lucius' mouth.

"Answer this, Emperor," said Lucius, confidently. "Why would Fausta be looking for a physician to end her pregnancy, if the timing was right?"

"She is doing that?" His breath caught deep in his throat, like an old wound.

Lucius nodded.

Constantine shook his head. "Again, this is a vile rumor. You expect me to believe that my son and my wife are at it behind my back? Why would they risk everything to do this? He is about to become emperor!"

"People do unexpected things."

"That was different. Things were very different back then. I was almost an outcast. I was about to die."

"Perhaps there are simple reasons here too. Sometimes things happen between a man and a woman if they live their lives next to each other and their age is similar."

"Fausta is older than him."

"Not by much, and she is a beautiful woman in her prime."

"And again, this is all vile speculation."

"Except for one thing."

"What is that thing?"

"Crispus wears the other ring of this pair." Lucius held the ring up. "You can ask him about it when he has recovered. Perhaps he will have a good explanation as to why the match of this lovers' ring is on his hand."

Constantine reached for the ring.

XXXVIII

Outside Rome, 326 A.D.

"I must go to the toilet," shouted Paulina, banging on the door. It opened after a moment. Two of the imperial guards were outside.

"Is there no toilet in this house?" she shouted at them. "Or should I spoil this room."

"Come, we will show you." They escorted her to the toilet room and waited as she sat and finished her business. They barely turned their backs, but at least they did not harass her.

On the way back she asked for wine, putting her hand on the arm of the guard who'd been drooling watching her.

She smiled at him. His eyes widened.

"Please, you bring it to me. It will help me sleep."

He nodded.

A little while later he came into the room with a red jug of wine and an earthenware cup. She was standing by the window, her dress half open at the front where she had untied the ribbons holding it together. He stared, transfixed like a rabbit before a swaying snake.

"What is the plan for me?" she asked, softly, leaning forward so her dress opened a little more.

Behind him the door to the room opened and the other guard called out.

"We are not to be with the prisoner."

The man blinked, turned, looked back at Paulina. "You are to have a visitor."

Paulina nodded. "In the morning, I expect. Please bring me some blankets." She smiled her thanks.

"She is to get nothing else," said the other guard.

The first guard shrugged and walked away with a heavy step.

Paulina sat in a corner of the room, then lay down on the floor, curled up. The night was warm, and the room was airless, so she woke with a headache in the dark and a longing to get out of the room. She sipped some of the watered-down wine. She knew what her captors were doing. Softening her up.

She wondered what the workers at Nero's Circus would make of her disappearance. They mostly had their tasks set out for them and the architect for the new building would be available to them, but she knew things would slow down without her. They'd be lucky to get the project finished.

Or was she fooling herself? Perhaps she would barely be missed.

She sat up and hugged herself. The early morning dragged as if it would never end.

Eventually, a hiss of chariot wheels pulled her to the window. She could see through the slats on the window shutters, which were nailed shut. Outside, a large chariot had pulled up. Someone important, no doubt, because of the gold frontage on the chariot.

Paulina smoothed her dress and her hair. She would not be desperate, no matter who came and what they planned to do to her. Her project on the first proper Christian church in Rome could not be stopped, even if they skinned her alive. She shivered.

The doors of the room burst open. Four imperial guards came in. They looked like Saxons, with their battle axes hanging from their belts. Behind them came Fausta, the empress.

"Why am I imprisoned here?" asked Paulina. "I have done nothing wrong. You must charge me with something or release me. You cannot just imprison me. Constantine will hear of this. He would not approve."

"He would certainly not approve of you breaking your vow to me," said Fausta, walking into the center of the room.

Paulina came toward her. Two blond Saxon guards took their axes and crossed them in Paulina's path, barring her way.

"You will show proper respect for my position or they will have your head from your shoulders and roll it around this room," shouted Fausta.

Paulina went quiet.

"You swore to me that you did not send any messages to Constantine, but I find out that Lucius went to meet him."

"Lucius decided to do that himself. I did not send him."

"Splitting hairs will not work with me. I expected more from you." Fausta looked away. "Now you present me with a problem."

"I am not the problem. I will not speak against you, Empress. I know what difficulties you've had to put up with."

"Do you know where my ring is?"

Paulina hesitated, then lied. "No, what ring?" She tried to look concerned.

"You are lying. I can see it in your face," Fausta screamed.

"I swear. I do not have your ring," replied Paulina, angrily. "And I've no idea where it is."

"You will stay here until I decide what to do with you." Fausta glared at Paulina. "Your work in Rome is finished."

Paulina shrugged, as if she didn't care.

"And if you try to escape think on this, your name and your description will be added to the watch list in all the towns around here, and in Rome. You won't get far."

Fausta turned, waved at the senior guard to follow her and headed out of the villa.

XXXIX

Paphos, 326 A.D.

The island loomed ahead after only a day out of sight of land. Distant mountains appeared and then tall white cliffs, which they skirted heading north with a salty wind at their back.

"Will we get to port by nightfall?" asked Helena, looking at the cliffs. "We don't want to founder on those rocks."

"The lights of Paphos will guide us in, Empress. I will call you when we see them. No need to stay on deck any longer."

Helena headed back into the cabin where Bina waited, looking at the scrolls in the box that had accompanied them from Jerusalem. It was a box Helena almost slept with, keeping it at her feet at night and covering over whenever anyone came into the room. Along with the scrolls inside, records from Roman governors and military commanders in and around Jerusalem, lay part of the central spine of the cross they had found. She had cut the cross into sections and left the remaining parts in Jerusalem in case anything happened to her on their journey.

Now that the cross of Jesus had been discovered it was vital that it never be lost again.

Already it had proven itself to have miraculous powers and there was no doubt it would help her son create a new capital for the empire, away from the deep layers of anti-Christian prejudice in Rome.

She had fulfilled her mission in Jerusalem. She was also aware that Bina caressed the cross, as if it gave her succor from the loss of her family.

"Some of these scrolls are recent," said Bina. "Why is that?"

"We need to have everything that records the life of Christians before our time. Some people claim the persecutions we suffered were minor or that Christ never walked among us. Everything that proves these people wrong will help us unify the empire at our new capital, New Rome."

Helena knew then it was the right thing to do to adopt Bina. She would make it official with an announcement when they reached New Rome. Some officials there still insisted on calling the city Byzantion, its Greek name, but with all the senators from Rome arriving for the dedication ceremony it would be New Rome from this year on.

"You will meet the imperial family. I will teach you all their names and how to address them before we get there." She stroked Bina's hair.

"Thank you." Bina looked up at Helena. "Is the imperial family a happy family?"

"Yes," said Helena. "We are the happiest of families. We love each other dearly and you will be welcomed by all."

XL

Polensis, 326 A.D.

Constantine held the ring Lucius had given him tight in his right hand as he walked back to the amphitheater. Four of his guard walked with him. They were going against the flow of people who were leaving after the last event, but the crowds parted easily. Everyone looked happy. Many people bowed as he made his way through them. Family groups often included old men and women and young children scampering around.

He envied them all. He envied the simplicity of their lives. No one spreading rumors and vying for power or succession. No one trying to burn to death the master of their house.

Had Fausta really started the fire?

She was certainly capable of it. She'd abandoned her father and her brother for survival. Abandoning your husband was not a big step after that.

But sleeping with Crispus. When had that started?

His mind went back to the battle of Chrysopolis. Fausta had visited Crispus at sea before she'd come to his camp on land in the days before the battle. He'd assumed that was because Crispus' ships were on her way.

But when he thought about it, she really should have come to him first. He'd been so preoccupied with planning the battle he hadn't thought of it. Had she been making sure that she would live if her husband died and her stepson became emperor? She'd been wily enough to ensure her survival after many other battles. For Fausta, such a move might even be considered logical.

The guards at the amphitheater bowed as he entered. Torches flickered along the arched passageway leading to the room his son was in. A group of people were hanging around outside. They all bowed. Two guards stood outside the closed door.

Constantine pushed open the door to the room. Crispus was sitting on the edge of the bed. He was holding his side. There was no one else in the room, which was lit by three thick candles on tall holders.

Crispus winced loudly. "Have you come to watch me testing if my feet still work?"

"No, something else." Constantine almost decided not to say anything to Crispus about the accusations against him, so strong was the feeling of pity that rose in him on seeing his son wounded.

"Who are all those people outside?" He pointed at the door with his thumb.

"The physician has brought his whole family and all his slaves. I had to throw them out. Too much chatter."

"Have you stopped bleeding?" he asked.

"Yes, a good while now. That bear's claws had been filled, thank the gods. That blow should have ripped me apart." He looked at his father. "You are right. I cannot do that again." He half smiled. "Turns out you are right about a lot of things."

Constantine looked at his son's hands. He was wearing the large imperial family ring with gold eagles embossed on it, which could be used for sealing letters. He was also wearing a thinner gold band. Constantine wanted to ask what kind of ring it was, but he couldn't say the words. He dreaded the reply, the break in the friendship with his son that could result.

Crispus saw him staring.

He pointed at the ring Fausta had given him.

"I'm meant to give this to you," he said. "The empress gave it to me to hold for you." He pulled the two rings off with some effort, handed the thinner one to his father.

Constantine's heart was pounding.

He looked inside the ring. Fausta's name was there. He had to say something.

"This is one of those love rings high-born Roman families give to their sweethearts." He paused, looked at Crispus.

"You are Fausta's sweetheart," said Crispus.

"No, we never were," said Constantine. He put out his left hand, with the ring Lucius had given him. "This is what Fausta wears."

Crispus looked at the ring, blinked. His face paled, or was that the candlelight flickering? He looked around the room. Then he turned back to his father.

"Where did you get the ring?" He still hadn't taken the ring his father was holding out for him.

"Lucius came with it from Rome."

"Someone is scheming against me, Father. If Fausta wears a ring like this, it must have your name on it."

"Look at the name on this one." Constantine held it closer to Crispus. His tone was commanding now.

Crispus took it, glanced inside. "At least a hundred women in Rome wear a ring with my name on it."

"So, this could be Fausta's?" He was trying to sound reasonable.

A sneer crossed Crispus' face. "Some bitch in Rome may have given it to her. Some bitches there think a ring will make them lucky, help them get pregnant from me."

Constantine hesitated. He looked at Crispus.

"Fausta is a bitch?"

Crispus' neck reddened. "What? You don't?" He shook his head. "Is Lucius behind these lies?" He stood. He was a little taller than Constantine, but equally well built. They'd been called a pair of bulls to their faces, though Constantine was older now, his hair graying, his shoulders a little down.

"What lies?" Constantine could tell when an officer tried to feed him garbage. It felt like a muffled bell going off inside him. He could feel that now.

But still he needed proof.

And if it was true, he would have to act.

"I heard Fausta has been trying to have her baby die inside her." His mouth was dry as he spoke the words.

Crispus would have an explanation.

Everything could go back to the way it had been.

Crispus looked in his eyes. His hands moved. A moment later he was swinging a dagger.

XLI

Outside Rome, 326 A.D.

"I am not the person you think I am," said Paulina. The guard who had taken a liking to her stared in through the open bedroom door. Paulina was sitting on the low bed, putting her long hair up into a bun.

"My duty is only to watch you," said the guard.

"And you do a good job at that," said Paulina, turning and smiling up at him. She stood. "Have any of your family become followers of Christ since the emperor made it legal?"

The guard looked down the corridor to where his colleague would come to relieve him.

"My brother did. I almost did myself after my wife died in childbirth."

"I'm sorry," said Paulina. "Did the child survive?"

The guard shook his head. He drew his breath in, hardened his face.

"You will have a place in our church and people to help you, if you join us in Rome when all this is over."

The guard glanced at her.

"If we ever get to finish our church, that is."

"I heard that every denarii the emperor has is going into these new churches."

Paulina shook her head. "We would not get far with what he has contributed. Contributions from ordinary people will make our new churches rise from the dust."

She lowered her head, covered her face with her palms. "I need to get back to Rome," she said with anguish in her voice. "I have to make sure all the emperor's coin is being used wisely. I have to find a way." She looked at the guard.

"I would do anything to find a way." She was pleading now.

XLII

Helena pointed ahead at the torch lights at the end of the breakwater that guarded the Roman port of Paphos. The land beyond looked flat in the light from the moon, recently risen, against a tapestry of stars.

"Why are we here?" asked Bina, looking up at Helena expectantly.

"Paul preached here. He was the best of all Christ's followers. He took on magicians and the priests of Aphrodite here. Coming here with the cross of Christ is a closing of the circle, Bina." She leaned down to her. "The empire he tried to convert, one crowd at a time, has at last come to follow his path, and all because of my son and his wife, the Empress Fausta."

"Tell me more about Fausta." Bina looked happy.

"She is one of the beauties of the empire, and high born. The daughter of an emperor and the sister of one too."

Bina glanced at Helena. "Will she like me?" she said.

"Of course, she will love you. How could anyone not love you?"

"We will dock shortly," said a voice behind them. Helena turned. The captain was there. "Where will you sleep tonight?" he asked.

"We will stay on board. I want the priestesses of Aphrodite to come before me at the dock at dawn. Send a man to their temple." She leaned toward the captain. "You should be happy. God will reward you for spreading the name of his son."

"I was hoping to sell some of our cargo here," said the captain.

"My son will pay for it all when we get to New Rome, no matter what state it is in."

He looked at her with an unbelieving expression.

"Do not fear. My son does what I ask. Always. And he never complains. You will get every denarius you are owed."

The captain smiled. "Your orders will be carried out," he said.

Helena looked at him, breathed out. "And find out where the baths are. We could all do with a visit."

XLIII

Polensis, 326 A.D.

Constantine reacted quickly. His hand went to grip Crispus' wrist. Then they were both up and glaring at each other.

"How could you even think I was with Fausta?"

"You wear her ring," said Constantine, bitterness filling his voice.

"You old bastard. You just want a reason to stay in power. Are you going to kill me, like you did your father?"

Crispus pushed with both his hands, forcing Constantine back.

"Guards!" shouted Constantine. The door of the room burst open.

Crispus swung his leg and caught Constantine's knee, sending him down and to the side. The knife came toward him but the momentum of Crispus' body falling on top of him sent the knife point into the stone floor with a sharp clang.

A moment later Crispus was being hauled backward by two guards. He was angrier than Constantine had ever seen him, and blood was seeping down his side from his injuries.

"You are a curse on us all," he shouted at Constantine, struggling against the two guards. "You cursed me with your name and your attitude like stone and your women fawning all over you, spying for you."

He stopped struggling.

Constantine was on his feet. His mind was racing like a chariot.

"Release him," he said. He pointed at Crispus.

"What about you? What kind of a son are you with a ring like that on your finger? Tell me the truth now and we can put this behind us. You are still my son. Stop this." He growled the words. "Tell me the truth. She will pay. Not you." His hands were shaking. His arms too. Every part of him shook, as if he had a fever.

"I'll tell you the truth. But send these men away. We do not want the whole town talking about us by midnight."

The men looked at Constantine. Both had concerned expressions.

"Go," said Constantine. "And take this." He reached down for Crispus' knife. One of the guards put a hand out. Constantine passed the knife to him.

"And send the physician in," he said.

XLIV

Outside Rome, 326 A.D.

"I am not the woman you think I am," said Paulina. She lay back on the low bed they had found while searching the villa for anything useful for her stay there. It was nearly dusk. The room was dim as the shutters were closed.

The guard at the door pushed it open a bit more, so he could see her properly.

"I know that," he said.

Paulina stood.

She looked around. "Who lived here?"

"A widow is what I heard," said the guard. He was standing inside the room now, his hands on his belt, from which his sword and his dagger hung.

Paulina went down on her knees beside the bed. "Come and pray with me," she said. She closed her eyes and began the Prayer for All Needs.

We beg you, Lord, help and defend us.
Deliver the oppressed.
Raise the fallen.

She felt a hand on her arm. He pulled her up, turned her to face him.

"No, you will do as I say," said the guard. "Or I will put my sword inside you." He laughed.

She leaned back. She could feel the hardness of him pressing into her.

"You want me?" she said, huskily.

He let go of her arm and pulled her to him. They fell onto the bed. It creaked. He was scrabbling around with his tunic, his other hand on hers, breathing heavily, like a bull.

She stuck out her tongue.

"Come on then," she said, raising her eyebrows.

Her hand slipped down to his belt. He had her dress up around her waist now. His rough hands were all over her. She shuddered away from his touch, repelled by him.

Her hand found the dagger, slid it from its sheath, turned it, pushed it quickly and hard into his side. No hesitation.

He grunted, his eyes widening in fear.

A gush of blood flowed onto her hand.

He screamed, grabbed at her. She wiggled and turned, desperate to get out from under him.

His hands came up for the knife.

"To Hades with you," she said, jerking the knife around inside him, hoping to slice as much of him apart as possible.

His hands went to her throat.

"Stop," called the other guard.

"He's trying to kill me. I'm injured," shouted Paulina.

The guard came over, his eyes wide. Paulina was half naked from the waist down and fully drenched in blood.

She held a hand out to the other guard, asking for his help. He didn't take it.

The hands at her throat squeezed. She pulled at his arms. They came away. She slipped out from under his bulk and held her empty hand out.

"I need a physician," she said, weakly.

"Marco," said the guard loudly, ignoring her. He pulled the shoulder of the first guard, turning him around to see his face.

Paulina pushed herself to her feet and headed for the door. Her hands were shaking, her breath catching in her throat.

She leaned against the wall as soon as she reached the corridor. In her hand was the guard's dagger. Her hand and arm were slicked red with blood. Her night gown was soaked with it. Her heart was beating like a drum.

She kept the blade up. It shook in the air. Over and over she recited. *We beg you, Lord, help and defend us. We beg you, Lord, help and defend us.*

The other guard rushed out of the room. Paulina stabbed at him. He broke her attack with an upstretched arm. Then he pushed her away.

"I'm not like him," he shouted. "There is no need to defend yourself. You have no chance."

Paulina let her breath out in a gasp.

"I saw him eyeing you up. We were told not to harm you, on pain of death, and it looks to me like you gave him his penalty."

"I must get back to Rome," said Paulina.

"There are ten men outside guarding this villa. You won't be able to get past them. Put the dagger down."

Paulina looked at the dagger. She put her hand down but kept it tight in her grip.

"If you don't drop it, I will be forced to take it from you." He sounded confident, and with his leather breastplate and apron it would be difficult to strike a killing blow against him. Paulina stepped back toward the stairs.

"Come, take it from me." She held the knife out, on her open palm.

He stepped forward. His sword up. As he reached her with his other hand, she dropped the dagger and grasped his wrist. She stepped back, pulling him with her, turning on her side as she did, and going into a ball, as she'd been taught long ago, head tucked in. She hit a step, then the wall.

Then the floor with a bone-jarring thud. The guard fell partly on top of her, his sword clanging nearby. For a long moment Paulina wondered had she broken something or had he cut her, the pain in her side and shoulder was so sharp.

The guard groaned. She pulled herself from under him, her shoulder aching, kicking hard at a hand that tried to grab her.

No one else had come. She'd been right.

He'd been lying about the other guards. Maybe they were due to arrive in the morning. She came to her knees, her head aching, spinning, a strange vibration inside making it difficult to think. She looked around. She had to get out of here.

The guard groaned, pushed himself up, shouted, as if he'd injured himself.

She ran for the front door. She was still wearing the blood-soaked night gown and had no sandals, but this was her chance. One half-dazed guard should be easy to get away from.

It was nearly dark outside, but she could see the vines and raced toward them. She tripped as she reached them, falling between two rows thick with grapes, her breath forced from her body, dirt in her mouth.

She looked back. The dusk had turned the villa gloomy, but she could see through the front door. The guard was stumbling out. She stayed down, scrambled and rolled and shimmied sideways until she couldn't see the front door when she looked back. She came up onto her knees slowly as she heard a voice, not that far away.

"I will find you and I will enjoy you," came the shout.

She started running, bent low, her head down.

XLV

Paphos, 326 A.D.

The sun was well above the horizon by the time the priestesses of Aphrodite arrived. They came in a long line. Twenty of them. All had golden wigs on with locks flowing about their shoulders, even the older ones.

The inhabitants of the town waited around the stone paved open area at the end of the breakwater.

The governor of the town had arrived before dawn, with guards carrying torches. Helena had made him wait until dawn before seeing him. Now, he was standing to one side of the large chair, not quite a throne, which had been set up for Helena near her ship.

Bina was waiting onboard. Helena's guards were behind her, one on either side.

The priestesses wore long red gowns. Carved ivory penises dangled from their necks.

They stopped twenty paces from Helena. Together they prostrated themselves.

Helena left them like that for a long time. The crowd watching began muttering. Helena watched them. One part of the crowd was staring back at her. Some of them were smiling.

She stamped her foot. "Silence," she shouted. The crowd went quiet. All that could be heard now were gulls swooping over the dock.

In the distance, trickles of smoke rose into a clear blue sky from the white-washed buildings of the town.

"Only the head priestess will come to me," said Helena. She kept her expression stiff. Change required firmness.

An older woman pushed herself to her feet and came forward, adjusting her wig as she did so. When she was about five paces from Helena she bowed, held her head low and waited.

"Your name?" said Helena.

"Aphrodite, great empress." The woman looked up. "What have we done to offend you?"

"Tell me what you do here, and I will tell you how you offend me."

The woman tried to smile, but it went away quickly as she looked at Helena.

"We attract people to our temple who need help, the lonely and the stricken. We give them succor." She waved her hands inwards, illustrating people coming to them. "What can be wrong with that? We have done this since time began, since the gods lived on earth."

Helena shook her head, groaned in disapproval.

"Stop with the lies," she said. "What is your real name?"

"Aphrodite," said the priestess. "I do not lie." A hint of anger could be heard in her voice.

"There are times, Aphrodite," said Helena. "When we must see ourselves for who we really are." Helena pointed at the other priestesses. "You are a troop of whores. Aphrodite's whores." She beckoned the woman forward.

"Tell me this. What do you do with the bodies of the babies you kill in the womb or soon after their birth by leaving them outside for the rats to feed on?"

The priestess stared at Helena, her face reddening and stiff with hatred.

"It is our decision what we do. These matters are for the temple. Each priestess decides herself if she wishes the burden of her child. This is how we live. All on this island approve of this." She waved at the crowd, as if daring Helena to go against all of them.

"Not all approve of your ways, priestess. I am here to tell you that your temple is closed from this moment, and that you are not to go back there ever. Not even once. Your day is over." Helena straightened herself in her chair and went on, with force in her voice.

"The governor has been told about this. His troops will ensure my orders are carried out, or we will send more troops to replace them all."

The woman's jaw dropped. A muttering started up among the priestesses. One of them with good hearing had heard Helena. A young priestess, a girl of no more than fifteen summers, came to her feet.

She reached inside her red gown and pulled a gold handled sickle from it. She strode toward Helena, the sickle held out wide, ready to strike.

Helena's two guards came forward, their swords swung and the young woman's head came off and rolled toward Helena, carried forward by her body's momentum. The body jerked and fell, two fountains of blood washing the stone breakwater all around it.

A gasp went up from the crowd. Most of the priestesses stood. Many of them also had sickles in their hands. They rushed for Helena.

Helena's guards stood still, their swords up. As the women came nearer the guards shouted.

"A good day to die."

Arrows, coming from behind Helena, spiked into them all, stopping many of them. The captain of her ship and three of his men were firing arrows directly at the priestesses. The older one fell with an arrow through her throat. Others shrieked and fell with arrows in their stomachs, necks, chests.

Some of the priestesses stopped, threw down their weapons.

"Get them to kneel," said Helena to one of her guards, who had turned to her for instructions. "Then ask the townspeople to decide their fate."

XLVI

Polensis, 326 A.D.

The physician cut a strip of yellow bandage. "Do not get up again," he said, waving a finger at Crispus.

He looked at Constantine. "Can you make him stay still, Emperor?"

Constantine shook his head. "I wish I could."

The physician slipped the wide bandage under Crispus' body. "There was a woman outside looking for you, my lord," he whispered to Crispus.

Constantine heard the comment. "Who was looking for him?"

The physician looked from the emperor to his son.

"Some old woman who lost her daughters." He shrugged.

Constantine looked at his son. Crispus had his lips pressed tight, as if trying to suppress something.

"Tell her not to come back. My son knows nothing about what happened to her daughters. And," he leaned toward the physician, "if she does come back, she must give me the gold coins I paid her earlier."

The physician nodded, headed for the door.

"And close the door after you," said Constantine. He turned back to Crispus. He'd pulled a faded red blanket over himself.

"Did you kill that woman's daughters?" he said. "It's time you started telling the truth, Crispus."

Crispus stared up at him. "Why do a few whores matter?" He sounded indignant. "They got paid extra for playing dangerous games." He snorted. "At least they went to the gods doing what they enjoyed."

"So you don't deny it," said Constantine. He expected now that Crispus had been involved with Seutonius too. If he liked such pleasures, admitted to them, this had to be the reason Seutonius had taken that apartment in that part of Rome.

He remembered a trick he'd used many years before to get to the truth.

"You killed Seutonius too."

Crispus looked up at him.

"Lucius brought a slave girl with him who overheard you talking to him the night he died," said Constantine. "I am going to hear what she has to say later. But it will be better if I hear it from you. Save me having to meet her." Constantine tapped his sandal on the stone floor.

Crispus' expression changed. He looked bewildered. "You cannot believe a slave over me." He put his hand up.

"I want to know what happened," said Constantine.

"I've always loved you, Father. That is the truth. I never schemed against you, as so many advised me to do. I commanded your troops again and again, and brought you victory at Chrysopolis, when I could have taken over the empire." He shook his head. "And now you want to ask a slave what she has to say about me."

"I won't speak to her, if you explain to me why you killed Seutonius."

"Father, come here. I do not want anyone outside to hear this."

XLVII

Paphos, 326 A.D.

"You have witnessed a lot of blood," she said to Bina. They were in the cabin of the ship.

"You were wonderful," said Bina.

"No."

"You could have killed them all."

"Mercy can work, too."

"Will the Christians here really take over the temple?" Bina was wide eyed.

"They may not. The governor said there were not many Christians here, but the temple will be closed. If the Christians decide to start a small church somewhere else in the town, everyone will know that it is with my blessing."

Bina stretched her arms. "Why do you want to close all these temples?"

Helena didn't reply straight away. It was a good question. It needed a reply to equal it.

"I suffered a lot when I was young, not much older than you, Bina. It's not a nice story. Best to leave the past where it is, gone."

"Please, tell me what happened." Bina's tone was soft, appealing, hard to resist.

Helena sighed. "I started working in a tavern when I was a little older than you. The men all told me how lovely I was, and the tavern owner did too. They paid me to do things. Do you understand?"

Bina nodded.

"There was a temple to Venus in the town. They didn't like our tavern taking away their business." She paused, stroked Bina's hair. "The priestesses burnt down the tavern." She snorted angrily. "It didn't matter that they threw newborn babies out the back of their temple in a hole in the ground for rats and foxes to feast on, the local magistrate protected them."

"That's terrible."

"There are too many women in these temples. Every year some of them give birth and often the babies are not wanted. They have too many mouths to feed already." She paused, shook her head.

Helena's voice slowed as she continued, "I went to the place where they threw the babies. I got sick at the sight. I will not tell you more, but the thought of it turns my stomach even now."

She could not tell Bina about the little skeletons, the little skulls and the half-eaten baby girl she'd seen. The sight was still burnt into her memory.

"That is why I became attracted to the followers of Christ. They stood against these temples. They call their practices wicked. They were persecuted for it, before my son changed everything."

"I would never become a priestess," said Bina.

"I hope you will never have to."

XLVIII

Polensis, 326 A.D.

Crispus reached out, held Constatine's hand. His other hand came out from under the blanket with a thin bladed knife in it. He swung it toward Constantine's neck.

Constantine, grunting in shock, moved his head back while reaching for the hand holding the knife. He barely managed to avoid the blade.

"Crispus, stop," he shouted, anger gripping every muscle.

Crispus' eyes were blazing with rage. He pushed Constantine back, then winced loudly, and wrestled his knife hand free, almost knocking Constantine off his feet, the knife coming again toward his throat.

Constantine's training took over.

There was only one thing he could do. He jabbed the knife back against Crispus with all his strength and let the weight of his body force Crispus' hand back, until suddenly Crispus winced again and his hand gave way and the knife sliced viciously across his throat.

His son looked at him, shock and surprise mixing on his face, his eyes bulging, his mouth stretched into a gurgling shout, while blood flowed like a fountain.

Constantine pulled the knife out of Crispus' hand. He hugged him, feeling the hot blood pumping again and again against his own neck as his son gurgled, tried to speak. He put his hand on the wound to stem the bleeding, held it against the wet skin, but he knew, with his chest tightening fast, that this cut could not be stopped.

"Fath..," Crispus gurgled. He blinked, tears rolling from his eyes. And then he was just staring, accusingly.

Constantine bent his head and wept, his body shaking, anguish knotting inside him, holding fast to Crispus, rocking, praying for this not to have happened.

When he finally did release him, it was because of the voice of the physician in his ear.

"My lord, my lord, what happened?"

Constantine did not answer. He released his son, stood, stared down at Crispus. He hated himself totally in that moment, contemplated taking the knife and stabbing himself through the heart.

He raised both fists. His hands were wet with his son's blood.

There had to be a way for an emperor to turn back the sands of time. He would pay any magician or any god whatever promise was needed from him.

A few moments before his son had been alive. How could he not reach back to those moments?

He should never have confronted Crispus.

No. No.

Crispus had attacked him.

He took a step back. Blood dripped from him.

"I'll get water," said the physician.

And he was alone again with Crispus. Constantine stood close to him. The battlefield smell of blood was overpowering. He closed Crispus' eyes, felt his forehead. He was still warm.

He touched Crispus' cheek, tenderly. "Why did it come to this?" he whispered.

The physician had returned. He was coughing.

Constantine turned, his face stiff. "Remember this," he shouted. "My son was executed this evening. He died for crimes against the imperial family. That is what happened here. He is to be buried where the outcasts are buried, outside the walls. No monument is to be erected over his grave. I do not want to see his face again. Make sure the body is gone tonight and tell no one where you take it." He spat the final words out.

"Yes, yes, Emperor."

"And do not ask any question about what happened here tonight. Understood?" he shouted.

The physician nodded.

Constantine put his hands into the large red bowl of water. "And find me another tunic right now."

XLIX

Paphos, 326 A.D.

They set sail the following morning. The journey north to Myra, a Roman port built around a temple to Diana, the huntress, was uneventful.

The priestesses at Myra were known for their modesty, so they were spared having to leave their temple, and it was made clear to all in the town that the small Christian community there would be supported from now on.

Next, they stopped at Lesbos, where the temple to Cybele had already been closed by a new governor, for outrageous public lewdness. After that they headed north through numerous islands basking in plate-calm blue seas, until they reached the narrow Hellespont where it rained non-stop while they passed through into the choppy waters of the Propontis, where they hugged the flat northern shore until they reached New Rome.

All the while Helena was teaching Bina Latin. She'd been taught enough by her father and mother to converse with Helena, as it was the language of the empire, but she wasn't as fluent as she would need to be at the imperial court.

Helena also taught Bina about the imperial family.

"Crispus will become emperor soon. He is a wonderful grandson and a great soldier and a leader. He will make us all proud as emperor. You had better be nice to him," said Helena with a smile one morning as they neared New Rome.

"Tell me about the Empress Fausta again," said Bina.

"Fausta is the most beautiful woman in the empire. I love her dearly. She is kind, clever and she will love you too."

Bina smiled up at Helena as shouts rang out from the small dock below the Imperial Palace, which was still under construction, at the point where the Bosporus opened into the Propontis.

Their trading vessel had Helena's pennant clearly visible on the mast, but still there were no obvious places to dock. Other boats were also waiting outside the dock to bring their cargo to land.

"Tie us up alongside the imperial galley," said Helena to the captain, who was standing nearby.

"Yes, Empress," said the captain.

Rowers began maneuvering the ship, and thin ropes, attached to thicker ones thrown onto the galley, were used to slowly draw the trading ship alongside.

"Is the emperor here?" asked Bina. "If that is his galley."

"We will find out soon," said Helena.

When the two ships were tight together, a wooden walkway was set up between them and the captain of the galley bowed as Helena and Bina, followed by their baggage, went ashore.

Helena thanked him. He smiled and tapped the purse at his belt in reply.

The master of the dock must have spied their ship approaching, as he was waiting beyond the galley with ten gleaming slaves, their smiles reflecting the beauty of that hot late summer afternoon.

"Is my son here?" asked Helena, greeting the master of the palace with a dismissive wave.

"No, my empress. He is not back from Rome."

Helena pointed at the boxes and bags coming off the ship. "Well, take everything to the palace. And if one thread is missing when I get there, I will have someone's head," she said.

She pointed back at the captain who was staring at them from his ship.

"Pay him a good price for his cargo and an extra ten aureus for the passage."

The master of the dock bowed and turned, issuing a string of orders. The slaves moved quickly to get the baggage.

"Where are we going?" said Bina.

"To the market. It is one of the best things about New Rome. There is a market for spices from the east, cotton from the south and wool from Britannia in the north, and," she bent down to Bina, "you will see slaves for sale, some as young as you are."

Bina's mouth opened.

The master clicked his fingers. A troop of ten imperial guards came forward from where they were waiting by the entrance to the dock, a high gate set between the Imperial Palace warehouses.

The master must have overheard Helena, as he asked, "What market will you wish to be escorted to, Empress?"

"The imperial bazaar." She looked down at Bina. "My son set it up on my direction. I must see how it has grown."

They headed up a steep hill, with building work going on all around them. It looked as if the whole city was being rebuilt. High walled buildings were replacing hovels, and thick stone towers were replacing wooden look-out posts. The city buzzed with activity. When Helena looked back down at the port a line of ships was visible in the Propontis and other ships approached from all angles.

This truly was the center of the world.

"I've never seen anything like it," said Bina.

"Wait until you see where we are going next."

L

Polensis, 326 A.D.

Paulina leaned against the mast of the ship that had carried her in pursuit of Constantine. She'd managed to find a man with a cart load of grapes on his way to Rome along a back road who was willing to help her. He was looking to avoid the traffic on the main road into the city. She'd stolen a short tunic from a washing line before waving at him from the narrow road.

After they reached the outskirts of the city, she went to a Christian friend's house. He gave her money for the journey. There was no way she could stay in Rome with Fausta's men looking for her.

The journey had been slow, as she'd used only back roads, but she also cut her hair and a slave went with her. They pretended to be two slaves on a mission for their master. Her hope now was that Constantine was still in Polensis.

The sea was calm as they rowed slowly into the dock. Paulina only had a few garments tied in a square of cloth and held under her arm.

She hadn't dared go back to her room in Rome.

"You'd better be here, Constantine. I am running out of coin to keep chasing you." She looked expectantly at the town, her hopes rising.

She asked the first man she met after they finally docked, after a long wait for a place in the port and was immediately bitterly disappointed.

"The emperor is long gone. He was here briefly. A terrible thing happened and he left soon after."

"What terrible thing?"

"His son, Crispus, was executed. We all went into mourning, but he ordered the mourning to end." The man shook his head. "They are a strange family."

"Where has he gone?" She blinked. It felt as if the world had moved underneath her feet.

"Ask at the governor's villa." The man pointed into the town.

Paulina, alone now as she'd sent the slave back to his master on the ship, found the governor's villa and told the doorman she was a friend of the emperor's looking to know where he had gone.

The doorman replied, "Do you know the emperor's friend, Lucius Armenius?"

Paulina nodded, happy at once to hear Lucius' name.

"He can tell you more about the emperor's plans than I." He looked Paulina up and down, assessing if she had weapons. Then he pointed at a passageway to the side of the villa.

"He's in the gardens." He leaned close. "He stares at the sky most of the time."

Paulina headed down the passageway and into a beautiful garden with a marble fountain in the middle, statues of the old gods around the sides and marble benches around the fountain. On one of them a man was lying on his back, a jug of wine nearby.

Paulina strode up and stared down at Lucius. He seemed not to notice her, and when he did, he simply waved her away.

"What is wrong, Lucius?" Paulina shook his shoulder. She'd had her hopes dashed and raised again. He had to answer.

Lucius continued staring up at the sky. Paulina looked up, in case she'd missed something, then pulled back her hand and slapped Lucius on the cheek, hard.

Her fingers stung, but she felt good.

He grunted. She kicked hard at the wine jug. It fell over. Wine splashed out onto the gravel beneath their feet.

That woke him up.

"What are you doing?" Lucius rose, straightened the jug. "That is the best wine from Greece. It's the best they have in this forsaken pit the gods have all forgotten." He glared at Paulina. His speech was slurred. "What in Hades name are you doing here?"

"I'm here to find Constantine. What in Hades name happened to Crispus?" she shouted at him.

Lucius shook his head from side to side, not stopping, then threw his hands in the air. "Disaster, Paulina. Total, stupid disaster." He looked at Paulina, a hollow look in his eyes, as if he'd lost everything.

LI

Perinthus, Autumn 326 A.D.

Constantine leaned forward. The horse he'd been given at the last post stop was weary. They had been riding hard all day. Perinthus, the next stop on the Via Egnatia, lay not far ahead. All afternoon the road had been lined mostly with vineyards, set well back, but now they were passing apple orchards, the trees set far apart.

A few of the people on the carts they passed had stopped and bowed, when seeing the purple flag his lead horseman was carrying, but many on their dusty wooden carts seemed uninterested. They wore drab trousers and had long Greek-style dark hair.

Many had probably been forced to contribute to one side or another in the wars, only recently ended, that had set Constantine on the unified throne of the empire. But he didn't care if people just stared as they cantered past.

They rode because the journey by ship, all around Greece, could take even longer, and he was determined to get to his new capital before news of Crispus' death arrived.

The mission to get to New Rome had grown in importance inside him every day since he'd left Polensis. He could not have stayed there even another night. He wanted to be as far from what had happened, from what he'd done, as possible.

And it would be another three days of hard riding before they reached their destination. He had ten guards with him, enough to fight any bandits on the road. There was no need for a larger force. All his enemies were dead. He had killed them. Every one of them.

The gates of the town of Perinthus were still open when they arrived. The governor, they were told, was in his stone palace in the hill above the port, located on a small peninsula on the north shore of the Propontis. They rode slowly through the dead looking town.

It was twenty days since he'd killed Crispus. They'd passed in a blur.

He'd eaten little each day and slept poorly every night. Killing people, even up close, rarely bothered him, but killing your own son leaves a peculiarly bitter taste.

In the immediate aftermath, he'd blamed Lucius for bringing him the news about Crispus and Fausta, but Lucius had pointed out that Crispus could well have succeeded in killing his father at another time, if he was willing to take up a blade against him when accused of a crime.

After that, he thought about Fausta's part in it all. And every morning now he woke up thinking about her. Was it true the baby was Crispus'? How could she have betrayed him with his son?

But deep down he knew.

He'd praised her talent for survival many times in conversations, and this act showed what she was really capable of. The next question was, what should he do about her?

Juliana, who had ridden beside him all the way from Polensis, didn't help with that question when he asked her.

"The gods will decide," was what she said. And then she went quiet. She'd been quiet for the most of their journey.

She didn't even complain about being left on the ship in Polensis, but she had been vocal when he told her to leave her Saxon guards behind.

He'd changed his mind and allowed some of them to come along, when she told them they were as good on horses as any of his own guards.

The governor of Perinthus greeted them in a large bright audience hall.

"We will feast tonight in your honor, Emperor. The dancing girls we have here are wonderful. They come from all parts of the empire." He smiled broadly, lighting up the room with his white teeth.

"No feast. No dancing girls. If you have soup and bread that is all I and my guards need." Constantine sat on a bench at the side of the hall, in the shadows.

Juliana was standing nearby with her two Saxons. His other guards were outside, arranging for a change of horses at the governor's stables.

Constantine looked around. "Bring straw mattresses and we will sleep here. The breeze from the sea is most welcome." He turned and pointed at Juliana. "This woman is my advisor. She is to get her own room."

The governor bowed, a perplexed expression on his face.

"Is there anything else I can do?"

"We must take your best horses tomorrow morning, early, but we are leaving behind the best from last night's stay."

The governor nodded. He looked at Constantine's grave face. "Has something happened?" he said.

"No, my eyes have been opened."

The governor stared at him for a long moment, then, with a low bow he left the audience hall.

LII

New Rome, 326 A.D.

Helena followed the tall guardsman who had been appointed to lead their party. She'd given him full instructions as to where to take them, but she still had regular comments about the route he chose through what had been the ancient sleepy port of Byzantion and was now rapidly becoming the capital of the empire.

It was a transformation that caused serious problems, both for the people who lived here, who hated the intrusion and the mess and the constant noise, and the new people who'd arrived, who hated that the city was still half finished and clearly not big enough or grand enough to be the capital of an empire.

"No, no, that is the wrong way," shouted Helena, tapping the guardsman on the arm. She pointed to the right. "The market is that way. Why are you taking us the wrong way?"

The guard looked at her as if he wanted to take her head off, but instead he gave a half smile, bowed and replied, "I only thought you would like to see the new entrance they have begun," he said.

Helena stiffened. "This way," she said, pointing to a narrow alley.

As they entered, the sky turned into a strip of blue directly above them. The buildings on each side were so close together, clothes drying lines hung between them with tunics and garments of all types and colors hanging from them. There was still a Greek feel to the city, many of the walls were whitewashed, but other walls were dark, newer buildings owned by traders from the east or the north. At the ground floor level, the Roman colonnade style of shops, set back under pillars, gave way to the Greek style of shops, with goods displayed on the road in front of the buildings.

The crowds grew thicker, the smells stronger; sweat, spices, the occasional sewer that hadn't been covered over. Her guards had difficulty keeping some of the people away. Shouts in multiple languages echoed as passers-by saw who walked among them. There were people of all types in the city, Roman patricians in togas, traders from the east with pointed or fur caps, Egyptians with long gowns, Africans with patterned skirts, and many Greeks with short tunics moving fast through the crowds.

Workers carried bundles on their heads and shouted for space to move or pushed handcarts with even more shouting. Bina clung close to Helena. All around looks of awe followed the empress. From some shops came cries asking her to stop and look at their wares.

Bina clung tighter to Helena's arm.

"It's not far," said Helena. "See that gate ahead?"

A brand-new Roman stone gate, with wooden scaffolding still clinging to one side, stood ahead on the right. Roman legionaries stood guard in polished round helmets, their spears upright, eyes roving. A shout went up when one of them spotted Helena and her guards.

More guards appeared from inside the gate and formed a line as they passed through into the imperial market.

The first street inside the market was lined with gold merchants, their wares gleaming on tables, muscled guards standing beside them.

"This is where your lovers will buy you presents," said Helena.

"I don't want lovers," said Bina, shaking her head, quickly.

Helena smiled. "You may change your mind some day. It's good to know the choices your love-struck admirers will have."

Bina looked around, wide eyed.

Helena waved at a table with thick gold necklaces and shiny arm bands. The trader greeted her like a long-lost friend, bowing again and again and ushering Bina forward first to pat her head and then offer them both an iced grape juice.

"Come inside, come, come. Everything is top quality. Perhaps a necklace for your young friend?" said the trader.

They went into the shop. Gold necklaces hung from every wall and from the ceiling in rows.

"Which one would you like?" said Helena.

Bina didn't reply.

Helena pointed at the trader. "Did you make the necklaces with imperial eagles I asked for?"

The trader nodded, pointed at a row of necklaces near the back.

"Our highest purity, created especially for friends of the imperial family."

"I need two," said Helena. "One short, one long." She looked down at Bina. "One for you and one for Fausta."

They waited as the trader selected two necklaces and showed them to them. Helena peered down.

"These are good," she said. "Send them to the palace and ask the chief treasurer for your fee."

The trader bowed.

"The iced juice has arrived," he said.

Helena looked at the tray. "One sip, Bina." She drank some, as did Bina.

They left the shop.

"Why only one sip?" said Bina.

"We show people we trust them with a sip. But it's enough." She leaned down. "And if we don't know the trader, we never take a sip. There are resentful people, who hate my son, but there are many more who love him and us. Be aware that we have enemies too. Always."

She stood, gripped Bina's hand. "The next thing I buy for you may shock you, Bina."

Helena pulled Bina forward.

LIII

Polensis, 326 A.D.

"Are you sure this will be the quickest way to New Rome?" asked Paulina. It was two days after her arrival in Polensis. They were walking toward the dock.

"We may get there before Constantine, if the winds are as favorable as the captain claims they will be." Lucius still looked glum, but at least he'd stopped drinking.

"We need to get there soon." Paulina had taken to biting her nails. Crispus' death changed everything. Constantine was still in danger from inside his palace. If something happened to him, everything she was working on, the new church in Rome, recruiting ex priestesses to follow Christ, and the work his mother was doing in Jerusalem, could all come crashing down.

"This galley was manned by friends of Crispus. It's why he came here." Lucius pointed ahead at a galley tied up at the dock.

"Why would they want to help us, if we're friends of Constantine?"

"I told the captain we plan to confront Constantine." Lucius didn't even turn his head.

"Are you mad?" Paulina nudged him hard. "What are we supposed to be saying to Constantine?"

"You can provide that information if we're asked," said Lucius. "I know how clever you are. And anyway, I thought it best we don't leave them here to spread lies about the emperor."

"You deserve a medal." She shook her head.

"I don't think the emperor will give me one."

A final few amphorae were being stowed away below deck when they arrived.

"How did you pay for this?" asked Paulina.

"I borrowed from the governor. I told him the emperor would pay and I told him why I was taking these men far from his peaceful port."

"I bet he agreed quickly."

Lucius smiled.

The captain, a Greek named Ajax, was waiting for them on board. He had multiple scars, including a long one on his face, and one of his eyes was half closed over.

"You take my cabin," he said to both of them after greeting them.

"Lucius will sleep on deck," said Paulina. "I'll need the cabin for prayers for our safe arrival."

"I expect a quick journey," said Ajax. He smiled at Lucius.

The galley pushed away from the dock and they rowed around the headland guarding the port, and then, as the wind filled their sail, they turned and headed south.

They sat with the captain near the rudder while they ate each day, listening to his stories about Crispus' exploits. How he had single-handedly turned the battle of Chrysopolis in his father's favor, jumping onto the lead ship of the enemy fleet and sending the navigator to his death and the ship spinning in the wind.

There were other stories too, all of which Lucius and Paulina lapped up with encouraging noises.

The journey through the Greek islands was fast, the days spent tacking with the winds until the sun set and the nights sheltering in bays.

A storm blew up on the sixth day and they waited all that day in a small bay with a fishing village. They bought olive oil and wine from the village head man and told the villagers tales of Rome and New Rome that night as they feasted in his stone house.

The wine was strong. The captain drank a lot. Enough to see him place a hand on Paulina's thigh. She swiped it away forcefully.

"I am sworn to Christ only," she said.

"Are you the priestess Crispus complained about? The one named Paulina who turned his father's head and made him leave the old gods?" The captain, swayed, smiled. There was a malevolence at the edge of his smile.

Outside, the rain pounded on the roof and seeped in along the walls.

"I am," said Paulina. She too had been drinking.

Lucius felt for his dagger.

"I thought as much," said Ajax. "You didn't hire us to tell your master he was wrong to execute Crispus, did you?"

Paulina looked in his eyes.

"You want to be saved, Ajax?"

He shook his head. "No, I want revenge for my friend. The man who saved my life." His face turned into a snarl.

Paulina leaned close to him. "Stick with us. I'll introduce you to the person who killed Crispus, up close, this close." She stuck her tongue out at him.

Ajax threw his head back and laughed. He gripped Paulina's shoulders and said, "If you don't do it, I will slice you from ear to ear and spoil that pretty face of yours."

"You'll have to come through me if you plan to do that," said Lucius, forcefully.

Paulina pushed at him with her fist.

"Do you know why I agreed to take you to New Rome?" said Ajax, leaning toward them.

"Because you fancy Lucius?" said Paulina.

Ajax shook his head. "No, following the emperor to New Rome, with two of his friends on board, gives me an opportunity to exact some portion of revenge." He slid his dagger out and placed it on the table, his hand around the handle.

"I've been talking to my crew about when we should do this."

"Do what?" asked Paulina. She slipped her own knife into her hand under the table. She'd taken the small apple-peeling knife from the governor's palace in Polensis.

Ajax swiped a finger across his throat.

"Why are you telling us this now?" said Lucius.

"Because we have come up with a better plan," said Ajax. "It is clear to all of us that you, Lucius, love this hard-faced woman." He waved dismissively at Paulina. "She is not my type. I like them younger. But I can see why you like her."

Paulina looked at Lucius. He was stony faced. If he did love her, he had never told her. She smiled at the thought that Ajax might be right.

"So, what is your plan?" asked Lucius.

"We'll keep Paulina on board when we get to New Rome and you will bring the emperor down to our ship. You will tell him that she's wounded and cannot be moved and asks for him." He leaned across the table to Lucius. "If you want, we can arrange this. We can cut her now, if you wish."

Lucius shook his head slowly. "Do not harm her, if you value your life."

Ajax grinned, showing broken teeth.

"And if I don't come back with the emperor?" said Lucius.

"We'll feed your pretty friend to the eels of the Bosporus."

Lucius glared at him.

Ajax banged the table. "Think hard upon my offer."

"What happens when Constantine comes on board, you'll try to kill him? You against a city?" asked Paulina.

The head man of the village had noticed the tense conversation going on and was standing by their table.

"My crew are agreed. If we all die to revenge Crispus, it will be a good thing. We die like heroes."

Paulina put a hand up to stop Lucius speaking. "You do not need to harm either of us, Ajax. We agree to your terms." She looked at Lucius. "I am sure Lucius will bring the emperor to you."

Ajax leaned close to Paulina. "If your friend doesn't come back with the emperor and just a few personal guards we will also, after we have killed them all, share you with every crewman again and again until your blood stops running." He slammed his dagger flat onto the table, making the red earthenware cups they were drinking from bounce.

"There will be no trouble in our village," said the headman. "You must all leave now."

Paulina looked at the headman and smiled. "Don't start a fight. My friend will just have to kill you all." She pointed at Ajax. "We will go. But bring one more jug of wine." She stared at Lucius, as if seeing him for the first time.

LIV

Perinthus, Autumn 326 A.D.

Constantine looked out at the rain through the doorway of the audience hall. The storm had begun in the middle of the night. Now, in the late morning light, it was raining as if the end of the world had come.

"Where is the governor?" he asked Juliana, who was looking out at the rain beside him.

"Nowhere to be seen. I asked his wife, when she arrived with the slaves to bring us the bread and cheese, but she hasn't seen him since last night."

"I don't like it," said Constantine. "This was one of the ports Crispus stayed at before Chrysopolis. He recruited here." He looked around "Do you think the guards told people what has happened to him?"

"You warned them not to." She touched his arm, lowered her voice. "You must stop blaming yourself for what happened to Crispus. He drew his weapon and attacked you, twice." She turned back to the hall. "Why don't we ask the guards if the word Crispus crossed their lips since they came here."

One guard put a hand up when they lined them up. "I didn't say his name, but I was asked about him. A young girl with a sad smile pressed me in the stables. She said she had been praying for his return. I told her not to." He blinked, shook his head. "But I never said his name."

"But you told her he was dead?" said Constantine.

The man nodded.

Constantine shook his head. "We make our way to the stables and leave now," he said. "I need to get to New Rome. I don't want any mourning rituals delaying us."

Juliana nodded, as did the guards.

"We take whatever horses we find in the stables and go."

They put on their belts with their swords, took a last swig of watered down wine, put on their helmets and went out of the audience hall heading for the stables.

The parade area in front of the stables was empty and the gate out to the town was closed. It looked as if the governor's compound had been deserted.

And then, arrows fell around them.

"Break the stable doors. Hit them together," shouted Constantine. They did, six of his guards smashing their leather clad shoulders into the door as one. It gave with a crack as the wooden bar holding it broke in the middle. Two stable men inside held their hands up as Constantine, Juliana and their guards raced inside. One guard had an arrow in his thigh. Constantine asked Juliana to remove it, then closed the doors, placing a wooden table against them.

Then he went to the two stable men. "Is there any other way out of here?"

They shook their heads.

"Where is the wall weakest?"

The men looked at each other. One man pointed at a far corner. "Some of the wall stones are loose there," he said.

"Why is the governor firing arrows at his emperor?" asked Constantine, grabbing the neck of the tunic of the older man.

The man shook his head. He looked bewildered.

"Please, please, my father is not well," said the younger man. "We heard Crispus was dead this morning and hoped you would leave quickly, before any trouble."

Constantine let go of the older man, pulled his sword and pointed the tip at the younger man. The edge looked sharp, its tip capable of bringing death with a flick.

Constantine was breathing heavily after his run across the parade area. He knew he should have been training for combat more frequently, but since Chrysopolis he'd stopped the daily routines. He tried to slow his breathing. He did not want his guards to see he was struggling for breath.

After a pause he said to the younger man, "Your governor was a friend of my son?"

The man nodded quickly.

"Someone's daughter is waiting for Crispus to return?"

The older and younger man looked at each other. The older man nodded, and the younger man swallowed and spoke. "This is a secret in the governor's halls. We do not speak about it outside in the town, but everyone here knows that your son took the governor's daughter to bed with promises when he visited here on his way to Chrysopolis." He paused, looked at his father. "Many of us thought he was coming back." He gave Constantine a fake smile. "I am sure he would have if he'd lived."

Constantine stared at them but didn't say anything.

Juliana gripped his arm. "We'll have to leave that one behind," she said, pointing at the guard, lying against a wall in a corner.

Constantine turned back to the younger man. "One of our men will stay here after we're gone. Tell whoever is in charge that if I find out any harm has come to my guard I will come back and kill him and all his family, his children and his parents." He leaned close to the young man, waved the top of his sword in his face. "Understood?"

Sweat trickled down the young man's brow.

"Now go to where the stones are loose and dig us a way out of here."

The man headed toward the far corner of the stables, pulling his father after him.

LV

New Rome, 326 A.D.

Helena pointed at a narrow alley leading off the main passage in the market. Two people could not easily pass each other in the alley. One had to turn sideways. The high walls were houses with doorways, mostly closed, but a few open, leading to dark hallways.

People were going each way, which slowed things down, though most people stepped into doorways or went back when they saw the empress coming.

The sky above was a thin sliver of blue. They turned again into a wider alley, and this time they could hear shouts ahead, as if there was a game of knucklebones going on. They approached a high iron gate with two fat bellied guards behind it. The guards opened the gate when they saw who was approaching. Helena and her entourage passed through with the guards bowing low around them.

An old stone doorway loomed on the right. They passed through it and were immediately at the end of a long gloomy room with tiers of seats on each side and a platform at the far end.

People sat in small knots on the seats. There were Egyptians with white headdresses, senior Roman slaves in pristine tunics, Greek merchants, and men with turbans and long beards.

On the platform were children aged from maybe four to about ten. The smell in the room was of sweat and fear.

"This is the slave market for children," said Helena, pulling Bina forward.

Bina looked horrified. Helena leaned down. "I am not going to sell you! Don't be afraid. We're here to buy you a companion. I can't be with you as much as I have been any more. You will need someone to play with and grow up with." Helena pointed at the children. Each had a red clay tablet hanging around their neck with white letters drawn on it.

"The tablets show if they have had any education, or if they have a talent for music or dancing or poetry or anything else," said Helena.

They sat in a prominent place in the middle of the benches on the left. Their guards sat behind them. Some of the children stared, dazed. Others looked away or at the sand covered floor. A giant with a whip guarded the door at the back. He had two swords on his belt.

"How did they end up here?" asked Bina, wonder in her voice.

"They may have been sold to pay off a debt or been captured in a raid or they may be the children of slaves and their masters need some money."

A slave boy began dancing on the platform. Some of the watchers clapped. An old man with long white hair called out something from the far side. A tall man with a long silver stick came from the back and called out a price, raising his stick and lowering it when no one else bid for the boy.

"Would you like a boy or a girl as a companion?" asked Helena.

Bina didn't reply.

"I think a girl will be better," said Helena. She pointed at the platform. "Do you see one you might like."

Bina's eyes widened.

Helena called the man with the stick over.

"Ask the girl with the best education to recite something," she said.

The man hurried to the platform, looked at the girls, then picked one. He shouted at her. She trembled as she stepped to the front of the platform, then spoke slowly and quietly in Latin.

"Speak up," shouted Helena.

The girl raised her voice a little. Helena leaned forward, then nodded. "Virgil." She turned to Bina. "Will she do?"

Bina nodded.

Helena waved the man over to her.

"What is the price for this girl?"

"You must make an offer. She is well educated, as you can hear and will make a fine house slave." He leaned closer. "I am sure she will also make a good bed warmer and become even more useful in the next few years." He grinned.

"That is not what we want her for." Helena pointed at him. "Has this girl worked in a whorehouse?"

The man put a hand to his chest. "No, no, I swear. We got her recently as a debt payment."

A man shouted from the far side of the room. "Two aureus."

Another man shouted. "Three."

The room went quiet. All eyes were on Helena. The man with the stick raised it.

Helena motioned him to her. The man looked around, as if waiting for a signal, then nodded and bent down to Helena.

Helena leaned forward. "I will pay three and I will try to forget that your own man sought to raise the bidding against me." She looked around. "Perhaps I should tell everyone here about your tricks."

The man bowed, went to the center of the room, lowered his stick and pointed it at Helena.

"Shall we bring her back to the palace with us?" asked Helena, leaning down to Bina.

Bina nodded. Her mouth hung open.

LVI

The Propontis, 326 A.D.

Lucius and Paulina sat with Ajax by the rudder. The days since they almost fought and killed each other had passed quickly, each late summer day as cloudless as the next as if the world had no cares, and all you had to do to live in it was cast a net over the side at the end of the day in a quiet bay and eat the bounty of the sea cooked over a fire of driftwood on the beach each night.

Twice they did this.

Other nights they stopped at white-washed seaside villages for fresh water and to share pots of lentil stew, which sometimes even had meat or fish in them.

Ajax was not a big talker, but this day, as the end of their journey neared, he'd started asking questions.

"Have you been to New Rome before?" he asked them both.

"Not me," said Paulina. She smiled at him. There was still a chance she might be able to get him wrapped around her finger.

"I have," said Lucius.

"Is it true the emperor picked the wrong side of the Bosporus for his city?"

Lucius shrugged.

"I heard that brought a curse on New Rome." Ajax stared ahead, as if willing New Rome to appear on the hazy line of the horizon.

"We will undo any curse when we anoint the city and all its temples as Christian," said Paulina.

Ajax shook his head slowly. "Crispus told us about the emperor's plan. He hated it all. He told me he would close the Christian churches when he became emperor."

Paulina spoke quickly. "Have you considered that Christ may have been at work to see Crispus' plan undone?"

"No, I don't believe it. The old gods are the most powerful ones. You will see." He held the handle of his dagger and smiled.

"There is hope of eternal life for all who believe in Christ," said Paulina, smiling back at him.

"And Hades for everyone else. I know the story," said Ajax. "Don't waste your breath trying to convince me. The empire needs the old gods, the gods of fire and war. We need to be strong, not weak, like Christ in the face of enemies, turning his cheek."

Lucius pointed ahead. A pale line was emerging on the horizon.

"We'll be there by nightfall. Is there a dock near the palace?" asked Ajax, pushing his hand against Lucius' shoulder.

"I will show you," said Lucius.

LVII

Perinthus, 326 A.D.

Banging echoed through the stables. "Emperor, there has been a terrible mistake," a voice shouted.

Constantine went to the barred door. "What mistake?" he shouted.

"The governor and his family have fled. I am the centurion responsible for the city watch. Please open up."

Constantine laughed, pulled his sword from its scabbard.

"We'll open the door. But if this is a trick I will cut your head off and piss on it."

He turned, pointing at the stable men digging at the wall in the corner. "Don't stop," he hissed.

He waved two of his guards forward. They moved the table blocking the door. Then they swung one side of the door open and stayed behind it, ready to push it closed again.

A centurion with ten city guards lined up behind him waited outside with his hands in the air.

"Come here," shouted Constantine.

The centurion strode in.

"The danger is over, Emperor. We checked all the walkways above. The men who shot arrows at you are gone or dead if they tried to stop us. The governor, his wife and daughter have fled." He bowed his head. "When I heard what had happened I roused the men on duty loyal to me. We killed two of the governor's personal guard. Their bodies are outside. There is no danger now, I swear, on my life." He bowed.

"What in Hades name happened to the governor?" said Constantine.

"He was hoping for Crispus to be emperor. He expected it."

Constantine looked out into the parade area. The bodies of two guards lay in the far corner.

"Who would have become emperor if their arrows had been better aimed and I was dead now?" he said.

The centurion shook his head.

"Thank you for what you did today, centurion. This will not be forgotten. Come and see me in New Rome."

He turned to Juliana. "I will go out first, with the centurion." He put his hand on the centurion's shoulder and wheeled him around.

"Let us go out and meet the men who saved an emperor."

The centurion took him down the line of men outside. Constantine walked past them, taking in each face.

He saluted them at the end and headed back to his own men waiting in the stables, a grim smile on his face.

"We are leaving. Pick horses," he shouted.

"You want to get to New Rome fast," said Juliana.

"I do. I expect that is where this governor has gone. He may incite others against me. I'm sure there are many who expected to benefit from Crispus coming to power."

LVIII

New Rome, 326 A.D.

Helena, Bina, the new slave girl and their guards walked past the circus, the home of chariot racing in the Greek town of Byzantion. The original circus was wooden with only two rows of seats and no seats at the ends.

On Constantine's orders a much larger stone building was being built with connecting walkways to the Imperial Palace, as it was done in Rome. A dusty storm of activity was visible all around the palace and the circus. The overseers knew the emperor would be back soon and that he'd developed a short temper regarding the slowness of the building work in his new capital.

Helena was greeted with bows at the side gate to the palace. A senior imperial family slave walked with them to the empress' rooms overlooking the point where the Bosporus and the Propontis joined.

"All of Empress Fausta's children are in Nicomedia," said the slave. "They were here earlier in the summer, but the building work is not good for them, the Empress Fausta said, and the air is better there at this time of year." He opened the high doors to the bedroom.

Slaves had already carried the empress' boxes here from the ship. Helena went along the line of boxes checking the hair she had wrapped around each wooden lockpin was still in place. They were.

"Will the emperor be joining us soon?" asked the senior slave.

"I do not know. Both my son and my grandson may come at any time." She turned and pointed at the new slave girl and then at Bina.

"Take them to the baths and have them washed and both checked for any sickness. And clothe them in the best we have. This girl is free born," she pointed at Bina. "And this is her slave companion, purchased this morning." She pointed at the new slave girl, who was staring around her fearfully.

Helena used her finger to call the new slave girl to her. "Do not be afraid. We will not abuse you. Be loyal and honest and you will have a happy life with us. Do you understand what that means?"

The girl nodded, but she still didn't smile.

"You are to teach my adopted daughter Virgil and anything else you know. You can read, yes?"

The girl nodded.

"Teach Bina," she put a hand on Bina's shoulder, "to read, and I will be very happy."

Bina looked awe struck. She'd been watching the other girl since they'd left the slave market.

The two girls were led away. Other slaves soon appeared. They brought watered-down wine, and ice in a small jug from the palace basement, where it was stored in an ice pit all year just for the imperial family.

Helena went to the balcony overlooking the imperial dock. Bina would be happier now. She would be a striking beauty one day and, if everything went to plan, she would do anything that Helena asked.

She spoke softly, to herself, "Come soon, my son and my grandson. We have much to celebrate."

She turned to look at the box which contained the piece of the true cross and opened it. The documents had moved around inside and a few flakes of parchment were lying at the bottom, but otherwise everything was perfect.

She put a hand on the dark, almost black wood of the true cross, bent her head and said a prayer,

We beg you, Lord, help and defend us.
Deliver the oppressed.
Raise the fallen.
Be with us now and forever and ever, amen.

She repeated the prayer three times, then paused, then repeated it again.

Finally, she pulled her hand away. The wood had been warm, almost alive, or was she dreaming it?

She closed the lid of the box and pushed it to the bottom of her bed. Then she went down on her knees and prayed for the safe return of her son and her grandson.

LIX

New Rome, 326 A.D.

Ajax waved at the port official. It was late afternoon. The official's blue tunic was streaked with dust. Sweat gleamed on his face. It had clearly been a long day at the imperial port. The city was stretching beyond its limit preparing for the return of the emperor.

A small skiff, with two men on board, came fast toward them.

"Let down the rope ladder," shouted Ajax. One of his crew threw a rope ladder with thick wooden steps over the side the skiff was approaching. One man came on board. He was wiry, brown skinned with deep crevasses in his face.

"Why do you seek landing at the imperial port?" he said to the captain, looking around the ship.

"We have friends of the emperor on board. One of them is ill," said the captain. "She is in the cabin."

He pointed at Lucius standing nearby. "This is the famous companion of Constantine, Lucius Armenius. He will vouch for all this."

The man went to Lucius. "Do you know the imperial password?" he asked.

"Last time I was here it was Build New Rome," said Lucius.

"When was that?" said the man.

"Before the summer."

The man went to the side of the ship and gave a thumbs up to the port official. The man waved a signal, moving one hand up and down.

"You are to tie up alongside that galley," said the man who'd come on board. "Our skiffs will tow you in."

Two skiffs were rowed toward them. Lines were thrown down and soon the ship was alongside the galley.

Ajax watched everything closely. Lucius stood beside him.

"They are good here," said Ajax.

"The best in the empire," said Lucius.

"We will wait on board for you to bring the emperor," said Ajax.

"What do I do if he's not here?" asked Lucius.

"Do not try to trick me. We made good time, but he should be here. He left Polensis before us."

"I won't trick you." He wanted to say, *I value Paulina too much*, but that might only endanger her.

Ajax looked at him. "If the emperor has not arrived yet, we will wait for him or maybe we will sail away together for another friendly voyage and come back later in the summer." He pressed the tip of his finger into Lucius' chest. "Just make sure you come back and tell me what's happening by tomorrow night and bring the emperor, or someone who can confirm he is not in the city." Ajax leaned so close to Lucius he could smell the fish paste and flat bread Ajax had eaten for lunch.

Lucius nodded. He did not feel good about leaving Paulina in the clutches of Ajax, but he knew she could take care of herself better than many men.

The men on the galley helped them tie up. Then Lucius crossed over the galley and made his way out of the port. Two of the port guards had seen him with Constantine previously. They allowed him through the exit that led straight up the hill to the Imperial Palace.

Slaves were carrying rubble in sacks down the hill from the building work that was still going on into the late afternoon. The men had bowed backs and faces streaked with dust. They did not look at him as he passed them, heading up the hill. Occasionally he passed an overseer cracking a whip. Some of them had small bronze balls at the end of their whips for gouging flesh when their whip was cracked against a body.

Lucius halted at the gate to the palace. He'd already been told the emperor had not arrived back from Rome yet. He knew the best chance he had of getting reliable information was from a member of the imperial family.

"Is the Empress Fausta here?" he asked at the gate.

"No," said the guard. "But the Empress Helena is here."

"Send a message to her that Lucius Armenius wishes to see her." He wasn't at all sure if Helena would help him, but she might.

"Wait on the bench," said the guard. "I will send word to the empress."

Lucius sat on the bench. The view of the Bosporus, twinkling with cresting waves, ships at anchor waiting to dock, and the shore beyond, thickly wooded for much of its length, was breathtaking, but he had no inclination to enjoy it.

How could he get Paulina free? And what would he tell Helena? Paulina and she were friendly, as they were both followers of Christ, but Helena always stayed away from Paulina, as far he could tell, and he had no idea why.

He also had to decide if and when he would tell Helena what Paulina knew about Fausta. He decided it would be better to do that after Paulina was freed. But what would he do if Helena didn't want to help, or she didn't want to see him?

She could make him wait until the next day too. He would have to just sleep on the bench. Late summer nights were warm and unless it rained, he could probably lie under the bench all night. The palace guards might tell Helena he had waited all this time to see her.

A trader, an Armenian man wearing a long feather-patterned cloak with a silver fringed hat, arrived at the gate. He looked at Lucius as if observing a beggar. He gave his name to the guard at the gate. The guard looked at a scroll he pulled from a leather pouch on his belt and opened the gate for the Armenian.

Lucius stood.

"Good friend, I too am from the mother country. Are you going to see the Empress Helena?" he said, in Armenian.

The man shook his head dismissively and headed through the gate.

"Please, I beg you, if you see Helena, tell her another Armenian waits at the gate for her. I am Lucius Armenius." The man was already through the gate. "You will be rewarded in gold," shouted Lucius.

The man turned and frowned, as if to say gold didn't interest him. The sun was gone, and the moon was up when the Armenian came out. Lucius had been given water and a crust of bread by a gate guard who'd taken pity on him, but he was lying on his side when the Armenian passed.

The Armenian spoke as he went by.

"I told her another Armenian waited to see her," he said.

Lucius came to his feet. "Did you tell her my name?" he said, softly, hope springing up inside him like a stream discovered in the desert.

The Armenian kept walking. He didn't look back. "No," he said over his shoulder.

The gate guard, who'd been listening to this exchange, closed over the gate with a clang. He put a giant wooden board against the inside of the gate so no prying eyes could see what was going on inside at night.

Lucius groaned in anguish. He looked down the hill. What might they be doing to Paulina? He paced in a circle. Was there any other way to get to see Helena? Should he try to get in over the palace wall? He looked at it for hand holds.

No, if he tried that the guards might consider him an enemy, a potential assassin or thief, and cut him down. His stomach twisted and his hands became fists in front of his face. Should he abandon his wait for Helena? Perhaps he could sneak back onto Ajax's ship and free Paulina himself?

No, no. Ajax would have his crew standing guard all night. This would be what he expected. He might get on board, but Paulina's throat could be cut in a moment. He had to play this out.

He lay down again and closed his eyes, tried to rest.

LX

New Rome, 326 A.D.

Constantine held the reins tight. His mount was frothing. They'd been riding all day, but still he kicked at its side. He'd had horses die under him because he pushed them too hard, but that was a long time ago. He prided himself now for knowing just the right pace to push a horse at without killing it.

Ahead, a dusty glimmer of light had grown as dusk descended. The misty torch light that showed New Rome after a day of building work grew nearer by the moment.

The new city wall lay straight ahead. He'd walked the route himself, but it was still less than half finished. It enclosed a much larger area than he'd been advised to set for the city limits, but the new size for the city would allow it to have farms inside the walls, as well as multiple ports in the years ahead.

The main gate had not even begun to be built, so nothing barred their way as they rode toward the walls of the old Greek town of Byzantion, which he had taken control of for his new capital.

The old wooden gate in the walls was already closed to travelers when they arrived. Two spluttering torches high up on the wall lit the gate, so that the guards could see anyone arriving.

Constantine shouted up at the guards manning the gate.

"Your emperor has arrived. Open up."

The doors opened slowly a few moments later. An older guard was shouting at the others, "This is your emperor, show some respect."

The torches on the inside of the gate showed four guards in a row, their spears upright.

"Thank you, centurion. What news from the city?"

The centurion of the watch came up beside his horse. "The city is abuzz with building work, Emperor. There are people from every part of the empire and beyond arriving every day. We need five interpreters full time at this gate. I do not know where they are all sleeping inside." He pointed his thumb over his shoulder at the city beyond. "Or what they have brought with them." He saluted and stood back.

Constantine, Juliana and their guards rode into the square parade area inside the gate. Around the sides of the square taverns were still open. Torches flared at their doors as people came and went. It certainly looked busier than when he'd come this way in the spring. His financing of the rebuilding work, with the treasure he'd won at Chrysopolis, was having a visible effect.

They passed through the square. Constantine looked back as they did. His guards were eyeing the taverns. They could enjoy them, after he was safely in the palace.

The long straight stone-paved road ahead went gently uphill. On each side of it were the high walls of villas and the occasional apartment block at crossroads. They also passed temples and markets, set back from the road, and the number of apartment blocks grew until they took up both sides of the road and went from two floors to four and even five as they neared the center of the city.

Statues of Greek gods stood tall in places, but no statue or church to Christ could be seen.

At the end of the road, where it opened into the old Greek forum, stood a giant statue to Apollo. Torches lit the square. Around it, taverns were serving sprawling families occupying tables on three sides of the forum. The fourth side had no buildings as it led to the new circus still being worked on by torchlight, even in the late evening.

Constantine pointed at the statue to Apollo. "We need a statue to Christ there," he said.

"A statue of you," said Juliana.

Constantine shook his head. "After all I've done, I don't think that's a good idea."

Juliana leaned toward him. "You united the empire, brought peace and prosperity and prevented more wars of succession. The people will remember that."

"Maybe, but I've also lost the son who I loved more than my own life." He spoke slowly. "The pain of that never leaves me. It comes back when I wake and again when I lie down to rest." He pointed his horse around the edge of the circus building work. They walked on in silence.

"It ended up that I was exactly like my father, keeping my heir in the dark, as if he might never become emperor," said Constantine, as they rose on.

"But you did not scheme against him, as your father did against you." Juliana spoke softly.

Constantine looked at her. Her face was lined now. She was near the end of her time as his guard, but he could not wish for a time when she would not be with him, close by, helping him, her presence bringing pleasure to each day.

"Juliana, we unified the empire, brought peace, but the price we paid has been high. My father and my son both died because of me, one way or another."

"I'm told the god of Christ is able to forgive," said Juliana.

Constantine, on seeing the torches at the gate to the Imperial Palace, got down from his horse and walked, with the reins in his hand.

Juliana slipped down from her horse and walked with him. His guards did the same. They walked in a slow line across the empty cobbled square, their sandals slapping on the stone.

Constantine stopped when the guards in the gate house spotted him as, with creaking noises, they pushed open the brightly painted wooden gate of his palace.

He turned to Juliana and said, "It is not forgiveness I seek, Juliana." His voice was tense. "I want only what is impossible. To bring them both back. To have them waiting there for me." He pointed at the palace. "That is how I failed and why there should be no statue to me. I united the empire and broke apart my family."

"What will you do about Fausta?" asked Juliana.

Constantine shook his head. "I will do no more damage to my family, Juliana. She is the mother of my children. None of them are old enough for the throne yet, but in another ten years they will be." He reached a hand for Juliana.

"What can I do about her?"

Juliana stared back at him, her leather breastplate gleaming in the light from the palace torches. "This is not about what I think," she said. "Do what you think is right."

Constantine put both hands together, as if in prayer. "I am told that Christ urged us to turn the other cheek." He sighed. "Perhaps that is the path I should take."

LXI

New Rome, 326 A.D.

Helena stood at the open window looking out over the Bosporus. It gleamed in the moonlight like a giant snake. On the far side glimmers shone from fires along the shore, where workers had set up camps on that side so they could be rowed across the water to work in New Rome each day.

A knock echoed.

"Who disturbs me at this hour. I said that Armenian must wait until morning," shouted Helena.

The door creaked open. A head peeked in.

"The emperor, your son, has arrived. I am sorry to disturb you." The young imperial slave looked around the room. Perhaps someone had told him that the empress had arrived back with two young girls and he expected to see them naked on the bed.

"My friends are not here," shouted Helena. "I thought when they made you a eunuch that also got rid of your desires."

The slave stepped inside, bowed low.

"I am sorry. I am not a eunuch," he said. "I was sent from the front gate."

"Well you'd better be careful, or I'll order they make you one," said Helena, her voice calming. "Where is my son now?"

"He has gone to his rooms."

"Who is with him."

"The warrior Juliana."

Helena snorted, spoke under her breath. "That one is too old to fight for my son." She waved. "Send for my dressing women. And send a message to Constantine that I am on my way."

She went to the next room, another bedroom, where two beds had been set up near each other for Bina and her companion. The two girls were in thin bed tunics and sitting on plump silk cushions, talking.

"I must go and see my son. You two wait here. I hope you will see him in one of the general audiences in the next few days." She touched her chest, where her heart lay, said a prayer in her mind that all would go well for the imperial family in the important days ahead.

She went back to her room and closed the door. Three older female slaves were already laying out long dresses for her to pick one from.

"Not those," she said, loudly. "Something uplifting. This is a joyous night. Let everyone know it." She smiled. Her son had returned. She should be happy.

More dresses were brought and a selection of diadems for her hair. She made her selection and let the slaves fuss around her.

When they were done, she said. "Leave."

They scurried away. She headed after them. The marble corridor that separated her from her son's rooms was long. It had an open colonnade style window on the right, with a view over the Bosporus. The corridor was lit by occasional torches which left black marks on the roof.

At her son's rooms, four guards waited outside, their spears crossed to prevent anyone going into the room.

"Let me pass," she said, as she approached.

The lead guard stepped forward. "We have explicit orders not to disturb the emperor," he said, firmly.

"I cannot disturb the emperor. I am his mother. I am sure he did not include me in that order," said Helena.

"He said no one was to disturb him," said the guard, turning to face to the side, a hand up, blocking her.

"You dare stop me seeing my son?"

The young man trembled a little, but he kept his hand steady.

"You must wait like all the others," he said.

"What others?"

219

The man pointed down a corridor opposite. A line of people waited all the way down the marble floored corridor, presumably all with a good reason, waiting for a private audience with her son.

"How long have they been here?" she asked.

"They came tonight, soon after he arrived." He leaned down to her. "We will send them all away."

"Why?" said Helena.

The guard shook his head. He had a grim expression as he spoke. "Some of them are sick. They must not be allowed bring their contagion into the palace."

A woman wailed from far down the corridor.

"They came quickly this time?"

"Many more will come too, all looking to see him at the audience hall."

"Why have the numbers grown so fast??" she asked.

"We were working to get the city ready for the emperor's return. That is what the emperor instructed us to do." It sounded as if he was complaining. He put a hand to his lips.

"I have said enough." He bowed.

"Indeed, so now you must do as I ask," said Helena.

"What can I do for you, Empress?"

"Let me pass, or I will make sure you regret this night." This time she spoke softly.

The guard paused, then stepped back and opened the door a little. Inside, her son's room was lit by spluttering candles in a line of candle holders at the far end of the room, where couches were arranged around a large window looking out over the Bosporus.

The room was empty. To her left were double doors leading to her son's bedroom. Along each wall were busts of previous emperors on marble pillars. The floor was pale green marble.

Helena walked to the bedroom door and rapped on it. She did not want to walk in on them. After a few moments she rapped again, harder this time.

"Who is it?" came a female voice, Juliana's.

"Helena."

There was a pause. "Wait, I will come out," came Constantine's voice. He sounded tired.

Helena walked to the window and looked up at the moon. Near it in the sky, glistening like a distant lamp, lay Venus. She sat on a couch. They must have been busy in there for it to take so long for him to get dressed.

A hand dropped onto her shoulder. "It is good to see you, Mother. What news from Jerusalem?"

She opened her arms. He bent down and hugged her. She half rose to him, her pleasure at seeing him clear on her face.

"I found the cross of Christ and records of his trial," she said, excitement in her voice at the chance to tell him her news.

"That is good. We must summon the bishop. Did you bring the cross here?"

She nodded and stared at him, her head on one side. Something was wrong. She could feel it.

"What happened? Somethings happened, I can see it in your eyes," she said. She raised her hands. Please God, don't let anything bad have happened.

Constantine looked down at the floor.

"Crispus is dead."

Helena put a hand to her mouth. She groaned as his words ran through her like a knife.

"No. Don't say that." She shook her head.

"But it is true."

"How, what happened? An assassination?" She clutched her stomach as if she'd been stabbed.

"I killed him, Mother. He pulled his dagger, lunged at me, twice. I had to defend myself." His voice was stiff, his face ashen.

Helena stood, went to Constantine and hit her fist into his chest.

"That is the most ridiculous thing I have ever heard. Where is he?" she looked around. Tears were at the corner of her eyes.

"Please don't say this is true."

Juliana was standing behind her. She shook her head in sorrow.

221

"I am sorry, it is true," said Juliana.

Helena took a step back.

She almost fell as her leg struck the edge of a silk covered couch. Juliana moved to help her. Helena waved her away viciously.

"This is a cruel game," Helena wailed at Constantine. She was bent almost double.

Constantine didn't say anything.

Her breath was catching in her throat.

"Where is he now?" asked Helena.

"Buried in an unmarked grave." Constantine's tone was hard, as if he didn't care what his mother thought.

"You did all this." Helena's hands became fists. "Crispus is your heir. How could you kill him? There had to be a way to avoid that," she shouted, anger clear in her voice.

"If you listen, I will tell you."

"Go on, tell me." She spat the words out.

"Crispus killed Seutonius in Rome and—"

Helena cut across him. "Who told you that? A pack of lies no doubt meant to divide our family. Who spreads these lies?"

Constantine shook his head. "I did not kill him because of that." He put his hand to his chest. It was trembling. "I killed him because he came for me with his dagger, twice, and tried to cut my throat here." He shouted those last words, his hand at his throat.

Helena groaned like a wounded wolf.

She turned to Juliana, pointed at her. "Was your Saxon warrior involved in any of this?" Her eyes blazed.

Juliana narrowed hers but did not reply.

"Juliana was not there when it happened," said Constantine.

"Who was?" said Helena, turning fast.

"No one else."

"So, we have to take your word for what happened."

"There is more," said Constantine.

"What, more?" said Helena staring.

"Fausta."

"She's not dead too, is she?" She almost laughed.

"No."

"So, tell me."

Constantine stared at her. Moments passed in silence. A night watchman called out from below. A laugh echoed distantly.

A knowing look stole over Helena's face. "No, no, you are mistaken. Is that why you killed your son? You thought he was sleeping with Fausta." She laughed, a sick, deformed laugh.

"You cannot believe such stupidities." Her voice was anguished. "This is a vile accusation."

"I have proof."

"What proof?"

Constantine reached for the purse attached to his belt. He opened it with the leather draw string and peered inside. He pulled a gold ring out. He held it up.

Helena walked to him and grabbed it. She peered at it.

"Fausta's name is here. That is your proof? Anyone could have made this. Your enemies are as numerous as the sands in the sea." She threw the ring onto the ground.

"We will have a memorial day to celebrate Crispus' life, and his victories." Helena turned to Constantine. "He helped you win the empire. How could you let this happen?" She turned to Juliana.

"I blame your advisors for letting our family be torn apart like this. I blame..." Helena's voice trailed into a sob. Her head bent as tears flowed.

Constantine looked out the window. He didn't go to her. He straightened his back, put his fist against the edge of the window, pressed it into the stone until his knuckles were white.

"No, there will be no memorial day. There can be no memorial for someone who tries to kill an emperor and usurp his throne."

"What about Fausta?" said Helena, quickly. "What will you do with her?" She glared at Constantine.

"You are worse than your father. At least he didn't have me killed when he wanted to discard me." She headed for the door, her dress swinging and glittering as she went, her wrist at her brow.

LXII

New Rome, 326 A.D.

Lucius walked down the hill to the port. Helena wasn't going to see him at this hour. His best bet was to be at the palace gate again at dawn.

The moon and Venus lit his way. Occasional torches spluttered at intersections where two streets met. At the gate to the port there were no guards and the gate was closed. He wasn't sure what he was going to do without Constantine or someone from the imperial household to get the gate open.

He peered through the bars of the gate. They were spears connected at the top and bottom and reinforced with other spears in a criss-cross pattern. He leaned closer, focusing his gaze past the spears, and blinked.

He could see the galley they had tied up to, but he couldn't see Ajax's ship. What was going on?

He rattled the gate. No one came. He rattled it again, harder.

"Let me in," he shouted. He shouted again.

He could hear the lapping of water in the dock and laughter from somewhere.

He screamed at the top of his voice. "Let me in!"

A rattling noise came from a small room to his left.

"Who wakes us in the middle of the night," came a voice.

"I am Lucius, the Armenian. Where is the ship I came in on? I was to meet them back here."

A shadow appeared from the room. A guard with his sword out, dangling from his right hand, moved slowly toward him.

"What ship?"

"We were tied up beside the galley. It's a trading ship under Captain Ajax."

The man was near enough now to slip his sword blade through the gate and cut Lucius open.

"That ship left at sunset," said the man.

"Where to?" said Lucius.

"No idea. We don't ask questions like that. Why should we?"

Lucius turned and headed back up the hill, his world falling apart.

Where had they gone? Where was Paulina? Would they come back?

LXIII

Nicomedia, 326 A.D.

Fausta walked toward the infirmary, a low stone building at the edge of the town, separated by a wide street and a high wall from the other buildings around it. Two personal guards accompanied her as well as a slave. The streets were almost empty, even though it was early morning and normally there would have been traders, fishermen, slaves and farmers passing by.

As soon as she'd arrived and heard about the sickness she'd ordered the gates of Nicomedia to be kept closed, until she understood what was happening. The council of elders for the town would, no doubt, be right now at the gates of the villa by the sea, waiting to remonstrate with her for the decision.

Her slave knocked on the door of the infirmary. A notice had been pinned to it with a red X.

The door opened just a little and someone mumbled from inside.

Fausta pulled the silk scarf around her throat up and over her mouth and nose. A doctor in Rome had advised her to do this when visiting sick legionaries' wives. "The smell can make your stomach sick," he'd said.

She waved at the guards behind her, motioning for them to enter the infirmary. They pushed past the slave and yanked the door open. A young man in a blood-stained tunic fell half-out onto the sandy gravel outside the infirmary. He looked up as her two guards went inside.

"What is going on here, physician?" said Fausta.

The man came shakily to his feet.

"We had ten dead overnight. A terrible pox is spreading in the town. We do not know yet if it is a curse from the gods and how many will die." His eyes looked haunted.

"Who brought this pox to us?" said Fausta, standing away from the man, holding her stomach, where her pregnancy was beginning to show.

He coughed, spluttered. "We do not know. Only the gods know."

The two guards came out. They both looked scared.

"All are dead inside this place," said one.

"Go back inside and clean the place, Doctor," said Fausta.

When the doctor had gone inside, she said to the guards, "Close the door. One of you waits here. The other to check for any other doors. Make sure no one comes in or goes out. Is that clear?"

The two guards nodded.

"A troop will be sent to relieve you later this morning. And," she dropped her voice and glared at the two men, "if you are asked, the infirmary is closed."

The two men nodded.

Fausta headed back with her slave. She clutched her gown to her. The sickness had to be stopped. All their lives depended on it, and the life of her unborn child. At the door to her villa there was a knot of six people, two older women and four men of varying ages. All were in wildly different outfits. One was covered in flour, another had a toga on, a third was wearing a leather breastplate.

"Come inside to the audience hall. I will hear you there," she said.

They followed her inside and headed for the audience hall, a large room with thin-pillared colonnades along the side walls and wooden benches in the center, where it was open to the sky. Fausta went out a back door to the parade area for the imperial guards stationed in the town. The centurion was summoned with a shout. He appeared quickly.

She spoke to him at the edge of the parade area. She made a fist with her hand and kept her voice steady as she spoke. This had to be done.

"Send a troop to the infirmary. Kill the doctor inside first, his mouth is a threat to us all. Then set the building alight. No one is to stop the flames. No one is to leave the building alive. Report to me when the whole lot is ashes."

The man stared at her, blinked twice, then saluted.

"Yes, Empress, at once."

Fausta headed back to the audience hall. She was no longer sick in the mornings, but her back hurt these days and the pains in her belly were sharper each day.

The people waiting for her were talking in hushed tones.

She went to the emperor's gilded chair at the top of the room and sat down.

"I speak for the emperor. Come forward one at a time and tell me how I can help you." Her tone was firm, official.

The older man in the toga came forward and bowed low.

"Empress Fausta, we must ask you to open the gates of the city. Traders and visitors are waiting outside."

"The gates will be opened, but anyone who shows any signs of sickness will not be allowed to enter. Understood?"

The man bowed. "I agree entirely with your wise decision, Empress. I too heard reports of a sickness. We must do all we can to stop it spreading."

A woman piped up from behind the man. "My son is the doctor at the infirmary. I am sure he can help visitors. We are waiting for him to come home after being in the infirmary all night." She looked around, smiled. "That is how dedicated he is."

"Does he often spend nights in the infirmary?" asked Fausta.

"No, no, only when he has very sick patients."

The others around her stepped away from her, almost imperceptibly, so that now she was standing alone, looking around.

"I am not sick," she said, startled at what had happened. Then she coughed.

LXIV

New Rome, 326 A.D.

Constantine looked out over the Bosporus. Galleys and trading ships were moving back and forth to the various docks around the city. It was a spectacle that could not be found in Rome.

The most senior imperial slave, the master of the Imperial Palace, stood beside him, half a step back.

"Emperor, I advise that we take action immediately." He sounded nervous. He was an old man. Nervousness came easy to old men. Constantine smiled. It was coming to him too.

"This type of thing happens every year in late winter and again in late summer," said Constantine. "Why should we close the fish market?"

"We don't usually get so many deaths this time of year. This year is different. We usually get slaves unable to work and traders falling ill, and the normal routine of women dying giving birth or men dying in fights, but many more people are dying and they are coughing blood and it is all connected with the fish market." He bowed his head. "I believe the head of the fish market did not pay his respects this year at the shrine to Poseidon. He will be punished for it."

"What does this person believe in, if not the old gods?"

"He follows Christ, Emperor."

Constantine turned to the man and pressed his index finger into his tunic embroidered with silver.

"No follower of Christ can be punished for his beliefs," he said. "Have you not read my edict on this?"

The man nodded. "I am sorry, Emperor. Your edict will be followed."

"How many deaths so far from this sickness?"

"Twenty-three, Emperor. And there was sickness in the imperial dock yesterday."

"Tell me more."

"A ship arrived. The passengers asked to see your mother. One stayed on board. She was the sick one. The ship left in the night. We are glad to see the back of it."

"Who were these people who came for my mother? Did you get any names?"

"Just one, Emperor, Lucius Armenius. He came off the ship."

Constantine pressed his fist into the palm of his other hand, wrapped his palm around it.

"Did you say this Lucius sailed away with the ship?"

"No. He is in the city somewhere."

"Find him," said Constantine. "Bring him to me. And keep the fish market open. We cannot stop them trading because a few people die, and someone didn't make an offering to the old gods.

"Anything else?"

"The Empress Fausta's ship was spotted heading for Nicomedia by a galley coming from there."

He stared out to sea.

"Make sure the fish market stays open," said Constantine. "Many of the poorest here rely on it."

The slave bowed, disappeared.

Juliana, who was sitting on a nearby couch was shaking her head slowly. "Are you sure that's the right call, Emperor? If there is any chance of sickness, we are always told to cut off the source, even if that means cutting off your own hand."

"I hope it won't come to that," said Constantine raising his hands and looking at them. "Why do you think Lucius is here? He said he was going back to Rome. There was someone he wanted to see."

"I can guess who that might be," said Juliana.

"He's fallen for someone?"

Juliana nodded.

"We'll have much to discuss then," said Constantine.

"What about Fausta?" said Juliana.

"I will send a messenger for her."

"I thought she'd come here."

"The children are in Nicomedia."

Juliana stood beside him looking out over the Bosporus. Her hand linked with his.

"What else will you do about the sickness?"

"We'll open the temples, put the sick in them, let the best physicians deal with them and set the bishops and priestesses to prayer." He pulled Juliana closer to him.

"Knowing you're with me makes this a lot easier." They hugged. He let his breath out. His anguish following the death of Crispus was still with him, but since telling Helena about the betrayal of Fausta something had changed in him. He'd understood their treachery more clearly and it had hardened him to what he'd done, and at the same time softened him to Juliana.

Up to this he'd stolen time with her but kept Fausta close to him too.

Those days were over.

LXV

Propontis, 326 A.D.

"Where are we going?" asked Paulina. The sea was a dark, flat, shiny skin, all around them. To their left lay a black ridge of land. On their right, not far away, lay the darker bulk of an island. Above the horizon the moon shone, turning the sea beneath it into a strip of silver.

"We're going to find someone," said Ajax.

"And you're not going to tell me who," said Paulina.

"Perhaps I will. Perhaps I won't. Come, drink with me." He pointed at the spot by the rudder where they'd eaten when Lucius was on board.

"I thought we had drunk all the wine a long time ago."

"One of the crew men came back with some jugs." He raised one up. It had an imperial double eagle crest on it.

"He stole them," said Paulina.

Ajax smiled. "I will talk to him about that."

Paulina sat down by the rudder, cross legged, and pulled her tunic down over her knees.

"And tell him he should have taken more?"

Ajax shook his head, sadly, mocking her. "You think we are pirates, no? We may be now, but we were Crispus' closest allies, his brothers in arms, the men would die for him. The men who were planning to do many more things with him." He pointed at Paulina. "But all our plans are thrown aside. What do you expect us to do, forget it all?"

"No, but don't blame me for your master's fate."

"We heard you talking about Fausta." Ajax leaned closer. "It seems you know a lot about her and Crispus."

"What do you mean?" She did her best to look innocent, pushed one bare leg forward to stretch it, then the other. She pushed her sandals off.

Ajax leaned forward. "We will find out soon enough what you know." He reached for her ankle. "I'm sure you will want to tell me everything after you get to know me better." He stuck his tongue out at her.

She pulled her legs back.

"If you rape me you will have many people coming to cut your balls off and make you eat them."

"But how will they know? You might be at the bottom of the sea." He laughed, moved a little closer.

"Look out," said Paulina. She looked over Ajax's shoulder. He half turned, only for a moment, but it was enough time for Paulina to slip over the side of the ship and almost without a splash, slide into the water.

LXVI

Nicomedia, 326 A.D.

Fausta blew out the candle by her bed. She would usually ask a slave to do it if she was in a palace in New Rome, but there were not that many slaves with her at their villa in Nicomedia. The house slave she usually kept near her had taken ill the day before.

That was the signal Fausta took to send her own children with their personal slaves to an imperial estate in the country, south of Nicomedia, on the other side of the bay. Few visitors went there and the instructions she'd given, that the gates of the estate be barred for the rest of the summer, should protect them from whatever pestilence had come to Nicomedia.

It was the same solution that had saved her grandfather when a pestilence struck Rome. Not having her children at the villa with her was a blow, but she was grateful that she had an excuse to send them away. What she had been doing with Crispus put them in danger too.

She sat up. A chill had come over her at the thought of Crispus. What had happened when Lucius went to see Constantine at Polensis? Had they met with Crispus? She took a deep breath. They would be talking about her, she was sure of that. But if any of them claimed she had done anything wrong she would deny it.

They had no proof.

She looked at her hand, where Crispus' ring had once been. That some slave had stolen it was a gift from the gods. It would not have been good for Constantine to point at it and ask her about it. She'd been a fool to wear it when she was with him in Rome.

She slid off the bed, walked to the window. Her second floor window looked out over the wall of the next villa to the hills beyond.

She must do nothing that would indicate her guilt. Constantine could not prove anything. She was the mother of his children. She would remind him of that. She took a deep breath to calm herself.

With good fortune Crispus would have laughed at Lucius' conspiracy theories. With better fortune, he would have found a moment to be alone with Constantine and do what they talked about. She put her hands together in prayer.

The old gods would protect her, they had to. And they would strengthen Crispus' hand at the moment that he needed it.

Soon, a knock would come at her door and a messenger would bring her good news.

LXVII

New Rome, 326 A.D.

Constantine woke with a blazing headache. He drank from the watered down wine jug and stood naked at the window, stretching. A slave cracked open the door of the room.

"Shall we set the breakfast for two?" the young man said in a Greek accent.

"Yes," said Constantine. He looked back at the bed. Silk cushions were strewn around it. Juliana lay beneath a purple silk sheet, the curves of her body visible. Previously, when they were in the city together she'd stayed in a room in the barracks of the imperial guard. Many people knew they were more than friends, but they always kept their involvement limited. He'd respected the rules of a happily married emperor, to have as many mistresses as you want, but keep them all out of sight.

If there was one good thing that came from all this, it was that he could now live openly with Juliana. Fausta could say nothing. Perhaps he would tell her to stay in Nicomedia and never come to see him again. That would ensure there were no endless arguments and the children he'd had with her could live with their mother. How often did he see them, anyway? She'd sent them away again this year and he'd barely seen them while he was campaigning.

He would suggest it to her when she came to New Rome. She could take whatever she and her slaves could carry back to Nicomedia and never return. And she could send the children to him for a month each year.

He slipped on the green tunic waiting for him on a nearby couch and walked into the connecting room where breakfast was laid out on a low, highly polished cedar table surrounded by couches laden with red, green and purple cushions. He pushed a purple cushion to the marble floor in a patch of sunlight and sat on it cross legged, then reached for a plump olive. A noise behind him made him look around.

Juliana was coming toward him wearing a short tunic, her hair wild around her and a smile on her face.

"You are happy this morning," he said.

"I am," she replied. "I don't have to run off. Fausta is not here to disturb us." She put her fist in the air, in a victory gesture.

"Yes, this has all worked out well for you."

She put a cushion beside him, sat on it.

"It's worked out well for you too. You survived an assassination attempt."

He shrugged. "I'm a danger to anyone who tries to kill me. I always have been. You remember when we met?"

"I do. You were a danger to everyone." She slid closer to him, pointed at the Bosporus. "What's going on there?" A ship, sailing away from the city, was burning. A column of dark smoke curled from it.

"I will find out soon, I'm sure." He drank some of the wine that had been poured for him.

They ate little that morning. The day had started hot. They went to the imperial baths together, and after it he prepared for an audience of those selected to present their petitions to him that day. The audience hall was controlled in New Rome by a hierarchy of eunuchs. The eunuch in charge was named Crassus.

"My emperor, my light, it is wonderful to have you back in New Rome," said Crassus, bowing, as Constantine came in through the door at the back of the audience hall. He was dressed in one of his light military uniforms, the one with a thin leather breastplate and only a few medals.

"Get on with it, Crassus," said Constantine. He walked to the gold-plated throne with jewels on its feet and its headrest. He was wearing the thin jeweled diadem that Persian kings preferred. There would be a change in style for Roman emperors he'd decided, as well as a change in location for the capital of the empire.

"The legate of the city watch may come forward," shouted Crassus.

At the back of the hall, behind a row of legionaries, their spears up and ready, stood a group of men in uniforms and togas.

The legate of the city watch strode up the room in his official uniform of round helmet, blackened leather breastplate, and black leg and arm greaves.

He prostrated himself before the throne.

"Rise," said Constantine.

The man came to his feet. "I'm here to report a jump in cases of the pestilence that has stricken the city, my emperor." He bowed again.

"What do you need?" said Constantine.

"Legionaries to guard the ports for a start, my lord. A mob attacked a trading ship and sent it, burning, out to sea this morning. They had reported one person sick on board after landing and a mob set them alight and pushed them off."

"What was the ship carrying?" asked Constantine.

"Grain."

"You will have your legionnaires. We have two cohorts we can use. One of them will be allocated to support you."

Constantine leaned forward. "How many are dying each day?"

"It is twenty, sometimes thirty, but the people are afraid it will grow if we allow more sick people to come into the city." He put a hand to his brow, sighed, then looked behind him.

"The heads of the main guilds are here, Emperor. They will no doubt press you to keep the gates of the city and the ports open, but," he spoke slowly now, "I cannot guarantee there will not be riots and even more deaths if you do this."

"Thank you for your work. I will decide this later. You are dismissed," said Constantine.

The man backed away, bowing.

"The head of the city guilds to come forward," shouted Crassus.

A thin man in a plain white tunic with only a gold arm band to mark his status walked forward. He too prostrated himself. When he rose and spoke his accent was Armenian.

"My emperor, the gold workers guild, who I represent, and all the guild leaders with me," he waved behind him, "appeal to you not to close the city. We must trade, or the city will die, families will starve."

"How many guild leaders are with you?" said Constantine.

"We are ten, my emperor. We are the guilds who employ most of the traders in this city." He had a confident air.

Constantine straightened. "Yes, the city will remain open, but you will each pay one tenth of the cost of the infirmaries we will set up. That cost will only be told to you after they have been closed. Until then, you must set aside funds to pay for the bill for all this." He waved at the city beyond the walls. "And no one who is sick will be allowed into the city if they arrive at our ports or our gates."

The head of the guild bowed. "Very wise, my emperor."

Constantine waved at Crassus to come to him. "This audience is over. I will tour the city gates now to make sure my orders are clear and are followed."

"There is one more person I beg you to see, Emperor," said Crassus.

"Who?"

"A friend of your son, who wishes to see you."

LXVIII

The Red Islands, Propontis, 326 A.D.

Paulina gripped the rock. The sea was barely moving, so the swim from Ajax's ship had been easy, but she knew it would not be long before he had his crew roused and scouring the shore for her.

She had to get inland and find somewhere to hide. She waited a few moments, steadying her breathing, then dragged herself up and out of the water, shivering as she exited. Her head felt light. The moon lit everything like a beacon. What she needed now was clouds, but there were none.

A shout from behind and the sound of oars slapping pushed her to climb faster. Big slimy rocks made it hard to go up. A whoosh sounded and something clattered below her. They were firing arrows. A giant rock loomed. It was half covered in pigeon shit. She went around it, squeezing between it and the next rock.

Another arrow clattered nearby. Shouts rang out. They were close. Move faster.

She pulled herself up and looked back. Their ship lay near. Ajax was visible, readying himself to get into the water.

She went on up until she reached the top of a low ridge, then started running. There had to be legionaries stationed on these islands to prevent pirates using them. But where were they?

She turned back. He hadn't topped the ridge yet, but it wouldn't be long. Her breath was ragged, and then she stumbled as the ridge dipped and rose. Where could she hide? There had to be somewhere. Then she saw it. A dip ahead was wider than the others. She looked into it. Tufts of grass sprung out on a ledge a little below.

Dropping down to the ledge, she lay tucked against its wall. It was a chance to catch her breath.

She was shivering again, her teeth chattering. Her mind wandered to what they would do to her, what he would do to her, if they caught her. The moon shone directly overhead. If anyone looked down into the dip, they would see her.

LXIX

Nicomedia, 326 A.D.

Fausta stamped her foot. "I said no one is to be allowed in through the gates," she shouted.

"He came by sea," said the slave.

"I meant the sea gate too."

"Will you see the messenger?"

Fausta glared at him. She could hardly refuse a messenger from the emperor.

"Yes, of course. Send him in," she said. She walked to the center of the atrium and sat on one of the wooden benches by the fountain. The heat of the midday sun had dried up the flower beds beside the fountain. It had been a long summer.

She kept her head straight as the messenger strode in. He bowed low and put his hand over his heart when he rose.

"My empress, I have a message from the emperor. You are summoned to New Rome at once to attend him, as he arrived there yesterday." He bowed again, looked at her expectantly.

Fausta coughed, covered her face with her purple silk scarf.

"Please, tell the emperor that I cannot come to him at this time. I have not recovered from my journey from Rome yet, and my doctors say I must rest. I will come to him when I can." She stood and with a halting step, headed out of the room. She held her pregnancy with one hand, supporting it as she went out.

The messenger stared after her, then turned and went out the way he had come in. When he left Nicomedia, Fausta was watching from a window slit in the guard room of the main gate heading north.

She gripped the hand of the man standing beside her. He was Arabian, handsome, tall, with curly black hair. His clothes were those of a low-level merchant, but the look in his eyes, assessing everyone around him, as if he was working out how to kill them, set him apart.

"Follow that messenger. Find out which palace he goes to. Then follow my instructions."

The man nodded, headed down the stone stairs of the guard block, picked up the reins of the horse waiting for him and headed out and after the messenger.

In her mind Fausta went over everything that could happen. She had given clear instructions to the messenger not to take action until it was proven that Constantine and Juliana were living openly together. The bitch had to be stopped.

And if Crispus was with his father, he was to be sent to her in Nicomedia. Until he arrived, she would have no idea what happened between him and his father and how much had been revealed about them.

Whatever happened, she had to make sure of one thing, that Juliana did not benefit from any of this.

LXX

New Rome, 326 A.D.

Constantine watched the young woman coming into the audience hall. He noted her beauty, and the sorrowful air that clung to her.

No doubt another of Crispus' conquests looking for information about him. Crassus should not have agreed to let her in.

The woman prostrated herself. Constantine looked away.

"Emperor, I beseech thee. Pray for me." She stayed down, her forehead touching the marble floor.

"Rise," said Constantine.

She didn't. Her body was shaking. Sobs echoed.

He sighed, waved at Crassus. Crassus came forward, bent down to the woman, whispered in her ear.

She looked up.

"I will not harm you," said Constantine. "I do not know what happened between you and my son, but if you need help when the baby is born send word to me."

Crassus took the arm of the woman and pulled her slowly to her feet. He guided her away. As she exited the room, she shouted through sobs, "Crispus should be emperor, but he is dead they say, and no one mourns him."

A hush descended, then a loud chattering broke out.

Constantine raised his hand.

"I mourn my son more than you will ever know," he shouted, each word distinct. "He was my heart. And now my heart is broken. Come back here."

The woman, sobbing, returned.

244

He pointed at her. "When the Empress Fausta comes here, I want you to visit her, and tell her your predicament. Do you understand?"

She nodded.

"The death of my son is an example of what happens to those who wish me harm." He glared around the room. "Let his death be a warning to all. It does not matter how close you are to me. Do not take up a weapon against me." The hall buzzed. The news of what had happened to Crispus would be in every tavern by noon.

He left the audience hall and headed for the stables. Juliana was waiting for him. She had two horses ready. Hers was black. His white. Around the stable yard a dozen imperial guards were mounted and waiting. Each had a glittering gold painted helmet and breastplate and a spear with a purple pennant.

"How was the audience?" said Juliana.

"The usual, complaints and beggars. And," he paused, "a woman who claimed Crispus made her pregnant, with her hand out."

"If you do anything for her, there will be a hundred such girls here with sob stories every week." She sounded angry.

"You don't think I should help her?"

"How would you know she's not lying? Every unwed mother who came within spitting distance of Crispus will put in a claim. And he enjoyed boys too. Will you pay them off?"

"I think I can tell a liar when I hear them."

"Was this girl a liar?"

"No, most likely not."

"You can judge the baby on how it looks when it comes out, like all others who have faced this."

"Fausta can do that."

He mounted up and they rode out, heading for the main land-gate in the north of the old city wall.

They rode side by side. People stood still, staring at them. Many would wonder who Juliana was, her Saxon leather breastplate different to any Roman military uniform and the jeweled hand axe hanging from her belt not Roman either.

They didn't speak most of the way to the gate, and she stood in the background as he gave orders to the gate commander and inspected the guard, finding fault with many small things, but always providing guidance on what to do. Most of the men under him revered him. He could change their life with a word and many of these guards had fought with him.

When the tour was finished, they stopped at a large tavern looking out on the Propontis. The tavern owner cleared the best table overlooking the sea and they sat and enjoyed the fried fish that was the tavern's specialty.

"My emperor, are you sure you want some of us to sit with you?" said the centurion who led the troop of guards that had accompanied them.

"This is my city. I expect no trouble here. I want to hear from your men. Select four to join us. The table is big enough."

The four guards smiled like children when they joined Constantine and Juliana. It took some pressing, but as the meal progressed, they spoke about their experiences in the city and especially about the problems at night in the taverns.

"I was nearly murdered the other night," said one guard, as he reached for his watered-down wine.

"What happened?" said Juliana.

"I was in a tavern and a fight broke out between followers of the old gods and followers of Christ." He shook his head. "Knives came out. Two men were stabbed. A few of us threw the bastards who'd started it out. They were claiming followers of Christ were bringing the pestilence to the city."

"You did good," said Constantine. "What else is going on that I've missed?"

The guard told them about the fights between workers from various parts of the empire and about the new brothels that had opened up near the circus.

"How are the girls there?" said Constantine. He raised his eyebrows.

The guard shook his head. "They bring pestilence into the city. No one can go there."

"Is there anyone else being blamed for the pestilence?" said Julianna.

The guard just stared at her.

LXXI

The Red Islands, Propontis, 326 A.D.

Paulina woke with a shiver. A wind had started up and was bending the grass. She turned, peered along the gully to the part of the sea that was visible. Fishing vessels rode the wind in the distance and a galley moved slowly heading east. There was no sign of Ajax's ship.

She crawled forward so she could see more of the coast. Still no sign of the ship. Her muscles ached from sleeping on the ground and her mouth was dry. She had to find water before the sun came up further.

She peered over the edge of the gully. There was nobody around. The island had a peak in the distance and a trickle of smoke coming from somewhere below it. She climbed out of the gully and began walking.

The coast curved and as she came out of a dip, she saw a fishing village below. Pulled up on a short beach lay four fishing vessels. Around them, men and women were mending nets. A little offshore lay Ajax's ship. She went back into the dip. She couldn't walk down there.

Moving along the dip she entered a thick pine forest, with a blanket of needles on the ground. Birds chirped as she walked quietly on the needles, looking for water.

The forest extended toward the village, but she found no stream or pool. She saw a young girl collecting firewood, but hid from her, and waited until she was gone before moving on.

The girl was most likely from the fishing village and the first thing she would do when she got home, if she saw Paulina, would be to tell her family. And they might well tell Ajax.

Her mouth felt like the inside of an oven now, dry and hot. The sun was high and the forest steaming with the smell of pine.

She reached the far edge of the trees at a cliff, below which stood a group of goats in a strip of land between the bottom of the cliff and the sea. She watched as a man with a red scarf around his head walked away from the goats and back along a path to the village. When he was gone, she followed the edge of the forest until it reached the path the man had taken and walked toward the goats.

They were gathering around a stone trough. She started running. There had to be water in it. Every part of her was consumed by a craving for water. But when she looked into the trough she groaned. Only a thin layer of dirty water lay at the bottom of the trough.

She had no choice. Her hand went into the dirty water and cupped enough to wet her mouth. When it went in she held it there, reveling in the relief, but sick at the taste.

A noise startled her. She spat, turned. The man she'd seen earlier was walking toward her, a long wooden stick in his hand and an angry expression on his face. The man had his head to one side. One of his eyes was closed by a scar. Paulina had seen many old injuries, missing limbs and the puckers of healed wounds, so she knew what this was. The man had been part blinded.

As he came nearer the man waved his stick, ordering her away. He grunted, like a bear.

Juliana put her hands up. "I am sorry. I was thirsty."

The man shook his head, pointed at the forest where she had been and waved at her to go.

Around his waist hung a water skin on a thin leather belt. She pointed at it. The man shook his head, waved his stick at her threateningly.

She took a deep breath, went to her knees and put her hands out in supplication. The man stopped swinging his stick, threw it down, raised his hands, as if appealing to the gods, then undid his water bottle and passed it to her.

As she was drinking the man came close to her and reached out to touch her hair. She grabbed for his stick. They wrestled for it for a moment, then she punched his kneecap and he went down.

A shout from behind made her turn. Two young men were coming toward her at a run. The man with one eye roared. His mouth bellowed open and she could see that his tongue had been cut off. He'd suffered more than a half blinding.

The two young men slowed to a walk as they saw her come to her feet with the help of the stick.

The larger of the two men smiled at her.

"You must be the runaway they're looking for," he said. "They didn't tell us you were a sister of Venus. But it makes sense now. We were wondering why they would offer such a reward for a slave."

"I am no slave. Ajax kidnapped me from New Rome. I am a priestess of Christ. He wants me for his own. I did not agree. If you take me back to the city you will be rewarded double what he offered." She looked from one of the young men's faces to the other.

They were both smiling.

"What did he offer you?"

The bigger man's smile turned to a leer. He reached to grab her.

She swung the stick in her hand and caught him on the forehead, sending him reeling. The other one shook his head, stood back.

The bigger one came for her again. She jabbed the end of the stick into him fast. He stopped abruptly and fell, clutching at his stomach. The old man was backing away. He turned then and ran toward the village.

"You are good with that stick," said the smaller of the two men. He looked at the old man running away.

"He is scared of you," he said. "So, tell me, how will you pay us, if I do get you away from your friend Ajax?" He looked her up and down. "I don't see any purse."

"I am a friend of the imperial family. You will have their thanks as well as payment."

"Your friend Ajax offered a gold aureus for you. You'll pay me two if I take you back to the city?"

"I agree," she said.

"How do I know you'll pay me at all?" he said.

"You don't, but Ajax is just as likely to cut your throat as pay you. Which one of us would you trust?"

She smiled at him, then picked up the water skin from where it had fallen.

"Don't drink from that. His tongue festers," said the younger man.

"What is your name?" said Paulina.

"Jason." He handed her the water skin dangling from his belt.

The other man was coming to his feet.

"Stay here and watch the goats," said Jason. "And the next time a woman appears in front of you don't grab her as if you haven't had a woman in a year."

"Forgive my brother, he is a bit slow." Jason waved at her to come with him.

"Where are we going?" she asked as she followed him.

"I'll show you where you can hide." He led the way to a sidetrack wide enough only for a goat and surrounded by thorn bushes.

She hesitated, looked back. The brother was not following. Should she go with him?

Jason waved her forward. "Come on. Ajax is probably on the path from the village already. That goat man cannot speak, but he can tell a story with his hands." He made a curvy shape like a woman in the air.

"Why should I trust you? Ajax could be waiting this way."

Jason sighed, shook his head. "What is waiting for you is a place you can hide until nightfall. Me and my brother will row you across to the mainland tonight and I will come with you for my reward." He smiled at her.

"You could still be a runaway, but I saw the fish tattoo on your arm so I will give you the benefit of the doubt."

Paulina pointed back at where they'd left his brother.

"What about your brother?"

"I'll go back there, after I've shown you where to hide. I will tell them, when they come, that you ran off like a wild horse when I tried to bring you back to the village."

"Do you follow Christ?"

He nodded. "We get blamed for everything bad that happens around here. They say the old gods are deserting us every time a goat bears a dead kid, or the water goes bad in a well."

He started walking, pushing past the thorns, his arms up. She followed, copying him, down the thin path until they reached a rocky open piece of ground with a goat herders hut at the side. The door stood open. They went inside. There was one room with stoppered jugs of water. She drank, washed her mouth out, spitting outside into the red dust. He passed her some bread from a small leather bag on his back. The bread was hard, but it tasted like the best bread ever. A tear of relief ran down her cheek.

Jason had already gone.

She explored around the hut. On one side stood a wicker pen to keep goats in and beyond the hut a path led to a cliff. She went back for more water and waited, sitting at the side of the hut, sheltering from the afternoon sun and going over her options again and again. Was she crazy waiting for him? Would Ajax and his men appear at any moment? She stood, walked around, listened. Then she walked to the cliff and looked for a way down.

LXXII

Fausta stared at the old priest. The afternoon had been as hot as any day that summer. She wore only a thin, almost see-through tunic. She'd noticed his eyes bulging when he came up the hall to meet her.

"I know you have curses you can throw and that can change people's luck, so when I ask you to curse someone you will do it without hesitation, yes?"

The priest nodded over and over, his hands out in front of him in supplication. "What name shall we write on the curse, my empress?"

"Juliana."

"What crime has Juliana done that we will call the gods to remedy?"

Fausta paused, took a step forward and placed her hand on the old man's shoulder. She whispered her reply in his ear. "If you tell anyone what I tell you, I will have your heart cut out and fed to the birds that flock to your temple. Understood?"

He nodded vigorously. "My lips are a seal," he said, drawing the back of his hand across his mouth. He stood still, staring into the distance behind her. "No word of your curse will go beyond our temple. Each of us, priests of Zeus, will curse Juliana with fire tonight. Now tell me what crime she has committed?"

Fausta pointed at him. "She conspires to steal something away from me." Her finger shook as she spoke.

"Is Crispus' name to be mentioned in the curse? What happened to him has shocked us all."

Fausta licked her lips. This was the moment she'd dreaded. She felt light-headed. "What have you heard about Crispus?"

The priest shook his head, sadly. "This morning a ship arrived from New Rome. They told us the news that Crispus is dead and that there'll be no mourning for him." He opened and closed his mouth. "I thought you knew."

Fausta felt weak. Her knees almost gave way. She wanted to vomit. A well of sorrow opened inside her. What had happened? A flash of muscle-twisting fear ran through her. She bent her head, put a hand out. He took it, steadied her.

"This too will pass," he said.

She wanted to hit him, wail, throw herself to the ground and cry to the gods. She didn't. She sniffed, then pressed her lips together.

"Be sure," she said, a few moments later, "that your curse mentions no one in the imperial family." She passed the gold aureus she'd been holding in her hand to him. "When your curse succeeds you will be rewarded again." She could barely finish the sentence. She turned and walked to the door at the back of the atrium, which led to the slave's quarters.

The priest shouted his thanks and hurried away.

Fausta sat on the low slave's bench just beyond the door to the slave's quarters. Usually there would be a slave sitting on it in the dark low corridor where the slaves moved about. But there wasn't. Many had gone with her children and others that should be here were back in New Rome with Constantine.

She knew why she had been summoned by Constantine. Juliana appeared to have won. She had been warned about that one. She should have listened. Crispus had been sure Juliana was behind the delay in him coming to power. He had claimed that he would die because she wanted him out of the way.

He'd been right.

And now the witch would try to rid Constantine of his empress. She could even now be twisting his mind against his wife, the woman who'd helped him gain legitimacy as an emperor.

Fausta looked around. The walls in the slaves' corridor were dusty red. The bare earth was red too. It looked as if the blood of all the slaves who'd died here had changed the corridor. She had to go back to her rooms. She had to find a way to stop Juliana destroying the imperial family.

There was only one way to do that. She had to tell Constantine what she planned with Crispus. She could tell him how they had been planning what they would do when Crispus came to power, how he'd pledged to her that her children would be placed as heads of provinces when they grew older and that her entire family, including Constantine when he was old, would be safe after Constantine abdicated.

They had met many times, exchanged rings. What could he say if she admitted meeting him? She was his step-mother.

She summoned the bishop of Nicomedia the next morning.

When he arrived, she met him in the same atrium she had met the priest of Zeus, but this time she wore the thick black stola of mourning.

"Rise," she said to the bishop, who had prostrated himself on the floor of the audience hall.

When he came to his feet, she pointed at him. "You must pray every day for all who are sick in the empire, Bishop. And ask all your people to pray for the imperial family. We all need Christ to intervene for us and protect us from harm."

The bishop nodded. "Yes, we are doing this already." He smiled, opened his hands, as if catching a bowl. "And soon we will have a sacred and powerful weapon to help us all."

"What weapon?"

"The bishop of Jerusalem sent letters addressed to all bishops. The true cross that Christ died on has been found. Praise be to Christ."

Fausta stiffened. "Helena, the emperor's mother, has been in Jerusalem. Does she know about this?"

"She found the cross, my empress. And she has taken a part of it to New Rome. It will protect the city." He opened his eyes wide. "Perhaps you could ask her to give a piece of it to Nicomedia, to help protect us too?"

LXXIII

New Rome, 326 A.D.

Constantine hugged his mother. They were in the garden of the Imperial Palace.

"I hear you have a gift for us," he said.

"It is a gift for the whole city," said Helena. She pulled away from him. Her robe and scarf were both black and her scarf was half pulled over her head to cover most of her hair.

"Mother," said Constantine slowly, looking at her, "I have ordered no mourning for Crispus. Please do not set a bad example."

"You cannot control who I mourn," she said, a sharp edge to her voice.

She looked away to where a fountain played in the middle of the garden. "And when Fausta finally arrives, I am sure she will agree with me." She stared at him. "You must not do anything against Fausta, do you hear me?" she said, her tone as hard as stone.

"I hear you."

"Well do more than hear me. The so-called proof about Fausta you told me about the other day smells like a jealous pack of lies to me." Her voice slowed. "I have never met a more decent and clean-living woman than Fausta." She laughed. It was a despairing laugh." I expect what you uncovered was Fausta meeting with Crispus to ensure her children would still have a place when you were gone. That they wouldn't all be slaughtered, as has happened in the past to the children of ex-emperors after their death."

Constantine looked down at the stone paving. He shrugged. "You may be right. I have not judged Fausta. I have not even spoken to her about these things." His voice was heavy with emotion.

"And I expect Fausta will be as shocked as I am about Crispus."

"Do not blame me for that, Mother." His voice hardened. "I regret what happened, but my hand was forced, by Crispus coming at me with a knife." His voice cracked. "I had to defend myself."

"You could not have taken the knife from him? I thought you were skilled in such things."

He thought about her question, then replied, "Crispus was still stronger than me. I had to do what I did. It was kill or be killed." He'd convinced himself that he was right. He'd played the fight with Crispus over in his mind hundreds of times since it had happened. He could, perhaps, have done something differently, but all his training said that you must take the first opportunity you get, and kill your opponent without hesitation.

She shook her head. "The cross of Christ has come at the right time, my son. You will need its power to help you. Killing a son is something few fathers have to do." She turned away from him.

"When will I see the cross?" he said.

"It will be displayed in the church of Eirene in one week, for all in the city to see and for all to know that Christ will save this city from this pestilence." She looked at him. "It can save you too."

He gave her a half smile, then grew serious again. "But why wait? Surely the people need to see it sooner?"

"A proper case is being made for it, which will allow it to be touched but no piece to be taken from it." She pulled her scarf across her face. "And I expect Fausta will be here by then. It will be good for you two to pray together for forgiveness for all you have both done."

LXXIV

The Red Islands, Propontis, 326 A.D.

Paulina waited almost all that night, alone and wondering if Jason would return with Ajax. After the sun set, she calmed down. If Jason had revealed where she was Ajax and his men would have come for her already. They would not want to try to take her at night and give her another opportunity to slip away in the dark.

The night brought another change too. Rolling clouds covered the sky, revealing only occasional glimpses of the moon. She hoped it might rain so the muggy air would be cleared, but all she got was a light drizzle, as if the gods were laughing at her.

The drizzle sent her back into the hut to rest, curled up behind the water jugs. She woke with a hand on her shoulder.

She shook the hand away, pushed herself up, her heart beating.

"We must go now. My brother and I often go fishing at first light. Come quick, there is a path down by the cliff."

The moon had come out and the clouds were moving away.

"What happened with Ajax?" she said.

"Nothing. No one took any notice of the goat herder. He dances for the villagers and makes all things bigger than they are. He cannot read or write, so he cannot tell people what happened. And he often attacks people who will not pay attention to him. Mostly they stay away from him." Jason put his hands up in mock surprise.

"But you should know that my brother tells me he will inform Ajax where you are, if you do not pay us. My brother can speak."

Paulina stared at him. "You will be paid. Now take me to the boat and let's go." She bent over. Her stomach hurt as if she had been punched.

Jason went ahead along the path to the cliff but turned off before it reached the end and headed through a thin gap in the thorn bushes to a gully which ran toward the cliff edge. He went down into it and Paulina followed. The ground was rough, but it led in a series of steps toward a thin sandy beach, where a fishing boat waited, pulled up onto the sand.

When they reached the boat Jason's brother was sitting in it. He got out and handed her some flat bread and a piece of hard cheese.

"This is to make up for yesterday, princess."

She ate. He smiled. It was as fake a smile as she had ever seen.

Jason stood behind his brother and shook his head. The meaning was clear. Paulina was not to deny she was a princess.

"Thank you. You and your family will be rewarded."

Jason's brother looked her up and down. "I am happy to help you, princess."

"No more talk," said Jason. "We need to get out to sea." He pushed at the boat. The two brothers slid it into the water.

Paulina got on board just as it started to drift, a current taking it. She ended up wet and panting.

"Lie in the bottom of the boat," said Jason. "We will be following our normal fishing routine. The sun will be up soon and everyone in the village, including your friends, will be able to see us."

LXXV

Nicomedia, 326 A.D.

Fausta stood in front of the temple to Zeus. The dawn was near, golden light trickling over the forest to the east. The high door to the temple was open. Torches inside cast a hazy light over the ground in front of the door. It was an arresting sight. The temple was a low square building with no columns.

The sweet smell of incense drifted out from the doorway. The three imperial family guards she'd arrived with stood still behind her, their red cloaks drifting a little in the breeze.

The head priest of Zeus was waiting for her at the bottom of the two steps leading to the temple. He was wearing a long black tunic and had a thin lightning rod in his hand.

"Wait here," she said to the guards. She walked into the temple.

In front of her was a pit. She did not look into it. She knew what it contained. Four heavy incense burners stood around it, but the stink from the pit was not entirely masked. To the back of the pit stood three young black slaves. They were naked. Each had a chain around his neck and his hands were tied. The chains were connected to a ring on the back wall.

"You will inspect the offering?" said the head priest.

"As you wish," said Fausta. She could see that each of them was well endowed.

"Make your decision," said the head priest.

Fausta went closer, walking around the pit and past the slaves, to just beyond where they could reach because of the chains around their necks.

One of the men glared at her. Another had a sullen expression. The third gave her a shy smile.

She went back to where the head priest was standing. Two other priests, wearing only loin cloths, stood with stiff faces and glassy eyes beside him. Each had a sickle with a gold blade in his hand.

"Praise Crispus, son of the emperor," said the head priest loudly. "We make this offering in thy name and remember with it all the good things you did and all the things that were taken from us when you passed into the underworld."

A jingle of bells rang out.

Fausta pointed at the middle slave, the one with the angry expression.

The head priest nodded and began reciting in old Greek. His voice went up and down, as if he were singing. The two younger priests went to the back of the temple.

Light was coming in now through a slit window in the back of the temple. They pulled the chain of the middle slave back, forcing him to them.

The slave tried to stop them, kicking at them and shouting aggressively as they came near him, but one of the priests swung his sickle at him and the black slave ended up on one knee on the red packed earth as he tried to avoid it.

The two priests came for him then. One dropped his sickle and jumped on the slave, pinning his chest to the ground. The other slashed again and again with his sickle at the slave's throat. Blood flowed and splashed as the slave's desperate screams turned to gurgles.

The other two slaves watched. The one who had smiled at Fausta kept smiling at her.

The dead slave was disconnected from the chain and dragged to the pit. The head priest went around to where the priests stood, holding the dead slave with his head up and blood flowing into the pit from deep cuts like new mouths.

A trumpet sounded and the head priest spoke.

"We make this sacrifice in memory of Crispus, an emperor's son, so that he has a slave with spirit by his side to help him in the underworld." He placed a hand on the back of the dead slave and pushed the body into the pit.

Then he smiled at Fausta and widened his eyes in a question.

She pointed at the slave still smiling at her.

LXXVI

New Rome, 326 A.D.

Constantine opened his arms. "Lucius, it's good to see you."

Lucius embraced him. "I thought you might still be in mourning," he said.

"I will mourn Crispus until my last breath," said Constantine. "What are you doing here, Lucius? I thought you were sailing back to Rome."

"Somebody came who changed my mind."

"I heard you had fallen for someone. Is that who came?"

"Who told you?" He stared at Constantine for a long moment. "Juliana doesn't know everything."

Constantine smiled, thinly.

"Paulina came to Polensis looking for you," said Lucius. "She almost died because of Fausta. She wanted to tell you what happened to her."

"Where is Paulina?" Constantine looked around the room. They were in his private rooms in the palace.

Lucius told him everything that had happened with Ajax and how she'd been kidnapped by him.

"So, now I know who you've fallen for," said Constantine.

Lucius put his hands out, appealing to Constantine. "Can you send messengers out for Ajax to be arrested, his ship searched?"

"I can, but I suspect Ajax has a plan. Why would he take her away if he was just going to hold her? He's up to something."

Lucius began walking back and forth. Constantine, who was standing by the window to enjoy the breeze from the Propontis, watched Lucius.

"That is what worries me," said Lucius.

"Paulina can take of herself. She is more capable of that than most men," said Constantine.

"So, we do nothing?" Lucius had a pained expression.

"I will include a call for news about them in my next message to governors of ports in all nearby provinces. And if news of her doesn't arrive by next week, when many will be gathering for the unveiling of the cross of Christ, I will send another and as soon as we get word where they are we will send men to release her."

Lucius stopped walking. "What about Fausta? What happens to her?"

"She will stay in Nicomedia and look after our children."

"That's it?"

"I will not let this madness with Crispus destroy my whole family, Lucius. Our children love her, and she had no part in Crispus' attack on me. She will not be with me. But I will do no more against her. This family has had enough bloodshed."

"I wish Paulina was here to tell you what happened to her because of Fausta." Lucius was angry.

"I do not want to hear any more about the crimes of Fausta," said Constantine. "She follows the way of Christ. If anything, she is a better follower than me. I cannot believe she conspired to do me real harm."

LXXVII

The Red Islands, Propontis, 326 A.D.

Paulina lay in the bottom of the boat all that morning as the brothers made their way slowly, following the shoals of whitefish between the mainland and the Red Islands.

She looked away as they pissed over the side of the boat and took the water bottle and more bread when it was offered to her. Eventually, Jason leaned down to her. "We will head ashore now. There is a village we visit, but we will not go there, we will stop at a cove beyond it."

Paulina lay still in the bottom of the boat. The queasy feeling in her stomach was getting worse. It was spreading through her body as if a black net had captured her.

When they pulled up onto the beach, she was able to jump onto the sand, but she was weak and stumbling and Jason noticed it.

"You are unwell?" He had a concerned look on his face.

"Get me to the city quick and you will be paid."

The brother grinned. "What happens if she dies?" he said.

"I won't die," hissed Paulina.

"And if you do," said Jason. "You will be treated as the followers of Christ are, with respect."

She nodded her thanks.

"Go back to the island and tell them I have gone whoring," said Jason to his brother. "And look out for a fire from this beach each evening. It will tell you to come over and get me."

"And remember," said Jason. "Say nothing about Paulina, as you agreed. They may well cut your throat if you tell them what we did."

The brother nodded and pushed the boat back out to sea.

They watched him row away.

"Can you trust him?" said Paulina.

"Yes, I bring a woman back to the island for him every month or two. There is no woman on the island who will have him."

He pointed at a path leading away from the beach. "This way."

"What about you," said Paulina. "Will no one have you either?" She made a shocked face.

Jason smiled, slowed to match her pace. "No, that is not my problem. For me, there is no one I want on the island."

Paulina looked at him. He was tall, well built and rugged looking. She could understand his willingness to help her. He wanted something different in his life. She had felt the same a long time ago when she left her village in Gaul.

They walked on in silence up a steep hill. Before they reached the top Jason turned to her.

"The road to the city is not far. We can claim to be master and slave for anyone who asks, or mistress and slave, if that is what you like." He grinned.

Paulina shook her head firmly. "We are traveling companions, that is all." She knew if she agreed to either of his choices, he would expect her to sleep with him. She kept walking, looking ahead, avoiding his eyes. She needed his help to get to New Rome, nothing else.

"Pity," he said. "We could have had a good time tonight."

"You don't want to sleep with me like this," said Paulina. She coughed, slowed down. "I could make you sick by morning."

"We sleep far apart then."

"How long will it take to get to New Rome?" she asked, coughing again.

"With you walking this slow we could be there tomorrow," he said. "The tavern we can stay at tonight has a woman who looks after sick travelers. She can see you. I will sleep outside your door." He looked down, then up at her. "I have never met someone who knows the imperial family or…" he looked away. "A woman as beautiful as you."

She poked his side. "I could be your mother."

"I don't care," he said.

She shook her head. They went on until they reached the road. A stream of carts and people walking and on horseback moved both ways along the road. The carts carried amphora, building materials, giant watermelons, and sacks of different shapes and sizes. Some carts had slaves attached to them by rope and others had slaves walking behind.

Riders came by, often in pairs, but also single legionaries, centurions and officers, and one troop of ten legionaries on their way at a double pace toward Nicomedia.

She thought about stopping them and asking them for help, but she had no proof of who she was, and she had come to trust Jason. The chance of any Roman officer giving his horse to her was slim, no matter how sick she was. She would just have to walk to New Rome.

Or die on the way.

It was starting to feel like that. The road had gone down hill for a while, and had thin, tall Cyprus trees lining it and fields of wheat and olive trees stretching around it and up ahead toward a line of tree covered hills.

Soon they were walking uphill, on a road through a forest of high umbrella pine. After a while she had to sit, holding her stomach. A passing wine merchant in a cart with some amphora offered her a lift.

"But your boy can walk," he said.

"I'm grateful," she said. "But I cannot pay you."

"No need," he said, his tone soft. "Just stay at the back of the cart and I will drop you at the next tavern. They can help you there."

It was afternoon when they reached the tavern and Paulina was lying flat at the back edge of the cart. The woman who cared for sick travelers was called. She took one look and told Jason and the wine merchant to carry Paulina into the stables.

"We have put all the horses into the back field," she said. "We've had a stream of ill people in the past few days." She looked down at Paulina, who was now lying on the folded-over blanket used as a mattress in one of the stable bays.

"This one looks real sick. Are you the husband?" she asked the wine merchant.

"No, just helping someone on the road," he said. Then he turned and left.

"Are you her son?" she asked Jason.

"No, I agreed to help her get to the city."

The woman looked him up and down. "This lady, and I can see she is a lady, will need a day or two to recover. She has the heat humor in her and may have the pestilence. I will give you soup for her, and a peppermint drink. Make sure she drinks it." She grabbed Jason's arm. "Who will pay for this? I see she has no purse."

Paulina's eyes were heavy, but she pointed at Jason and then at herself. Jason smiled down at her.

"I will pay. How much is it?"

They argued about the price and at the end Jason put a hand in the small purse on his belt and handed her two silver coins.

Paulina watched him and called him to her with her finger. He bent down to her.

"I'll never forget this," she said.

He shrugged, followed the woman from the tavern and returned soon after with a warm honey and peppermint drink and a thick red blanket.

He helped Paulina to sit up and gave her the drink. She fell asleep after.

The tavern woman was watching from the doorway. As Jason stepped back from Paulina, he put his hands together in prayer. The tavern woman touched his back. He turned.

"I do not know if your friend will live or die," she said. "But she would certainly die if she did not have you. We find bodies by the side of the road every year."

LXXVIII

Nicomedia, 326 A.D.

Fausta took the scroll from the messenger. She read it, then threw the scroll at one of her slaves. "Get my things ready," she shouted. "We are going to New Rome tomorrow."

She went to the table where her breakfast lay, mostly uneaten.

"And find that Bishop Eusebius who came here to see me. I want him here."

"The bishop is waiting for you in the audience hall, Empress," said the slave.

"Fetch him." The slave left in a hurry. Fausta headed through the connecting door into her bedroom. She selected a black stola and a thin black scarf and had her slaves dress her in them. The new slave held her mirror. He nodded eagerly and smiled at her as she looked at herself.

A knock sounded on the door. A slave put his head in. "The bishop Eusebius is here," he said softly, then withdrew.

Fausta looked at herself one last time in the mirror, pulled her scarf down more over her forehead and went through to see the bishop.

He prostrated himself on the floor as soon as she entered the room. "Rise, Bishop, there is no need for that," she said, softly, but inside she enjoyed the respect the prostration showed.

"How can I help?" she said. She moved a little to get more comfortable on the yellow silk couch. She didn't ask him to sit.

"I am honored to meet you again, Empress." He bowed low.

"Why are you here, Bishop?"

"There is a dispute in the church in Alexandria. I hoped you might persuade the emperor to intervene."

"Have you been cast out of the city?"

"I came here with only good intentions, Empress. I know you wish our Christian church well." He bowed.

"You might come with me to New Rome and present your appeal directly to the emperor, Bishop. I leave later today."

The bishop put his hands together. "That would be wonderful. Will you bring me directly to see the emperor, or will I wait with the others seeking an audience?"

"I will bring you directly to him." She smiled. It was not a pleasant smile. It had a dismissive edge.

"That is wonderful. I should go now and pack my things and get ready." He bowed and started walking backward to leave.

"Bishop," said Fausta.

He stopped. "Yes, Empress."

"I hope you will do just one small thing for me."

"Of course, Empress. Whatever you ask."

"Remind the emperor, when you see him, that he must cast aside those around him who are not Christian." She walked to him. "I'm so afraid for the emperor these days. Will you do what I ask?"

"Yes, yes, of course." He bowed. "Is there someone in particular you believe might lead him astray?"

She paused, wondered for a moment if she was right to name her enemy. Then her eagerness to say what she'd been thinking overcame her doubts. "Yes, this person is a liar, and a threat to the imperial family. The emperor should know your doubts about her."

"Her name?"

"Juliana."

"The Saxon?"

Fausta nodded.

LXXIX

New Rome, 326 A.D.

Constantine walked down the center aisle of the infirmary by the shore of the Bosporus. He'd granted the imperial physician a large storage block, used for storing wheat in the winter, to treat the ill in the city. The building was separated from others by an open area, so the risk that a miasma of corruption from the sick and dying would reach others could be reduced.

Inside the building, sick people lay on folded blankets, which were used as mattresses. The physician walked behind Constantine as he toured the site.

"Are we doing all we can for these people?" asked Constantine. He held his red scarf over his mouth.

"We have prayers three times a day. We will do one more from tomorrow. That is the quickest way to deal with the sickness, Emperor."

"Anything else? I am sure there is more you can do."

"We have a policy to let the sickness take its course, Emperor. The fates will decide who is destined to live, and whose thread will be cut at this time."

The emperor looked over his shoulder. Juliana, with her axe dangling from her belt and her leather breastplate shining in the light streaming in from the high windows, was standing impassive behind him. She too had a scarf around her mouth and nose. The physician turned to walk on. Juliana gave Constantine the thumbs down.

Constantine caught up with the physician at a row of patients at the end of the room. People were lying flat out. Many looked almost dead. They had been placed beside patients sitting up.

"What is this?" said Constantine angrily.

"A patient who is well can encourage the sickest of our patients to get better, by their words alone. That is why the recovering patients are put here before they leave."

Constantine looked along the line of sick people. Two men, at the far end, were carrying a body away toward a back door.

"Do many die from here?" he asked.

"My assistant knows that," said the physician. "I do not concern myself with numbers. Praying to the gods is a more effective way of managing illness than counting."

"Remind me how you came to be my physician," said Constantine.

"I am related to the empress," said the man, smiling.

"Do we have the sickness under control in the city?" Constantine watched as more patients came in at the other end of the room.

"Only the gods can answer that."

LXXX

The Road To New Rome, 326 A.D.

Paulina was still sick the following morning, but she insisted they had to travel. Jason brought her flat bread and another hot drink from the lady of the tavern.

The drink made her sleepy.

She lay down on her thin mattress and went quickly into a deep sleep. She began to dream.

She was back in Rome. It was the night before the celebrations for Constantine's twentieth year in power. She was searching the palace, running from one empty high-ceilinged room to another. Curtains drifted in the breeze. It was dark, and she was following someone. A woman. She had to move fast to keep up with her. She was getting away. Then the woman turned a corner and Paulina knew who it was.

She was following Juliana.

And it wasn't the first time she'd followed her. She went around the corner and saw them.

Juliana had her arms wrapped around his neck and her legs up and around his body.

He had her up against the wall. She was groaning in ecstasy.

"Faster, Crispus, faster," Juliana called out. She looked directly at Paulina and smiled, as if she had something she knew Paulina wanted.

And then the dream was over, and she woke, with Jason looking down at her.

"Shall we wait until tomorrow? You do not look well," he said.

Paulina's mind was somewhere else. She was trying to work out if her dream had been a memory or a vision.

"Let's stay here today. What was in that drink you gave me?"

"Juice of the poppy." He smiled down at her, clearly relieved that they would not be traveling again soon.

LXXXI

Nicomedia, 326 A.D.

Fausta struck the floor with her sandaled foot. "Do not tell me you can't do it. I am the empress. You will do what I say."

"But we cannot rebuild the infirmary in one week, Empress." The physician's hand trembled. He'd probably heard what happened to the last physician in charge of the infirmary.

"How many men do you need?"

"It's not about…"

"How many men are working there now?"

"Twenty."

"You will have a hundred legionaries working for you tomorrow, including engineers used to building legion forts in a few days."

"Thank you, Empress." He bowed.

"Has your family moved into the villa I allocated them?"

The physician hesitated. "No… I mean we will soon."

The empress walked up to him. She pressed the tip of her finger into his pristine white tunic.

"Make sure you do. I insist on those who work with me bringing their families within easy reach."

The man swallowed. His Adam's apple bounced in his throat. "My wife wanted to stay at our home until the schools restart."

"What kind of a man are you? Tell her no. You have two young girls, yes?"

The man nodded.

"It is for the best if your family are near." She closed her eyes. "Best for all of us. Is that understood?"

He nodded. "Yes, thank you, Empress." He looked away. He clearly wanted to leave but Fausta was not finished with him yet.

"I also want you to make a potion for me."

Silence descended. The physician stared, his eyes slowly widening.

"What kind of potion?"

"A potion that can kill a horse in one night."

He spluttered. "I'm not trained in such things, Empress. I am sure there are people in the market."

"But you know how to do this?"

He nodded.

"Bring it here tomorrow."

"Can you not have someone take a sword to the horse?"

"I want no one to know how the horse died. The effects must not be clearly poison."

The physician's expression changed. "Aaah, I see."

"And you will tell no one about this. Not even your family. Do I have your word?"

"Yes, yes, you have my word."

"Good, I would hate something to happen to your lovely family."

The physician went, bowing all the way to the door.

Fausta's face remained hard. She had done many things to protect herself and her children. Whatever it took, she would survive, and they would too if she did. Staying alive in an imperial family took more than waiting for things to happen. Emperors were fickle, they could not be trusted.

LXXXII

New Rome, 326 A.D.

Constantine walked along the line of prisoners. They were on their knees, their tunics slit so that their backs were exposed. Their hands were tied firmly behind their backs with thick rope. In front of them lay the parade area inside the palace wall. The prisoners were kneeling on the stone paved path at the edge of the sand covered area.

Each of the twenty prisoners had a legionary behind him.

Constantine reached the end of the line. Faces crowded a nearby gap in the wall with bars across it. The gap was there to allow people outside the palace to see the emperor's guards training, but also, on days like this, to see traitors being executed.

Constantine lifted the scroll in his hand and began reading from it. The list of names included the rank of the accused legionary. There were two centurions on the list.

He recited the standard form of words used before an execution.

"By the power I possess as emperor of all, and because of your treason, I order your head to be struck from your body and your blood to flow out to feed the sand of this parade area, so that others might know what awaits all who stand against their rightful emperor."

The men waiting were the last to be rounded up after the battle of Chrysopolis. Their action in not coming forward when he offered an amnesty proved their intentions could be to reveal themselves at a later date, and act against him.

A failure to deal effectively with all traitors had resulted in the deaths of other emperors in the past. Kindness to such men would, without doubt, be seen as an opportunity to overthrow him, as traitors to his cause could expect leniency.

He looked up at the sun. Any moment now the city watch would blow a trumpet to signify mid-day and Constantine would shout the order to spill blood.

He looked up to the walkway where the man with the trumpet stood. It rose to his lips.

"I ask for time for you to hear me," came a voice from the line of prisoners.

Constantine stared at the trumpet player. The man had the trumpet to his lips but was not blowing it. Calls for an execution to stop often happened. Appeals to leniency or the gods and tearful accusations against others were common.

"There is a conspiracy against you, my emperor," came a shout.

Constantine looked down the line of men. Only one man met his eye. He was rocking back and forth.

The trumpet blared.

"Let their blood flow," shouted Constantine.

The legionary standing behind each prisoner pulled out his sword and swung it, fast.

"Julia. . ." came a cut-off shout from the prisoners, amid grunts and roars, as twenty heads were taken from shoulders and twenty bodies fell forward, so their necks pumped blood onto the parade ground sand.

LXXXIII

Three day's walk from New Rome, 326 A.D.

Paulina sat down on the parched grass near the road. "I can't go on," she said.

"We are nearly there," said Jason. "You can't give up."

"I'm not giving up," said Paulina. "I'm resting. I don't feel well." She groaned and lay on her side.

A voice called out from a cart, about to pass them. "If the lady wants to be carried in the cart, put her in quickly."

"Ask him what he wants," said Paulina. Her voice was low.

Jason ran to the cart, which had slowed. There weren't any carts right behind his, so he could probably even stop to let Paulina on board.

Jason returned with the good news. "He asks for nothing," he said. He bent down and lifted Paulina. She tried to protest, but she didn't have much strength, so she just accepted being carried.

He placed her on the back of the cart, near some sacks. The driver whipped his mules and their pace picked up. Jason walked behind. After a while the driver of the cart turned to her.

"Are you heading for New Rome to see the true cross?" he said.

"I'm going to see the emperor," said Paulina. She pressed her lips together. That was all she would admit to. But she had been thinking about Lucius. And a lot of things made sense now about how he hung around her, and it all made her smile, as if she'd rediscovered something that had been lost a long time ago.

"Yes, that's what we all want," said the driver. He pointed behind him. The road had been heading up hill and they could see a long stretch of it behind them. It looked busier and busier the further away the carts were.

"You must have set out early," she said.

"Before dawn," he replied.

"What is this true cross?"

"The cross Jesus died on has been found. It is a wonderful miracle. That is what it is. We will see it when we get to New Rome. And we will all touch it too." He turned and smiled at her. "All us followers of Christ are saying the true cross will cure anyone who believes in our Christ god. That is why I stopped for you. You are going to New Rome for a cure for your sickness, yes?"

Paulina nodded. One way or another it was true.

"When did you find out about this?" she said.

"Only yesterday. A rider is passing by all the estates whose masters follow the way of Christ."

"You came quickly."

"Yes, this is such a wonderful day. I wanted to be among the first to kiss the true cross and get the blessings of Jesus. This is the first open gathering we have ever had. Ever!" He smiled, as if his heart would burst.

A wave of nausea distracted her. Paulina put her head down in the back of the cart as it passed through her. A little while later she leaned up and asked the driver, "What ails you?"

"We are waiting for a child." He lowered his voice. "If we do not have a child, everything we have built up on our farm will be lost."

He coughed, looked at his hand and wiped it quickly on his tunic. The stains on his tunic were all blood red, and a new one was visible now. She looked at Jason and called him to her with her finger.

"Do not go near the driver. He is sick," she whispered.

Without turning, the driver spoke. "We will all be cured by the true cross. Have no fear, shake my hand." He put his hand behind him for Jason to grasp.

Paulina shook her head at Jason, but Jason shrugged.

"I believe it," he said. He walked up and shook the driver's hand.

When he returned to the back of the cart Paulina motioned him close. "What he has is different to me. I am not coughing blood," she hissed.

"All sicknesses are the same," said Jason. "And they cannot be passed from hand to hand. Sickness starts within. It is an unbalancing of the humors."

Paulina wanted to scream at him, but she did not have the energy for it. Jason gripped her shoulder.

"We are blessed. You will recover," he said. "Soon we will be in the presence of the true cross." He came closer to her. "Christ can resurrect us from the dead if you believe. Do you believe?"

Paulina nodded.

LXXXIV

Nicomedia, 326 A.D.

Fausta took the small red earthen-ware vial from the physician. She looked around the room. The new black slave was the only other person with them. He was waiting by the door to her bedchamber.

She walked to the window. The physician followed her.

"How much is needed to kill a horse?"

"A few big drops. You can kill a whole stable with this vial."

Fausta gripped his bare arm. "You have told nobody about this?"

"Nobody, I swear, on my life."

"Good, then you must forget about this vial and get on with your duties. How is the new infirmary coming?"

"You sent the right people. They will have the building finished next week. They even know how to run it. The man you sent was a legion physician for many years."

"We women are not as useless as some people think."

"I am not one of these, Empress. I know what women can do," said the physician. He looked away.

"Thank you for your tireless work," she said. "I will come and see you when I return from New Rome."

The physician bowed, backed up and left the room. When he was gone, she called her new slave to her.

"This will be your big test," she said.

He looked eager, his eyes gleaming and a smile playing at the corner of his mouth.

"Your wish is my command," he said.

She held the vial tight in her hand, looked around. "Do you remember the face of that man who was just here?" she said.

He nodded. "I could not forget it, even if I wanted to."

"Well, follow him and do not come back to me until his neck is cut and his days are over and," she leaned close to the slave, "bring me back that snake ring on his finger as proof of his death and I will reward you."

The slave nodded and hurried toward the door the physician had exited by.

LXXXV

New Rome, 326 A.D.

Constantine walked slowly with Juliana around the palace garden. It was late morning. They had eaten breakfast together. The sun was high, and a white haze lay across the sky, as if the gods had decided to mask the heavens.

"What do you need in the market?" asked Constantine.

"Things," said Juliana.

"Can you not send one of the slaves to get everything?"

She looked at him. "The bazaar here is supposed to be the best in the empire. The street of jewelry makers is without doubt the best. I must see it again. I cannot stay in the palace the whole time."

"The best jewelry makers will come here. All I have to do is call them and ten will arrive tomorrow morning with their best pieces. There is no need to leave the palace. Everything you can possibly need is here." He waved around him at the painted statues, the fountains and flower beds. The pounding of hammers echoed from the direction of the circus.

"I cannot be stuck in here all the time," she said. She sounded frustrated. "Is this a prison?"

He looked at her. "No, of course not. You decide when and where you go. I always swore that to you, and I will not break my word."

"Good," said Juliana.

"Let me send a troop of men with you. You'll need a proper guard. If anyone finds out you are going around alone they may want to hold you against my good behavior. And that will not end well."

"I am just another of your guards as far as most people know in this city, Constantine. And anyway, I will have my axe and I will bring one of the imperial slaves."

"To carry your purchases."

"To carry my purse."

Juliana kissed Constantine's cheek, then kissed the other side and left him in the garden staring after her. She had already told one of the young female imperial slaves that they were going to the market. The slave was waiting, excited, by a side door into the palace grounds. It was the door slaves and imperial guards used. The slave was carrying a wicker basket.

They went out through the door and passed through the gate beyond it and soon were walking down the hill to the bazaar. Juliana turned twice, as an instinct made her skin crawl, but seeing no one following them she put it down to a reaction to being out in the city and watched by men on all sides.

They may not know who she was, but the sight of a woman in a leather tunic, even the soft one she wore, with a war axe dangling from her belt was unusual.

They headed first for a fig merchant the slave had assured Juliana was the best in the city. Juliana had enjoyed figs during her childhood, but the ones in Treveris and Rome were often hard. Here she could get the freshest in the empire.

The shop also sold sweet confections, a mix of date and fig and a light flour, sweetened with rose syrup, which was what Juliana had asked the slave about, and which had started her desire to go to the market.

"Are they not the best fig sweets in the empire?" said the fig merchant as he passed a silver tray under Juliana's nose.

"If you let me try one, I will answer you," said Juliana.

He held the tray for her to pick one. She did, popped it in her mouth, then groaned in ecstasy.

"Please come inside. We have many kinds of confection like this." He looked at her axe. "But please, leave your weapon at the door. My assistant will hold it for you."

The assistant was a giant half as tall again as Juliana.

"I do not give up my axe for anyone," she said.

"You do not have to, but it will help you to sit and enjoy our cushions and the Persian lemon drink we offer here."

Juliana gave her axe to his guard and sat on one of the stools at the back of the room, set around a circular table. The lemon drink was served in small green glasses. She instructed her slave to sit beside her and drink as well. As they sipped at the sharp tasting liquid the owner of the shop brought samples of figs for them to taste.

"You are from the palace, yes?" asked the shopkeeper.

Juliana nodded. She looked at the wide doorway leading out. A crowd had gathered. The slave beside her was smiling. Juliana followed the slave's gaze. A young man was beaming at her.

She knew then how stupid she'd been. The slave she'd brought with her was well known here. She probably visited this market regularly. Everyone nearby would have heard that they had a visitor from the Imperial Palace, someone important enough to have a slave of the imperial family with her.

As Juliana watched the faces peering in at them, the crowd parted in the center and a young, bearded man came through. He was dressed in a green tunic and had a green phallic amulet dangling from his neck.

He bowed at Juliana from the entrance to the shop.

The shopkeeper waved the man forward. "Praise be, my spiritual guide has arrived just in time." He bowed to Juliana. "This is Alexander of Tarsus. He has the gift of prophecy and healing and has helped many in this market to stay healthy in this time of crisis."

Alexander bowed, then went further and lay down on the rush mat floor, his forehead on the mat.

"It is an honor to meet Juliana the Saxon. You are a blessing to our lands," said Alexander.

"I am not from the imperial family," said Juliana. "You are very mistaken to do this. Get up."

Alexander rose slowly. "But I have heard you are the consort of the emperor. That makes you a part of the imperial family in my eyes."

"And who are you, Alexander?" said Juliana.

"I am a poor servant of the people," said Alexander, placing his hand to his chest, holding it there in a sign of peace. "I knew today would open a door for me to help my people. It was written in the wind this morning." He bowed.

"You read the wind?" Juliana spoke slowly. She'd heard of such people when she was a child, living on the frontier between the Roman and the Persian empires.

"I am blessed with a small ability for that," said Alexander. He pointed at an empty stool near her. "May I join you?"

Juliana nodded. "I won't be staying long, Alexander, but tell me what the wind speaks for our city." Stories of people dying from the pestilence were going around the palace every day now. Good news would be welcome.

Alexander shook his head. "I cannot tell such things." He looked down. "It is not for me to spoil such a beautiful smile."

"I insist," she said.

He bowed.

In the doorway the crowd had grown. All were quiet now, listening to the conversation. Juliana knew what it was like at palace ceremonies to have everyone listening, but this felt different. Perhaps it was the luminous blue of Alexander's eyes or perhaps it was the radiance of his smile. It warmed her. She looked away.

"If I may take a sip from your lemon water," said Alexander. "I will tell you all you wish to know."

Juliana didn't look at him. She waved her hand dismissively.

She saw his hand, brown and hairless, reach for her drink and heard him sip it, slowly, savoring it. Then he spoke.

"If the emperor does not know what is happening in his New Rome, then please, you must tell him." His voice went lower. "More than one hundred bodies a day are being buried in pits outside the city walls. Some say the pits will extend the length of the walls this time. Did you see the pits when you came into the city?"

Juliana shook her head. "The emperor is aware that people are dying. It troubles him greatly," she said.

Alexander leaned forward and put a hand out, as if wanting to touch Juliana. The shopkeeper grunted his disapproval.

"What people ask, Juliana," said Alexander, "is why our wonderful emperor will dedicate his new city to the Christ god." He looked around. Heads nodded while others repeated the conversation to people behind them.

"The Christ god can help this city," said Juliana. "If we stop the pestilence here, it will save countless lives. We've had too many gods. The emperor is doing this, setting the one God over us, to save his people." Juliana looked in Alexander's eyes. They were blue pits she might fall into. She looked away.

"We will find out soon enough if this is true, sweet Juliana." He reached closer to her.

"And if the Christ God does not save the city, it will be clear to all that is because the old gods are angry at their temples being taken and their priests and priestesses discarded." He sighed loudly. "There are stories coming to us about temples all over the empire being destroyed.

"I do not believe the Christ God can save us, Juliana. Tell him to cancel the dedication. If he continues with it he will bring a curse on this city. The cross of the Christ god must not stay here."

LXXXVI

Two day's walk from New Rome, 326 A.D.

Paulina leaned up. The cart had stopped. She'd been taking shelter from the afternoon sun by positioning her head in the shadow of the sacks. The day had passed like the journey of a snail. Her mouth was parched. The number of carts and riders heading toward New Rome had grown beyond reason that day, slowing all progress.

Now they had come to a stop as distant shouting crackled through the air. She turned and looked for Jason. But he was gone. She slid from the back of the cart and walked around it, holding her stomach. As she reached him, the driver put a hand on her shoulder and said, "No further. This is bad."

She leaned up, so she could see over the heads of the people in front.

"Come up here, you'll see better," said the driver. He patted the spot beside him.

She pulled herself up with his help. In front of them was a line of unmoving carts. Behind one cart further along there were men standing in a row as if they were legionaries, but none of them had helmets or spears.

"Who are they?" she said, leaning toward the driver.

"Followers of Zeus. I was wondering if we would find some of them joining us. See, they all have black scarves or arm bands. That is how we know them."

More shouts filled the air.

"What is the arguing about?"

"What is it always about with these people, Paulina? They want us all to go back to the old gods." He put his mouth close to her ear. "I would not be surprised if they are going to New Rome to cause trouble." He spat across Paulina and onto the ground. She moved back a bit and out of the line of his spittle.

"Look, your friend Jason is coming back." The driver put out his hand. "What news, Jason?"

Jason came up beside him and looked up at them.

"Not good," he said. "Followers of Christ are arguing with the followers of Zeus. They will not listen to each other. I think they will come to blows soon."

"Are they trying to stop us going to New Rome?" asked Paulina. A stomach cramp made her groan.

"Looks like it," said Jason.

LXXXVII

Nicomedia, 326 A.D.

Fausta took hold of the guide rope and walked up the gang plank to the galley.

"The wind is good for us?" she asked the captain, who was waiting, bowing on the deck.

"Yes, Empress. We can be in New Rome in two nights."

The black slave carried the first of her traveling boxes. Three other slaves followed with boxes of different sizes. Behind them came Bishop Eusebius. He had two young priests with him. They all carried large leather shoulder bags. Eusebius was shown to a windowless cabin below deck. The empress was given the captain's cabin in the aft of the ship. The captain would sleep in another, small windowless space below deck.

As they rowed out of the harbor at Nicomedia the empress stood near the captain in the center of the galley, below the mast.

"We will do all we can to make your trip fast and uneventful," said the captain. He looked around. "Will all your slaves be sleeping below deck with the rowers?"

"All except my black companion. He sleeps inside my door," said Fausta.

The captain nodded and made no further comment. Soon after, Bishop Eusebius appeared.

"I will pray for our safe arrival and for your baby," he said. He opened his hands and began to whisper. The captain stood beside him, his head bowed.

Fausta waited a few moments, then left them to it.

She ate alone, with just her black slave in the cabin that night, and the following day stayed there until the gently bucking waves drove her onto the deck to see what was happening.

"Forgive us for the rough journey," said the captain. "The wind has picked up and we must ride the waves while we can." He put a hand out to steady Fausta.

She brushed his hand away. "Is there any danger, Captain?"

"There is always danger at sea," said Bishop Eusebius, who had appeared beside the captain.

"You should join us in our prayers to Christ at noon," he said. He smiled at Fausta.

"I do my own prayers," said Fausta.

"With your personal slave?" said Eusebius.

"Yes, he helps me pray." The edge of a smile crept to her mouth, but she suppressed it.

"He tells me he is a follower of Zeus," said Eusebius. "Have you converted him to Christ, Empress?"

She didn't reply. She squinted, looked at the distant shoreline to their right.

"We seem very far from land, Captain," she said.

"We travel further out going north, Empress. That allows the ships going south to take the inside line," said the captain.

"I want to be nearer the shore, Captain. See to it."

"Yes, Empress."

He went to the bare-chested man holding the rudder and soon they were heading along a line nearer the shore. Their purple imperial pennant flapped noisily from the top of the mast. Fausta went to her cabin, ate half a dry biscuit and vomited soon after. She lay down on the floor, the black slave rubbing her back, and tried to stop thinking about the sea all around them, but the ship was creaking and moving side to side and up and down now. She held her hands together and pressed them to her forehead.

A little after midday she went back out on deck to see if land was near. She was relieved to see it much nearer, to the right.

"There are not many ships coming south, I think we made the right call," she said to the captain.

He pointed ahead. "This one is coming straight for us," he said.

"They will see the imperial pennant and turn aside, won't they?" asked Fausta, anxiety growing inside her.

"Yes, I am sure they will," he said, grinning, showing blackened stumps for half his teeth.

They watched as the ship sailed directly for them. It seemed that the captain of the other ship was determined to wait until the last minute to turn.

The slap of waves against the side of their galley grew stronger suddenly, as did the noise of the wind whistling through guide ropes. The crew were silent. Most were below the main deck sheltering from the sun and the constant spray when the ship was moving fast.

"You must turn aside, Captain," said Fausta.

"It is not our place to turn, Empress," the captain replied. "We may just make matters worse by us both turning the same way."

Screams of seagulls filled the air.

"Do as I say, Captain. I have a bad feeling about this." Fausta clutched at her pregnancy with both hands. The baby kicked on.

"I will do it at the last moment," said the captain. "That will at least give them an opportunity to get out of our way or tell us which way to turn."

The other hands on deck were all pointing now at the galley bearing down on them. Fausta tasted salt on her lips. She looked over the side. The sea was a deep-dark green. She had no idea how to swim. She'd seen a few young boys swimming naked near their family villa but had never been allowed into the sea with them.

A shiver rose through her spine. The kicking stopped.

The captain stood at the back of the ship holding the rudder.

The other ship was not changing direction. What were they playing at?

The imperial galley heeled to one side, sending Fausta across the deck as they skewed. They were heading out to sea again. Seagulls cried and the grunt of rowers filled the air. She looked to the right. The other ship, moving slowly under oar power, passed by in a shower of spray from its oars. A giant of a man stood by the mast. She remembered him from somewhere, but she couldn't remember where.

LXXXVIII

New Rome, 326 A.D.

Juliana stood. "I've heard enough," she said. She pointed at the crowd outside the shop.

"I may need your help getting through this lot."

Alexander stood, walked to the door and spoke softly. She could not hear what he said, but she heard some laughter as the crowd dispersed.

"Thank you, I will take a bag of your best fig sweets, shopkeeper." She reached into her purse and pulled out two silver denarii. "Take this."

The shopkeeper bowed, smiled, and almost scraped the floor with his hand movements as they left his shop.

"May I escort you back to the palace?" said Alexander, as they went out into the street.

"No need," said Juliana. "I am safe with this." She held up her axe, which had been passed to her on the way out of the shop.

Alexander nodded and stared after her as she and her slave headed back down the street.

Juliana wasn't concerned, but she sensed they were being followed. Beggars were always about, and some did follow you if they thought you had a gullible face, but she didn't usually feel threatened by them.

But things could be different now. She was much more of a target as she was openly the consort of the emperor. It felt very different to the last time she'd been walking around the city.

She picked up her pace, turned into the main street heading up hill to the palace.

A noise made her turn.

An Arab man, handsome, tall, with curly black hair, wearing the clothes of a low-level merchant was walking fast toward her. The look in his eyes spelt trouble.

She'd heard of women being kidnapped in the street in the city, one the daughter of a senator. She picked up her pace, waved the slave to come faster. The circus was just ahead. Once they were within waving distance of the guards at the gate, she could call them to her, if he tried anything.

"Juliana, don't be afraid," a voice called out.

She did not turn. The patter of running feet echoed. She couldn't help it now. She looked around.

The Arab man was near. His hands were high, indicating he had no ill will. Juliana shook her head, kept walking.

"I have a message for you, please listen, Jawlayna," he shouted, mangling her name.

Juliana looked back. He had stopped following her. The gate to the palace was within a spear throw. She stopped and called him forward. He came.

"Stop there," she called when he was ten paces from her. Her hand rested on the head of her axe. She could have it out and his head off his shoulders in the time it took for a long blink.

The Arab man smiled. "You are a difficult woman to catch," he said.

"What is your message?"

"The Empress Fausta sends you good wishes. She hopes you will be a guide-mother for her baby, when it comes."

"Why do you tell me this in the street?"

The Arab took a step forward and looked around. "The empress does not trust everyone," he said. His smile was false, extending only as far as his lips.

Juliana put her hand up and pulled her axe a little from the leather holder that held it to her belt.

"Come no nearer, if you value your head."

"I do," said the Arab.

"Is that all you have to tell me?"

"One last thing. She hopes you will see her when she comes here. Alone."

Juliana shook her head. "You and your bullshit message can go to Hades," she shouted.

The man stepped back and walked away.

LXXXIX

One day's walk from New Rome, 326 A.D.

Paulina held her bowl out to Jason. He shook his head. "If you cannot eat, nor will I," he said.

She handed the bowl to the driver. They were camped in a clearing at the side of the road. Many others were around them. It was dusk and a red sun was lowering quickly behind the high umbrella pine trees the road passed through. They could see the last tree-covered ridge ahead before the road dropped down to the Bosporus.

"We should not be sitting here," said Jason, looking over at the nearby group of young men, the followers of Zeus.

"They are no danger," said Paulina. "If they were going to draw blood they would have done so yesterday. There wasn't even a broken nose. They were just exercising their lungs."

Jason shook his head. "I saw their leader calming them. He was telling them to wait, that they would have their chance to fight later."

"You have good hearing," said the driver. "I reckon they didn't fight because they were outnumbered."

"By women and sick people?" said Jason.

"And carters," said the driver, pushing his chest out.

"Will you take your olives across the Bosporus tomorrow?" said Paulina to the driver.

"I will sell some olives on this side and then take a ferry across if I need to sell the rest. There are two ferry ships. I will show you."

Paulina put her head down on the folded-up sack he'd given her to use as a pillow and pulled the thin blanket, also made of sacking, up over her shoulder. Her stomach cramps were still there and she still felt woozy, barely able to think. She knew what she needed, a proper bed and the care of a physician.

She drifted away, wondering what had happened to Lucius.

***

The following day, as they came down from the ridge overlooking the Bosporus, they were greeted with a disappointing sight. Crowds of people, lines of carts and horses, filled the road ahead. A flat ferry ship was taking on passengers, but the crowd around it was as dense as flies on a new corpse.

Jason took her hand. "We'll be better off trying along the coast. There are other ferries near the dark sea."

Paulina looked at the driver. He was half-way around in his seat.

"You go ahead whatever way you want. I didn't expect any payment from you anyway. Your story about knowing the emperor was an obvious pack of lies, but you were entertaining. Good fortune." He coughed, looked at his hand, wiped it on the front of his tunic. Another red stain to add to the others.

"Will they let you cross if you are sick?" said Paulina.

"A little of this," the driver held up his finger and thumb in a circle to indicate a coin. "And I could buy my way into heaven." He laughed, waved goodbye.

Jason put his arm under Paulina's and took her off the cart. He walked with her in his arms for about fifty paces, then put her down. "We walk straight through the trees here," he said. "There is a road that runs along the Bosporus we can connect with. This will lead to it." He pointed at a gap between the trees. A sheep's skull lay against a tree at the opening. "Drovers use this," he said.

"How far?"

"Not far. But you will have to walk. We will walk together." He put his arm around her shoulder. They headed into the trees. Catcalls and whistles from people on the road followed. "She could be your mother," came one. "You deserve a healthy girl," was another.

They ignored them all. The path through the trees was flat, at least, but it was not short. It took half the day for them to reach the Bosporus. The good news, when they glimpsed the waterway through the trees on their left, was that there were no crowds milling. They reached the road, which curled around a small bay, and sat down beside it. There was almost no traffic here, just a single rider, a man in a post service uniform.

As he came near, Paulina stood and put up her hand. "What news," she called out as he came toward them.

He passed without stopping, waited until they were behind him before shouting over his shoulder. "The ferries are closed to all who are sick."

Paulina straightened herself and pushed her hair behind her ears. "We're not sick," she shouted after him.

The post messenger just turned and glared at her.

"He's probably on his way to tell the ferryman in the next fishing village not to take people across," said Jason.

"We have to keep going," said Paulina. "I need to see a physician." She held her stomach. The cramps were worse and her head felt stuffed up. The walking had not helped.

Jason held her tight and half carried her as they walked on.

"We'll get across, if I have to swim with you on my back."

She managed a small smile for that.

When they reached the fishing village two men with swords stood barring the road.

"Go back," shouted one of the men. He pulled his sword. "Only traders we know are allowed to pass." His companion, a younger man, pulled his sword too.

XC

One day's sailing from New Rome, 326 A.D.

Fausta looked behind. The ship they'd passed, which had turned to follow them, was about a league behind them.

She pointed at it.

"Are they following us?"

"Yes, Empress. Maybe they have a message for you and saw our imperial pennant." He smiled. "Perhaps it's the emperor. Should we haul down the sail and wait for them?"

Fausta looked at the ship sailing after them.

"The emperor would have been on deck with his hand up if he'd come to look for me. No, don't wait."

The captain nodded. They kept sailing, the wind picking up as they neared the red islands and passed between them and the mainland. The ship pursuing them was getting nearer, but the captain assured Fausta that they would dock at New Rome before the other ship came within boarding distance.

He was right.

But a man on the foredeck of the ship following began launching flaming arrows at their galley as they entered the waters of the Bosporus, tacking north. One arrow struck the aft deck.

"You must go to your cabin," said the captain. He was fuming, his fist raised, shaking it at the other ship. "That ship must be full of pirates. They are scum doing this to an imperial vessel."

Fausta looked back at the only man visible on the other ship. He was standing alone with a bow and firing arrows rapidly at them. She could almost make out his face.

"Is he suicidal?" said Fausta. "Doesn't he know we can cut out his eyes and make him eat his balls for attacking an imperial vessel?"

"The ship is probably stolen. There are lots of disaffected sailors around since Chrysopolis. I thought they should have been executed, but the emperor was too lenient," said the captain. "That's what comes from being a follower of Christ."

An arrow whistled down onto the deck near them.

"To your cabin, now, Empress."

The empress complied and the rest of the journey was accompanied by the smell of burning wood and the shouts of men firing arrows back at the other ship or dousing flames.

Finally, their speed dropped and shouts from the shore could be heard. Fausta went on deck. The other ship was nowhere to be seen.

"Where did he go?"

"Into the Bosporus. By the time we find someone to look for him he could dock and be gone with his crew into the city."

"The emperor will hear of this. I am surprised you didn't find a way to send him to the bottom of the Propontis." Fausta was shaking with anger at how near she'd been to a fiery death.

The captain put his head down. "I could have waited for him to come alongside and fought with him man to man, but I followed your orders and you are safe, Empress. There was no chance of him boarding."

She walked up to him and pressed her finger into his chest.

"You should have taken his head," she shouted, then pulled her hand back and slapped him hard across the face.

He grunted and his hand, near the sword on his belt, moved toward it, but it stopped. She knew why. Any attempt on the life of a member of the imperial family could have you and your whole family killed. Every generation.

XCI

New Rome, 326 A.D.

Juliana hurried into Constantine's apartment in the palace on the top of the hill overlooking the Bosporus.

"What's the news about Fausta?" she asked.

"Her ship was attacked on the way here," said Constantine. "She went straight with Bishop Eusebius to the church we're building at the temple of Eirene. She says she will pray there until nightfall." He banged his green wine glass on the long table by the couch.

"It's a ruse," said Juliana. "She's sending a message for me to clear out before she arrives. I should go."

"Stop," said Constantine. "You will not leave. I will decide these things, not her." His voice rose.

"I will be here when she arrives," said Juliana, her voice rising. "You know what she's like. She will be spitting fire if she can even smell me."

Constantine shook his head.

"We have more important things to worry about than Fausta," he said. "We had over two hundred dead yesterday because of the pestilence. The new infirmary is not ready, and I have to decide whether to close the ports and the city gates." He pointed at the window and the city beyond.

"Close them all," she said. "And tell Fausta to go back to Nicomedia."

Constantine stared at her. "I can't do that. I have to find out what happened between her and Crispus. I want to hear it from her mouth. Her denial or her admission."

Juliana stood behind him and put her hands on his shoulders. She pressed with her fingers through his thin tunic.

"She will lie to you, you know that, blame everyone else but herself. She's always been like that. She's a patrician and expects everything to revolve around her."

"This goes way beyond being a patrician."

"No, no, this is exactly what patricians do if they can't get their way. They try to eliminate whoever defies them. That's me."

She looked up at him.

"One of the prisoners I executed this morning claimed there is a conspiracy against me," he said, softly. "Your name was mentioned."

"Not for the first time."

"True, but I still don't like it."

"It reminds me of what the imperial soothsayer said, that there are always three conspiracies against an emperor. One by someone with no hope of getting near you. One by someone you know, who hates you, and is close to you, but is incapable of being a danger to you, and finally, one by someone you know who is capable of being a danger."

"Who is that person?" said Constantine.

Juliana shook her head. "Not me. I'd rather die than raise a hand to you." She bent up and kissed his cheek.

He pulled her to him.

"Fausta will never part us again."

She pushed him back onto the couch and kissed him, hard. They rolled over and soon their tunics were off. As he groaned, she wondered how long she could hold him in her spell.

A servant knocked at the door as they were finishing. Constantine roared for whoever it was to go away.

Soon after, they were drinking watered down wine and looking out over the Bosporus, catching the late morning breeze. A knock came again at the door.

"Come," shouted Constantine.

Crassus entered, bowed.

"What is it?"

"The empress awaits you in the audience hall."

XCII

New Rome, 326 A.D.

Paulina put her hand up and smiled at the guards. Out of the side of her mouth she said to Jason, "Be quiet while I talk."

She took a step forward and addressed them. "We need to get across the Bosporus. We do not mean you any harm." She made a sign in the air.

"Then go back the way you came," said the older of the two men. "There's a ferry that way." He pointed at the road behind them.

"Is there no other way across?"

The man shook his head. "No."

"We will do what you say," she said.

"Come, let's go," she said to Jason.

He shook his head, turned with her as she pulled him around. As they were walking back, she whispered in his ear. "We'll take a rest after the bend in the road."

The road bent inland and soon they were out of sight of the village guards. Paulina pointed at a spot where the grass was thin. The sun was lowering now. A smell of pine trees came down from the forest on the ridge. Jason took some dry bread from the leather bag he carried and passed some to Paulina. They ate hungrily.

"How much water do you have?" asked Paulina.

He shook his head and pointed at the water skin he'd given her to carry earlier that day.

"There isn't much left," said Paulina. She poked Jason with her finger. "We'll wait until nightfall and go around those bastards."

Jason smiled. "Did you see the stream coming down from the hill, just beyond where they were standing."

"That's why they picked that spot," said Paulina.

They lay on the dry grass and waited as the day ended. Soon stars were coming out above them and soon after that the sun was gone completely. The rustle of animals came to them from the woods, foxes foraging most likely.

"Do they have bears here?" said Paulina.

"They're mostly further north," said Jason. "But if we do see one stand still."

"Go back up to the road and see if those friendly guards are still on duty," said Paulina.

Jason wasn't gone for long.

"They have two torches burning by the road now. They can probably be seen in New Rome."

"Good, that means they won't see us when we go around them." She stood, holding her stomach. "But we'll have to be quiet."

"I can do that. We have to be quiet fishing. The whitefish can hear fishermen."

"I think they just see your shadows." She touched his arm. She felt like complaining, but she had to keep their spirits up.

"No, if my brother talks, I can see them skittering off down through the water."

They crossed over the road and headed up the side of the ridge overlooking the Bosporus. Just before it got steep, they turned left and skirted what was now almost a cliff. Barely able to see, progress was slow as their feet got caught in fallen branches or hit rocks and fell into holes. It was frustrating going and at times Paulina bent forward with her hands to feel the way ahead. It took every portion of her determination to keep going.

Looking downhill she could see the torches of the guards flickering through the trees. She had a bad dry taste in her mouth and her stomach was queasy, but she said nothing to Jason.

"The stream has to be near," whispered Jason. They were scrambling across a steep area of shale, beyond some trees. The thin rocks threatened to move underfoot and send a wave of debris down the hill.

"What's that?" hissed Paulina. She stopped moving. There it was again, a bubbling noise. She smiled, for the first time in a long time. She could almost taste the clean water ahead. She looked back. Jason's dark bulk was right behind her and then she saw the flash of his teeth.

"Keep going," he hissed. "I'm going to lose my footing."

She stepped into the stream a few steps later, but she didn't care that her sandals got wet. She bent down, cupped her hands in the water and drank. It tasted like sweet wine. No, better than sweet wine. She closed her eyes with the pleasure of it.

Jason was beside her doing the same.

"Wash the water skin and fill it up," she said, passing the skin to him. Her hands were trembling. She wasn't sure if she'd be able to fill it.

"Are you suffering?" he asked, as he put the water skin into the water and rubbed at the drinking end with his hand.

"I'm going to be sick," she said. She bent to the side and vomited onto the grass.

He put a hand on her back and rubbed it.

"We'll get through," he said.

She nodded, unable to speak, as waves of nausea passed through her. All she wanted to do was lie down. Drinking the water had made her worse. How could that happen?

"Let's get across and down the other side of the village," said Jason.

They crossed the stream, Paulina bent over, and headed down hill on the other side. They walked parallel with the road for a while until they came to a thin path. All the time they'd walked slowly in the near darkness, with just the stars illuminating the ground.

It was slow going.

They needed the path.

"Let's see if we can find a boat," said Jason, softly. He had his arm around her again. They headed down the path, walking as quietly as possible. Their eyes had adjusted to the darkness so much that when they did see a light ahead, it was like watching the sun rise as they came toward it. You couldn't stop looking at it.

They stopped at a stone wall and looked into the low house from whose window the candle shone. There was no other light beyond the candle, so they assumed it had been left out for someone returning.

"That'll be the guard's house," said Jason, nudging her. "We'd better keep moving."

They did and passed other similar houses, all in darkness, as they made their way down to the water. Jason almost fell head first into the Bosporus when they did reach it, but Paulina held him back.

"Are you looking ahead?" she said.

He pulled her tight to him. "I was looking at the stars," he said.

"Well don't."

The edge of the Bosporus here was a lip of land about a man's height above the water, which stretched away like the back of a giant water snake, shifting darkly.

"Shall we go that way?" said Jason, pointing left, to where they had come from.

"No, not that way, too near the guards," said Paulina.

She turned, kept walking along the lip as it curved to the east, the shape of two houses visible inland. Soon, the lip went down until the water was lapping near their feet and she spotted the distinct shadow of an upturned boat.

"We can take that."

"It might have a hole in it," said Jason. "I'd rather find one in the water."

They kept going until there were no more dark shapes of houses.

"We have to go back and try that boat," said Paulina.

"We might drown."

"I need a bed," she said. "Or I might die."

They went back, slowly. Jason turned up the boat and slid it into the water. "I get in first," he said, and he did. It didn't sink.

"There is a leak," he said. "But I think we can make it across. The current should take us." He smiled at her. She knew because she saw his teeth.

She had to wade a little into the cold water to get on board and ended up lying at the bottom of the boat, shivering. She knew then that if they sank, she would be dead, fast.

A sliver of moon rose as Jason rowed with his hands to move them out into the Bosporus. Then the current caught them, and they were pulled toward the middle of the waterway, heading back toward New Rome. They passed the point where the guards waited at the edge of the village as their speed picked up.

It felt at times as if the boat was going to spin, the current was so strong. And then they rounded a corner and ahead shone the torches along the city walls of New Rome. All Paulina had to do was put her head up to see them. They were a welcome sight. They meant proper care and a warm bed.

And that was when they came to a complete stop. The water around them glistened but didn't move.

"What's happening?" said Paulina, putting her head back down.

"I have to row fast with my hands now," said Jason.

XCIII

New Rome, 326 A.D.

Fausta paced back and forth. The light from the mass of candles at the end of the room lit the audience hall as far as the top of the pillars that lined the walls. Beyond that, darkness gathered.

She turned as the door at the back of the hall scratched open and stormed toward Constantine as he came in. "Why did you leave me here all day? Why?" She put her face close to his, then drew back. "I suppose you were with your witch."

Constantine raised his hand. "Do not speak to me like this. I have been touring the city gates and preparing for the dedication. You must know there is a pestilence killing people here. Do you only ever think of yourself?"

Fausta stepped back, bowed, mockingly. "Forgive me for being the empress," she said. "I thought you might want to tell me that Crispus is dead. But how did that happen?" She raised her voice. "Please, go on, tell me."

Constantine's expression was unmoving. "Why did he have your ring?"

Fausta tipped her head backward and laughed. "What? You think I was with him?" She stepped forward.

"Yes, I was, as a matter of fact. I spent a lot of time with Crispus in Rome. We exchanged rings too. It's true." Her voice went higher with each word, until she was screaming. "I did this for my children, so that when Crispus took over the empire he would not have all their throats cut." She sliced her hand across her throat.

Constantine shook his head. "That would not have happened. The edict making him emperor made that clear." He pointed a finger at her. "Explain this, how was I nearly burnt to death in Rome?"

She snorted. "I expect the witch Juliana was behind that. You were meeting Paulina." She pointed at him. "And she is now trying to blame me! Ha, has she poisoned your mind completely?" She paused, then spoke again, spitting out each word. "And still you haven't told me how the heir to your throne, your son, Crispus, died."

She put her hands together as if in prayer. "And why in the name of all the gods can we not mourn him? What happened?"

"He raised his knife to me," said Constantine.

"And you had to kill him? You have guards around you. Why did they not disarm him?"

"We were alone." He walked toward her. "It had to be done. I do not have to explain my actions to you."

"No, but you will have to explain them to the gods."

"There are many things you and I will have to explain to the gods," he said. "For instance, whose baby are you carrying?"

Her knees bent, she put her hand to her brow, her other hand going to a marble pillar to hold her up. "Whose baby? How could you even think that? It is yours."

He shook his head. "If we conceived the baby here before the spring you should be near your confinement." He pointed at her belly. "Instead, you look as if that's months away."

She bent her head forward and whispered, "There is something wrong with our baby, my emperor. Believe me, it is not developing properly." She looked up at him, tears in her eyes. "Do not blame me for something I did not do."

He looked away, then back at her and sighed, his anger dissipating. "I will not turn against you, Fausta. You know that. We are together too long."

He put his hand out. She took it, came toward him, a small smile flickering across her face.

"Do you wish to stay in the palace?" said Constantine.

"No," she shook her head. "I will stay with Bishop Eusebius. He is teaching me many things."

The two of them stared at each other.

"Tell him to come with you to the unveiling of the cross of Christ, tomorrow. I am sure he won't want to miss that."

She smiled. "Helena found it?" She shook her head, as if amazed.

"Yes."

"She is here?"

"You will see her tomorrow." Constantine took a step back. "She is one of your biggest supporters. Who would have thought that?"

"Your mother is wise," said Fausta. "Has she…" she stopped herself.

"Has she what?" He sounded frustrated.

"Has she told you about the threats to disrupt tomorrow's ceremony?"

"Threats from followers of the old gods?"

"Yes."

"They will not succeed. The dedication tomorrow will change everything. After tomorrow the empire becomes Christian, not just this city. Perhaps not everyone believes in the Christ god, but enough do."

Fausta shook her head. "There are very few followers of Christ in this city. You are risking the wrath of the mob, Constantine."

Constantine spoke in a low determined voice. "The old gods did not help us win our battles, Fausta. The Christ God did. I will never forget that."

"It wasn't Christ who helped you at the Milvian Bridge," she replied. "It was his followers."

"Them too, and they will be rewarded as long as I am alive," he said. "It is time you embraced this."

XCIV

The Bosporus, 326 A.D.

Paulina looked at the trading ship becalmed like them in the middle of the Bosporus. A candle glimmered on the deck. Three sailors were around it, playing knuckle bones, or so it sounded from a distance of fifty paces.

"Should I paddle to them?" said Jason.

"No, we must reach the other side before dawn. They are not going anywhere soon."

He nodded, began paddling with his hands again. Slowly they moved to the far side of the Bosporus and eventually the hills on that side were towering over them.

"The Golden Horn is just around the next bend. We can take it slowly and arrive like the other fishing vessels returning after an early morning trawl of the Bosporus."

"Do they do that?" asked Paulina.

"Look around," said Jason.

She did. Soon the shapes of five or six boats like theirs appeared out of the gloom.

"We will not have to go through the city gates?"

"No, fishermen are never refused entry at any of the docks. They never have been."

"But we have no fish."

"No one checks," he said. "But you must stand straight as we go ashore. The dock masters are always on the look out for people with a pestilence."

As the dawn rose behind them, they paddled into the Golden Horn and Paulina got to see why it had been given that name. The sun

311

threw a gold streak on the waterway at the entrance, which was cut off by a stone fort on the eastern shore and the hill behind it.

A shout greeted them as they approached the dock on the western side of the Golden Horn.

"No vessels are allowed dock in the city. You must go to the end of the horn to dock."

"We have fish," shouted Jason.

"Only fishing boats with the city pennant are allowed come ashore here," came the voice. Paulina could see who was shouting now. It was a man with a round metal hat and a large belly. Behind him stood four legionaries with spears and shields, drawn up in a line.

"Not as easy as you thought," said Paulina, nudging Jason.

"Nothing on this trip has been easy," said Jason.

Paulina rocked in the bottom of the boat. She was close enough to the city to smell it. She would not give up. "Go to where he's saying," she said. "I have to get into this city."

They made their way slowly up the narrowing waterway until they passed the end of the city walls on their left. Beyond it lay a bare stretch of scrub land with only bushes growing. Further on there was a new dock and a cleared area of ground extending away into the distance.

"I heard the emperor is starting a new wall. Why he needs it so far from the city I have no idea. This must be where it will be," said Jason. "But who will live in that place?" He pointed at the scrub land.

"Constantine has invited the senators of Rome to bring their families to live here. Perhaps they will live there."

"I don't see any senators wanting to live this far from everything. There are no temples or baths out here. That's what those people like."

Paulina sat down. There were small fishing craft milling around at the dock, but as they approached no one shouted at them, though she did see some men in dark uniforms watching them from the shore, their leather breastplates gleaming in the early morning sun.

One of them came to where they pulled up by the low stone wharf. He shouted down at them as they touched against the stone wall.

"Did you steal that craft?"

"No, master. We did not," said Jason. "I took my friend out for a visit across the Bosporus last night and we lost our oars." He pointed at Paulina. "She's a wild one."

The man looked at her. Paulina smiled up at him and pulled her tunic up a little, exposing her bare knee.

The man laughed. "I don't know what you pair have been up to, but we will see what the city guard makes of your story. Come ashore." Behind the man three legionaries had appeared. They looked down, grim faced, at Paulina and Jason.

All they had with them was one leather bag, which Jason was carrying. It could have been used for supplies for a night out on the water. The guard at the half-built gate to the dock asked them what was in the bag and eyed them both as if they were thieves.

When he saw that the only things in the bag were an empty waterskin, a second tunic and some dry bread wrapped in a dirty cloth he did not look happy.

"You weren't out on the water for a good time," he said. "Where are the wine skins? You're trying to bring someone into the city without permission, isn't that the truth?" He threw the bag back at Jason. Then he pointed at Paulina.

"I reckon he's smuggling you back in." He looked her up and down. "They didn't let you in at the main gate and you need to get home, is that it?" He grinned. "Your husband waiting for you with a stick?" He pointed at a purple bruise on Paulina's lower leg.

"Where did you get that?"

"Yes, I fight with my husband," said Paulina. "And I like to get out of the city. What is wrong with that?"

"Nothing, but we'll have to get your husband to come here to swear for you," said the guard. "What is his name and where does he live?"

Paulina looked at him for a long moment, then said, "Send someone to ask for Lucius Armenius at the Imperial Palace. Tell him his wife Paulina is waiting for him."

The guard shook his head. "The Imperial Palace? I hope you're not wasting our time. It's a long way to the Imperial Palace from here. It will be afternoon before a messenger gets back." He looked at Jason. "Is your friend lying?"

"No," said Jason.

"We have done nothing wrong," said Paulina. She was struggling not to show she was ill. "Jason helped me. My husband will reward you."

"I have a room you can wait in," said the guard. "Bread and water will be brought. You cannot say we have treated you badly."

"Why can't you just let us pass?" she said.

"Emperor's orders. Directly from his mouth. And especially for today, with the ceremony up by the palace. There'll be a lot of people trying to sneak into the city."

"What ceremony?" said Paulina.

"They say they found the cross that some god was crucified on. I don't believe it myself, but the emperor seems to, so maybe I should too?" He grinned.

XCV

New Rome, 326 A.D.

Fausta walked into the Imperial Palace without being stopped. The centurion in charge of the main gate knew her well.

"Will you need an escort to the ceremony this afternoon?" asked the head of the imperial family guard unit, walking fast to keep up with her, his red cloak swirling behind him.

"Yes," said Fausta. "Ten of your best men. I want them by the main gate waiting for me and," she looked at the man, "each of them is to be made aware that threats have been made against my life, so they must act with speed to cut down anyone who threatens me or the emperor. If any man fails to draw blood quickly he will pay for it with his own."

"Yes, Empress. They will be here waiting for you. Our best men."

Fausta swept on. Behind her strode Bishop Eusebius. Two priests who had accompanied them from the bishop's villa were waiting outside. They had escorted them to the palace and would escort Eusebius to the temple of Eirene, where the ceremony to welcome the cross would be held. The ceremony would also mark the transfer of the temple to become a church of Christ.

They reached the entrance to the imperial family rooms, a large triple-floored block, with pillars outside, and inside a string of atriums with rooms around them for up to seven imperial family members, with a long garden at the back overlooking the Bosporus. Half the building was unfinished, with mosaics incomplete and the underfloor heating only finished in Constantine's rooms, which were at the back of the building.

Fausta did not head there. She went to the atrium that Crispus had used and sat on the couch overlooking a side garden with a view of the Propontis. Two slaves were putting Crispus' uniforms into long boxes, most likely to send them to be altered and reused.

"Leave us," Fausta shouted at the slaves. As they departed she added, "Send Crassus here at once and the best wine and grapes."

She smiled at Eusebius and pointed at the couch opposite. It shone with dark-purple silk.

"Don't be afraid to sit on it. Crispus had expensive tastes, but he loved everything to be used." She put her head up. "Do you hear something?"

They both went still. Distant banging and the sound of a saw came to them, and the faint buzz of insects and tweeting of birds from the gardens, but no sounds from anything nearer.

Until a sob came from Crispus' bedroom.

Fausta stood and ran to the door to Crispus' bedroom. She shouted, "Come out at once whoever is sniveling in there."

The sobbing stopped. Eusebius joined Fausta. They went into Crispus' bedroom and looked around.

"Do not be afraid," said Eusebius. He walked to the left, around the giant bed.

A young boy in a purple silk tunic was curled up near the bed. The boy had curly golden hair and nut-brown skin. His eyes were red from crying. He stared up at Eusebius, as if he'd never seen a priest of Christ in a rough, dark woolen tunic all the way to his ankles.

"Why are you crying?" said Eusebius.

"Don't ask him that. I know why he's whining," said Fausta. "He needs to go back where he came from."

The boy sobbed at that and put his hands up to Eusebius.

"Do not touch him," said Fausta. "We must leave this creature to be dealt with by the master of slaves." She pointed at the boy. "Stop crying or I will make you eat your own eyeballs."

The boy went quiet.

"Come, Eusebius," said Fausta. "Crassus has arrived."

In the other room, and out of breath, Crassus waited, looking around.

"Get rid of that crying boy in there," hissed Fausta, pointing with her finger back to the room they'd just come out from. "Why is he even still in there?"

Crassus looked shocked, like a child who had just been caught pleasuring himself. He shook his head. "I don't know, Empress. I'm sorry. So sorry."

"I never want to see his golden curls again," said Fausta. "Do you understand?"

Crassus nodded. He bowed. "Is that all, Empress?"

"Fetch the Saxon Juliana to come here," she said. "After you have taken that idiot boy away." She pointed at the other room.

Crassus walked fast and returned a few moments later with the boy under his arm, struggling and whimpering and using Crispus' name in appeals for clemency.

"Do treat him properly," said Eusebius.

Crassus slapped the boy across the face, hard. That almost shut him up. Just the sound of pained, heavy breathing could be heard as Crassus left the room with the boy under his arm.

Eusebius sat down on the couch. "I would have taken the boy," he said. "I still can, if you wish."

"I am sure you could find a good use for him, Bishop, but the eunuchs have a special way with young boys, which I cannot disagree with."

"But many of them die when they cut them."

Fausta shrugged. "Tell me your plans for today, Bishop. Will you be at the altar when the cross is revealed?"

Eusebius looked at the mosaic floor. "No, I will not. The bishop of New Rome is not a man who likes to share his moment in the sun."

"But you should be there, surely?"

"I'm not a big believer in the power of dead wood or rotten cloth. You would not believe how many people have come to me with shrouds they claim Jesus wore or wood from seats or tables he sat at."

"But no wood from his cross arrived before?"

"No, not to me. You do know some people will expect their relatives to be raised from the dead, if they pay us enough, after listening to stories of Jesus raising Lazarus. I can only imagine what they will pay to touch where Jesus' blood soaked in."

"It'll make for a steady stream of pilgrims at the temple to Eirene."

"No doubt."

A creaking sounded from the door as it was opened. In walked Juliana.

"Greetings, Saxon," said Fausta. She did not rise, but Eusebius did.

XCVI

New Rome, 326 A.D.

Paulina walked the perimeter of the stone walled room. There was only enough space for three long steps one way and two the other. Jason was sitting on a bench at the back of the room.

"I hope your friend Lucius comes," said Jason.

"He will," said Paulina. "The two of you will get on well. He is a good man."

"How long have you been married?" said Jason.

Paulina didn't reply. She kept staring at the floor.

Jason went to the door. It was made of thick planks and had a bar across the outside, which prevented it from opening. A finger-thin gap between the wall and the wood of the door allowed them to see outside into the busy, but small parade area in front of the half-finished gate which led out to the city. They could even see out through the open gate toward scrubby bushes, a few houses and the wide road to the main part of the city.

A flow of pack horses and carts were coming both ways on the road. Occasionally riders could be seen, but no one looking as if he'd come from the Imperial Palace had arrived while Jason had been watching. And now they were both hungry and thirsty.

Jason banged on the door. "Bread and water. We were promised bread and water," he shouted.

Someone laughed outside. He banged again. "Lucius Armenius will have your heads off your shoulders when he comes if you do not treat us well," he shouted.

Paulina gave him the thumbs up. She did not feel well enough to do more.

There was no laughter outside the door after that. Jason banged the door again after a while. Then banged it more. Eventually, a shadow passed outside, and they could hear the bar on the door being removed. The door swung open. Two guards were outside, their spears ready. A thin slave had a wooden board with bread on it in one hand and an earthenware jug in the other.

The slave kept his head down as he brought in the bread, and the jug. The door closed behind him with a bang when he departed.

"At least we won't starve to death," said Jason. He carried the bread and water to Paulina.

"I can't eat," said Paulina. She gripped her stomach.

"Don't let them see you like that," said Jason. "They'll never let us into the city."

They waited, watching a line of sunlight on the floor moving. The crack between door and the wall was now also giving them a way to measure time. Paulina stared at it, wishing it to move.

Why was he taking so long?

Shouting outside made her look up to the door. The bolt was moved and then the door opened, and a rush of sunlight made her shield her eyes. Someone was coming. She stood, hope growing inside her.

It was Lucius. Thank God.

She put a hand out toward him. He came to her and hugged her.

"Husband," she said.

"Paulina, I was worried for you." He kept her in his arms.

"Who in Hades name is this?" he said, turning to look at Jason.

"He helped me get away from Ajax," she whispered. In the doorway stood the guard who'd put them in the room and behind him two other guards with spears.

Jason stood up and smiled at Lucius.

Lucius let go of Paulina, pulled his fist back and smacked it straight into Jason's cheek.

A cheer went up from the guards outside.

Paulina couldn't rush to Jason, as Lucius was supposed to be her husband, but she wanted to. She glared at Lucius instead.

Jason reeled back and fell against the wall. He screamed, raised his fists and bent into a defensive crouch.

Lucius grunted mockingly, grabbed Paulina's arm and pulled her toward the door. They walked straight through the grinning men and out through the nearby gate, which was crowded with people heading into the city. When they'd passed through the gate, Paulina pulled away from Lucius and looked back.

Jason had also been released and was staring after her.

She motioned with her head for him to follow.

"What did you do that for?" she asked Lucius, slapping his bare arm.

"I did it to get you released." Lucius grabbed her arm again. "You look like shit. The head of the guards was laughing about you looking like you've been kept up all night by your friend. I had to pay him and that had to be done or they'd never have believed I was your husband." He kept walking. "Is your friend coming after us?"

"Yes, he needs to be paid too for helping me escape. Did I tell you that?"

"No, and I suppose you think I should be the one to pay him." Lucius stopped, looked back at Jason coming toward them.

"Are you two lovers?" he said, when Jason was nearer.

Paulina shook her head. "He's way too young for me. And anyway, you know I'm not in need of any man. I've had my fill of men." She bent forward and groaned.

Lucius waved Jason forward. They were out of sight of the guards on the gate. Jason was holding his face when he came up.

"I didn't punch you that hard," said Lucius.

"Hard enough." Jason raised a fist. "Expect one back some time."

"Just help me with Paulina. And remember, you got released because of what I did to you, and the bribe I paid, and my knuckles are probably as sore as your cheek." He put an arm under Paulina's.

Jason looked at them, shook his head, as if at his own stupidity for coming with Paulina and put his arm around the other side of her.

"Where are we going?" asked Paulina.

"There are chariots for hire up ahead," said Lucius. "Then we take you to a physician I know."

"And Jason comes with us," said Paulina.

"Yes, yes, understood. You are your own woman."

It was late morning by the time they were finished with the physician. He gave Paulina a steaming hot drink and a small bag of herbs to bring away with instructions to go straight to bed and stay there for a week.

When they came out of the physician's shop, near the circus, Lucius said, "I can pay you off, Jason. You don't have to stay around." Jason had waited outside the shop on a bench where relatives and other patients were all waiting.

Jason looked at Paulina.

"Do you want me to go?" he said.

She smiled at him. "I will need your help for one last thing."

"What's that?" said Lucius, angrily.

"I want to go to this ceremony they are having at the temple of Eirene."

"Why?" said Lucius.

"Something a cart driver said to me."

"What cart driver?"

"I'll tell you on the way."

"What did he tell you?"

"I'll tell you that on the way too."

XCVII

New Rome, 326 A.D.

Juliana walked slowly toward Fausta. She stopped about five paces away and kept her right hand on the top of the axe attached to her belt.

"What do you want to see me about?" she asked, staring at Fausta, a hard look on her face.

Fausta made a humming sound, shifted on the couch. "Meet Bishop Eusebius, Juliana, one of the most important bishops in the empire, possibly the most important."

Juliana nodded toward Eusebius.

"But you don't care much for followers of Christ, do you?" said Fausta.

"So, you begin with total lies, like the last time we met," said Juliana.

"Stop it, Juliana. We could at least be polite. Come, sit down and drink some wine with us." Fausta gestured at the table.

"I have no time for sitting around," said Juliana. She glanced at the table. A red earthenware mug had been set on the table in front of the only place where she could have sat.

"What is it you want to talk about, Empress?"

"You mean aside from you stealing the man I love?" Her voice crackled with emotion.

Eusebius shifted in his seat. The tension in the room was like a pulled bow waiting to be released.

"I have told the bishop about you and Crispus," said Fausta.

Juliana shook her head. "Just more lies, Bishop."

"There is a witness who saw the two of you together in Rome in his rooms, Juliana, playing the beast with two backs game. You can stop denying it." Fausta pointed at Juliana.

Juliana took a step toward Fausta, who pulled back in her seat and waved a hand in the air. The black slave who went with her everywhere these days, rushed forward, his hand near a dagger on his belt.

Juliana looked at him. "Go on, spread your lies, Fausta," she said. "But Constantine believes me." She opened her hands to Fausta, then made fists of them. "He is mine."

"Not for much longer," said Fausta.

Juliana headed for the door. She turned when she reached it.

"And Constantine knows all about your plans to cause disruption today, Empress. We know about the priests of Zeus you have paid to come here. But you will not succeed. Today's ceremony will go ahead as planned."

XCIII

New Rome, 326 A.D.

Constantine lifted the edge of his ceremonial gold breastplate with his thumb. It was cutting into his collarbone.

"This is heavier each time I put it on. Are you adding more sections?" he asked the slave in charge of his military uniforms.

"No, Emperor," said the slave, who smiled for a moment, then suppressed it.

"Are you thinking I'm getting weak?"

"No, no, Emperor. I didn't think that." The slave sounded scared.

Constantine motioned for the slave and the others helping him to go. Only Crassus remained.

"You do not want to get there late, do you, Emperor?" said Crassus.

"I cannot be late, because it won't start until I arrive," said Constantine. He looked around.

"Where is Juliana?"

"She will come later, that's what she said." Crassus bowed. "We can go now, if you wish. Our messengers tell me the temple is full and the flute players are repeating their program already."

"Good," said Constantine. "Has Helena arrived?"

"She is waiting for you at the gate."

"Let's go."

He strode out of the room and along the marble floored, pillar lined corridor which ran through the center of the imperial apartments. Light from the late morning sun streamed in through an opening in the roof high above. Life sized statues of previous emperors ran down the middle of the corridor.

When he reached the end, palace guards in polished silver breastplates flung open the double doors. They took up their places behind him as he went down the three wide marble steps to the open area in front of the gate. Helena was waiting there with her own small entourage of slaves. Four of them, one at each corner, were carrying a long black wooden box. Their faces were grave, and each had blue fish symbols painted on their bare arms.

It had been a long summer and though soothsayers had been predicting a change in the weather, it hadn't come yet.

Constantine was sweating already.

"You look wonderful," said Helena. Beside Helena stood a young girl dressed in a pristine white tunic with a gold band in her long black hair, which sprayed out from her, as if she had just come from the baths.

"This is your new adopted daughter?" said Constantine, smiling at Bina.

"Yes, she is a follower of Christ and can give witness to how the cross came from Jerusalem."

"No one will dare question you," said Constantine.

"No, they won't, but Bina telling her story, even briefly, and being here, will help to persuade the skeptics who never believe anything they are told until they see the evidence."

"Like Thomas."

"Indeed. Shall we go?" said Helena.

"Bina will be between us." He patted Bina on the shoulder. "She is a symbol of the future, which the Christ god will make better for us all."

Helena, Bina and Constantine climbed into the golden imperial covered wagon. It had gold eagles on its sides, a sculpted gold eagle on its roof and each of the four wheels was decorated with jewels.

Four black horses waited patiently. Their handler was soothing them with words. As soon as the door to the wagon was closed, he jumped up to the driving seat and flicked the reins. The wagon moved on slowly. Ahead of it, a troop of fifty imperial guardsmen, their spears held tight in front of them, moved out of the palace gate. Behind the wagon came Helena's slaves with the box and another fifty guardsmen, similarly dressed, wearing black breastplates and leather aprons, with bare arms and purple scarves, the thick type used to stop the dust swirled up by marching men from filling mouths.

As soon as the gate opened, a roar went up from the crowd waiting outside. Constantine had ordered the chariot races to stop a few days before because of the pestilence, so the crowds, who might normally have been waiting at the circus for it to start, were all now lining the Imperial Way, which ran alongside the circus and ended at the Temple to Eirene and the sacred grove beyond, at the corner where the Bosporus met the Golden Horn.

The distance they had to go was only three times the length of the circus, and should not have taken long, but because of the crowds it was slow going.

Constantine banged on the roof of the wagon and the driver opened a hatch in the roof and gave a thumb's up. "Emperor, our legionaries are pushing people back up ahead."

Constantine looked out through the grill on his side. Faces stared at the imperial wagon. Many did not look happy. It looked as if the dregs of the city had been forced to attend. The stench of sweat made his nostrils twitch.

Someone shouted from the crowd, "The temple is ours, not yours."

Someone else screamed, "Eirene will be angry, Emperor, if you take her temple."

"Long live the emperor," someone else shouted. Others took up that call.

The crowd hushed then, and for a moment all that could be heard was the clop of horses and the grinding noise of the wagon wheels moving over the stone paving.

And suddenly a multi-throated gasp sounded and Constantine could not resist. He looked out again.

XCIX

New Rome, 326 A.D.

Juliana walked down the underground passage that connected the Imperial Palace to the half-built senate building. It would be used by Constantine when the building, an exact copy of the one in Rome, was finished.

She reached the point where the passage was without a roof and found the stairs that led up to the platform overlooking the building work, most of which was still only at the foundation level.

She went up. In a corner of the small wooden platform, at the point where it overlooked the imperial way, stood Crassus, observing the crowds waiting for Constantine and the cross of Christ.

Crassus didn't turn around as she approached. "The emperor would be better off staying in the Imperial Palace while this pestilence is about," said Crassus, gently, as Juliana came to stand beside him.

"He's not an easy man to control," said Juliana.

"It's his mother I blame for all this, not the emperor," said Crassus. "She wants to show everyone what she found on her travels."

"You don't believe the cross will bring good luck to the city?"

"If I believed everything people tell me I would be a babbling wreck before noon."

A distant thud sounded. Then another.

"They're throwing rocks," said Crassus.

"The imperial guards will protect the emperor," said Juliana.

"I expect many of those people throwing rocks only came to New Rome in the last week," said Crassus.

"Should we send reinforcements?"

"The guards can handle a few rock throwers," said Crassus. He looked around.

"It's not the crowds here I worry about," said Crassus. "It's what's going to happen when Constantine stands up in the temple and tells everyone it's now dedicated to the Christ god." He sniffed, as if disdaining any mention of Christ.

"Did you do what I asked?" said Juliana.

"Yes," said Crassus, "but there will be a lot of unhappy people in the imperial family if you go through with this."

"We have no choice. This must happen publicly," said Juliana.

"What will we do after?" said Crassus. "If your plan works."

"The baths will be open this afternoon?" she said.

"Yes."

"Have a room set aside for us."

"The room usually used for these things?"

"Yes."

"Will you need all the tools and a man to use them?"

"Yes."

"You do know if it gets out what you are doing, it will never succeed?"

"That's why I rely on your discretion," said Juliana.

A roar came from the direction of the crowds. "This is a very determined mob," said Crassus.

"They must have been paid well," said Juliana.

"And my reward?" Crassus had a smile on his face, but his eyes were black pits, which you could have sacrificed the innocent in.

"As agreed, your tormentor will be gone forever."

C

New Rome, 326 A.D.

Fausta sniffed the incensed air. The large square, high-ceilinged central room of the temple was filled with richly dressed patricians and the senators who'd arrived early from Rome.

She leaned toward Bishop Eusebius, who was standing beside her.

"Tell that scrawny priest that his empress will speak to start this ceremony, or he'll be washing the feet of the sick by nightfall."

"Which priest?" Three priests in long robes stood at the top of the hall. Each was dressed differently, though two were clearly Christian, as one had a blue fish symbol painted on his forehead and the other had a small wooden cross in his hand.

The third priest was dressed in green and holding a green stick with both hands.

"The head priest of Eirene," said Fausta. "The one with the wand." Her voice trembled with anticipation.

"He will speak before you?"

"He's the one going to hand over his temple, so yes."

Eusebius stepped forward and whispered in the ear of the head priest of Eirene. Fausta looked around. The young flute players at the side of the hall were still playing. Many people were watching them. The hall was full now, perhaps two hundred people, all standing in rows, with a gap down the middle of the room. The ceremony should be quick, to prevent too many of the older people from falling down, but as usual, when the emperor was supposed to attend, they were all waiting for him.

The high priest stamped his sandaled foot on the pale gray stone floor.

"My people," he called out. He said it again, louder.

The two Christian priests glared at him. They were clearly astounded that he was starting so soon, without the emperor.

"We are here today to mark a change in the destiny of our beloved city," said the priest. "This, our most important temple, set up by our ancestors to the goddess of peace, Eirene, will be handed over to the followers of Christ." A murmur in the hall grew louder as he spoke.

"But first, the Empress Fausta will speak." He motioned Fausta to come forward.

Fausta went to the top of the room and turned to face the crowd. She waited for silence, one hand up. Her tongue felt dry. The words she had practiced were drifting from her mind. She looked for a friendly face. The patricians and senators she mostly never spoke to all had hard faces, showing little sympathy. But then, she found her friendly face. Her black slave was standing by the main door, his arms folded across his giant chest. He smiled at her. She could not help but smile back.

"I am with you all to mark this day." She paused, looked at Eusebius. "A day that I never thought would come. I am your empress, and I appeal to you to stand up for what you believe in, not to always go along with what you are told to think or told to believe." Her voice grew more confident as she went. "It was the wish of Crispus, the heir to our beloved emperor, to stand here in front of you on this day." She raised her hand, pointed it at the crowd. "But I can tell you what Crispus planned to say."

From the back of the room, a shout echoed.

"Empress!"

A murmur grew like a wave and all heads in the crowd turned to see what was happening.

CI

New Rome, 326 A.D.

Constantine listened, his head to one side, as stones hit the wagon. At first only a few, then a lot, sounding like hail. As the sound diminished Constantine threw open the door of the wagon, put his greave covered arm up to his face, and jumped from the wagon.

He stumbled as a rock hit him in his side but pulled his short sword from its scabbard as he rose. It had a jeweled handle, and was meant for show, but the blade was sharp enough.

Another rock struck his thigh. He felt it through the leather apron he was wearing. That was the last rock to hit him. Members of the imperial guard from behind and in front came into a circle around him and the wagon. Many of these men, who'd fought with him for years, stood close around Constantine, their shields up.

He tapped many of his men's shoulders with his free hand, acknowledging their presence, whispering their names.

The crowd, on seeing the emperor and his willingness to take a stand, stepped back.

After a long moment, the sound of stones stopped and Constantine ordered the men around him to lower their shields. He stepped from behind them and slid his sword away.

"Listen, my people," he shouted. He raised his hands. Voices hushed. Behind him Bina and Helena poked their heads out of the wagon.

"I am here to help you. A distribution of coin will be held this afternoon at the circus. All who have been sick or who have any need will receive my personal support from my treasury." He banged the breastplate covering his chest with his fist. "I swear this to you."

"What about the temple?" cried someone in the distance.

"The name of your temple will not change. It will still honor the goddess Eirene," shouted Constantine. "And you can still go there and pray to her." He pointed at faces, one after the other.

"The followers of Christ help all people too, not just the patricians who cross their palms with gold, like the old gods do. They help the poorest, the sickest and the slaves. You will benefit. This is not just talk."

The mood of the crowd shifted.

"Hail, Constantine," someone shouted. The cry echoed. Many in front of him put their heads down in shame at having attacked the wagon.

Constantine waved the driver to go on. He stepped back up into it as it moved. One of his guards pushed the door closed behind him.

"You are lucky, my son," said Helena. "You could have been stoned to death."

"I have been lucky for a long time, Mother," he said. "I think by now you must accept it is the will of the gods."

"The will of God," Helena corrected him. She leaned forward. "We will miss Fausta's speech now. I wonder what she will say?"

Constantine straightened. "Fausta is not supposed to speak without me being there," he said. He rapped the roof of the carriage.

"Faster," he shouted.

CII

New Rome, 326 A.D.

Juliana pushed her way through the crowds. As she went, she watched for troublemakers, men who looked like they were on a mission. She'd rarely thought about the power of foresight which had helped her in her early days with Constantine, but in the past few weeks her dreams had changed, and she'd remembered them more easily after she woke.

She'd seen magpies gathering many times in her dreams recently and knew from her childhood, and from her time with the Saxons, that they gathered in her dreams to warn her.

She knew where the danger would come from. She knew who had to be stopped.

Whatever the price.

A shoulder high stone wall marked the edge of the temple precinct. The gate was manned by imperial guards. She strode straight past a line of people waiting and pointed at the small gold medallion at the center of her breastplate. It had Constantine's silhouette on it and told anyone who saw it that she was on the emperor's personal business.

They let her through the gate. With tension building inside her, she joined the stragglers pushing to get into the temple through the double-height main doors.

Flute players could be heard playing as she waited for the press of people to move on. And then they stopped, and voices came to her on the breeze. Was that Lucius' voice?

No, it was someone else.

She pushed her shoulder hard into a young woman and managed to get past her as the woman was still turning to remonstrate with her.

"I need to see the emperor now," said Juliana, loudly. People around her all turned and stared.

And then she was near the door and she saw him.

The black slave who went around with Fausta was just inside the door.

She glanced around. The two large slaves Crassus had nominated to follow her were not far behind. Just far enough not to be automatically seen as guarding her, but near enough to be ready if she needed help. Juliana nodded, then turned back to the door and pushed on.

As she came near him, about to pass him, she put her left hand up in a peace sign, looking beyond him, and with her right she pulled her dagger out slowly, the people around her covering her movements.

This was the moment of greatest danger.

A tremble ran through her. Doubts loomed. Had he seen?

But he showed no signs of being aware of any danger, until the very last moment, as Juliana slammed the handle of her dagger into his thigh.

"Empress," he screamed.

The shout brought silence to the crowd. They stepped away from him and Juliana.

The black slave fell back, to get away from the knife, his arms flailing, clutching at his leg, his mouth wide, looking down for blood. People shouted. She pulled her dagger back.

The two slaves Crassus sent came up quickly beside her and held Fausta's slave. They dragged him away under their arms as if they had come to save him. Juliana put her dagger in its sheath and reassured all these around her with calming gestures.

Then she followed Crassus' slaves.

Outside, the black slave was shouting and groaning loudly, calling out to nearby imperial legionaries for help.

Juliana came up behind him and tapped the slave hard on the skull with the blunt end of her dagger.

He groaned, fell forward, needed to be held up, but he stopped shouting.

Crassus' slaves who were half carrying him knew their destination. The room under the baths. As they went around a corner Juliana caught sight of the Imperial Way and the crowds streaming toward them.

CIII

New Rome, 326 A.D.

Constantine jumped from the wagon as soon as it stopped. His imperial guards were forming up around him.

"Six men tight with me," he said.

The men knew what to do. They formed up, two ahead, one on either side of him and two behind. They kept one hand on the pommels of their swords. Their other hands carried the new lighter oval shield, which Constantine had approved the previous year.

Together, they walked through the crowd which had gathered around the temple of Eirene. It was ten thick around the walls and more people were coming from the circus.

The crowd parted as they approached, like flesh under the blade. As they entered the temple, Fausta's voice echoed.

"That is what Crispus wanted to say to you today."

Faces turned at the noise of Constantine's entry. Fausta paused, then said, "Please welcome our beloved emperor, Emperor of all the world."

Constantine, surrounded by his men, walked up the center of the temple. Shafts of sunlight filled the room from thin windows high above. Doves, which had been allowed live in the eaves of the temple, cooed, while an insistent muttering could be heard from the crowd outside. In the temple, the stink of sweat was only partly masked by the incense coming from giant candles burning in a row at the top of the room.

When he reached Fausta he turned to the crowd.

"Thank you, Empress, for your fine words. Now let us talk about the future." He raised his hand. "My mother, Helena, will join us soon with the cross that Christ was crucified on. This cross will bring good fortune on you, the citizens of our empire and all our descendants." He pointed at Bishop Eusebius.

"I call on my friend, Bishop Eusebius, to welcome the cross into our city."

He stepped aside, put a hand on Fausta's elbow and guided her down the hall. She looked at him, hesitated for a moment, but then went with him, as if he was taking her out with her agreement. His men formed up around them. Faces peered at them until they were outside, when Constantine swung left and walked fast along the outside of the temple, to beyond where the crowd had gathered.

"Why did you start without me?" he hissed, still holding Fausta's elbow.

"I was preparing them for you," said Fausta. She sounded innocent. Then she pulled away from him with a shove of her arm and her tone hardened. "And it's important someone mentions Crispus' name today. He was going to be their emperor." Her voice rose.

"What did you say about him?" said Constantine.

They stopped walking under a cedar tree, the first of a line of cedars, which marked the beginning of the sacred garden behind the temple.

"I told them he'd planned to be here to wish them all good fortune in the years ahead."

"You mean wish the blessings of Fortuna on them?"

Fausta looked straight at him. "There is no shame on calling on the old gods to bless us."

He pointed at her. "No, but this was not the right time to do it." He made a fist and shook it between them. He'd had enough of her defiance. "I warned you not to talk about Crispus. What made you defy me?"

Fausta looked over his shoulder.

"What does he want?" she said, spitting out each word and pointing.

CIV

New Rome, 326 A.D.

Paulina, Jason and Lucius had reached the circus. A stream of people were walking toward the temple of Eirene.

"Are they all going to see the cross?" asked Paulina. She held an arm across her stomach.

"I think you should go to the palace," said Lucius.

"And do what, rest?" said Paulina. She put a hand on Jason's arm. "You tell him what I've put up with to get here on time."

"She nearly died," said Jason. "But I am with you. She needs rest." He held Paulina's arm. "I can carry you there."

Paulina looked from Jason to Lucius. "The two of you are to stop it, at once. I will decide what I will do." She kept walking, but faster.

The crowd thickened as she went, and it became difficult to make progress. The basement level of the unbuilt senate building was to their right, set apart from the road by a thick rail. A staircase led to a platform overlooking the building work and the road. Someone was standing on the platform watching everything.

"Who is that up there?" she said, pointing.

"I can't see," said Lucius.

"Let's get closer," said Paulina. They pushed sideways through the throng until they reached the thick rail around the senate building site.

Paulina looked up again. "It that Constantine's slave?"

"Crassus, the head slave?" said Lucius. "Yes, I think so. He'll know what's going on." Lucius waved up at Crassus.

Crassus seemed not to notice him.

Paulina screamed, "Crassus." Her voice was louder than you'd imagine coming from a thin woman.

Crassus' gaze remained fixed on the temple in the distance.

"Shout with me," said Paulina.

"Crassus," they all shouted as one. People stared. She didn't care.

Finally, after even more shouting, and a few other people joining in, Crassus looked down at them and waved.

"What's he doing up there?" said Lucius.

"If I know Crassus, he's directing everything from up there. Let's go and see." Paulina went under the bar blocking them from the building site and headed toward the platform. She looked up. Crassus was shaking his head and pointing behind them. Paulina turned. A group of people were pushing their way through the crowd.

She looked back up at Crassus. He was pointing at the group, who were now disappearing up ahead.

Crassus raised his hands in despair as they watched.

"Let's go after them," said Paulina, pulling Lucius and Jason with her.

"This is a stupid goose chase, isn't it," said Jason. "First we chase one. Then we chase another. Then another."

They pushed through the crowd. All they knew was the direction the group had gone in, until the crowd thinned and they saw who they were following.

Juliana was at the head of the group, leading slaves toward the baths. Paulina started running. "Juliana," she called out, but Juliana didn't hear. The noise from the crowd, shouts and mutterings had become louder with all the pushing.

Jason ran ahead. He was waiting at the entrance to the baths when Paulina and Lucius arrived.

"Which way did they go?" said Paulina. She bent over, her breathing coming fast.

"In that door, but it's locked," said Jason.

Paulina looked at it. "The two of you smash it in with your shoulders. I bet you can break it."

At the first attempt the door just rocked a little. At the fifth, it sprung open. An earth lined corridor, the type slaves used, led to a staircase down. Voices echoed from below.

Three slaves barred their way at the bottom.

"Go back," one said. He had a gnarled stick in his hand, the type used for inflicting beatings.

"No," said Paulina, shaking her head. "Go, find Juliana and tell her that her friend Paulina is here. We will wait."

The slave disappeared, and soon after he returned. He took them into a long room with manacles hanging on the walls, tables with torture instruments and, tied to a wooden wheel, a black man with blood flowing down his leg.

Juliana came straight to them. "You must go. We don't have much time. I need to find out what this slave has been up to."

"Whose owns the slave?" said Paulina.

"Fausta. I heard someone talk about him."

Paulina put a hand up. "If you want to get him to talk, I know what to do," she said.

CV

New Rome, 326 A.D.

"I promise not to mention Crispus' name again," said Fausta. She was staring at one of Crassus' assistants, who was hurrying toward them.

Constantine looked at her. "I don't want us to be at each other's throats," he said.

Crassus' assistant bowed as he reached them.

"Emperor," he said. "Forgive me, Juliana the Saxon waits for you at the baths." He glanced at Fausta.

"Tell her I will come after the ceremony," said Constantine.

Fausta laughed. "That Saxon is shameless." She put a hand on Constantine's arm. "Come, let us do this together. People will already be wondering where we are."

They arrived back in what was now a church just in time to listen to Eusebius talking about unity in the empire and the promise of what Christianity would bring to all the people in every land.

"Christ is a religion for all, the slave and the emperor. Doing to others what you would want them to do to you, is the cornerstone of Christ's teaching. Let us celebrate this day when a temple became a church." He raised his hands and looked to the roof.

At that, yells sounded from the main door.

"Kill the Christ loving emperor," came a shout. Other similar shouts echoed from beyond the door. The distinctive sound of swords clashing and the yells of the injured followed.

Constantine and Fausta went to the side of the hall, near the door. His small troop were lined up in front of them.

"Out of the way," shouted Constantine. "We'll deal with this." He tapped the shoulder of the centurion in charge of his guard. "Swords up. Let's send these bastards to Hades and get out of here."

He looked at Fausta. "Stay behind me and out of the way of my sword."

She nodded and smiled tentatively. He enjoyed the thought of her seeing him in action, but he knew he was a lot older than most, so the encounter might not go as he wished. But he'd never shied away from a fight. He wasn't going to start now with his life and that of his empress at stake.

He'd never be able to walk among the people of his city again if he did run or hide. Most men in the empire were judged by their ability to fight and draw blood when the moment demanded, no matter their age.

Patricians stood back as his small troop made their way to the main door, screams and the clash of weapons filling the air. The door was clear of people now. When he reached it he could see why.

Imperial guards and other men with swords were fighting outside, grunting, slashing, shouting. He looked at Fausta. Her mouth was open. She'd gone pale. As he watched she fixed her face and glared at him.

"Stay back," he said to her. Then, with a tap on the shoulder of the lead centurion and pointing his finger they headed out into the fight. What confronted them was not what he'd expected. Many of his personal guards lay dead. The last of them, fighting near the door, were facing a large mob, some with cudgels, others with swords. As soon as Constantine stepped out of the church an animal roar broke from many throats, as if their prey had finally been flushed out into the open.

CVI

New Rome, 326 A.D.

Paulina held the dagger tight. She went up to the black slave and pointed it at his stomach.

"I'll rip you open and pull out your intestines so you can see them and wrap them around your neck if you do not talk, fast."

His mouth opened. His face contorted in despair.

Juliana, Lucius and Jason watched from one side. Jason was shaking his head, as if shocked by how different Paulina sounded.

Paulina placed the point of her knife just under the slave's belly button. It moved back as the slave pulled his stomach in fast.

"You will beg me to finish you off and you will tell me everything as well, when you feel it all coming out." She swung the knife from side to side slowly, its point grazing against quivering black skin.

"Do you know how long it takes to die with your intestines out?"

The slave's eyes were wide. He looked appealingly at Juliana who looked away, and then to Lucius, who shook his head.

"Last chance," said Paulina. "I'm looking forward to cutting you." She licked her lips. "It's been a while and there are a lot of extra torments I'd like to try on a big boy like you."

The slave shook against the ropes binding him, his stomach in and his face twisted in terror.

Paulina lowered her knife a little. "Perhaps you'd like me to start a little further down, smear you with honey and leave you here overnight as a feast for the rats." She made a chomping sound.

"Stop, stop, I will tell you everything," shouted the slave.

Juliana stepped forward.

"Tell," she said.

"The empress mounts me every night. Is that what you want to hear?" He was shaking now, rattling the wheel, his voice rising higher and higher. He'd probably seen slaves being tortured to death and knew Paulina's threats would not be idle.

"What else?" said Juliana.

The slave's eyes widened. He stared one way, then the other.

"I overheard her plotting against the emperor." His head went down on his chest. "She paid the priests of Zeus to send men here to attack the emperor at the ceremony today. They plan to kill him." His arms shook. "She has poison too in case her plans don't work."

Juliana headed for the door. "Come with me, Lucius. Wait here, you two." Paulina and Jason nodded their reply. The black slave began crying. Paulina patted his arm.

When Juliana left the baths by the small door they had entered through, it was eerily quiet at the entrance, as if a pestilence had killed everyone in the city.

Then she heard it. The sound of swords clashing. They ran toward the temple. As they came near, they slowed, so their breathing would be steady when they started to fight.

"Where are the rest of Constantine's men?" shouted Lucius.

"Blame him," shouted Juliana, pointing at the platform in the distance where Crassus was standing, staring down at the fighting.

Juliana had her axe out. She swung it at a black robed man who'd turned to face them, his sword up.

The axe loped his arm off. Blood spurted. The man stared at the arm falling to the ground, as if he couldn't believe it was his. With his other hand he pulled a dagger and flung it at Juliana. She ducked and swung her axe back around so it caught the man in the side. The man screamed as he fell.

Two other men were facing her now, their swords up and ready. Both were smiling at the chance to take on a woman.

Their smiles didn't last as her axe flew across both their faces, cutting across one man's eyes and into the forehead of the other, sending him backward.

Constantine was ahead. He shouted, "What took you so long?"

"This way," she shouted. She pointed over her shoulder.

Two imperial guards fighting close to Constantine must have heard her, as they headed in her direction, stabbing their swords at the men blocking them. Behind Constantine, Fausta stood, her head up, looking this way and that, her eyes wide.

Lucius shouted, "Watch out."

Juliana leaned back. A sword gutted the spot where she had just been.

"Come on," she shouted. Faces beyond the men they were fighting showed there were many more men, mostly dressed in black, waiting to get a chance to fight them. She knew that if they had to fight and kill one man after another they would tire eventually, and someone just starting to fight would cut them down.

"Come quickly." She swung her axe again and now Constantine was to her left and behind him Fausta.

"Kill the emperor," shouted someone. The cry was taken up by others, adding urgency to the clash of weapons.

"I'll stop them following you," shouted Lucius.

"No," shouted Constantine. "We all fall back together."

And so they did, walking backward, pressed and harried by sword thrusts. And still no reinforcements arrived and in the distance, by the temple, there was a mound of bodies and behind them a line of patricians in togas watching everything.

"This way," shouted Juliana, pointing at the door to the baths.

She was rewarded by a sword thrust slicing into her upper arm. The cut felt like fire. Her axe fell. A cheer went up from their enemies.

She stepped back. She knew if she didn't escape from the fight now she would die. And probably be raped soon after, while she was still warm. Some men became aroused while fighting a woman and would see it as their just reward.

Only something like a knife in their eye would stop them.

She picked up her axe with her left hand and flung it at one of the men approaching her. He laughed as it missed him.

Constantine was beside her. "Run, show us where to go. We will follow you," he said.

Juliana turned and ran. She reached the door to the baths and looked back. Fausta was behind her. Lucius was with her. Behind them Constantine and three of his remaining guard were walking backward, swords up, not even fighting now as a mob of about twenty men gathered around them.

She opened the door, checked for the locking bar and shouted at Constantine, "Run."

He did. Another cheer sounded and mocking laughs.

They piled in through the small door, stumbling on top of each other, everyone splattered with blood. She pushed the door closed. Lucius put the bar in place. As he did a blade came through the gap between the door and the wall. It almost went into his throat.

"Burn them out," came a shout from outside.

"Down the stairs," said Juliana.

The stairs into the basement of the baths had been cut into the rock of the hill.

Lucius was at the back as they went down. Juliana was at the front. At the bottom of the stairs lay a corridor. The door to the torture room was open further along. Constantine went in, followed by Fausta.

"I'll wait here with the guards," said Lucius. "When those bastards come down, I'll let you know."

"Release my slave," Fausta shouted from the torture room. Juliana followed into the room. Fausta was pointing at her black slave.

"Release him, at once." Fausta's shriek had more than outrage in it. It also had the tremble of fear.

Constantine looked at Paulina, then at Juliana.

"Why are you questioning the empress' slave?" He was angry too.

Juliana pointed at the slave. "This slave is not only taking your place in the empress' bed, he also told us that it was the empress who paid for the followers of Zeus to rampage above us."

"That's beyond ridiculous," said Fausta, her tone calming. "You just want rid of me. You've been planning this for a long time." She appealed to Constantine. "Don't believe a word she says."

Paulina stepped forward. "We all heard this slave tell us what Juliana just told you," she said.

"It's all lies. That slave would say anything to protect his life, like all slaves." She pointed at Paulina. "The word of a tortured slave has little value in a Roman court. My word counts for more."

"What else did this slave say?" said Constantine.

"They're coming," shouted Lucius from the corridor. Shouts echoed.

Paulina walked over to Constantine. "The slave told us everything he said can be proven if you speak to the high priest of Zeus."

Fausta screamed. "Your Christian priestess is a liar. I can prove it. She walked fast to the black slave. A dagger appeared in her hand. She stabbed it into the stomach of the slave and pushed the knife upward in his chest as blood flowed down her arm and his body shook.

"No," screeched the slave. Then his head jerked and his body thrashed against the ropes holding it.

Fausta dropped the knife. "I did that because he dared lie about me," she said. She pointed at Paulina, then at Juliana. "They are all liars. They both want to control you. Do not believe a word they say, Constantine."

Constantine looked from face to face.

More shouting echoed from outside the room.

"Do you have proof that Fausta conspired against me?"

"She carries a vial of poison to slip into your drink, if you survive this attack today," said Juliana.

"Where on her person?" said Constantine.

"Wrapped to her thigh."

Fausta waved her arms in the air. "I always carry poison," she screamed. "That proves nothing."

Jason, who was at the back of the room, spoke softly.

"No, it proves the slave was not lying."

"Who are you?" said Constantine, turning on Jason.

"I live on the Red Islands. I heard all the slave said. I believed him."

Paulina put a hand up to stop Jason speaking. "Fausta also tried to kill me near Rome. She wanted to hide what I'd found out, that she had been trying to have her baby aborted."

"That's a lie," shouted Fausta.

Paulina shook her head.

Constantine looked at Fausta's belly. It was definitely not as big as it should be if it was his. If it had been his it would almost be ready to be born. More shouts, some closer, forced his hand.

"I have to help them outside," said Constantine. "Search her for this poison."

Juliana followed him. In the corridor a vicious fight was taking place. Two men had forced their way down into the corridor and two others were lying dead at the bottom of the stairs. Someone was shouting from up above. "Keep the emperor."

"Come down, follower of Zeus, we have what you want," shouted Juliana.

An older man dressed all in black appeared at the bottom of the stairs.

"Stop fighting, followers of Zeus, the emperor is surrounded," shouted Juliana. She raised her axe and held it up, as if to strike Constantine.

"Juliana?" shouted Constantine, in a confused, angry tone.

"Come and watch your victory over the first Christian emperor, priest of Zeus."

The older man had a gold tipped stick in his hand, which he pointed at Constantine. "You will not make this empire Christian," he shouted. "Kill him, Juliana the Saxon."

Juliana pulled the axe back and flung it.

It missed Constantine and landed in the middle of the high priest's chest. He screamed like a frightened child, then fell back with blood spraying all around him.

Constantine growled and bared his teeth at the men he had been fighting. They took in what had happened and headed for the stairs.

"Good throw," said Constantine. "But you almost took my head off."

He looked down the corridor. "There are steam rooms down here," he said, softly.

"I'm told you could die in one of these rooms, if the attendant stokes the fire below too much."

He went back to the torture room. Fausta was standing at the far wall. She was shaking her head slowly from side to side.

Jason was holding her. Her gown was torn as if there'd been a struggle.

"No, Constantine," said Fausta, fear in her voice. "You must believe me. You must."

He grabbed her arm and pulled her toward the door. "Your mistake was killing this slave," said Constantine, firmly. "He spoke the truth. The followers of Zeus were trying to kill me. I don't know if you also tried to burn me to death in Rome, but the evidence against you cannot be ignored. Treachery cannot go unpunished. This rule has kept me alive. You will die without the shedding of imperial blood. The hot room is waiting for you."

"There is no evidence," she whimpered. "You cannot kill the mother of your child to be." She let herself fall, forcing Constantine to drag her. He pulled her with determination.

"The child is not mine. It would bring shame on us all."

Lucius went to help him.

"I know what you tried to do to Paulina," said Lucius, grabbing Fausta's other arm.

She twisted her hand away from Lucius and plunged it into a tear in the thin green gown she was wearing. As Constantine pulled her to the door, she pulled out a small earthenware vial and put it to her mouth.

She spat out the stopper and lunged the vial toward Constantine's mouth. He turned his head, clamped his mouth shut just in time. The contents fell on the floor.

Lucius took a hold of Fausta's arm again. The vial dropped and smashed on the ground.

"Bring her," he said coldly.

They pushed and carried a wailing Fausta to one of the small steam rooms at the end of the corridor, used most often in deep winter, when the snow fell.

The steam room had a wide bench and a long bath big enough for one person. The walls were curved inward and covered in mosaic tiles.

Fausta wailed as she was taken to the room.

"Please, please. What about the baby? What about your children? I beg you. Let me live."

But Constantine had hardened his heart. And he had no choice. To allow a conspirator in his own family to try to kill him and not retaliate would see twenty conspiracies hatched against him by the end of the week. And he would not be able to stop news of what happened here getting out.

This way, he would hold onto his life and the empire would not sink into rebelliousness and slaughter.

As soon as they released her, Fausta ran to Constantine. Lucius pulled her away. She was sobbing as he held her.

"Put her in, close the door. I do not want to hear her voice again, ever." Constantine pointed at Fausta. "You betrayed me. Accept your fate."

Fausta's wailing went up another notch. She struggled wildly, flailing at Lucius.

Juliana and Paulina went to help him.

"Your son was right. Your God will ruin the empire," shrieked Fausta. "He would have saved it. That's why we wanted you out of the way. To save the empire."

"Stop," a voice called out. All heads turned. It was Helena. She was coming down the corridor.

"What are you doing to the empress?" Helena called out.

"Fausta tried to kill me," said Constantine. "She has to die. We cannot have a traitor in our midst."

"She is pregnant with your baby," said Helena, loudly.

"It is not mine. Fausta knows that its birth date will betray her. She tried to kill the baby," said Constantine.

"It's lies," screamed Fausta. "Believe me, Helena."

Lucius squeezed his arms tight around her and pushed her into the room.

No one said anything as he slammed the wooden door shut. He wedged a piece of wood to stop it opening.

From behind the door Fausta could be heard banging it and screaming. "You will curse this city if you do this. You will curse your family if you do this. I was only defending myself. Let me out."

"Stay here, Juliana. Make sure it is done. Find the bath slaves. They know how to heat these rooms."

Fausta was still banging on the door.

He turned to Helena. "Is the cross damaged?"

"No," she said. "But the ceremony was interrupted." She sniffed. "I had to send Bina back to the palace."

She turned to Juliana. "So, you will be the new empress?"

Juliana shook her head. "That is not what I want. All I ever wanted was to save Constantine from the empress' scheming." Her voice rose as she spoke. "At least three times she tried to kill him. He unified our empire, gave hope to everyone, from patrician to slave, and they all believe in him. He has beaten every enemy, on the battlefield and in his own house. If he'd died your true cross would probably have been thrown into the sea and the empire would have gone back to the old gods."

Helena hugged her.

Epilogue

Constantine walked down the corridor and out into the parade area in front of the palace. Helena and Bina were waiting for him. Bina was leaning against Helena. It was seven days after the riot and death of Fausta. Bina was wearing a purple tunic, signifying her new status as a member of the imperial family.

Juliana was behind, at the palace door, talking to Crassus.

"Thank you for protecting me after what happened to Fausta," said Crassus.

Juliana looked into his eyes. "We protect each other. We both know too much to have one of us fighting the other."

Crassus nodded. "I wondered for a long time why you asked me to tell Crispus that Constantine would never give up his throne." He smiled. "You made all this happen, you know that, Juliana."

"You give me too much credit. They made their choices," said Juliana. "I saw it as a test. If Crispus had come to power, it would have been a disaster for many. He'd have had all our throats cut in a year."

"Getting me to tell Crispus that Seutonius was about to inform everyone about Crispus' tastes was your master stroke, Juliana, worthy of a great general."

"And you will tell everyone who asks that Crispus died by poisoning to ensure peace in the empire." She pushed a hair away from her forehead. "What happened to Fausta's body?" she asked.

"They flushed it down the drains where the unwanted babies go," said Crassus.

"Good, there must be no place for her children to mourn her. I look forward to many years of peace here in the palace," said Juliana.

"Not total peace. You heard Jason and Lucius were fighting last night."

"Yes, Paulina should pick one of them."

"She can decide. That's the problem. She was supposed to pay off Jason, so he could leave, but she hasn't."

"She was always slow to pay her debts," said Juliana.

Constantine turned. He raised his hands in exasperation at Juliana holding back and talking to Crassus, then looked ahead again.

"He needs you with him," said Crassus.

Juliana smiled, briefly.

"You are the empress now, Juliana," said Crassus. He bowed slightly to her.

"I will never be that."

"But you have everything an empress has."

"I only have what I wanted."

"Your son Axel is expected later, I heard," said Crassus. "You were wise to keep him away until all this was settled."

"Yes," said Juliana. "I forgot to mention, Axel will be adopted as a member of the imperial family."

"A good move, Empress Juliana." Crassus bowed again. "Your story will give hope to every slave, everywhere."

Juliana walked toward Constantine, her hand out to take his.

Before You Go – Two Things

I hope you have enjoyed this book. If you can be persuaded **to write a reader review on Amazon, I'd really appreciate it.**

Reviews on Amazon are critical to the success of an author these days.

To join the mailing list and receive news of the forthcoming box set with maps and a concluding short story, click this link or put it
in your browser: **http://bit.ly/TSOTBseries**

Printed in Great Britain
by Amazon

59006363R00215